OATH BOUND

Also by Richard Cullen

Steelhaven (as R. S. Ford)
Herald of the Storm
The Shattered Crown
Lord of Ashes

War of the Archons (as R. S. Ford)
A Demon in Silver
Hangman's Gate
Spear of Malice

OATH BOUND

Richard Cullen

An Aries Book

First published in the United Kingdom in 2021 by Head of Zeus Ltd
This paperback edition first published in 2021 by Head of Zeus Ltd
An Aries book

9 7 5 3 1 2 4 6 8

A CIP catalogue record for this book is available from the British Library.

ISBN (PB): 9781801102049
ISBN (E): 9781801102032

Cover design © Nick Venables

Typeset by Siliconchips Services Ltd UK

Head of Zeus
First Floor East
5–8 Hardwick Street
London EC1R 4RG

www.headofzeus.com

The stream of Time, irresistible, ever moving, carries off and bears away all things that come to birth and plunges them into utter darkness, both deeds of no account and deeds which are mighty and worthy of commemoration; as the playwright says, it "brings to light that which was unseen and shrouds from us that which was manifest".
— Anna Komnene, *The Alexiad*

Place Names

Amblesberie – Amesbury
Ánslo – Oslo
Berchastede – Berkhamsted
Boseham – Bosham
Bretagne – Brittany
Brien – Brean
Canterburgh – Canterbury
Coleselle – Coleshill
Coppethorne – Copthorne
Cudessane – Shefford
Dunheved – Launceston
Exonia – Exeter
Hedeby
Hereford
Hooe
Leofminstre – Leominster
Lundenburg – London
Mathrafal
Merleberge – Marlborough
Rhuddlan
Scipene – Shippon

Sudweca – Southwark
Tatecastre – Tadcaster
Walingeford – Wallingford
Walsingaha – Walsingham
Worle
Recordine – Wrockwardine
Yorke – York

PROLOGUE

SENLAC HILL, 14TH OF OCTOBER 1066

Carrion crows led a path to the dead. They had filled the distant sky, a cloud of them wheeling and cawing before the feast. Bedel and Wyg passed men stumbling across open fields and through the trees in their ones and twos. Neither lad could tell if the bloodied wastrels were their own countrymen fleeing for their lives or the invaders, and they weren't of a mind to stop and ask.

Bedel glanced back through the darkened spinney, seeing Wyg struggling to keep up, blundering his way from the shadows. The sky had been turning to grey when they'd set off from Hooe, but even after running most of the five miles they hadn't managed to reach the hill before sundown.

'We shouldn't be doing this,' Wyg said for the tenth time as he ambled up to his older brother. 'Mam's gonna kill us.'

Bedel ignored him, but Wyg was right: their mam *was* gonna kill them, but this was too good an opportunity to miss. Everyone in Hooe knew what was happening. The Franks had come across the sea, looting and burning until the king could take no more. He'd raised the fyrd and gone to face them, and by now it would all be over, one way or the other. Bedel might have missed the scrap but he was damned if he was gonna leave all that loot lying around for the crows.

'We should go back; it's too dark,' Wyg moaned.

'Go back then,' Bedel snapped. He'd just about had enough of Wyg's whingeing. He should have left him back at the village, but then his little brother was always dogging his tracks like a waif. Besides, Bedel was the eldest and he'd never in his life done what his little brother asked.

Wyg glared around at the dark surroundings. 'I can't go on my own, can I. What if I get –?'

Bedel shushed him, raising a hand to his brother's mouth. 'Listen,' he whispered.

Carried across the field beyond came a sound. Voices raised on the wind. Singing.

The longer they listened, the more Bedel could make out. Those weren't English voices. The invaders had won. King Harold was beaten.

For a moment he thought turning back might not be such a bad idea. Caught looting the dead by Harold's men and they'd be in the shit for sure. Caught by an invading army...

Bedel dismissed the thought. He hadn't come all this way to leave empty-handed.

Silently he led his brother through the trees to the edge of the spinney. It was a bright enough moon to see by and the view made something twist in his guts. Dark shadows peppered the field. Corpses lay like abandoned sacks of dirt all the way across the flat expanse and up the hill. And atop that rise stood a camp, tents all along the dark horizon, flags flying, fires burning.

'Is that the king's men?' Wyg whispered.

'Course it ain't the bloody king's men, idiot. Listen to them. Does that sound like any king's men you've ever heard?'

Wyg's silence told Bedel his brother understood perfectly well they were not king's men.

Just as Bedel was wondering whether this was a good idea after all, a spot of rain landed on his face. In moments that spot had turned to a spatter and then to a torrent as the sky opened up and it started to piss down.

A smile crossed Bedel's face. Those Franks would be less likely on the lookout for looters in this, and the sound of it beating down would hide any noise the pair of them might make.

'Right,' he said to Wyg. 'Best be quick about this.'

He darted from beneath the trees, Wyg at his shoulder. Under cover of dark they reached the first mass of corpses sprawled out on the field. To Bedel's eye they reminded him of how his father had often looked those years ago, just before he'd drunk himself to death. That useless bastard had spent a lot of his time lying around like a dead man. Bedel could only hope the dead he ransacked tonight would grant him more of a legacy than his sot of a father ever had.

Their skin was stony pale in the moonlight. Not that the dead bothered him; he'd seen enough of them in his few short years to know there was nothing to fear from a corpse.

Bedel searched the first body, but there was nothing to find; no coin, no jewellery, no nothing. He moved on to the next. This one had nothing on him either, apart from a leather belt at his waist. Bedel saw the buckle was iron, might have been worth something. After a quick fumble, he managed to get it undone, but it was wedged tight underneath the bulk of the corpse.

'Help me, will you,' Bedel said to Wyg.

He struggled again, yanking at the belt but it wouldn't come free. Turning, he saw Wyg watching him.

'Don't stand gawping,' he said. 'Come and help me.'

Wyg just stood there in the rain, useless and shivering.

'If you're not going to help, you might as well piss off.'

'I don't like it,' said Wyg too loudly.

'You don't like what?' Bedel asked, feeling his annoyance growing.

'This is wrong,' Wyg said. 'We should be helping bury this lot, not robbing them.'

Bedel stood up fixing his brother with a stern glance. 'You knew what we were coming for. If you weren't going to help you should have stayed at home.'

'Well maybe I should,' Wyg snapped.

Before Bedel could say anything else, his little brother ran off into the dark.

Bedel cursed. He knew he should have made Wyg stay home, but it was too late now. Well, bollocks to him. Without giving his brother another thought, he turned back to the body – grabbing the belt again and giving another yank. It came loose and he eventually managed to slide it out from under the corpse. Holding up the buckle in the moonlight he realised it wasn't made of iron at all, but tin. Pretty much worthless.

Despondently, he moved on to another one of the corpses,

finding nothing of value. Then another, and another. Most of the dead had already been stripped of any worth, and Bedel got the sinking feeling his brother was right. He shouldn't be here at all. And now Wyg had run off into the night and there was no telling where he was. This had been a stupid thing to do.

He squinted through the dark, trying to see where his brother had gone.

'Wyg,' he uttered into the night as quiet as he could so as not to bring attention from the singing Franks. There was no reply.

Bedel moved through the field of dead, picking his way across the corpses. 'Wyg?' he whispered again. Still no answer.

There was a rising sense of panic in his stomach. If he returned without his little brother there would be hell to pay. His mother would beat him to within an inch of his life. Just as he began to despair, he heard laughing in the distance. Straining his ears, he made out a little voice he recognised coming from the camp at the summit of the hill.

No, it couldn't be.

Bedel began to make his way towards the sound of his brother's voice. Fires were lit all along the hilltop and he could see the silhouettes of foreign soldiers moving around in the dark. They were drinking and laughing, as the bodies of their enemies rotted in the night only a few feet away. In the midst of it all, he heard his brother babbling on about something or other as the Franks laughed along.

Stupid bloody Wyg. Never could keep his mouth shut, never could stay out of trouble.

Bedel had reached the edge of the camp. He heard his

brother's voice louder than any other. He was telling one of his stupid stories, but the Franks seemed to find it amusing for some reason. Then, from the edge of the dark, Bedel saw him.

Wyg was standing on a chair, and beside him a man sat eating at a table in the middle of the field. Warriors surrounded him, still in their mail coats, and Bedel could tell this was the man in charge. Everyone was showing him respect as he sat eating his fill from a big wooden table. And next to him stood Wyg nattering away.

'…and then we came all the way from our village,' Wyg said. 'We wanted to see, that's all. Me and my brother.'

The leader just sat eating, tearing at a chicken carcass and ignoring the boy. It reminded Bedel that all he'd eaten since breakfast was mouldy bread.

Half of him wanted to run off and leave Wyg with his new friends. But something inside him knew there was danger here. He had to take his brother home. He had to find the courage to step into this nest of snakes.

Bedel walked towards the table and the man who was eating from it. He stepped into the torchlight, passing the laughing warriors. He could see that every last one of them had been in a fight. Some were wounded and still bleeding, but none seemed to care.

As Bedel reached the table, the man looked up, fixing him with a stern gaze. His hair was cropped at the sides, his chin clean-shaven, a dark moustache hanging down past his sullen mouth.

'Wyg, we have to go home,' Bedel said, eyes still fixed on the man, unable to look away.

His brother stopped his talking, and an uncomfortable

silence fell over the group. The warrior wiped his mouth with the back of his hand. Then he spoke in another language, talking to Wyg as though he should have understood.

'Eh?' Wyg answered.

Bedel wanted to scream at his brother that they were in danger. That there was every chance they'd soon be as dead as the corpses lying on the field, but the words were stuck in his throat.

'He asks that you sit beside him, little one,' said a man at the edge of the gathering. Bedel saw he was dressed as a priest, but for the mail he wore under his robe. A silver crucifix hung about his neck, beneath a handsome smiling face.

With a nod, Wyg obeyed, sitting down on the chair beside the table. The warrior spoke again in the Frankish tongue, as though Wyg would suddenly understand him. Once again, the priest spoke for his leader.

'He says he has come to this land to conquer. He wants to know if you think he will be welcomed by your people?'

Wyg furrowed his brow. 'What do you mean?' the boy replied.

Bedel clenched his fists, fighting the urge to run, but how could he? If he left his brother here his life wouldn't be worth a spit.

'He has come to take your lands,' the priest said. 'So tell us, will your father bow down before his new king? Or will he fight against him?'

'Our dad's been dead years now,' Wyg replied.

The priest conveyed his words in Frankish, and the warrior shrugged before speaking again.

'Tell us, boy,' asked the priest. 'Will you give your fealty?'

Again Wyg furrowed his brow. 'I don't know what fealty is.'

'It is loyalty,' the priest replied. 'Undying devotion to your king.' He gestured to the warrior at the table. 'This man intends to rule over these lands. Will you bow down before him? Will you pledge your loyalty to your new master?'

Wyg looked at Bedel. He was unsure of what he was supposed to say.

Bedel took a step forward. 'We will both bow down before you, my lord,' he said, unsure which of the men he should address.

The priest seemed unmoved by Bedel's willingness to please, but still he gave the answer to the warrior at his table, who laid down the chicken carcass and said more words.

The priest regarded Bedel with a smile. 'Then let us hope that your countrymen are as eager to accept their fate as you are.'

That seemed to be it, as the king at his table went back to filling his belly.

'Can we go now?' Bedel asked, keen for this to be over with.

'Of course,' the priest said. 'Go. Live your lives. But do not forget the face of your new king. He will not forget yours.'

'Let's go, Wyg,' Bedel said.

Surprisingly, Wyg seemed only too happy to do as he was told this time, and he moved from behind the table. Bedel grabbed his brother's hand, and as they made their way from the camp, back towards the field of bodies, he could hear the Frankish warriors laughing once more.

He all but ran across the battlefield, pulling his brother along behind him. The rain was pouring now, and a distant storm was closing. Bedel felt it in the air just before the distant horizon suddenly lit up. A few seconds later there was an ominous rumble of thunder. He didn't stop running, pulling Wyg through the dark, dodging the bodies strewn in their path. Before they had crossed half the battlefield, Bedel's foot caught on something on the ground and he tripped, sprawling in the dirt.

'Come on we have to go,' Wyg said, hopping from one foot to the other, his hair and clothes drenched.

Bedel pushed himself up to his knees, looking down at the corpse he had tripped over. It was among a pile of dead men, their faces shining white and pitiful in the moonlight. He looked closer at the hulking body in front of him. Around its thick neck was an iron band, and as he reached out and touched the metal Bedel realised it was a torc. He had seen its like only once before, a piece of jewellery worn by a passing tinker. The man had told him how old and valuable such things were, and Bedel got a sudden warm feeling in his gut. Perhaps he might salvage something from this after all.

He took hold of the torc in both hands. There was another flash of lightning, and Bedel briefly saw that two wolf heads had been carved into each end of it. He yanked at the neckband, trying to free it, but it was held fast about the dead warrior's neck. As he yanked again, the thunder rumbled.

A hand grasped his arm in an iron grip.

Bedel heard Wyg yelp behind him, before his brother ran terrified into the night. Bedel could only watch in horror as the corpse pulled itself from the pile of bodies, still grasping tight to his arm. Arrows protruded from his mail; his hair and beard were matted to his face by blood and rain. He dragged himself to his feet, until he stood tall amidst the carnage of the battle, a terrifying giant back from the dead.

The corpse looked down, regarding Bedel with eyes filled with rage. Caught in that gaze, Bedel wanted to scream, wanted to beg for his life, but his voice would not come. All he could do was stare up at the giant and wonder if his last moments would be filled with agony, or if death would come mercifully quick.

Without a word, the warrior released him, and Bedel fell back to the mud. There he wallowed, as the giant stared up at the moon, face framed in the pale light. Bedel shivered, wondering what this warrior from the grave might do. Then, ignoring Bedel completely, he lumbered away into the night.

Bedel could only watch as the giant disappeared. Above the sound of the rumbling storm, the Franks began to sing louder.

'Let's go home now?' Wyg's voice pealed out through the rain, and Bedel saw him waiting at the edge of the battlefield.

For the first time in his life, Bedel did what his little brother asked.

PART ONE

THE IRON COLLAR

I

HEDEBY, DENMARK, WINTER 1050

The crackle of the fire was the only sound in the tiny hut as the boy sat on his mother's lap. He toyed with one of her golden braids that lay draped across his chest.

'Tell me again where I came from, Mamma,' the boy asked.

The woman squeezed him all the tighter, gathering the furs about them. He snuggled closer, warm in her embrace.

'Again, Styrkar?' she replied. 'I have told you this a thousand times.'

'But I like it,' he said, the flames from the fire dancing in his frost-blue eyes.

His mother sighed. 'Only five winters old and yet you already cause me trouble. Very well, but then you must go to bed.'

She ran her fingers across his thick red mane of hair and kissed his forehead. As Styrkar watched the flickering fire, his mother began.

'It was not so many years ago,' she said. 'Your father was

away on the hunt, and I was left alone to wait for him, as I often did. It was already bitterly cold and there was a hard winter coming. When the morning came I wrapped myself in a bearskin and went out walking towards the mountains. The sun was bright, but there was a frost on the ground. The last of the summer flowers would soon be dead and I wanted to pick them and make the house pretty for when your father returned. As I carefully chose snapdragons, orchids and daisies, I spied a flower I had never seen before. It was blue as the ocean, petals like the wings of a butterfly. I picked it to smell its sweet fragrance. Never had I seen anything more beautiful. Then I spied another, and another after that. So I picked another, and another, until the trail of flowers led me to the woods. I didn't stop until I had a whole bunch of beautiful blue flowers in my hand, but then I realised I was lost. I'd been so bewitched by the beauty of the flowers that I had wandered far into the woods. It was then I heard the baby crying.'

'Is that me, Mamma?'

'Patience, Styrkar.' She ruffled his hair to quiet him. 'We will get there.'

The boy laughed at his mischief as his mother continued.

'I forgot the flowers and the cold and the fact that I was lost, and I rushed deeper into the woods. It was dark and I could still hear the crying, but the noise seemed to be coming from all around. I searched and searched, but could not find it. I began to panic, so sad it made me weep. It was cold, and I knew if I did not find the baby soon it would freeze. I did not stop. I looked and looked, and just when I thought I would never find the baby something stirred just through the trees. In the shadows I could see the red glow of two eyes staring at me. The eyes of a wolf.

'My heart stopped beating, and we stared at one another. I did not know if the wolf would attack or run, but there was something about it that made me forget my fear. Then, just as quickly as it had come, the wolf was gone. Something in me knew I had to chase this creature. I followed, rushing through the ferns until my legs were sore but eventually I found it: a baby lying on the ground, skin pale, eyes blue like the winter sky, hair red as flame and a voice loud as thunder.

'I picked him up and covered him with my bearskin cloak. Your father and I had wanted a child for so long, but we had not yet been blessed by Freya. As I held this child close to my breast I knew then that I would keep him forever.

'Alone in the woods I began to wander. I was hopelessly lost, and dusk was starting to fall, but through the trees I saw something.'

'The wolf,' Styrkar said, unable to stop himself.

'Yes, the wolf. He guided me back through the trees, all the way to the edge of the woods. As I made my way back home, I knew this was no ordinary animal. The wolf who had guided me into the woods and shown me the way was Fenrir, the son of Loki. And he had given me a precious gift. From that day, I knew that he would watch over me as I watched over his precious child. So there, is that what you wanted to hear?'

Styrkar smiled as he looked into the fire. 'Yes, Mamma,' he said.

'Good. Then now it is time for bed.'

Before the boy could protest, the door to the hut burst open. His mother turned with a sharp intake of breath, clutching her son tightly as the hut was filled by the chill night air. In the doorway stood Styrkar's father, a look of horror on his face the boy had never seen before.

'Raiders,' he said, rushing to take up his axe.

Styrkar's mother stood, placing her son down in front of the hearth. She drew a knife and followed her husband to the door. As his father rushed out into the night, Styrkar's mother paused at the door. She turned, looking at her son standing next to the fire.

'Hide yourself,' she said. 'Do not let them find you.'

With that she rushed out into the night.

The boy stood there as the wind whipped through the hut. The fire behind him was agitated by the flames, growing angry at the intrusion. Styrkar could hear distant sounds from outside: screams of alarm, bellows of anger. There was a ringing sound that reminded him of the blacksmith as he hammered his steel. And all the while Styrkar waited, looking through the open door and out into the night.

He would never remember how long he stood there, as the sounds of violence gradually faded. Despite what his mother had said, Styrkar did not hide. Instead, when he had waited long enough, he walked to the door and stepped out into the night.

Fires raged all around the town of Hedeby.

In the moonlight he could see men rushing from dwelling to dwelling, their swords and axes flashing in the night. Despite the danger, the boy began to walk, searching for his mother among the carnage.

He passed a spear thrust into the ground. Atop it was a

head he recognised but couldn't quite place, the face hanging slack, blood still dripping from the severed neck. A scream alerted him to the sight of a woman being dragged into a nearby house by her hair, two bearded warriors taking a grim delight in her misery. Somewhere a dog was barking incessantly until it was suddenly cut off with a strangled yelp.

Styrkar wandered in a daze, somehow managing to reach the edge of the town unmolested. Perhaps he should have run, but he had not yet found his mother among the slaughter. What was he to do without her?

When he reached the waterfront he could see the whole town. Ships were burning in the harbour, the flames rising so high they blotted out the moon. Fires raged all across the settlement as its people screamed and died. Styrkar could only watch the life he had known crumble to ashes.

As the chill of night began to creep into his bones, someone approached. They stood beside him at the flaming waterside, joining him to witness the town burn. Styrkar looked up at the man, seeing a grizzled stranger, sword at his side, shield across his back bearing a black painted raven. He was old, his eyes wrinkled, his beard long and thick. A more brutal face Styrkar had never seen. The warrior watched for some time as the flames danced in his eyes.

'Do not be troubled,' he said eventually, his voice deep and forbidding. 'This was always meant to happen.'

When Styrkar did not answer, the man knelt down beside him, as though imparting some nugget of deep wisdom.

'Your people were always fated to be slaves.'

Styrkar turned to look the warrior in the eyes. He saw no remorse, no emotion in that face, and in return did his best to show no fear.

'Some people are meant to be slaves,' the warrior continued. 'Others destined to be conquerors. You, boy... you are now a slave. And you always will be.'

Styrkar turned away, taking in the sight of the burning town for the last time. Before he was eventually taken away aboard a ship bound for a foreign land, he made himself a single promise.

He would never forget what he saw this night...

And he would never forgive.

2

ÁNSLO, NORWAY, SUMMER 1055

The smell of cooking pig made Styrkar's stomach grumble in appreciation, but he was forbidden to eat it. No feast of meat and ale for young Styrkar – he would get only scraps. The hounds that lounged at the king's feet were better fed than he was.

The court of Sigurdsson was a dour place, a dangerous place, but Styrkar had managed to survive well enough. He watched from a corner of the kitchen as Ingerith and her cooks prepared the feast. There he sat, waiting to be called, along with the other slaves. He raised a finger, pressing it between the iron collar at his neck and the flesh beneath. It had long since hardened, a callous around his throat that had set like a scar.

You will always be a slave, Harald had once told him. Styrkar had no reason to believe he was wrong.

'More ale,' came a shout from outside the kitchen.

Ingerith hurried to fill a jug, looking over to where Styrkar crouched.

'Quickly,' she said.

Styrkar scrambled to his feet, taking the heavy jug and carrying it across the kitchen. On his way he saw a discarded bone at the edge of the table, only a few strands of gristle remaining on it. As he moved past he swept the bone into his kirtle and carried on, out into the open air.

He was suddenly hit by the sound of raucous laughter from the mead hall. His bare feet squelched through the cold mud as he crossed the path from the kitchens, and he heard a yap as Three Legs came limping up to him. The sorry-looking hound had been one of Harald's best hunters a few years before, but after being attacked by a wolf he had lost a leg, along with the favour of his master. Three Legs wasn't the most inventive of names, but the dog didn't seem to mind it.

Styrkar paused, reaching into his shirt and offering the bone he had pilfered. The dog sniffed at it, then gently took it in his jaws and slunk off to a quiet corner to eat.

So much for the gratitude of hounds.

As Styrkar opened the door to the mead hall he was almost overwhelmed by the stench of stale sweat and beer. There was a boisterous racket. Harald laughed loudly with his jarls. Someone was lying on the ground, beaten and bloody, but that was not an uncommon sight in the court of King Harald. These events usually ended with a fight or two, and on extreme occasions with a corpse.

Styrkar knew it was best not to think on such things. Better to worry for his own safety.

He moved around the table, pouring ale into waiting tankards, unnoticed and unacknowledged, just the way he liked it. Harald held court, and all eyes were on him. Some of the faces Styrkar recognised, others were strangers from different parts of the kingdom, most likely jarls or warriors of note come to curry favour with the king. Young Magni, Harald's son, sat close to his father. Though not that much older than Styrkar, he was still a trusted aide and considered a warrior. Styrkar had to subdue his envy for the boy's position and not think on what might have been had fate treated him differently.

In his heart, Styrkar was still the spawn of Fenrir, despite his lowly position. That one story his mother told by the fire all those years ago had stayed with him. It was the only precious thing he had to hold on to.

'We will strike up a fleet the likes of which the oceans have never seen,' proclaimed a particularly drunk warrior. Styrkar did not recognise him.

'And will you take the head of Sweyn himself?' another of the warriors said with a laugh.

'I'll piss in his eyes,' said the man, and he was joined in boisterous laughter.

Styrkar did his best to pour more ale without spilling it but the task was difficult with such rowdy behaviour. As the laughter subsided, the man seemed heartened by the encouragement of his fellow warriors and continued.

'Then I'll take that crown from his head and proclaim myself master of all Denmark.'

He laughed, but his was the only voice raised this time.

Styrkar took a step back. In all his years in service to Harald he had learned to sense the coming of violence. When directed at him, he had taken every balled fist and open palm with gritted teeth, facing the pain and humiliation without complaint, but he also had the sense to take to the shadows when someone else was the target.

All eyes had turned to Harald, who did not move, did not speak, but merely stared at the warrior with the loud mouth.

'I did not mean…' the man began, but in that withering gaze he could not even manage to apologise.

'Yes you did,' said Harald, his gravelly voice slurring from too much ale. 'So tell me what you'll do with that crown.'

The man slowly stood. Styrkar could see the fear in him, despite his efforts to disguise it. There could be no show of weakness among these men, and it would be a tough task for him to back down and still save face.

'What I mean is, I would take that crown and lay it at your feet.'

'So you would be the kingmaker?' Harald said. 'And I your puppet?'

More uncomfortable silence. Styrkar could only watch as the man considered the king's words, trying to formulate a way he could get out of this in one piece.

'I would…' The man was struggling.

Styrkar knew something bad was about to happen. Some of the men around the table were watching keenly, looking forward to the spectacle.

Before Harald could react there was a piercing shriek from outside. Styrkar heard laughing, and the whining of a dog. Three Legs.

Forgetting the prospect of violence within the mead hall, he dropped the jug of ale and rushed outside. Further along the pathway were a group of warriors he didn't recognise, the followers of a visiting jarl. One of them had tied a rope around one of the dog's remaining legs and was dragging him along the path.

Styrkar felt a red rage burning inside. For years he had tried to hide it, to keep his mouth shut at every blow, quelling his anger at every injustice he had suffered. All that was gone in a single moment.

He ran towards the men, heedless of what might happen to him. As he approached, Three Legs snapped at one of the warriors clamping jaws to the man's thigh. He yelled in pain, kicking out at the dog and Three Legs yelped. The hound shied away from the man, who kicked him again.

'Stop,' shouted Styrkar rushing towards him and trying to push him away, but he may as well have been trying to push over the tree.

The warrior backhanded Styrkar and he fell into the mud.

'Are you mad, boy?' he snarled. 'You must be, risking your life for this useless mutt?'

He kicked Three Legs, and the dog whined for mercy, tail between its legs, head bowed. Ignoring the pitiful squeal the warrior kicked Three Legs again and again.

Styrkar leapt to his feet rushing forward with a cry of anger. He wasn't thinking now; he was just filled with hate. He forgot the collar around his neck and his duty to his master. Forgot he was a slave with no higher standing than the dog he was trying to protect.

There was a knife at the warrior's belt, and Styrkar grasped it, pulling it clear of the sheath and stabbing at him. The blade plunged into his thigh almost up to the hilt. The warrior growled, staggering back. Surrounding him, the men who had been amused at the display were laughing no longer. One of them grabbed Styrkar by his red hair and held him up, exposing the boy's throat as he drew his own knife.

'Enough!' A voice Styrkar recognised.

King Harald and his jarls had left the mead hall to see what the commotion was about. Styrkar was still held by his hair as the king approached.

'He stabbed me,' said the warrior. 'This little bastard stabbed me.'

The king looked over the scene, then fixed Styrkar with a glare.

'You allowed yourself to be attacked by this little heathen slave?'

That seemed to shame the man, who had already pulled the knife clear of his thigh and had a hand clamped over the bleeding wound.

'I would have justice,' said the warrior. 'This boy, this slave, needs to learn obedience.'

Harald nodded. 'That he does,' he replied.

The warrior took a step towards Styrkar, bloody knife still in his hand. There was no doubt what he was about to do with it.

'And I will decide what that punishment is,' said Harald.

That stayed the man's hand, and he stood waiting for the order to strike, eyes burning with hatred.

Harald looked down at Three Legs, whining on the ground, and then at Styrkar. 'You would risk your life for this dog? Are you stupid, boy? You want to die?'

Right now, Styrkar didn't care one way or the other. He

was ready for this to end and he would face death if he had to.

Harald could clearly see the defiance in his eyes. 'If you like dogs so much, maybe you should live like one.'

He took Styrkar from the warrior and dragged him up the path. Styrkar already knew where he was going; he could hear the sound of the hounds barking in the distance. As Harald dragged him past the kitchens he saw Ingerith watching. She was powerless to help even if she had wanted to, but she held her tongue, fearful of what might happen to her if she spoke out. Styrkar couldn't blame her for that. He had kept his own silence many times when a fellow slave was being abused.

The hounds were howling at the prospect of being fed. Styrkar's heart beat faster the closer he was dragged to the cage they were kept in.

'You want to be a hound?' Harald said. 'Let's see what's left of you after you spend the night with them.'

He pulled open the door to the cage and flung the boy inside. Styrkar was plunged into darkness. Outside there was laughter as Harald and the rest of the warriors left him to his fate. He could hear the hounds growling and sniffing in the dark, and quickly crawled to one corner, putting his back to the wooden enclosure. In the scant light he could see he was surrounded. At any moment he expected the hounds to leap at him and sink their jaws into his flesh, but instead they fixed the newcomer with sullen eyes, watching him from the shadows. He wondered how long it would be before they overcame their curiosity and decided to eat their fill.

Styrkar sat and shivered in the dark. All the while the hounds glared until one of them approached, sniffing at Styrkar's legs. There was a low growl rumbling in its throat and Styrkar should have been afraid, but as he looked at this beast, shut away in its cage, he realised they were much the same. This was their lot, to be slaves to a wicked master. In that moment both boy and beast knew they were exactly alike.

Slowly, Styrkar reached out a hand to the beast. It sniffed his fingers, then licked them, most likely tasting the remnants of the bone he had stolen from the kitchen earlier. Styrkar scratched the dog's face, tousled an ear and his hand touched upon the collar at the dog's neck. It was thick leather, but may as well have been forged from the same iron as the one about his own throat.

On seeing this hound get so much attention, another head peered from the shadows. The second dog whined in its throat as it came closer and Styrkar reached out his other hand. Before he knew it he was surrounded, the pack sniffing and fussing him, jostling one another for his attention. One of them lay beside him, another putting its head on his lap so he might stroke it. Perhaps none of these dogs had been shown such attention before. Perhaps they thought Styrkar was just another of their number and were welcoming him to the pack. Either way, he spent that night warm among the bodies of hunting hounds until the light of morning broke the dark.

'They won't need feeding this morning,' said a voice from beyond the cage, stirring Styrkar from his slumber.

Two men laughed. 'That was harsh, even for Sigurdsson. Boy can't have been much more than ten winters.'

'What do you care?' The bolt of the cage door slid open. 'Anyway, let's get these beasts out and on the hunt. King's got a sore head this morning and wants to clear it out in the forest.'

The door squeaked on its hinges as it opened. From within the cage, Styrkar could see the legs of two men standing and waiting for the hounds to come bounding out. Instead they remained, crowding around Styrkar in the dark.

'What's going on? They're usually howling up a storm by now.'

One of the men bent to look inside. Styrkar moved forward, and crawled his way out of the pen.

'Christ preserve us,' said one of the men, taking a step back. The other ran off as though he'd seen some kind of ghost.

Styrkar stood squinting in the sun as the rest of the hounds padded out of the cage, to sit at his feet. As his eyes adjusted to the light he could see men approaching from down the path, King Harald and the warrior he had stabbed among them.

'What's this?' said the king as he arrived.

The man who had released Styrkar from the cage could hardly find his words.

'I just opened the door and he walked out.'

Harald stared at Styrkar as though doubtful that was the truth. Surely this boy had not survived the night among his fiercest hunting hounds.

'There's not a mark on you, boy,' he said. 'How?'

Styrkar wouldn't have known how to answer had he wanted to, and so he stood in silence with the dogs at his feet.

'This is no justice,' said the warrior Styrkar had stabbed the day before. 'He should be punished.'

'No, Father,' said Magni. Harald's son stepped forward, looking Styrkar up and down. 'I would have him.'

'You?' said Harald. 'And what would you do with him?'

'You have your hounds, Father. I would have mine… until I am of an age where I inherit the pack.' He gestured to the rest of the hunting dogs.

Harald barked a laugh. 'You see,' he said to his men. 'Magni has ambition, just like his father. Very well. It will do you good to learn how to control a hound. But be careful – this one has teeth.'

He laughed as he gestured to the wounded warrior and the bandage that covered his thigh. The rest of the men joined him and soon every voice was raised in mirth. All but Magni and Styrkar.

The two boys stared at one another. A master and his new hound.

3

THE IRISH SEA, SPRING 1058

The ship rocked under a cloudy sky, floating like a dead man on the waves. When they had set out days before there had been a lively atmosphere aboard the ship. The journey had started with singing, men pulling at their oars with relish in anticipation of the riches to come.

Now the oarsmen sat in dour reflection, a pall of gloom hanging over every one of them.

There was a crew of thirty, all watching as Kjartan glared at the waves, squinted at the sky, licked a finger to test the wind. Nothing. They were utterly lost. The rest of Magni's fleet was nowhere to be seen; they had lost sight of them a day ago when cresting the northern peninsula, and now they were alone with nothing but the fog for company.

Styrkar sat towards the rear of the ship, his eyes averted from the rest of the crew. He was the only slave among them, the lowliest of the bunch, and as such it would serve him well to not draw attention.

He had taken out the piece of wood in his kirtle and the

small knife he was allowed to carry, and begun to whittle. Over time, the shape of the wood had revealed itself. It was always the same – there was no plan to what he created. Styrkar would simply let the knife unveil the carving one knurl of wood at a time. Already he could see what was taking shape. A crow was slowly appearing: a beak, a wing, a tail. As he carved at the wood he would add little intricacies: the sharp groove of a feather, the deep set of an eye. It was not long before it would be complete.

Beside him, Ragi snatched the carving from his grasp. Styrkar could do little to stop the hulking warrior, and he sat in silence as Ragi turned the wood over in his hand.

'What the bloody hell is this?' he said, his voice surprisingly high-pitched for such an imposing man. They had been oar-mates for the last few miles and it was the first thing he had deigned to say to Styrkar.

'Just a bird,' Styrkar replied.

'It's shit,' Ragi said, flinging the carving into the sea.

They sat in more silence as Kjartan continued to work out where they were.

Styrkar had hoped this would be his one chance. He was still a slave, but joining a raid would give him the opportunity to prove himself, to show his worth as more than just another oarsman. Magni himself had allowed Styrkar to come along, and for a brief moment Styrkar had hoped he would have the opportunity to fight. That chance was looking slim now. He had helped load the ship and been given an oar, but no one had thought to gift him with sword, shield or axe. It seemed he was just here as a beast of burden; always the faithful hound.

Styrkar glanced to the back of the boat. Ordulf stood

impatiently at the steerboard, waiting to be told what to do next. As Styrkar gazed at the man, Ordulf's eyes fell on him and he was quick to look away. He did not want to catch the eye of any of these warriors, least of all the man in charge of the ship. The less attention he brought on himself, the less chance he had of ending up in the sea.

Perhaps when they found land he would have his chance to prove himself – to show these warriors he was more than just a slave. To show them he was worthy enough to join their ranks. It was not unheard of; men had risen from slavery before by their strength of arms. All Styrkar needed was the chance.

'Well?' said Ansgar. He was the biggest of their number, a brute of a man who loomed two rows in front of Styrkar. 'Where are we?'

'I'm working on it,' Kjartan growled back. He held up the sun-shadow board to the grey sky, closing one eye and staring at it as though willing it to show him the way.

'We should never have agreed to come on this fool's errand,' Ansgar continued, talking to everyone and no one all at once. 'We have followed a boy. A bloody boy to the arse end of nowhere. Who thought that would be a good idea?'

Indeed they had followed Magni, and now it seemed they were regretting it. Though little older than Styrkar, he had built a fleet and a loyal following among the warriors of Harald Sigurdsson, but he was yet to win the renown his father commanded. This was his way of doing it – to join with the rebellious Welsh and plunder the coast of England. So far there had been little plunder and a lot of aimless rowing.

'Shit!' cried Kjartan, venting his frustration by pitching the shadow-board into the sea. 'That way,' he said, pointing in what was obviously a random direction. Styrkar was pretty sure they had already come from that way, but he made no complaint. As the rest of the warriors groaned and moaned their discontent, he took up the oar, and together they began to pull.

After days of rowing Styrkar had grown used to the labour. At first his back and shoulders had burned like fire from it, but now he was used to the work. Though still considered a thrall to his master, he had grown big enough to rival any young warrior.

They carried on rowing through the mists for more endless hours. Kjartan continued to stand at the prow, glaring out into the grey, but there was nothing to see but endless fog.

Eventually, Styrkar heard the screech of a gull before it landed right beside Kjartan. The navigator glared down at it, as though the bird had just insulted him. Then his eyes widened.

'See,' he proclaimed. 'I told you we couldn't be far away.'

'There!' shouted Topi, a young warrior a little older than Styrkar. 'I see it.'

Everyone followed his gesture, seeing the looming shape of cliffs appear through the haze.

'And our prayers are answered,' Kjartan said, though Styrkar doubted any of them had been praying for land. Maybe cursing Kjartan and planning his murder, but not praying.

Ordulf shifted the steerboard and they began to row closer to shore. More gulls wheeled and screeched atop the cliff edge and the sky began to brighten, lifting the fog to reveal the green hills ahead.

Styrkar felt some relief. The atmosphere on the boat became less oppressive, but there was also anticipation among the warriors. This was what they had come for – to plunder and grow their reputations.

They reached a small cove, and the boat slid up onto the beach. Kjartan was quick to jump down, sword drawn, eyes scanning for any witness to their arrival. Styrkar felt a sudden twinge of sympathy for anyone who happened to be on the beach when they arrived, but there was no one here. The place was deserted, and he placed down his oar with Ragi and followed the rest of them off the boat.

They milled about on the beach, stretching stiff backs and legs. Days aboard ship had left them used to the weft and wane of the sea, and Styrkar felt unbalanced as he trudged up the beach.

'Where are you going?' Ragi said.

Styrkar turned to look at the hulking warrior. For the first time since they had set off he was conscious of the iron collar that sat tight about his ever-thickening neck.

'I was just—'

'Get the boat unloaded, shithead,' Ragi ordered.

Styrkar knew better than to complain, trudging back down the beach and onto the ship. He began to grab their supplies: dried meat, berries, nuts for the journey. Tent poles and bedrolls, a pot for cooking. As he grabbed a set of spears he heard Ordulf muster the men around him.

'You all know why we're here,' he said, his voice hoarse and thin from a wound he'd taken to the neck some years before. It had left a vicious scar across his throat and given

Ordulf a peerless reputation for survival. 'Magni called this raid to aid the Welsh. To harry the king of these lands. To seal an alliance. Well, forget that. We're not here to follow some boy.'

Styrkar could hear noises of approval from some of the warriors, Ansgar the loudest among them.

'We're on our own now,' Ordulf continued. 'There is no one to help us, but neither do we need them. These people are weak, this land has riches for the taking and there's nothing to stop us. If we think smart, move fast and fight hard we can take these easy pickings and be back to the sea before the local lord even knows we're here. Are we of the same mind?'

'We are,' shouted Kjartan, a little too eagerly.

His voice was soon joined by the rest of the men, and Styrkar could feel the bloodlust rising in each of them. A couple of the warriors even drew swords, waving them around as though there might be someone to fight on the empty cove.

'Right,' said Ordulf. 'Then we'd best make our way. We won't win gold and renown farting around on this beach.'

The warriors turned and made their way back towards the boat, picking up their armour and weapons, placing helmets on heads, slinging spears over shoulder, taking up shields.

Styrkar could only watch with envy as they prepared for war. He was not to be honoured with armour and the only weapon he carried was a blade barely long enough to kill a rabbit. He picked up a heavy sack full of supplies and followed the eager warriors.

As they trudged their way up the beach towards a grassy

path through the rocks, Topi came to stand close by. The lad was tall, eager. This was his first raid and he'd insisted on coming aboard Ordulf's ship rather than join his father and brothers. He wanted to make his own way. Styrkar could only dream of such ambition.

'Your time will come,' Topi said.

Styrkar nodded his acknowledgement. He knew he was almost as strong as any of these veteran warriors, and he would grow much stronger yet. Given the chance he could learn to wield axe and sword and spear as well as any of them. But that opportunity looked slim.

'Soon, I hope,' Styrkar replied.

'I can't wait for my chance,' Topi continued. 'These people are feeble; everyone knows it. Since the reign of Cnut they've grown too pious. Their blood mixing with the mongrels, becoming weak. This'll be easy. We'll return laden down with silver and slaves. People will speak our names for years.'

Speak your names, Styrkar thought. Would anyone ever speak his, he wondered? As he adjusted the pack on his back to make it more comfortable, the collar at his throat feeling tighter than ever, he already had his answer. No one ever spoke the name of a pack mule with anything but disdain.

Ordulf led the raiding party across the coastline. There were only thirty of them – not a large force, but more than enough seasoned fighters to take on even a well-populated settlement. As the day wore on, the sky brightened, and Styrkar began to sweat under his burden, the enthusiasm the warriors had displayed on the beach beginning to wane.

Up ahead, Styrkar saw Ordulf raise a hand. There was a copse of trees not too far inland, and they all hunkered down, eyes scanning for any sign of life. As they waited, a man appeared from beyond the tree line, carrying a sack across his shoulder. He was foraging most likely, and he stopped as he saw the grim party of shaggy warriors watching him from yards away.

For some moments they simply stood and stared at one another. Then, ever so slowly the man raised a hand and waved. Styrkar could hear a couple of the raiders laugh.

Then the man dropped his sack and sprinted off into the trees.

Ragi moved to give chase, but Ordulf grabbed the collar of his mail shirt and stopped him.

'Let's give him a head start,' said their leader. 'We don't want to catch the rabbit before it leads us to the warren.'

Ragi nodded his agreement, but his eyes still burned, yearning for the hunt.

As one, the warriors loped after their prey.

4

WESSEX, ENGLAND, SPRING 1058

They ran. Styrkar's bare feet ached as he followed the fleeing warriors towards the coast. They had passed through a strip of thick woodland, the briar cutting into his soles and slashing his legs, but he ignored the pain. Yielding to it would be the death of him.

Ordulf led their flight, closely followed by Ragi and Kjartan. Topi was with them too but wounded as he was, he struggled to keep up. Styrkar paused for a moment, turning to wait for the young warrior. When he caught up, Styrkar took him by the arm, dragging him along. If the lad was grateful he didn't have the strength to mention it.

Thirty raiders had fallen on the settlement like wolves on a lamb. Styrkar remembered the screams, the violence, the barking of dogs and the wailing of children. It had been nothing like he'd expected. There were no valiant warriors to defend the village, just a mob of frightened farmers desperate to survive, pleading for mercy in a language

Styrkar didn't understand. But he supposed the sound of begging villagers was much the same in any language.

From the stories he'd been told of daring raids along the coast, anyone would have thought it the most heroic thing a man could do. All Styrkar had seen was butchery.

Long-forgotten memories had come back to him as the burning started. Memories of his own hometown reduced to ashes. He had been a fool to expect anything different this time. Only there was a difference.

Ordulf had spoken of a lightning attack, of them pillaging the settlement then moving on. But that had not happened. They had tarried too long. Glutted themselves on the settlement's food and ale and women, carousing well into the night. They had awoken the next morning not to an empty village of beaten farmers, but to warriors waiting to avenge themselves on these invaders.

The fight had been brief. Styrkar had followed as the warriors fought hard to escape, but these were not the weak English he had been taught to expect. They fought with all the fury and skill of any Norseman, and Ordulf's men had been no match for them.

Styrkar had run with the survivors and now only five of them remained. A glance back through the trees told him their pursuers were not ready to give up yet, but if they could just reach the boat even a crew of five might be able to escape.

They burst from the thick canopy, out onto an open field. Ahead Styrkar could see the vast blue of the sea, and smell the salt in the air. They weren't far.

'Come on,' Ordulf wheezed at them from up ahead. 'Faster, you dogs.'

Ragi and Kjartan sped on past, and Ordulf watched as Styrkar helped Topi along. For a moment Styrkar thought he might also help the young warrior, but instead he turned and ran after the other two.

Sparing another glance back, Styrkar could see their pursuers crashing through the brush in the distance. They weren't far behind, and he pulled Topi along more eagerly.

When they'd almost reached the beachhead, Styrkar could smell something other than the sea. There was an acrid stench of smoke in the air, of something that had been burned just a few hours before. As he reached the headland he stopped, glaring down at the beach.

'Shit!' Ragi shouted at the sky. 'We are cursed.'

The five of them looked down at the remains of their ship. It had been set on fire, the front half now little more than charred timbers, the rest floating uselessly in the sea. There would be no escape.

Ordulf drew his sword, still panting from their flight. Ragi pulled his axe and Kjartan just stood, hands by his sides, his weapons lost in the earlier fight.

'Remember who we are,' Ordulf said as Styrkar laid Topi down on the ground. The young warrior was pale, his flesh clammy as he gripped the wound in his side. Blood had poured down his thigh, soaking his leggings. His sword was still in its sheath but he looked in no condition to wield it.

'We will not die like farmers or fishermen,' Ordulf continued. 'We are warriors.'

If Ragi or Kjartan shared their leader's enthusiasm for a noble death, neither was in the mood to say so.

Styrkar stood with them, facing the trees, awaiting their fate to come rushing out to cut them down. But it did not rush. The English knew they had the Norsemen cornered. There was no longer any need for haste.

Three warriors came forward carrying shield and axe. Then another three. Then a half dozen. They stood a few yards away, watching, as though unwilling to take on the beaten and wounded raiders.

'What are you waiting for?' yelled Ordulf as loud as he could manage. 'Which of you will fight me?'

A few of the English glanced at one another in confusion, a couple of them shrugging.

'I don't think they understand you,' said Kjartan.

Ordulf fixed him with a withering glare, eyebrow raised. 'I can bloody well see that,' he replied.

Styrkar heard the snort of a pony from within the wood. From beyond the trees walked a black horse, its rider staring intently. The English warriors made a gap for him to ride through and he sat atop the mount, glaring at the beaten raiders. His chin was clean-shaven, a dark moustache drooping down past his mouth, giving him a grim aspect.

Another rider came to join him and they both regarded the raiders. Styrkar felt his hands begin to shake and he balled them into fists. He was determined to show no fear, even at the end... especially at the end.

'I will fight you,' said the mounted warrior. He spoke the Norse language like a native.

As he climbed down from his horse, the second rider began to protest. Styrkar could not understand what was being said but it was clear he was not happy with this man rising to Ordulf's challenge.

Despite the protest, the warrior ignored the other rider, taking his shield from his pony's saddle and drawing his sword. Ordulf stepped forward, sword in hand, hefting his own shield. He planted his feet in front of the English warrior and raised his head.

'If I beat you, will your men grant my freedom?'

The warrior shook his head. 'You will die here today,' he replied. 'All that's in question is how… fighting for your life, or begging for it.'

That was all Ordulf needed to know, and he roared as loud as his hoarse throat would allow, charging forward, sword raised.

The English warrior braced himself as Ordulf smashed into him. It barely knocked him back a step and he countered, smashing his sword once, twice, three times against Ordulf's shield. Styrkar watched as their leader stumbled under the blows, staggering back against the power of his enemy.

Shaking his head, Ordulf charged in again. This time he tried to batter the warrior back with his own shield, but the Englishman moved aside, the impetus of Ordulf's charge making him stumble forward. The warrior hacked in with his sword, opening up the back of Ordulf's neck.

The raider staggered, desperate to stay on his feet but his legs would not obey him and he fell to his knees. The English warrior did not gloat in his victory, wasting no time as he struck again, severing Ordulf's head from his shoulders.

He turned to face the rest of them. 'Who is next?' the warrior asked.

Ragi and Kjartan looked to one another, unsure of what to do. Kjartan shook his head, splaying his hands to show he was unarmed. Ragi looked to the row of English, realising this was his last day, that there was no other way than to die. For the first time Styrkar saw fear in these men's eyes and it sickened him to his stomach.

All their talk of great deeds, all their talk of dying a hero's death was nothing more than wasted air. They were just like any other men. They were not great warriors. They were cowards.

Styrkar knelt by Topi, who lay silently in the grass, and pulled his sword from its sheath. Stepping towards the warrior in his bare feet, with no armour but the iron collar at his neck, Styrkar said, 'I will fight you.'

There was some laughter from the watching English. They didn't take him seriously, but then why would they? What could he do against this mighty warrior who had just bested the fearsome Ordulf as though he were some worthless sheep farmer?

The English warrior was less amused though, and he regarded Styrkar with a curious look. It took some time before Styrkar realised he was being shown respect. For the first time in his life someone regarded him as an equal.

'Begin,' said the warrior with a nod.

Styrkar charged. He raised the sword high, aiming at the shield but intending it as a feint. If he could strike low when the warrior raised it perhaps he had a chance.

The warrior struck forward with his shield before Styrkar had a chance to bring his sword down. The rim smashed against his jaw and he went down, dazed, the grass soft against his face.

Rage bubbled within him, threatening to consume him. He had lived his life as a dog, scrabbling in the dirt to survive. There was no way he would die in the same manner.

Picking up the sword once more, he charged again.

This time the warrior parried his blow, sending the sword spinning from his grip before driving the pommel of his weapon into Styrkar's nose.

Stars flashed before his eyes as he fell backwards. The copper tang of blood filled his mouth. Styrkar floundered, expecting the final blow to come, but as his eyes focused he saw the warrior was waiting patiently. Though his hands were shaking, Styrkar was no longer afraid, just furious. He would not die like this. He could not die like this.

'Come on,' he said, as he staggered to his feet. 'Kill me. Come on.'

The warrior stood unmoving. It only served to fill Styrkar with yet more anger, and he bellowed from the bottom of his lungs, charging like an animal, unarmed, unarmoured. This would be his death, but anyone who cared to witness would not see him die a slave.

He didn't even see the shield coming this time. It took him in the side of his head, driving him to the ground. All the strength was gone from his limbs, and yet he still tried to drag himself to his feet. A kick drove him back to the dirt, and before he could think to rise once more, the warrior planted a heavy foot in his chest.

'You have courage,' he said. 'But my horse has more skill with a sword.'

'Let me up,' Styrkar snarled, writhing with all his strength, but he could not move, barely able to breathe beneath the weight of the warrior.

'What's your name, boy?' the warrior asked.

There was no use fighting it now. He was powerless. Best this was over with.

'My name is Styrkar,' he said.

'Not much of a raider, are you, Styrkar?'

'I am...' The word was lost on his tongue for a moment, but Styrkar knew what he was, better than any man. 'I am a slave.'

The side of the warrior's mouth turned up for the briefest moment and then the smile was gone. 'You have much courage for a slave. Are you loyal to these men?' He gestured to Kjartan and Ragi, who stood watching silently.

'My master is Magni,' Styrkar replied.

'And where is this Magni now?'

Styrkar shook his head.

'If he is not here, then you are a slave with no master. And I can claim you for my own. What say you? Will you die here on this hill, or will you be my slave?'

It was no choice at all.

'Yes,' Styrkar replied. 'I will be your slave.'

The warrior took his foot from Styrkar's chest and offered his hand. He pulled Styrkar to his feet and clapped a hand to his back. The rest of the English warriors closed in on the other three surviving raiders. Styrkar could not help himself, and he turned to watch. As the English advanced, Ragi ran to meet them but he was hopelessly outnumbered and cut down in an instant. Kjartan and Topi could only wait for the end.

Styrkar did not feel any pity, not even for young Topi. They had come bringing death with them – it was only fitting this was how it ended.

The English warrior pressed his sword pommel to Styrkar's bruised chin, turning his head away from the killing. 'Don't feel bad for them, Styrkar the Norseman.

They knew what they were facing when they landed on these shores.'

'I am no Norseman,' Styrkar replied. He knew where he came from; he had never been allowed to forget it since the day he had been taken by King Harald. 'I am a Dane.'

'I am Harold, son of Godwine. Jarl of Hereford. And you fight like you don't care if you live or die, Styrkar the Dane. So tell me, do you wish for death?'

Styrkar was unsure how to answer. Before that day he had never been asked his opinion on anything. Living and dying meant little to him, but there was one thing he knew for sure.

'No, I do not wish for death. I only wish to be free. And if you take this iron from my neck I'll serve you of my own free will until I am dead... or you are. Whichever comes first.'

Harold nodded. 'All in good time,' he replied. 'First I need to teach you to fight.'

5

BOSEHAM, ENGLAND, SEPTEMBER 1062

The hall stank of sweat and embers. The place was stifling in contrast to the crisp air outside, but for some reason they had chosen to do this indoors. Forty men, all crammed together, the feasting table moved aside to make a space for the fighters.

Styrkar wore his mail shirt but no helmet. In his hands he gripped an axe. Almost five feet of haft topped with a steel head. He remembered the first time he had lifted one of these weapons, how heavy it had felt in his arms. Now he wielded it as though it weighed nothing, but he had grown much in the past few years. Though barely out of his youth, Styrkar was bigger and more powerful than most of Harold's housecarls.

Opposite him stood Wistan, sword and shield gripped tightly, mail shirt, helmet, that keen angry look he always wore on his face. Styrkar would have thought him a friend, but he knew Wistan had never cared for him. Most of the housecarls treated him as one of their own, but some still considered him a slave. An animal. Harold's faithful hound.

'Come on, boy,' Wistan barked. 'Let's have it.'

Styrkar just stood and waited. He couldn't let Wistan bait him, no matter how loud his bluster. It wouldn't be long before the man lost patience.

There were shouts of encouragement from the crowd as the men were watched eagerly. Styrkar knew this was a test, but he would not let the occasion get the better of him. He had to take this seriously. Though they were not to strike a wounding blow, Styrkar knew well enough that mistakes were often made in practice fights, and he doubted his opponent would lose any sleep over hacking off a sliver of flesh with his blade.

Wistan bellowed. It filled the hall, and might have served to frighten a lesser man, but Styrkar had faced much more fearsome foes. He had rowed with them, run with them, seen them die. Wistan might make the noise of a devil, but he was a man like the rest.

Styrkar braced himself as Wistan came at him, shield held to the fore. His arm was up, sword raised as he peered over the shield. Raising the axe, Styrkar timed his strike to perfection, bringing it crashing down against the shield. It stopped Wistan in his tracks, sending splinters of wood flying.

Wistan retreated, reconsidering his actions. He was losing face, and to nothing more than a freed slave. Styrkar could see the anger in his eyes, the helmet doing little to mask the man's annoyance.

'Come on,' he shouted again, his frustration growing.

He ran in again, this time slower, more measured, but

it gave Styrkar the opportunity he'd waited for. As Wistan brought the shield within range, Styrkar hooked its edge with the axe, yanking it aside and leaving Wistan open. Before the housecarl could retreat Styrkar had brought the haft around, smashing it into the front of Wistan's helmet.

The housecarl fell back on his arse to a tumultuous cry of approval from the watching warriors.

'The bloody Red Wolf!' someone cried.

It was a name they'd chosen to grant Styrkar over the years, as much for his red mane of hair as his quick temper. Though he would never admit it, he liked it.

'Arseholes,' Wistan barked, rising to his feet.

He looked ready to go again, and Styrkar took a step back, raising the axe. Before the next attack came, a familiar voice shouted, 'Enough!'

The hall fell silent. Even Wistan lowered his arms, taking a step back towards the edge of the hall.

Harold came forward from the crowd, standing before Styrkar, looking him up and down. It was a relief when he finally nodded his approval.

'Good work,' Harold said. 'You've come far. No longer the animal I chased down on the coast a few years ago.' That got sniggers from some of the men.

'He was lucky, this time,' said Wistan. 'That boy has the luck of a saint.'

Harold shook his head. 'He didn't seem lucky to me. But if you say it's so, maybe I should test it.'

He held his hand out to Wistan, who obediently handed over his sword and shield. Styrkar felt the hairs prickle at the back of his neck. Harold had taught him sword, axe and spear over the years. They had sparred many times, but never in front of such a crowd. He had never been tested like this.

'Shall we get to it?' Harold said.

Styrkar didn't wait. Later he would have no idea what came over him, but it was as though the wolf inside knew it had to attack or be defeated. He didn't roar to signal his move, just threw himself forward, axe raised high.

Harold raised the shield, catching the axe as it came down. More splinters of wood went flying, but Harold stood his ground. He batted the axe aside, sweeping the sword at Styrkar's head. It only just missed, Styrkar ducking to avoid having his skull caved in.

The gathered housecarls were silent now, watching intently. The sense that this was mere practice was gone, and Styrkar knew if he didn't defend himself as though his life depended on it, he could end up dead.

He struck with the axe again. Harold knocked it aside, but Styrkar was conscious of the counter, darting aside, not relenting, attacking once more. There was a crack as the shield split, and Styrkar knew he had the advantage. He brought the axe down, but Harold dropped his shield, reaching up and grabbing the weapon's haft, his sword arm moving swifter than Styrkar could comprehend.

He stood frozen, the blade an inch from his eye. All he could do was stare at the rune-carved steel. There was no noise in the hall – everyone was watching, waiting, seeing what their earl would do.

Harold lowered his blade and grinned. It cut through the dread atmosphere, and the housecarls cheered with delight.

Styrkar breathed a long sigh as Harold clapped him on the arm.

'Much improved,' he said. 'The Red Wolf is a warrior to be feared, but you still have a way to go before you can challenge for the earldom.'

More laughter. The thought of any man challenging Harold, whether they could best him in a fight or not, was preposterous. He was one of the most powerful men in the country, second only to King Edward himself. Anyone who took on the son of Godwine had better have the devil's help. Or an army.

Harold took the axe from Styrkar's hand and flung it to one of his housecarls. He clapped Styrkar on the back and led him from the hall. As they left there was the sound of more raucousness, as challenges were called and men argued for who would be next to fight.

Outside, Styrkar felt the crisp air cool the sweat on his brow. Harold led them through the settlement, returning nods from the townsfolk they passed until eventually they reached the bank of the river that flowed south to the harbour. Across it a man fished, casting his net in the water. Further downstream another man rowed his swill tub, foraging for samphire in the reeds.

Harold sat on the bank, watching the river as it flowed past, listening to the sound of it. Styrkar was unused to such moments of reflection, but he sat down next to his earl nonetheless.

'Are you ready for what's coming?' Harold asked him.

Styrkar knew exactly what he meant. The power of the Welsh had risen in the west. King Gruffydd had stood as a threat for many years, and Harold's patience had run dry.

'I've never been more ready,' he replied.

'You are one of my most loyal, Styrkar,' Harold said. 'Though you have only served me a short time I would rather have you at my shoulder than many men I have known all my life.'

'I owe you more than I could ever repay.' Styrkar remembered that day he had been spared, and all the days since.

'I hope that's not the only reason you serve me.'

It wasn't. Harold had been like a father to him. The father he had barely known. He had taken a worthless slave and fashioned a warrior. Styrkar had never expected to be treated like a son by anyone, let alone a man such as Harold.

'No,' he replied.

'That's good.' Harold clapped a hand to Styrkar's shoulder. 'Because you are no slave. You were never a slave to me. I would have your faith and loyalty freely given. Not because it is demanded.'

'You have it,' Styrkar replied.

That seemed to satisfy Harold. He picked up a stone lying nearby and flung it into the river, watching the ripples it made disappear, dragged away by the flow of water.

'You still have the collar?'

Styrkar lifted the sleeve of his shirt. Around his wrist was twisted the iron collar he'd worn since he was a boy. It had long since grown too tight to fit his neck and Harold had kept his word, removing it and letting Styrkar serve out of choice rather than obligation.

'You should throw that thing away,' Harold said. 'There is no value in keeping it.'

'It was a part of me, my lord,' Styrkar replied. 'A symbol

of my bondage. Now it serves to remind me not to let myself become a slave again.'

'As you wish.' Harold gazed across the river. The fisherman was pulling in his catch. From the lightness of his net it was obvious there was little in it. 'You once told me a story. One your mother told you, of the wolf.'

'Of Fenrir, yes.' Styrkar remembered it well. It was the last memory he had of his mother and one he hoped would never leave him.

'You still believe it? That you are the son of the wolf?'

Harold worshipped his Christian god and had never put any store by the gods of the Danes, but neither had he demanded Styrkar forsake them.

'As strongly as you believe in the Christ,' Styrkar replied.

Harold reached inside his tunic, taking out a ring of iron.

'I have a gift,' he said. 'A trinket fashioned in the old ways, a symbol of your heathen gods.'

He handed the ring to Styrkar. It was an iron torc, and at each end had been carved the head of a wolf.

'I... I don't—'

'You don't have to,' said Harold. 'Wear it. Or don't. Fling it in the river if you like. But never forget who you are, Styrkar the Dane.'

Harold rose, briefly touching Styrkar on the shoulder, before leaving him by the river.

The fisherman cast his net once more. The forager pulled his swill tub from the river.

Styrkar felt the weight of the torc in his hands. It was a precious gift. Worth more than anything he had ever been given. But the value of things was only weighed by their meaning.

He forced the torc around his thick neck. The fit was snug, but not stifling like a slave collar.

As the river flowed by, Styrkar felt as though he had regained something lost in Hedeby all those years ago. For the first time in so long, he had a sense that he belonged.

6

OFFA'S DYKE, WELSH BORDER, SEPTEMBER 1063

'You will never forget the first man you kill,' Harold had told him. 'His face will forever haunt your dreams and you'll always remember those eyes staring in disbelief as you send him screaming back to God.'

It wasn't true. Styrkar had already forgotten that first man's face. Nor could he remember the second, or the third. After the fourth he'd even stopped counting the number of corpses he left rotting in those snow-covered mountains.

The Welsh were a savage people who lived for war. Many greased their hair into spikes, wearing nothing but war paint of pitch and chalk. And shit from the stink of them. Others were noble warriors; armed, armoured and skilled with blade and shield. But Styrkar had stolen the life from the noble just as readily as the savage. He had not cared how bravely they fought nor how kingly they looked. The Red Wolf had risen up and devoured every man who stood against him just the same.

Harold had been true to his word, allowing Styrkar to

prove himself worthy of his freedom. They had struck out into the grim Welsh countryside, destroying any who might dare to face them. Harold had gathered a lightly armoured force, easily able to match the enemy for speed and mobility. They had pursued the Welsh King Gruffydd all the way to his fortress of Rhuddlan. Upon finding his enemy already fled, Earl Harold had become enraged, burning the place to the ground and slaughtering every prisoner. Styrkar had never seen his master sink to such barbarity, but he had not balked at it. Indeed, it had stirred him to even greater feats of violence.

Men were looking at him differently now. Men he had thought his friends gave him a wide berth. Others who had previously treated him with disdain now acknowledged him with respect. Or was it fear? Either way he had been proud to finally earn the name Red Wolf, determined that he would gift the head of this upstart warlord to his master. But it was not to be.

Word had been sent that Gruffydd was dead. Murdered by his own followers for fear of what Harold would do were the Welsh king allowed to retake his seat in Gwynedd. Now they awaited proof of the deed.

Offa's Dyke spanned the length of the Welsh borderlands. It was barely more than a ditch. Whoever this Offa was, he had known little about how to defend a border.

Their ponies whickered impatiently as they sat waiting under the dark grey sky. They were hardy beasts, but not as hardy as their riders. Harold had chosen a dozen of his best to join him. Every man a veteran of his campaign against the Welsh. But the fighting was done. Now they sat and waited as the wind whipped across the flat grassy field, watching to the west, eager to know if the slaughter they had wreaked was to be rewarded.

As a group of horses appeared in the distance the men sat more upright in their saddles, braving the winds that whipped their cloaks about them. Styrkar's hand strayed to the sword at his side as the riders drew closer, but when he saw they only numbered four he realised they had not come to fight. These were a beaten people. All they had left to show was their fealty.

The four horsemen mounted the ditch, slowing as they neared the dozen gathered before them. Three of them bore the hulking build of warriors beneath their cloaks, where the fourth was slight, face hidden beneath a hood. Harold waited at the front of the group, observing their approach in silence. A grim-looking Welshman reached for a bag strapped to his saddle. With little reverence he opened it, pulling out a severed head and raising it up for all to see. The slack-jawed face of King Gruffydd stared at them with the one glazed eye that remained in his rotting skull.

A second rider dismounted, untying a heavy bundle from his saddle and bringing it forward for Harold. Kneeling, he pulled back the cloth wrapping to reveal a ship's prow carved into the crude likeness of a dragon head. Most likely it was from the ship Gruffydd had used to flee Harold's wrath.

As two of his men dismounted to take the prizes they had won, Harold turned to his housecarls.

'It is done,' he said. 'Let's away.'

But the Welsh were not done yet. One of the warriors nudged his horse forward next to the slight figure who rode with them. He grasped the hood of the cloak and pulled it back to reveal the face of a woman. Her hair was black as night, billowing about her shoulders in the wind. Styrkar was taken with how beautiful she was, but there was steel in her eyes. She looked as though she would have murdered every man present had she the strength.

'Very well,' Harold said. 'Bring her.'

The rain began to patter on their cloaks as they took charge of the woman and turned their horses south. The sky only continued to darken on their journey as Styrkar found himself unable to stop glancing at this woman, curious to know who she could be and why the Welsh would consider her as valuable a gift as Gruffydd's head.

When finally they reached the shelter of a town some miles from the border, Harold ordered the woman be given her own chamber and had his men watch over it with vigilance. The horses were tended, and the men offered meat and ale as their cloaks dried and beds were prepared. When night drew in, Harold took a place by a fire in the steward's feast hall. Styrkar sat by his side, in silence at first, but he could not hold his curiosity at bay.

'The woman?' he asked. 'Who is she?'

Harold stared deep into the fire as though it troubled him. 'She is Gruffydd's widow. Alditha, daughter to Aelfgar of Mercia. A most troublesome thegn, when he lived.'

'She had no children by Gruffydd?' It seemed curious the Welsh would hand her over without them.

A smile curled up one side of Harold's mouth. 'The Welsh have clearly seen fit to keep Gruffydd's issue for themselves. They are kin to the princes, Bleddyn and Rhiwallon. Most likely they will keep their nephews close lest they try and stake claim to Gruffydd's crown in years to come. Let them.

The Welsh are cowed. It doesn't matter who rules them now.'

'And what fate awaits Gruffydd's widow?'

Whether it was a sparking flame from the fire, or a stirring within him, a sudden light flared in Harold's eyes. 'She is beautiful, is she not?'

Styrkar could not disagree, despite the concern he felt at Harold's reaction. 'Any man would be fortunate to have her as his bride.'

Harold nodded his agreement. 'Fortunate indeed. Her father Aelfgar was a powerful man. Now he is dead, her brothers, Edwin and Morcar, have inherited that power. I doubt it will be long before she is wed again. Her new husband will gain much favour in the north.'

Styrkar could hear the yearning in his master's voice. His eyes remained focused on the fire and it was obvious his thoughts were of nothing but Alditha. Was it lust for her beauty, or greed for what he could gain from a union with her?

'Do you plan to take her for yourself?' Styrkar asked, wary he could be overstepping his mark. 'You are already wed.'

Harold shook his head. 'My marriage to Edith has never been blessed by the church. It would be of little consequence were I to take a wife...' Styrkar was about to point out Edith was the mother of his children, a woman he had made vows to, when Harold shook his head again as though ridding it of thoughts of Alditha. 'No matter. King Edward may yet sire an heir with my sister, and I would be uncle to a prince. That would make me powerful indeed. What more could any man want?'

Despite Harold's reassurance, Styrkar could see the hunger that still lingered in his eyes. He had just defeated a king. Laid waste to a whole country. Would such a man be satisfied with his nephew on the throne of England as he played protector? With every battle he won, and the more influence he gained, his claim to an empty throne of England was stronger. For the first time, Styrkar began to worry about what such temptation might do to his master. He could only hope Harold could resist it.

'So what is to be done with the woman?' Styrkar asked, hoping to divert Harold's thoughts from what might happen to the crown once King Edward was gone.

'She will be sent back north to her brothers,' Harold said, a hint of reluctance in his voice before he looked away from the fire and stared Styrkar in the eye. 'And you will be the one who takes her. I need a man I can rely on with this. There is no one I trust more than you.'

'Of course,' Styrkar replied, as keen to get this woman away from Harold as he was to obey his order.

'That is not all I would ask of you,' Harold continued. 'From here I am to travel to King Edward and deliver proof of our victory. Once you have seen Alditha safe, I would have you travel to Walsingaha. You will join Edith on her estate and watch over my family.'

'No,' Styrkar said. 'My place is at your side.'

Harold's brow furrowed. 'Your place is where I tell you to be,' he snapped. Then he sighed, laying a hand on Styrkar's shoulder. 'We have fought long and hard this past year. You have served me more faithfully than I could have asked. More than any other man. But we are nearing troubled times. King Edward is old; his health is failing. If he dies with no heir there will be more than one contender for the crown of England. And whether I like it or not, I am one of those contenders. Others might see some advantage to threatening the life of my wife and my heirs. I would see they are protected by someone I can trust.'

Styrkar realised the honour Harold was granting. The responsibility was a heavy one, but Styrkar would bear it.

'All right,' he said. 'I will do as you command.'

'Then it's settled. Get some rest. You have a long journey ahead.'

Styrkar did as he was bid, choosing a spot close to the fire before succumbing to sleep. He awoke to the sound of slaves sweeping the floor before laying fresh hay. As he stood he barely acknowledged that these poor souls were in the same position he had been a few short years before. But Styrkar had risen from his bondage. He had little pity to spare them.

Outside their horses were already saddled, the cloud having cleared to reveal a bright blue sky. Harold's men mounted their steeds as the door to Alditha's hut opened. She held herself with dignity as she was led to a waiting horse and climbed atop it. Styrkar wasted no time in leading the way, accompanied by two more of Harold's housecarls as they struck north.

Before they left the town, Styrkar noticed Alditha's steel gaze fall upon Harold as he watched them leave. It was difficult to read her expression as she looked upon the man who had ravaged her husband's lands and made her a widow. The man who was about to present her husband's head to the king. The man who might have harboured ambitions to marry her.

It would have been a strange union indeed. And a betrayal of all Harold held dear. But Styrkar would no longer question it. It had never been his place to doubt the motivations of jarls and kings. For now, he would simply obey his master's word.

7

WALSINGAHA, ENGLAND, AUGUST 1066

He brought the axe down with precision. Styrkar's practised swing split every log cleanly, the sound of it as crisp as the weather. This was his time, his chance to be alone with nothing but the axe, to build up a sweat, keep himself strong.

He could hear the three boys laughing in the distance. Their horseplay sounded good-natured for now, but he knew at any moment it could turn nasty. But what could he expect from the sons of Harold Godwinson? Their father had recently been crowned king of all England, and they were now heirs to the throne. Better they play out their animosity now than let it fester until one of them wore a crown and his brothers took up their earldoms.

Another swing, another split log and Styrkar considered his work complete. He put down the axe, grabbing a handful of logs, and made his way back towards the main hall. It was an impressive building, stone walls supporting a thatched roof. Other than the churches that were rife throughout this land, it was one of the most impressive constructions he had ever seen. Though that was to be expected considering the standing of the woman who owned this place.

Styrkar entered, greeted by the welcome smell of stew cooking over the fire. The great table was laid out for eight. Edith, her six children and him. As he placed logs in the hearth and stoked the fire to a rage, he couldn't help but feel more than the fire's warmth. He felt at home.

A stone bounced off the side of the hearth, and Styrkar turned. Beneath the long table he saw a dirty face peering at him, a grin splitting it from ear to ear.

'What was that?' Styrkar said.

Ulf giggled from his hiding place. As Styrkar began to wander the hall looking for the stone thrower, he felt someone slap his behind. He turned sharply, seeing Gunhild standing there, her smile almost as wide as her brother's.

Styrkar grabbed her, throwing the girl over one shoulder and tickling her ribs. She giggled noisily as Ulf ran from his hiding place to attack. In an instant Styrkar was rolling on the floor, wrestling with the two children who were reduced to fits of laughter.

'Don't get them too excited before we eat.'

Styrkar stopped his play-battle as he saw Edith looking down at them. She was the most beautiful woman Styrkar had ever known, though her face had become more careworn in recent months. Young Gytha was smiling by her side, too old to join in with her younger siblings, but still young enough to find their antics amusing.

'Go tell your brothers supper is ready,' Edith said to Gytha, and the young girl scurried off obediently.

Styrkar stood, feeling not a little foolish. Though the mistress of this estate treated him well, he still had to remind himself he was not her son. He was Harold's servant, and as such he was here to protect this family, not become a part of it.

'Shall we sit?' Edith said, as her maidservant began to stir the stew on the hearth.

Styrkar did as she asked, and not for the first time felt awkward in the seat. As he watched the maid at work, he was reminded of how far he had risen. He sat at the table of a king, no longer scurrying for the scraps beneath it. Styrkar the Dane had come a long way.

There was an uncomfortable silence as they waited for Edith's eldest sons. Edith had always been kind to Styrkar but he still did not know how to speak with her. Then again casual conversation had never been his strength.

He meant to tell her how sorry he was for recent events, but simply didn't know how. She had been Harold's handfast wife, their union blessed under ancient pagan laws, but now she was abandoned. Despite his vows, the king had taken Alditha as his wife – a union that bonded England's earldoms by marriage. In Harold's absence Styrkar had been ordered to stay with Edith, to watch over the family, but he was conscious his presence was a constant reminder of what she had lost. Neither of them had any choice in this.

The silence was broken as Gytha entered, followed by her brothers.

Godwin was the eldest, a man grown and recently granted

lands in the south. He was tall, serious, just like his father. Every inch the king he might one day become.

Edmund was coming into adulthood; a sallow youth, moody and mean-spirited. Styrkar had never taken a liking to him and he was sure the feeling was mutual.

Last came young Magnus. As he sat down, he winked at his sister Gunhild and tousled Ulf's hair. In response, Ulf batted off his hand and vainly tried to flatten down his brown mop.

'Shall we?' Edith said, when they were all convened.

Harold's family closed their eyes, clasping their hands in prayer. Styrkar bowed his head, but he would not join in with the giving of thanks. These were his people now, but he would never worship their Christian god. If he was going to offer thanks to anyone it would be the deer they had butchered to make their stew.

When Edith had finished, the maidservant began to dish up. Ulf and Magnus wasted no time digging in. While Edmund tore a hunk of bread and teased the stew in his bowl, Godwin sat back and regarded Styrkar curiously.

'Any word from my father?' he asked.

Styrkar began to feel uneasy. This was a ritual that was often played out, and one he doubted Edith would appreciate.

'None,' Edith replied, before Styrkar could speak.

'I'm sure it won't be long,' Godwin said. 'They say the Frankish duke is mustering an army. That he intends to force father off the throne and he has God on his side. War is inevitable.'

Styrkar had heard the rumours. Duke William of Normandy had laid claim to the throne of England. He alleged the previous king, Edward, had promised it to him, and the duke was determined to take what he saw as his right.

'The Bastard has no claim,' Edith said. 'We all know it to be false.'

'But father made an oath,' Edmund said, looking up sullenly from the bowl he had not touched. 'That's what they're saying. He went to Normandy and swore it before the duke himself.'

'Even if he did, such an oath should never be honoured,' Godwin replied. 'Wulfnoth is still William's prisoner. Any oath made under threat cannot be recognised in law.'

Harold's younger brother Wulfnoth, and his nephew Hakon, had been taken as hostages some years earlier. When the king had tried to bargain for their release, Duke William was rumoured to have made Harold vow that the crown would pass to him on King Edward's death. Whatever had been said, Harold had only managed to secure Hakon's release. Despite his brother Wulfnoth's imprisonment, Harold had taken the crown and now William was determined to have it for himself.

'The Lord God knows the truth,' Edith said. 'He will determine the victor. Any invasion will fail, your father will see to that.'

'Still so much faith in him?' said Edmund. 'After what he did to you?'

'Show some respect,' Godwin snapped.

'Respect?' Edmund replied, voice dripping with contempt. 'He abandoned our mother for a northern whore. That's what oaths mean to him.'

Godwin pushed back his chair and rose to his feet.

Edmund did likewise. Styrkar considered getting in between the hot-headed youths but Edith was faster.

'Enough,' she said. 'Sit down both of you.'

Her sons obeyed.

'You know I'm right, Mother,' Edmund said, unable to keep his mouth shut.

'No,' she replied. 'You're wrong about him. He has not abandoned me. Nor any of you. He has done his duty to the crown of England. For peace.'

Less than a year before in the north, the brothers Edwin and Morcar had risen in revolt against the sitting Earl Tostig, Harold's own brother. Instead of backing his brother, Harold had instead chosen to back Edwin and Morcar, sealing the alliance with a marriage to their sister Alditha. Edith had come to accept the arrangement, but it was clear her sons had not.

'He has done his duty all right,' said Edmund. 'She is with child already. The great King Harold doesn't waste time staking his claim to anything.'

Styrkar was on his feet as Godwin went for Edmund once more. The brothers grappled, knocking the table and spilling their wine cups. Before Styrkar could get between them, Godwin had Edmund about the throat.

'Leave it,' Styrkar said as he took Godwin about the shoulders.

Harold's eldest son was growing into quite the man, but he was still no match for Styrkar. Realising he could not win in a battle of strength he let go of Edmund.

'Take him outside to calm down,' Edith said.

Styrkar obeyed, all but dragging Godwin out of the house and into the crisp air.

'Let go of me,' Godwin snarled, pushing Styrkar away.

He was impetuous and prideful, and that was to be expected from the son of a king. But if he was ever to take on the mantle of rulership he would have to learn to temper his rage.

Styrkar followed the boy as he made his way towards the nearby wood. He breathed heavily but he was already calming himself.

'Do you think it's true?' Godwin said. 'Do you think my father is an oath breaker?'

Styrkar shook his head. 'I think your father is the most honourable man I have ever met. I think everything he has done is for the good of these lands.'

'Even when taking sides against his own brother? My father placed Tostig in exile. Do you think that an honourable thing to do?'

Styrkar shrugged. 'That depends on the brother.'

That brought a smile to Godwin's face. 'I am glad you're here, Styrkar. You have always been more a brother to me than anyone.'

'And I feel the same,' Styrkar replied.

But deep inside he knew that wasn't true. Harold was his master and his sons would rule these lands eventually. Godwin would never be his brother, no matter how much he claimed differently.

Before they could speak further, a rider galloped into the estate. Godwin and Styrkar went to greet him as he reined in his steed. From the weathered condition of his garb he looked like he had ridden hard for days.

'Have you news from my father?' asked Godwin. 'Have the Franks set foot on our shores?'

'Not yet,' replied the rider. 'But the king is gathering the fyrd and has summoned his housecarls.'

'Then we fight,' Godwin said. Styrkar could sense the relish in his voice.

'I have been sent for Styrkar,' the rider said. 'The king has ordered that you remain here.'

Godwin shook his head. 'No. I will fight at my father's side. These are my lands and I will defend them.'

Edith had come to join them now. She laid a gentle hand on her son's shoulder.

'Godwin, you must honour your father's wishes. If anything were to happen to you this land would lose its future king.'

'But I can—'

'For once, you have to do as you're told,' she snapped.

Styrkar could sense the fear in her voice. 'Godwin,' he said. 'If you have any faith in your father, you have to obey him. He knows what is best. You can defend your lands when the time comes. For now you have to trust Harold's judgement.'

Reluctantly, Godwin nodded. 'Very well,' he said. With that he clapped a hand on Styrkar's shoulders. 'I envy you, brother. You go to war. Promise me one thing: when you have secured victory you will bring me the Bastard's head.'

'I will do my best,' Styrkar replied.

A servant had already brought a saddled horse for him and as he climbed atop it, Styrkar gave Edith one final nod.

'Bless you, Styrkar,' she said. 'Bless all of you, and may you be spared from harm.'

He nodded his thanks, then reined his horse around and followed the messenger towards the south road.

As much as he appreciated Edith's blessing, Styrkar knew it would do him little good. The Christian god would not see him spared from harm.

Only his axe would do that.

8

ISLE OF WIGHT, ENGLAND, 8TH SEPTEMBER 1066

The frigid north wind lashed across the grassy hillock. Some of the housecarls pulled their cloaks tight about them, but Styrkar had been used to much worse cold than this in his youth, with little more than a cloth tunic for warmth.

As the wind whipped his hair into a red fury he watched with the rest. King Harold stood at the edge of the cliffs, staring south across the channel. To his right was his brother Gyrth, the taller and more serious of the two. They leaned into one another, their conversation intense. Gyrth was the more animated, the more desperate. Harold shook his head, which seemed to exasperate Gyrth even more.

To Harold's left stood their younger brother, Leofwine. He was uninvolved in the discussion, taking in the scenery as though he didn't have a care in the world. Leofwine would follow whatever decision his elder brothers made. Like Styrkar, all he wanted was the chance to fight.

As he watched the three brothers, Styrkar thought how

much alike they were to Harold's sons. The taciturn Godwin, the quarrelsome Edmund, the carefree Magnus. They mirrored one another perfectly, but then they were family.

'What are they saying?' whispered one of the housecarls behind him.

'Why don't you wander over and ask?' said another.

Neither was going to interrupt their leaders when they were in such an animated state, but Styrkar could guess how the conversation was going. The sky was dark, the weather had been inclement for days, and still there was no sign of Duke William. If he had not appeared by now there was little chance he would arrive in the next few days. Harold had called his fyrd and his housecarls, but they could not wait forever. There were fields to reap, communities to feed.

Harold turned to his brother Leofwine and spoke calmly. Leofwine listened intently before nodding his head and turning to walk towards the housecarls.

'There is no reason for us to wait,' he announced. 'The Franks are not coming. Return to your homes but be ready. The Bastard will not give up so easily. You will all receive the call soon enough.'

There was grumbling assent from the housecarls. They had waited weeks for sign of invasion, stirring themselves into a battle fever, ready to face the enemy, but now it seemed their preparations were for nothing.

As the rest began to move away from the windswept hill, seeking shelter before they took their boats back to the mainland, Styrkar waited. Leofwine came to stand beside him.

'You will come back to Lundenburg with us, Styrkar. Harold wants you by his side.'

'What will he do now?' Styrkar asked.

Leofwine shrugged. 'Knowing my brother, he will pray.'

Harold and Gyrth had turned to make their way back down the hill. Styrkar followed, hearing Gyrth cursing to himself all the while. When they reached the bay, it was alive with men loading up their ships. The sense of discontent was palpable. They had gathered a fleet, ready to pursue the invaders wherever they might try to land, but now they were bound for their homes. Weeks of waiting had seen many of them neglect their lands and their crops, and they were eager to salvage what they could.

Harold wasted no time, climbing aboard his ship. Styrkar boarded behind him, taking his seat and gripping an oar. It brought back memories he would sooner forget, of pulling an oar for men who had enslaved him, but experience had taught him there was little point dwelling on the past. Now he rowed for a different master, one who was worthy of the title.

As the steersman gave the order for them to row, Styrkar saw that Harold kept his eyes focused on the channel to the south, towards the man who coveted his lands and would stop at nothing to take them.

The crossing was brief, the journey to the capital took two days and they were weary by the time they crossed the wide river at Sudweca. No sooner had they entered the fort, than Styrkar could tell there was trouble. As Harold dismounted, a mournful-looking reeve approached.

'Sire, we have received word from the north.'

'The north is the least of my worries right now,' he replied.

'I am sorry. This cannot wait. It's your brother.'

Harold shook his head. 'Tostig? He is in exile.'

'No, sire. He has landed on the coast with a huge force of Norsemen led by Harald Sigurdsson. They have sailed up the River Tyne and now harry towns and settlements all across the north.'

At the mention of the Norwegian king, Styrkar felt his grip tighten on his horse's reins. Likewise, he could see Harold gritting his teeth. His lands were beset from all sides. He had only just disbanded an army and now he would have to ride to war once more.

'Send word to my brothers and all my housecarls. Gather my royal messengers. We will raise the fyrd and march north tonight.'

Harold walked inside as Styrkar handed the reins to a stable boy, then followed. He expected the king to make his way to his chambers – the man must have been exhausted – but instead he headed to the small chapel housed within the building.

He knelt, clasping his hands together in prayer. Styrkar considered leaving him in peace, but he was here to guard his king, and he would do his duty. While the king prayed, Styrkar stood watch as darkness fell. An attendant lit candles as Harold held his vigil, casting flickering shadows on the wall.

Styrkar had no idea what Harold was praying for. His god could not help him now. Tostig, the king's own brother, had declared war. And he had brought with him one of the most vicious warriors in all the world. Styrkar knew better than anyone what a brute Harald Sigurdsson was and he relished the prospect of facing the man who had enslaved him as a child. He could only hope the king would grant him the chance for vengeance.

The sky had turned black by the time Harold stood from his prayers. He turned to face his faithful housecarl and shook his head.

'I have no answers,' he whispered.

Styrkar had none either.

Harold sat on one of the benches lining the wall, staring into the flickering light of a candle.

'I will have to fight Tostig. But how?'

'He has betrayed you,' Styrkar said. 'His intentions are clear. He would have Sigurdsson take your crown. There is no other way but to face him in battle.'

'May God once more rid me of my troublesome kin,' Harold spat.

It seemed a curious curse. Harold looked up, seeing the confusion on Styrkar's face.

'This is not the first time I have been plagued by a wayward brother. You would have only been a child at the time, and he is little spoken of now. My elder brother Swein was a brute, a murderer. And yet our father still held him in favour, even after he slew our cousin.'

'You fought him?' asked Styrkar.

Harold shook his head. 'Thankfully I never had to. He died on a pilgrimage to wash away his sins. It seems he received his judgement from God on the road from Jerusalem.'

'Then your god is with you,' Styrkar said. 'It is obvious who he favours.'

Though Styrkar did not believe in Harold's god, that seemed the right thing to say. He hoped they were the words his king needed to hear.

'I will be judged for this,' Harold replied. 'By both God and man. If I can end this without Tostig's death then I will.'

'And Sigurdsson?' Styrkar asked.

Harold fixed him with a grim countenance. 'I take it you would not approve if I offered him similar mercy?'

'I will accept any judgement my king decides.'

That brought a smile to Harold's face and he stood, gripping Styrkar's arm tightly.

'You know as well as I do King Harald will accept no terms. He will ask for no mercy nor give it. You will have your chance for a reckoning. Just be warned – he is not an easy man to kill.'

'Neither am I,' Styrkar replied.

'I know, my friend,' Harold said, gripping Styrkar's broad shoulders tightly. 'I have made sure of that.'

9

TATECASTRE, ENGLAND, 24TH SEPTEMBER 1066

They entered the fort to the sound of cheering. Farmers and peasants had gathered from far and wide to greet their king. It seemed news of Sigurdsson's invasion had spread across the north, and people were rightly fearing for their lives. With King Harold's arrival they considered themselves saved, but the Norse army was not beaten yet.

Royal messengers had been sent in advance of their journey, riding throughout the north to gather the fyrd ahead of the king's march. Harold had also summoned his housecarls to him, and the further north they travelled along the road, the more his army swelled. Now they rode into Tatecastre with a force of ten thousand men, all eager to force out the foreign invaders and bring the king's troublesome brother to heel.

Night had already fallen and their way was lit by torchbearers. Once inside the boundary of the town they were greeted by a thin man, greying at the temples. He was surrounded by armed warriors, and Styrkar reached a hand to the axe slung at the side of his saddle.

'Sire,' the man said. 'I am the steward of Tatecastre. It is good to see you have arrived so quickly.'

Harold dismounted, and Styrkar, along with the other housecarls, did likewise. He wasn't sorry to climb down from his horse after so many days of riding.

'Do you have news of my brother?' Harold asked.

'I do, sire. If you would follow me.'

The steward led them into the main building, a longhouse of timber and thatch. Styrkar had noticed the dwellings grow more primitive the further north they travelled, reminding him of the rudimentary hovels built in his homeland. This whole place was more reminiscent of the lands of the Danes than anything he had seen in the south of England.

Once inside, the steward bid the king sit and rest, bringing ale, meat and bread for him and his men. Styrkar could tell Harold was wary of the hospitality, and with good reason. Though these were still the king's lands, the northern territories had remained violently independent. Tostig had been earl here, and the northern thegns and magnates had been so discontented with his rule they had rebelled.

Styrkar remained standing, watching from the shadows as the king sat and regarded the steward.

'What is your news?' asked Harold.

The steward took on a grim expression. 'There was battle at Fulford, sire. The earls Edwin and Morcar were defeated.'

'And where are they now?'

'Fled, sire. To where I know not.'

Harold nodded as he considered the news.

'You have not chosen to take up with my brother and

the Norsemen, I see,' the king said, having neither eaten nor drunk what was offered.

The steward looked uncomfortable. 'You will find none who support your brother here.'

'And Sigurdsson?'

The steward shook his head, his discomfort gone now, replaced by grit. 'We've had our fill of foreign rulers. You are the rightful king, sire. We are your people.'

That seemed enough to satisfy Harold, and he skewered some meat on a knife. 'What do we know of the enemy?'

'They are camped at Stamford Bridge, a few miles from Yorke. Their ships are moored at Riccall. Three hundred, if my scouts have counted right.'

'So they are not expecting us?' Harold bit into the meat on his knife and began to chew.

'No, sire. No one has sent word of your arrival and no one will.'

Harold finished chewing the tough meat, before washing it down with a cup of ale. When he placed the cup down he began to nod.

'Very well. I thank you for your hospitality. Now I would talk to my men.'

The steward quickly glanced about the room at the grim gathering surrounding the king, before rising with a tug of his forelock and leading his own men out into the night.

'We should send word to Tostig now,' Gyrth said. 'He will see reason and we can end this madness without further bloodshed.'

Harold considered the words as he stared into his cup. 'And then what?' he replied. 'I grant him back his earldom in the north? I pay Sigurdsson to leave?'

'Paying the Norsemen would be less costly than a battle. As for Tostig... we can grant him some lands in the south. He would be satisfied with that, surely.'

'Anyone else?' Harold asked.

Styrkar could see the king's thegns and his most trusted housecarls were unsure. It took the oldest of them, Aethelnoth, to speak up.

'Gyrth could be right. Sigurdsson has brought a formidable army. Three hundred ships. That's a mighty force of arms. It wouldn't be the first time the Norse have been paid off, and Sigurdsson is as wise as he is vicious. He will see the sense in riches over slaughter. As for your brother... could you really take up arms against him?'

Harold fixed Aethelnoth with a grim look. 'You doubt my resolve?'

The old housecarl quickly shook his head. 'No, sire. I was just... I would not want to fight my own brother. Not least because the church would see it as a sin.'

'Let me worry about the church,' Harold replied. 'But you are right. Battle is not the only way we can resolve this. Styrkar, what say you?'

All eyes turned to Styrkar as he stood in the shadows. He saw the thegns and housecarls glaring at him. Some of them were obviously wondering why the king had asked this lowly warrior, this slave, what his thoughts were. But none of them had spoken up when they had the chance.

He stepped forward into the torchlight so they could all see him. See he was not afraid to speak, even in such esteemed company. But what should he say? Styrkar had no idea who was right in this. All he could offer were his own thoughts.

'We should slaughter them to the last,' Styrkar said.

'Ha,' laughed Stoki, another old housecarl. 'The Red Wolf speaks. And of course he wants battle. What else?'

The gathered warriors laughed at that. All but Harold.

'Why should we do that?' Harold asked.

Styrkar had not expected to have to justify himself, but now all eyes were on him once more. Was it just his lust for vengeance? Or was it the right thing to do?

'I was first brought to these lands by men in search of plunder,' Styrkar replied. 'Men who wanted to write their names in legend. Every one of them worshipped Harald Sigurdsson more than they worshipped the Christian god. Growing up here I have seen powerful men. Rich men. But none of them have riches to compare with Sigurdsson. He does not seek gold, or slaves or hides; he does not need them. For as long as he has been alive he has wanted to reclaim the kingdom of Cnut. His eye has always been on these lands while he plundered those of the Bulgar and the Rus and the Dane. He will not stop until he has them… or until I kill him.'

'There,' said Harold, rising to his feet. 'There is your answer.'

Gyrth shook his head. 'Brother, you cannot just take the word of—'

'Of what, Gyrth? Of my most faithful servant? Who should I listen to? You? These men here? My priest? Or should I listen to a man who knows this invader better than any of you? Tomorrow we march north, and by the Holy Cross we will catch these bastards while they lie glutted on the meat they have pillaged from my lands.'

The thegns and housecarls banged on the table with their

fists in agreement. Gyrth still looked reluctant, but he knew he was beaten.

They all filled their bellies with the steward's meat and ale until eventually Harold led them away to their beds. As Styrkar made to follow his king from the longhouse, Gyrth leaned into him.

'You will have your chance to stand by your word soon enough, Red Wolf. You made a persuasive argument. I just hope you're as sure of yourself on the battlefield.'

'I know little,' Styrkar replied. 'But of that, I am sure.'

Just north of Tatecastre, Harold had gathered his fyrd, his thegns, his housecarls. It was a grey morning, though the sun was trying its best to burn through the clouds.

The king stood on a promontory, looking over his ten thousand. The only sound was of whickering horses and an inclement crow, untroubled by the sense of occasion. Harold took a breath before he addressed his army.

'We have travelled hard,' he said. 'As we moved north we gathered men from the dales and meadows and shires of these lands. I have sent the call and you have answered.' A sudden gust of wind whipped through their ranks, making the dragon banner of the House of Wessex flutter proudly. 'A few miles north of here an army has come, looking to take these lands from us. Some of you may have heard they are fearsome. That they cannot be defeated. The rumours that they have already sent two of my earls scurrying into the wilds are true. But I am no earl. I am a king. I am the son of Godwine, appointed by King Edward and the Lord God. And you…'

He drew his sword and slowly swept the blade across the field of men as though anointing them all.

'...you are more fierce than any rabble from across the seas. You are Englishmen. *My* Englishmen, and I will lead you all to victory.'

A sudden cheer went up from the crowd. Styrkar did not join in with them, but still he felt the rush in his stomach and the hairs on his neck bristle.

'Now we march,' Harold said. 'We march to war.'

He spun his horse northward, accompanied by thegns and housecarls alike. And his army followed.

10

STAMFORD BRIDGE, ENGLAND, 25TH SEPTEMBER 1066

They gathered on the eastern side of the bridge, the Derwent flowing fast at their backs. Harold's housecarls were at the vanguard, the king's Fighting Man banner flying alongside the Dragon of Wessex. The second rank was made up of the fyrd: common men and their thegns drawn from across the northern territories.

Blood had already been spilled. The corpses of Norsemen littered the bridge. They had been few, but determined to delay Harold's advance across the Derwent. The warriors had given their lives so that their brother Norse could muster in time to defend themselves. Styrkar had admired their courage, but that hadn't stopped him cutting his way through them without mercy. He now stood front and centre, next to the king atop his horse. Across the field the Norse had hastily organised a shield wall and were stirring themselves into a fury.

Styrkar had come at the behest of his king, but this was

not a battle he fought out of loyalty. He was here to face the man who had slaughtered his family, enslaved him, beaten him, turned him into an animal. Styrkar would face him on the field and there would be a reckoning. He could see Harald's raven banner flying. Could hear him bellowing in the distance, a head taller than anyone else on the field.

Glancing across at Harold, Styrkar willed him to give the order to advance, but the king merely sat there on his horse, waiting. It took all his will not to strike out on his own and take the fight to the Norse.

'Someone's coming,' said one of the keen-eyed thegns. 'Perhaps they might surrender.'

Styrkar could hear the hope in his voice, but the prospect of the Norse bargaining for terms gave him no relief. He wanted a fight, and no amount of negotiating would stop him.

Harold climbed down from his horse, his brother Gyrth doing likewise.

Instinctively, Styrkar joined them as they made their way forward. Two more housecarls along with Oswulf, thegn of Bernicia, strode from the ranks of fighting men to join their king.

In the distance, Styrkar could see a single rider trotting towards them. He brought no warriors with him, and there was only one man who would break ranks with the Norse and strike out to parlay with the enemy.

Tostig was neither as handsome nor as well-built as his brothers. Even in armour he had the frame of a boy rather than a warrior. Harold worshipped his Christian god with great vigour, but Tostig was almost priestly in his devotion.

Styrkar had always been wary of him, and in recent days those suspicions had become justified.

Harold stopped, waiting patiently as Tostig struggled to rein his horse to a stop. Styrkar found himself distracted, staring out across the plain at the Norsemen, who were filled with disquiet at the prospect of battle. Either they had little faith in the parlay, or they were taking no chances.

'Brother,' said Harold.

'Harold,' Tostig replied.

'This is your king,' grumbled Oswulf. 'You will greet him as such.'

Harold held a hand up to silence his zealous thegn.

'I see you have brought allies,' Harold said.

Tostig glanced over his shoulder at the Norse shield wall. 'I had to cross the seas to find them. It is obvious I have no friends on these islands.'

'That is not true. You have family on these islands. We are brothers, Tostig – it should not have come to this.'

'No, it should not. But you made your loyalties clear the day you sided against me.'

'Tostig, it was the only way. Do you think I wanted an alliance with Edwin and Morcar? Do you think I relished the thought of marrying their sister? Of abandoning the mother of my children?'

'I think you would do anything to strengthen your grip on power,' Tostig replied.

Gyrth made to speak, but once again Harold raised a hand to order silence.

'Think about what you are doing,' Harold said. 'What would our father say? Our mother?'

'Why don't you ask her? If you get the chance.'

Harold closed his eyes, looking down at the ground. He was torn between defending family or kingdom. It was an impossible choice.

'All right,' Harold said finally. 'I will give you what you ask.'

There was a rumbling of discontent from Gyrth and Oswulf, but Harold held firm. Styrkar could see his fists were clenched and he had all but spat the words through gritted teeth.

Tostig seemed surprised. 'You will return me to my seat in the north?'

It seemed like madness, but Harold nodded. 'I will grant you an earldom, Tostig. All will be as it was.'

'You will break your oath to Edwin and Morcar? Do you realise what you might provoke?'

'Edwin and Morcar are already cowed. Your allies have seen to that. Let me worry about the consequences. Just put an end to this.'

Tostig considered his brother's words. None of them had expected this from Harold, but Styrkar could understand. Tostig was his brother. How could he hope to face him on the field?

'And what of Sigurdsson? What will you offer him?'

Harold's expression darkened. His eyes scanned the field, taking in the Norse shield wall in the distance, and Harald still bellowing at his men.

'What will I offer him?' Harold asked.

'What lands would you grant the King of Norway to end this costly war?'

There was silence. Styrkar could tell that Tostig had

gone too far. Harold was a forgiving brother, but Harald Sigurdsson was not his kin.

'I tell you what land I will grant... seven feet of soil. And tell him I will dig the hole myself.'

Tostig nodded, as though he had expected the response. As though he had wanted it.

'Very well. I will give Harald your answer...' He paused, as though he had more to say. Instead he tugged his horse's reins and rode back towards the Norse shield wall.

'Looks like we're fighting,' Oswulf said.

'Looks like we are,' Harold replied as he turned to lead them back to their men.

Styrkar gripped his axe tighter, unable to quell his sense of relief. He had not followed Harold in the hope he would bargain terms. He had come here to kill.

Styrkar ignored the ache in his shoulders. His forearms burned as he raised the axe again, bringing it down with a crunching impact against the Norseman's shield. The wood cracked, splitting almost in two as the warrior stumbled beneath Styrkar's might.

He screamed, his voice hoarse. Had he been bellowing all this time? Styrkar could not tell. He was lost in the killing now. He had submitted to the rage.

Another strike and the Norseman fell, half his shield dangling, held on by a flap of cowhide. Styrkar could see his eyes wide in terror behind his helmet. This man had come with his king to conquer these lands. He might have expected to die for the cause, but at the end he feared it. Everybody did.

Styrkar showed no mercy. Screaming from the pit of his lungs, raising the axe with a vigour that belied his aching limbs. The axe crashed down, splitting the Norseman's shoulder, sinking deep, his cry for mercy lost as the impact cut through him.

There was no time to gloat. No time to revel in yet another corpse sent to the dirt at his hands. Styrkar planted a foot against the dead man's chest and wrenched his weapon free.

The Norse shield wall had buckled. Their resolve was giving out. Though they fought furiously, Harold's arrival had caught them unawares and they had been given no chance to don armour. It was like cutting through hanging meat. Slaughter of the most callous kind. Styrkar was all too happy to play the butcher.

The English housecarls charged again. Styrkar sprinted to catch them as they hit the shield wall, in no mood to be left out. He could hear the thunderous impact as swords and axes smashed against the row of shields. The wall collapsed, men falling back, others panicking in the face of the English charge and fleeing for their lives.

Styrkar could see a gap in the defence. He dashed through, an arrow flashing past his head to thud against a nearby shield. As he led the charge, the rest of the housecarls pushed past, closely followed by the men of the fyrd.

The Norse line had crumpled; there was no order to their defence. This was a fight to the death, with warriors attacking their nearest foe, heedless of the man standing next to him.

Styrkar swept his axe from left to right, attacking anyone who got near, but none would face him. The mettle of the

Norsemen was close to giving out and a full rout was near at hand.

His foe had to be close. Through the mass of confusion he scanned the battle, breathing hard, trying to stay calm enough to focus. Blood was coursing fast through his veins, his forearms a mass of cuts and grazes from the Norse weapons, but he ignored the pain.

There was a roar of fury as a breach appeared among the fighting men. Harald Sigurdsson stood tall amidst the slaughter, his sword striking with venom. Styrkar just had time to see him cut down a charging housecarl before stirring himself into a fury. He raced forward, bellowing something unintelligible, desperate to face the Norse king, to kill him and take his vengeance.

Sigurdsson looked up, his eyes ablaze. He was consumed by the berserkergang, lost in the ecstasy of battle, but he still had the sense to defend himself against an enemy of equal ferocity. The Norse king planted his feet, his chest heaving as he prepared himself to face Styrkar's attack.

'Come on,' raged Harald, raising his blade, ready to parry the huge axe Styrkar held aloft.

An arrow swept past Styrkar's ear, a soft breath against his cheek. It struck Harald in the throat before he could get within ten feet.

The Norse king stumbled, one hand grasping the arrow shaft as he slowly lowered his sword. Rage drained from his eyes, replaced by a look of bewilderment. His sword fell from weak fingers, his lips moving as he tried to speak, but all that came from his mouth was blood.

'No,' Styrkar growled, rushing at his enemy, but Harald had already fallen to his knees.

All thoughts of vengeance were gone now. Stolen from him in an instant. All he could do was watch a dying man.

'Look at me,' growled Styrkar as he stared down at his enemy.

Harald spat more blood, hand trying to stymie the gout of crimson pouring from his neck.

'Look at me, bastard,' Styrkar roared.

The Norse king slowly met his gaze, eyes glassing over as blood dripped from his mouth. They glared at one another as Harald's expression turned to confusion.

'Do you recognise me? I am Styrkar. Known as the Red Wolf. I am the son of Fenrir.' Slowly recognition seemed to dawn on Harald. 'And I am no longer a slave.'

Harald tried to speak but all he could do was gag, more blood spilling from his mouth before he pitched forward to die on the ground at Styrkar's feet.

There was no sense of triumph – he had been robbed at the final moment. All the years of hungering, clamouring for his revenge, and now it had been snatched away.

Styrkar suddenly felt the weight of fatigue on his shoulders, the hours of battle catching up with him. He almost lost his grip on the heavy axe, his mail shirt weighing him down as though it were trying to pull him to the ground beside Harald's corpse.

'The king is dead,' shouted a single voice above the din.

It took Styrkar a moment to realise it had been said in the Norse language. The fighting around him had died down, the enemy shield wall reformed, but the Norse looked beaten. News of their king's death began spreading through their ranks and they knew there was no hope left.

The housecarls and fyrd formed up around Styrkar, and Harold stepped to the fore.

'Tostig!' he bellowed. 'Tostig, come and face me!'

Styrkar scanned the enemy line but he could not see the king's brother among their ranks. If Tostig was still alive he was not willing to face his fate.

'Your king is dead,' Harold shouted. The field had all but fallen silent but for his voice. 'But I will grant you mercy. Throw down your weapons and vow never to trouble these shores again, and I will allow you to return to your ships.'

Silence but for the groans of the wounded. Styrkar watched what remained of the shield wall, waiting for one of the Norse leaders to come forth and accept the king's terms. Instead, a spear was flung from behind their lines, skewering the ground at Harold's feet. It was the only signal the housecarls needed.

With a roar they attacked once more, Oswulf of Bernicia screaming the loudest, leading the countercharge.

Styrkar was not to be left out. He was weary, but this battle was far from done, and he raced forward, axe smashing against the shield wall as they pressed the Norsemen back.

Despite the death of their king they fought on, shields pressing together to repel the English attack. There were thousands still alive, determined to fight to the death, and the battle soon turned to a press of bodies, men crushing up against one another, the occasional scream pealing out as a man was hacked by an errant blade or sliced by a spear tip. The ground was turning to mud, and Styrkar could barely stand. A thin mist of vapour began to rise from the crush as men struggled for survival in the cold autumn air.

'To the south,' someone cried. 'Look to the south.'

Styrkar could sense a panic infesting the English lines. They had looked on the brink of victory but something had shaken them from that certainty.

He pulled himself from the fray, glancing to the south-east to see more ranks of Norsemen approaching.

'Bloody reinforcements,' Oswulf said, hefting his shield. He had lost his helmet, his face spattered with blood. 'The day is not done yet,' he bellowed, and he rallied some of his fyrd.

Styrkar joined them as they rushed to face the newcomers. He could see the Norse shield wall had collapsed to the north, and men were already fleeing the field, heedless of their own reinforcements, but these newcomers had a determined look to them – a desperation.

'Form on me,' Oswulf shouted. He was joined by more thegns, bellowing to rally their fyrd. Gyrth came too, surrounded by his own housecarls. Soon the English had formed their own rank and planted their feet to face the coming onslaught.

The day had been long but still Styrkar knew he had to fight. He had been robbed of his revenge, but he would not be denied his justice. Harald Sigurdsson brought these men to English shores to conquer. If Styrkar could not avenge himself on his enemy then he would make sure his followers would regret the day they showed fealty to the bastard Sigurdsson.

The Norse charged, but even as they threw themselves against the English shields it was obvious they were exhausted. They must have run for miles to reach the battle, and now they were too late. Despite having fought for hours, English blood was up, and Harold's housecarls led the counter, hacking down the Norse even as they came to rescue their fellow invaders.

Styrkar hacked down on a shield, yet another hammer blow, more cracked wood. The Norseman fell back under the onslaught and Styrkar pitched himself forward, his practised arm swinging with relentless ease.

There was an almighty crack, and Styrkar felt the haft of his axe judder in his hand. Raising the weapon he saw the steel head had split from the haft and he was left holding nothing but a useless stick.

The Norseman facing him saw his chance, eyes wide with delight as he raised his sword. Styrkar gritted his teeth in readiness. He would not falter here at the last. He would face his fate.

With a howl, an English sword hacked in. The Norseman was taken at the base of his helmet, blood spouting from his neck as he was smashed sideways. Styrkar recognised Harold, face creased in fury, fighting like a raging baresark.

Under the tirade, the Norse reinforcements suddenly broke, fleeing before the onslaught. Styrkar scanned the ground, picking up a fallen sword and shield. All thoughts of mercy were gone now. These invaders had been given their chance.

Harold rushed to the fore. 'Chase them down,' he howled. 'Do not let them reach their ships.'

Styrkar looked about him. The Norse were in full rout. Thousands of fyrd and housecarls alike were already giving chase, pursuing the hapless Norse east towards Riccall. He rolled his shoulders, feeling the ache of his labours but choosing to quell them.

The day was won, but the killing was not over yet.

11

YORKE, ENGLAND, 29TH SEPTEMBER 1066

His wounds were still raw and aching, fresh stitches lined his arms and sealed a cut on his chin, but Styrkar ignored the physical pain. The bruises on his flesh were nothing to the ache he felt in his heart. He had placed so much importance on the battle, he had not even realised how much vengeance meant to him. It had been a chance to cast aside demons from the past, to finally settle the score that had been festering within him for half a lifetime. And in the end he had been thwarted by an errant arrow. Styrkar tried not to think on it, tried not to let it plague him, but somehow this place made it all the worse.

The building stank of incense and piety. Though the men surrounding him might have considered him a heathen, they gave no sign that it bothered them. But then who would challenge the mighty Red Wolf? The fierce axeman who had led the charge against the invading Norse?

It was a vast church – the biggest building Styrkar had ever seen. Despite their differences, King Harold had chosen to honour his brother with a burial befitting a man of his stature. But then Harold was nothing if not magnanimous. At Riccall he had spared many of the Norsemen, allowing the survivors to sail home in their ships, though they had only filled a fraction of the three hundred they had arrived in. Even Harald Sigurdsson had been granted honour in death, his body handed over for burial in his homeland.

That last honour should have bothered Styrkar more than anything. Had it been up to him he would have left that body to rot, but still, despite his ire he had not thought to question his king. It was not his place to do so. Instead he stood in this foreign place of reverence, watching the proceedings, biting his tongue as worshippers of a god he did not believe in buried an enemy as though he were a beloved brother.

The place was packed with men of all types, rich and poor, master and slave, Dane and Englishman. Yorke was a strange city indeed. Some Saxons called it Eoforwic, some Danes Jorvik, the clergy Eboraco, but still they all flocked together as one within its ancient walls. And all had come to pay their respects to Tostig... or perhaps not.

There was little grieving here. During his time as earl of these lands, Tostig had been hated by the northerners. Most of those who had come to witness his last rites had done so out of respect for King Harold, not to mourn the dead.

For his part, Harold stood firm during the ceremony. Like many of the others he did not grieve for his brother. Not even a single tear, unlike his brother Gyrth, who wept most of the way through.

The priest had finished his sermon now, and Harold

stepped forward to witness his brother's burial. Dark-robed monks lifted the body, conveying it from a side door to be buried in the churchyard.

Styrkar had seen enough. As the congregation followed the burial procession, Styrkar stood and watched them go. When he finally turned to leave through the main doors there was one other who had waited.

Oswulf nodded at Styrkar and they both stood in the centre of the empty church.

'I've had enough too,' Oswulf said. His eye was black from a blow he'd taken during the battle, the flesh at the edges yellow and puffy. 'I think we've all wasted enough time on Tostig fucking Godwinson.'

Styrkar felt a little guilty. 'We should honour the king's wishes.'

'You don't think we've honoured the king enough for now?'

The notion hadn't occurred to Styrkar. 'I think we are his servants.'

'Ha! I'd heard the Red Wolf was loyal. I didn't realise how much.'

'I owe—'

'And trust me, you've paid. So… the Red Wolf can fight. But can he drink?'

Styrkar shook his head. 'What do you mean?'

'We've been in Yorke for two days and I haven't yet had the chance to sample its ale or its women. What about you?'

'I don't—'

'That settles it then. We find them together.' Oswulf stretched an arm around Styrkar's broad shoulders. 'By Christ you're a big one.'

With that he led Styrkar from the church and out into the cold afternoon air.

Styrkar stared out at the river. His vision was fuzzy about the edges and he had a warm feeling in his belly. Inside the mead hall he could still hear the sound of laughter and carousing. Oswulf certainly knew how to celebrate a victory – he and his fellow thegns had attacked the ale and mead with more ferocity than they'd fought the Norsemen. Brawls had broken out, but somehow no one had managed to die. It was a strange release, but now Styrkar had drunk his fill.

He stood and watched as the river flowed by, the noise of it weirdly comforting as night fell. The sudden sound of footsteps approaching through the mud made him place a hand to the knife at his waist.

'Have you not killed enough men in the past few days?'

Harold walked from the darkness, unaccompanied.

'My apologies, sire,' Styrkar replied, dropping to one knee in the wet filth.

'Get up, my friend. It was a joke.'

Styrkar rose unsteadily to his feet, feeling more than a little foolish.

'I am sorry I left the church, sire. I should have stayed by your side.'

'The ceremony was a dull affair,' Harold replied. 'But that's what funerals are like, I suppose. You missed nothing. Better you reward yourself.' He looked Styrkar up and down as he swayed at the riverbank. 'Though I see that mead does not agree with you.'

'To be honest, sire, I find it agrees with me very well.'

Harold laughed. 'I'm sure. It is less than you deserve. So I would reward you for your loyalty, Styrkar. How would you feel about that?'

'You rewarded me plenty the day you set me free. The day you gave me this.' He touched a hand to the iron torc at his neck.

'No. I gave you what you deserved. And I would do so again. You have been loyal to me. More than I could hope from any of my housecarls. And so I would reward you as I would any of them.'

'Sire?'

Harold placed a hand on Styrkar's shoulder. 'Lands. How would you like to own an estate?'

'I... I wouldn't know the first thing about how to run an estate.'

'You wouldn't have to. You will have tenants for that. Men who would call you "master". It is the least I can do. I know you entered the battle out of more than mere loyalty. You wanted to take the head of Sigurdsson for yourself and you were robbed in the attempt. Well, let me compensate you for that loss.'

'I don't know what to say.'

'Say *yes*, Styrkar. That is the usual response.'

Before Styrkar could offer his thanks, there came a shout from the bridge nearby. A man came running, calling for the king, and Harold turned to greet him. As he moved into the light Styrkar could see it was one of Harold's messengers, muddy and sweating from the road.

'Sire, there is news from the south,' he said, bowing his head before the king.

'Speak it,' Harold said.

The messenger looked up, fear in his eyes. 'The Frankish Bastard has landed on English soil. Already he plunders the southern coast.'

'Raise my brothers,' Harold replied immediately, as though he had expected the news. 'And gather my housecarls. We take the road south at first light.'

With a bow, the messenger ran off to relay the king's orders.

Harold turned back to Styrkar. 'It looks as if your rise in status will be delayed, my friend. Can you wait a little longer for your lands, and fight by my side one more time?'

He would never have admitted it, but the thought of another battle alongside his king filled Styrkar with more relish than the prospect of owning any amount of land.

'I once told you I would fight by your side until my last breath,' he replied. 'But first, I will bring you Duke William's head.'

Harold clapped a firm hand to Styrkar's shoulder. 'Not if I take it first,' he said.

He left Styrkar at the river to plan their journey south.

It would be a long road, at the end of which would be another battle. The Frankish were fierce warriors, or so it was said. Again, they would have to repel a foreign invader, but Styrkar was sure of one thing...

...with King Harold to lead them, this victory was certain.

PART TWO

REVENANT

12

SENLAC HILL, ENGLAND, OCTOBER 1066

Ronan waited atop his horse. His head was fuddled from the wine – they'd drunk all night long and he'd not yet slept. Now it was starting to catch up with him.

Wine was all he'd wanted, anything to stop the shaking in his hands. They'd laughed and sung in their victory and not one of them had mentioned the friends lost, the slaughter. In the stark light of morning they had found a pile of horsemen lying dead beyond a low wall, their mounts broken. They had set off in pursuit of the fleeing English and not seen the stone wall sitting just before them in the dark. It had been their doom. Still, no one talked about that. They were flush with their victory – filled with too much anticipation for what they would soon gain.

'Hurry her up,' said an impatient voice. His irritation was easy to understand. Every man was starting to feel the effects of the previous day, whether from the wine or the battle.

Ronan looked to see the woman kneeling beside the

body in its sack. It didn't take a scholar to work out who was in there, but they were all forbidden to speak of it. A vanquished king shouldn't be mentioned when his successor was within earshot.

Not that Ronan cared to speak of anything right now. He was just glad the fighting was over.

The woman wept. She was a more beautiful thing than Ronan had ever seen, or at least it felt that way after the weeks of waiting with a group of stinking, sweating knights. He couldn't remember what repulsed him more – those men or their horses. It was a close-run thing. Now, seeing this woman weeping over her dead husband, he remembered what he had missed after all this time.

She gripped something close to her chest as they sewed up the remains, sealing them inside that sack. The woman bit back her tears as she stood, and she watched the men carry the body towards Ronan. All the while he couldn't take his eyes off her.

'You know what you have to do?'

Ronan looked down to see Brian standing beside him, his face serious. But then Brian was a serious man and, as heir to the Count of Penthièvre, had much responsibility. He, much like all the rest, looked weary from the battle, his face still marred by blood and mud.

'Take it somewhere quiet and burn it,' Ronan replied.

Brian nodded. They had been friends for years, and the nobleman knew that Ronan could be trusted with this. It was a task too ignominious to be given to a prominent knight, but one of Ronan's standing was perfect. He could take on this responsibility and would not be insulted by the mundanity of the task. Or such was the general feeling. In reality, Ronan felt he was doing the work of a lowly serf, but knew better than to complain. His time would come eventually, and he had been so very patient.

They secured the body to a saddle. Ronan had six men to accompany him, but that was more than he should need, especially with the hulking figure of his friend Aldus among their number. Though the English would have given anything for this body – indeed the king's mother was rumoured to have offered its weight in gold – they had been put to flight. There would be no one to stop them now.

Brian had also insisted on them being accompanied by a priest. Ronan had no idea what prayers had already been said over this corpse, but it was clear the Duke of Normandy wanted to make sure he was well and truly committed to the earth.

Before he reined his horse around and led his men off, Ronan spared the woman one last glance. She stood watching, gripping that sword to her breast. Her tears had stopped now and she regarded him with hate in those cold, beautiful eyes. For the briefest moment he wondered how many more times he would see that look as they made their way through these lands. With any luck it would be few, and these people would quickly realise what was best for them. Deep down, Ronan knew the chances of that were slim.

They struck south. Seven horsemen and a priest making their way through the countryside. The air was crisp but the rains had stopped. That was one small mercy at least. The further south they travelled, the more Ronan could smell the salt tang of the sea, and he knew they were nearing the coast. They made the journey in silence until one of the men rode up beside Ronan. He was young, a squire most likely and flush with the glow of victory.

'We are truly blessed with this task,' he said. 'The Bastard must think you a trusted servant to have granted you the honour.'

He was chancing his arm calling the duke "Bastard" but Ronan let it go.

'Who are you?' he asked.

'My name is Mainard. I am—'

'You think this an honour, Mainard? Scurrying away like robbers secreting their stash?'

'But surely we are chosen for this because of our—'

'We are chosen for this because the duke knows we will keep our mouths shut about where we burn the body. I suggest you prove him right.'

The young man looked down, suddenly shamed by his over-exuberance.

They had been tasked with destroying King Harold's body and telling no one of the whereabouts. If the English had a ceremonial place to worship their dead king it could be the spark that ignited a rebellion. Duke William would never allow that.

'You are the son of Rivallon of Dol-Combourg, yes?' asked Mainard.

'I am his illegitimate bastard. A bastard, just like the duke, as you seemed so eager to point out.'

'I didn't mean...'

'I know,' he said, taking pity on the lad. 'No one ever does. My name is Ronan. Just Ronan.'

As a bastard he had never been entitled to use the family name, unlike his half-brothers.

'You acquitted yourself well on the field yesterday.'

Ronan thought back. He could remember nothing that would have made his performance notable. He had remembered the screaming, the terror as he rode with the rest, smashing sword and lance against that impenetrable shield wall. Had he even killed a man? He couldn't remember. Perhaps it would come back to him later when he'd had a chance to sleep.

'We all did,' he replied. 'That's why we won.'

The lad laughed. 'We won because these English don't know how to fight.'

Ronan couldn't see why that made sense. The battle had taken hours. Had the English not been fooled by a false retreat and broken their lines, chances were William's army would have lost the day.

'We'll find out soon enough,' Ronan replied.

'What do you mean? We have beaten them. They are a defeated people.'

'We have invaded their lands and killed their king. That does not make these people defeated. Do you think they will so readily submit to a foreign master?'

'But Duke William is their king by right. He was granted the crown of England by the Confessor. That is why we're here.'

Ronan shook his head at the lad's naivety. 'There were more than two claimants before this all started. Now Harold is dead, even more will come crawling out of the woodwork. Nothing is over. This has only just begun.'

Though he hadn't meant to, Ronan had taken the shine off Mainard's morning, and they continued to ride in silence. As they reached the coast, the cliffs dropping away below them, Ronan gazed out across the channel and wondered when he would get to return home. If Duke William could subdue this land quickly then perhaps he'd be back within a year. If there was a complete surrender and they could shore up their defences, maybe even before then. But Ronan knew there was no point in wishing. He would just have to wait and bide his time.

As the bastard son of Rivallon of Dol-Combourg, Ronan would gain no lands or titles by birthright. He would have to earn them. That, after all, was the only reason he was here. Joining William had been the expedient thing to do, and this land was ripe for the picking. The promises William had made had seemed solid – he was a man of his word if nothing else. Many of his men had sailed across the channel out of loyalty to their duke. Most had come for the plunder.

Ronan would find out in good time whether that plunder was worth risking his life for, but then what other choice did he have? Return to Bretagne and live the rest of his life in quiet ignominy? No, this was a much better option.

The sky ahead grew darker and Ronan ordered them to stop. 'This place is as good as any,' he said, viewing the coast as it curved away to east and west. There were no witnesses other than the gulls that circled them, and he was hardly going to spend the whole day finding the perfect spot.

His men dismounted, taking the tree branches and slats of wood they had cut from the woodland to erect a small cairn. Ronan watched as Aldus stood by his side. His friend was a silent giant, his most loyal companion, and Ronan always felt safe with him near. Even in this foreign land, with enemies in every shadow, he knew he could rely on Aldus. They had grown up together, the cripple and the mute. Shunned and belittled by most other squires, they had formed a bond, and over the years learned to compensate for one another's weakness.

Without ceremony the knights placed the body atop the pyre. One of them tried to light a fire beneath, but the sparks were blown out to sea by the errant wind. Ronan began to lose his patience, but there was little he could do to help – he was hardly going to light the fire himself.

Eventually they managed to spark the kindling, and the cairn went up surprisingly fast. The priest got as close as he could, offering last rites and trying his best to sprinkle holy water, but it blew away on the stiff breeze.

'Do you think there's a special place for kings?' said Mainard, standing close by. 'You know... in heaven.'

Ronan shook his head as he watched the priest struggling with his sacrament. 'He's not a king now. He'll end up in the same place as everyone else.'

Ronan and the rest of the men stood and watched for some time as the body burned. The stink of cooked meat and charred wood assailed the air, and Ronan took a moment to appreciate the pyre and the relief it gave him from the chill morning. Eventually it burned down to cinders, and within an hour they were looking at nothing but a pile of burnt wood and bones.

'Pitch it into the sea,' he said. 'And let's get out of here.'

His men obeyed, and by the time they had finished there was no evidence of what they'd done other than a blackened patch of earth.

Ronan walked back to his horse, limping on his twisted foot, feeling it ache in the cold. He ignored it as best he could; just one more curse with which he was afflicted.

As they rode back there was a solemn silence. Ronan hadn't expected it to be so – why would any of them mourn such an enemy – but something about watching that proud king burn, anonymously at the edge of a cliff, infected him with a melancholy. Maybe he was just tired.

By the time they reached the battlefield, Ronan could see much had changed. The camp they had erected the previous night had been broken and most of the Frankish dead had been buried in mass graves. For the English no such luxury, and they still lay strewn about the hill where they had died.

'Is it done?'

Ronan turned to see Brian standing nearby. He was a stern young man, his severe brow making him look much older than his years. The heir of Penthièvre was not a man to be crossed, but he was one who could be trusted. Throughout his life, Ronan had relied on him the most.

'It is,' he replied, climbing down from his horse. 'Now, where can I rest?'

Brian shook his head. 'No time for that, my friend. We withdraw to Dover.'

'For what? Surely our duke will want to ride for the capital and demand the church recognise him as the new king.'

'William thinks it more expedient to await the surrender of the English nobles.'

'He what?'

Brian shrugged. 'I can see the sense in it. We have a defensive bastion at Dover. And it is a show of strength to force the defeated to come to you.'

'And he honestly believes the lords of England will just stand aside and let him take over?'

'Of course not. But they at least have the chance.'

'And when they don't?' Ronan asked.

'When they don't we will take up our lances once more, mount our horses and ravage this place until it submits.'

With that, Brian left him with Aldus. Ronan glanced up at his friend, and the giant looked back, his dolorous expression giving nothing away, as always.

'Looks like the fight's not over yet,' Ronan said.

Aldus did not disagree.

13

COPPETHORNE, ENGLAND, OCTOBER 1066

He woke from a troubled dream, body drenched in sweat. The cloth sheet covering him was sodden and he flung it aside. Styrkar could see little in the dark room, but there was a soft breeze blowing in from somewhere. The draught served to cool his fevered body and he shivered in the dark.

Was this his tomb? Had he awoken from death? Returned by the gods to…

To what? Styrkar could barely remember his own name, and as he tried to grasp onto his memories they slipped away like smoke.

He tried to move, immediately feeling the stinging pain in his shoulder, in his ribs, his thigh. Every muscle ached and his breath came shallow and weak. His throat was parched and he tried to clear it but only succeeded in coughing up a ball of phlegm. The effort sent more pain coursing through every fibre, and he lay back on the bed defeated.

Gritting his teeth, Styrkar tensed his stomach, feeling

it growl in its emptiness, before he grasped the wooden bedframe and swung his legs over the side. He grunted as he sat up, instantly regretting the effort when his head began to swim. Bile rose in his mouth, stinging his already sore throat.

Atop the bed was a sack stuffed with hay, soaked through with sweat. Styrkar could smell his rank body odour, the stink of it turning his empty stomach, and his first thought went to his wounds. If they had begun to fester he would not have to suffer this indignity for much longer.

He reached a hand to his shoulder, touching the cloth bandage that bound it. The material had hardened, a crust forming where the blood of an arrow wound had dried. His ribs were likewise bound, along with his thigh.

Finally, reaching a hand to his face, Styrkar could feel the flesh around his eye was puffy and swollen, tender to the touch.

The room had stopped spinning now, and he tried to stand. As he did so there was a flash of pain in his thigh and the spark of a memory was ignited.

He was standing amid the slaughter of the battlefield. The sound of horses and dying men filling his ears. Through the cacophony he could hear Harold bellowing for his housecarls to rally, and Styrkar rushed to heed his master. As he did so, an arrow pierced his thigh and he fell to one knee…

Styrkar sat back on the bed, reeling from the sudden image. Outside he heard a crow caw as the first sign of morning light crept beneath the door of the hut.

It was suddenly difficult to breathe, and Styrkar forced himself to stand this time, ignoring the screaming pain, grasping the sweat-sodden sheet that had been covering him and wrapping it around himself. As he did so he felt the sharp pain in his shoulder burn hotter, and another memory was kindled by it.

Arrows bit into the mud. Harold's brother Gyrth fell to the ground. His other brother, Leofwine, was already lying dead nearby. There were few of them left now, the fyrd already fled, the surviving housecarls putting up a valiant last stand but they fought a battle they could never win. Styrkar dragged himself to his feet, desperate to reach his king, but another arrow hit him in the shoulder, driving him back. He growled against the pain, snapping the shaft and almost dropping his axe…

He shuffled towards the door, suddenly desperate to breathe the open air, but he could barely walk, shambling like an old man beneath a heavy burden. As he took a faltering step the pain in his ribs screamed as though he had been stabbed.

Frankish knights raced towards Harold. They had lost their horses, but were still bedecked in mail, shields braced and weapons raised. One of them struck the king a blow and Harold staggered, raising his sword to fight back, but a second knight hit him with an axe, a blow that drove him to the floor. Styrkar bellowed, raising his own axe high to defend the king, but something struck him from the side, and he fell, ribs cracked, hardly able to breathe…

He managed to grasp the handle of the door, wrenching it open, and letting the cold dawn air greet him. Through his swollen eye he could barely see anything, his fuddled mind beginning to race.

Styrkar struggled to his knees. Harold was surrounded, his weapon lost. The knights did not relent, attacking as though they were taking down a wild beast. Styrkar bellowed to his king, a cry of loss and anguish cut short as something struck the side of his head...

He grasped the doorframe, desperate to stop himself falling. A laboured sob left his parched throat as memories of his murdered king came rushing back. The king he had vowed to protect. The king he had failed.

The crow cawed again, and Styrkar gazed out, eyes focusing on the grey landscape. The hut was in an isolated spot. Somewhere he could hear a river flowing and there was woodland rising up beneath the dull morning sky.

Outside the house was a bench, and he struggled towards it, sitting heavily and pulling the sheet about him for warmth. His feet grew cold on the damp ground as Styrkar sat there shivering, feeling the pain and loss more keenly than any of his wounds.

There he sat till dawn as the sun began to peer over the treetops. The light was warming but it brought him no solace. He fought back the tears, still shivering, wondering what he would do now the man he had vowed to protect was gone.

The sound of someone approaching brought him out of his misery. Perhaps it was whoever had helped him and tended his wounds. Perhaps it was an enemy.

He felt suddenly weak and exposed. What if it was a band of roaming Frankish, come to finish the job they had started at Senlac? Styrkar could barely walk, let alone defend himself.

When an old man came shuffling into view through the trees, carrying a sack across his humped shoulder, Styrkar realised he had been gripping the bench with all his might. He sighed with relief, settling back as the man approached.

When he saw Styrkar shivering on his bench, the old man shook his head.

'This morning is full of surprises,' he croaked. 'I thought I'd get back to find a corpse.'

Styrkar had no words. Besides, his parched throat probably wouldn't have let him speak even if he'd tried.

'Not the talkative type? Just my luck. I've spent the last ten days with a sleeping man and now he's awake he's got nothing to say.'

'Ten days?' Styrkar managed to mumble.

'Or thereabouts,' the old man said. 'I lose count.'

He stepped inside the house. Styrkar could hear him clattering around until he reappeared with a cup.

'Drink this,' the old man said.

Styrkar took the cup with a shaking hand. As he pressed it to his lips he could smell it was some kind of fermented brew, stagnant and rank, but he was too thirsty to refuse. The first mouthful stung his gums and burned his throat. The second he swallowed with gusto.

'The Franks?' Styrkar managed to say when he had finished the cup. 'What of the invaders?'

'Moved on east to Dover, by all accounts. Waiting for the English thegns to come fall to their knees and surrender. You're safe, for now. And you're some way from the battlefield. It's more than two days' walk to the coast from here. That's before you collapsed in the wood. It was lucky I was wandering by or you'd most likely be rotting there right now. It was the devil's own work getting you inside, lad. You weigh as much as a bull.'

Styrkar's stomach gave an audible rumble, and the old man opened his sack, pulling out a hunk of cheese. With a knife he expertly hacked off a sliver and handed it to Styrkar. It tasted salty and stale but he managed to swallow it down.

'You kept me alive for ten days?'

'Or thereabouts. Managed to get the arrows out of you too. With any luck there's no pieces of 'em still in there, but I guess you're mostly over the fever so that's a good sign.'

The old man took a seat on the bench. In the morning light, Styrkar noticed he bore as wrinkled a face as he'd ever seen, eyes rheumy, back bent with his years, but there was a sinewy strength to his limbs and his mind seemed to work well enough. Certainly well enough to have made sure Styrkar hadn't died.

'Why have you done this for me?' Styrkar asked. 'You owe me nothing.'

'Maybe I do, maybe I don't,' said the old man with a shrug. 'But I couldn't just leave you dying in the woods, now could I. Especially when I knew it was the Red Wolf who was lying there.'

'You know me?'

The old man pointed to the iron torc about Styrkar's neck. 'I like to keep my mouth shut and my ears pinned. I might live in the middle of nowhere but I still hear things in town. There's only one man who wears the wolf collar. King Harold's champion.'

Styrkar lifted a hand to touch the wolf head torc at his neck. It felt loose and heavy. He should have torn it free and thrown it into the grass, for he was king's champion no longer, but he had neither the will nor the strength.

'What other news have you heard? What of the thegns? Have they mustered an army to turn back the Frankish?'

'Rumour has it there's going to be a witan at Berchastede. They'll choose their new king then.'

Styrkar struggled to his feet. 'I must go there. I must join them in their fight.'

He stumbled and the old man reached out to stop him falling. 'You're fit to drop, lad. Berchastede is days away from here.'

Despite the pain that seemed to infect every inch of his body, Styrkar gritted his teeth and stood. 'I need to get dressed. I need to get to Berchastede.'

'I had to burn your clothes, but I have an old tunic from when I was a younger man. It'll most likely fit you. But at least let me give you a wash first. You stink to high heaven.'

Styrkar wanted to waste no time. 'Just the clothes will do,' he replied.

The old man nodded, reluctantly. 'All right then. I don't suppose I'll argue with the Red Wolf, even if he does look ready for the grave.'

They both entered the house. With some difficulty the old man helped Styrkar into clean clothes. He had lost some of his bulk over the past ten days, but the old man's garb was still a tight fit. Better he suffer the discomfort of poorly fitting clothes than walk the roads naked.

Styrkar managed to limp outside. He ached in every limb, but he was determined to make it to the witan. It was the only hope he had to redeem himself.

'How do I get there?' Styrkar asked.

'Through the trees,' the old man replied. 'There's a road not far on the other side. Head north. It's a two-day walk, lad. You'll be lucky to make it halfway.'

Styrkar just nodded. He would force himself to make it, or die in the attempt.

'Take this,' said the old man, before he could leave. Styrkar took the sack of supplies. Looking inside he saw the rest of the cheese, a waterskin and some apples.

With a nod, he left the old man behind and focused on putting one unsteady foot before the other. If there was to be a witan, he had to be there. Harold would have wanted that. Would have wanted him to pledge his loyalty to the new king and defend him against the Franks. He had to get there. Had to do his duty.

It took him most of the morning to make his way through the trees and onto the road. It was only then, as he gazed northward, that Styrkar suddenly remembered he had forgotten to thank that old man. He had been shown an act of kindness by a stranger, and he hadn't even bothered to ask his name.

Too late now. He would have to save his thanks for another day. All he could think on now was reaching Berchastede, determined that this fight was not over yet.

14

SUDWECA, ENGLAND, NOVEMBER 1066

The familiar stink of woodsmoke hung in the air. Another day another burning village. How many had that been now? Ronan had lost count, but at least the screaming was over. The flames had died down quickly thanks to the rain and now all that remained were charred embers and the corpses of animals and peasants.

Ronan watched from the hill, thinking back to how they had come to this. Duke William had waited at Dover for days for the English to prostrate themselves, and when they had not come he became enraged. If these upstart thegns would not see sense, then William was determined to provoke them into action.

The duke set off on a campaign to ravage the southern towns and Ronan had joined in, at first enthusiastically, but now his zeal for the butchery was waning. There was no glory in this, no sense of victory, and it had not taken long for Ronan to grow weary of the slaughter. Likewise, Aldus stood beside him, his silent companion, watching with emotionless eyes. Ronan could not ask him his thoughts, but he guessed they were much the same as his own.

'I'm sorry for bringing you here,' Ronan said, not expecting an answer. 'Pointless murder wasn't what I expected either. When we reach the capital, I'm sure things will get better.'

Aldus said nothing, not even acknowledging he'd heard, but that didn't matter. Ronan was talking to himself as much as his oldest friend.

The dumb giant had followed Ronan wherever he led since they were children. Though it had always been known that Ronan was high-born, it had never felt like that. He had been an outcast, despite his heritage. A pariah in some circles. It was only natural that his closest friend would be from humble beginnings. He had found Aldus as a boy, ridiculed and mocked by the other children of their town. Something in Ronan had wanted to protect him, despite his size. Aldus had seemed impervious to the barbs shot at him by the townsfolk, and it had fallen to Ronan to take those insults personally. He had defended Aldus, sometimes violently, and in return the giant boy had become his loyal follower. Ronan knew better than anyone that loyalty such as his was not to be spurned.

And so here they were. Two soldiers in a war of devastation. Ronan had made Aldus promises. Told him they would rise together. It didn't seem like there was anything lofty in their deeds right now.

Half of William's army had already made their way further north. He had left a contingent in Dover to guard their backs – an escape route should they find themselves on the run – but so far English resistance had been pathetic. The news of the English king's death had travelled on swift and dark wings, and it seemed the people of this land no longer had the will to fight.

Nevertheless, the duke was determined to ravage the countryside until the English magnates fell at his feet and proclaimed him the new king. So far there had been little sign of them, but perhaps they were simply biding their time.

At the garrison in Dover, many of the duke's men had fallen ill. A few days into their advance north, William himself succumbed to sickness. Though he still led his men it was obvious he was suffering. It seemed that their righteous and holy invasion had taken a turn for the worse. Perhaps they weren't blessed in their endeavours after all, and if the English magnates waited long enough William and his invading force would succumb to disease before a rebellion were even necessary.

A call went up from somewhere, stirring Ronan from the grim prospect of death. It was time for them to move on. The knights had salvaged everything they could from the town – the pickings had been slim and it had taken little time to loot the place. Livestock had already been slaughtered; survivors fled across the hills.

Before Ronan and Aldus could make their way to the waiting horses, a weary figure came towards them up the hill. Brian appeared to have aged in the days since they had arrived. He looked as unhappy with their current predicament as Ronan was.

'We are headed for Canterburgh,' he said, as he came to stand by Ronan's side. 'Rumour has it the English will surrender there.'

'And has any other rumour been true so far?' Ronan replied.

'We can but hope this one will turn out to be accurate. I for one could do with a bath.'

'Of that there is no doubt,' Ronan replied without thinking.

To his relief, Brian smirked, seeing the funny side. Though they were friends of old and part of the same conrois, Brian's position as the son of a count gave him certain privileges. Not having to suffer mockery at the hands of one of his knights was among them.

'The sooner these English accept God's will, the better,' he said, looking out onto the devastated town.

Ronan had heard the assertion many times, but still wasn't sure how much of it he believed.

'God's will? Or the duke's?' he asked.

'You doubt the righteousness of our cause?' Brian replied.

'That's why you're here? Righteousness?'

'The crown of England is William's by right. It was promised to him, under oath. He has the backing of the pope. We do God's work, of that there is no doubt.'

Ronan gestured to the blackened timbers dotted with corpses. 'This is God's work?'

'Don't be so blind, Ronan. We defeated a false king on the field of battle. You don't think God was with us that day?'

'I don't doubt we were blessed with victory. I was there, Brian. I fought. Our horses and lances sealed that victory. If God was there he was just a keen spectator.'

'Victory is victory. If we won, it was God's will.'

'And yet the English have not yet acknowledged their defeat.'

'That's just a matter of time. God is on our side. This is what he wants. This is why we follow Duke William.'

Ronan sighed. 'Sometimes I think you even believe that.'

Brian clapped Ronan on the arm. 'Our faith keeps us strong, Ronan. Of course I believe it. Now, let's go north and spread more of God's righteous anger. Who knows, before the day is out we might have a gaggle of English lords begging for mercy at our feet.'

Brian made his way back to the horses. His weariness looked to have already left him and Ronan knew, despite his claims, that it was not his piety and religious fervour that kept him going.

They had all been offered rewards. This was not meant to be a mission of enlightenment; accompanying God's chosen to claim his throne. That was merely the excuse. William had promised lands and power to his followers, and Brian was set to claim what he could. Not that Ronan blamed him. He had similar ambitions, as did every man who had crossed the sea to be here.

None of them had been forced into this. Ronan was well aware that he could leave if he wished to. He was under no obligation, but what was there back on the mainland for him? He was the bastard son with nothing to inherit. If Ronan wanted lands and titles he would have to take them, just like William.

He and Aldus made their way to where the horses were tied. Ronan struggled as always on his crippled foot, but he gritted his teeth and took the discomfort. Already the rest of the knights had mounted and followed the trail northwards. Ronan took to the saddle, watching as Aldus climbed atop his huge warhorse. He remembered well how the stallions had protested at being transported across the sea but they had been necessary, if not imperative to their victory. It wasn't as though they could use the tiny English ponies indigenous to this island. Aldus for one would have struggled to find one that could carry his weight.

As they rode through the devastated town, Ronan tried his best not to take in too much detail. He'd always considered himself to have a strong stomach for war, but this was no war he had ever been privy to. This was slaughter, pure and simple.

He saw a soot-covered face peering at him from the wreckage. Could have been a young girl, could have been a boy, it was hard to tell. These people didn't put much store by their appearance. Either way it was most definitely a child, a sole survivor scrabbling amongst the wreckage of his or her life. Ronan wanted to look away but he found himself staring as his horse conveyed him from the town. For the first time, he considered that perhaps he was on the wrong path after all. There would be much more suffering before this ended, much more misery to witness.

But despite the burning stink the town left in his nostrils and the sour taste it left in his mouth, Ronan knew he could not turn back now.

15

BERCHASTEDE, ENGLAND, NOVEMBER 1066

One foot in front of the other. That had been his constant refrain for so many miles now. Styrkar could barely feel his legs and his breath came in shallow gasps, but still he carried on.

One foot in front of the other.

Berchastede rose up before him, a huge wooden wall surrounding its boundary, but Styrkar did not allow himself to feel any relief. He was not there yet. Every step pained him, and as he neared the end of the journey his body was in danger of letting him down at the last moment.

He could not give in to collapse. Could not let his weak body fail him at this final obstacle.

Folk of all kinds milled about the place as he entered the wide-open gate. Peasant and warrior alike filled the streets, and in the distance he could hear the rowdy gathering he had come so far to witness. He was thankful the witan was not over. At least that was one bit of good fortune. Now all he had to do was stay on his feet long enough to see how it ended.

People stared as he staggered up the road, but that was to be expected. Styrkar knew he must have looked a sight – his red hair and beard in a tangle, stumbling like he'd just crawled from the grave. Despite his condition, no one raised a hand to help him as he made his way towards the huge longhouse that stood at the centre of the town. He could hardly blame them.

The crowd thickened as he drew closer to the longhouse, and the sound of shouting grew louder. Styrkar paused at the edge of the throng. His eye was drawn to a trough of brown stagnant water, and he could not stop himself from lumbering over and submerging his head, drinking in a long mouthful. If it tasted rank he could not tell, his mouth was so dry.

The cold water did its trick and he felt momentarily revived. After wiping the wet from his face and slicking back his hair, he began to push his way through the crowd.

He realised how weak he'd become as he struggled to push against the tightly packed mob. Styrkar found himself being jostled, where before his bulk would have seen the crowd part before him easily. Once he'd managed to make his way inside the huge hall he was hit by a cacophony of noise. The place was packed to the rafters with rowdy men, and the sound of it made Styrkar grit his teeth. For a moment he was back on the battlefield, his senses assailed by the sounds of screaming and dying men, but he forced himself further inside, all his strength of will making him focus on the task at hand, nailing him to the here and now.

Everywhere were thegns and magnates, jeering and cheering. Styrkar recognised some of the faces, though he could not put names to them. Others he had never seen before as they bellowed for attention. What was certain was none of them had been present on Senlac Hill. Not one of them had stood beside his king, but now they took it upon themselves to choose his replacement. Styrkar was sickened by their sense of entitlement. They should have been mourning Harold, not clamouring to pick his successor.

As he scanned the crowd, Styrkar's gaze fell upon two nobles he recognised. King Harold had formed an alliance with these men, and betrothed himself to their sister to seal the pact – the sister Styrkar had delivered safely back to their care three years before. The earls, Edwin and Morcar, were very different brothers. Edwin, the elder, was a serious man. Handsome in his way, his hair neatly trimmed. His younger brother Morcar was a shaggy affair, every inch reminiscent of the brutish north over which they both ruled.

Styrkar clenched his fists on seeing them. They had been as much to blame for Harold's death as anyone. The king had gone north to aid them in the fight against Norse invaders, only to find they had already been defeated. After Harold dispatched Tostig and Sigurdsson, Edwin and Morcar had pledged the king their support against the Duke of Normandy, but they had not arrived in time for the battle at Senlac Hill. Now both men stood front and centre, as though it was they who had secured victory in the north. As though they were the lords of this place.

A voice rose up amid the clamour, a long and soulful bellow that gradually silenced the crowd. From among the throng stepped an elderly man, long beard hanging down over his priestly white robes. Archbishop Stigand regarded the crowd with an air of superiority. Styrkar had always despised him; a man who expressed such devotion to his god, but had always forgone the self-sacrifice he demanded of others.

'I would thank the earls, Edwin and Morcar, for their contribution,' Stigand said, his voice still powerful despite his years. 'The witan has now heard entreaties from all present, and we will decide who will take the crown of England and lead us against this Frankish duke. What say—'

'I have not spoken.'

A single voice from the crowd silenced Stigand. The priest looked annoyed at the interruption, not least because the voice was that of a woman.

As Edith stepped forward to stand in the centre of this gathering of men, Styrkar felt a cauldron of emotion roiling within him. She was the first friendly face he had seen since Senlac. Harold's true bride had been like a mother to Styrkar. She had always carried the strength and bearing befitting the wife of a king, but now she looked small and frail amid this gathering of nobles. The death of her husband had clearly affected her deeply, and Styrkar wanted to walk forward and embrace her, to tell her how sorry he was, but the shame of his failure and the weakness in his body held him back.

'I have heard you all speak of rights,' Edith said. Though her voice was small, every man present was silent. 'I have stood and listened, while men who professed their loyalty to King Harold have argued and bartered for a crown that is not theirs. I have heard men talk of war who refused to stand by their king when he called upon them.'

There were rumblings of discontent from the crowd, but nobody dared to interrupt her. Styrkar looked across at Edwin and Morcar, seeing that even they were silent, though it was obvious they were the target of Edith's barb.

'Everyone here knows who the rightful heir is. My son Godwin is next in line to the English throne. It is he who now demands your support. He who will turn back the tide of Frankish invaders.'

'So where is he now?'

A single anonymous voice from the crowd. It sparked a murmur of indignation, and Styrkar felt his heart drop, sensing the gathered thegns agreeing with the sentiment.

'Your son has fled,' shouted another voice. 'Gone to seek protection from the High King of Ireland rather than face the Frankish bastard. What kind of leader is that?'

'He had no choice,' Edith said, but Styrkar could see she was foundering amidst the hostile crowd. 'It is because of your inaction, your cowardice, your failure to support Harold, that he had to escape these lands.'

Edith was quickly drowned out by the scornful voices of the thegns. They had turned back to their base state, jeering like animals, and it was not until Archbishop Ealdred stepped forward that they stopped.

Ealdred was younger than Stigand, though his hair and beard were still white as winter. He placed a consoling hand on Edith's arm, and called for calm from the crowd.

'We have gathered this witan to choose our king, and can only select from those who have honoured it with their presence. Godwin has a claim, of that there is no doubt, but it is clear he does not carry the support of those present.

England needs a king, here and now. Harold's sons have fled across the sea and we cannot wait for their return.'

Styrkar could see the fury in Edith's eyes, but she knew she was beaten, powerless to do anything. With her sons gone there was no one to represent the line of King Harold, and she backed from the centre of the hall, leaving Ealdred to continue.

'The choice of who will be king is clear. He has the support of the standing earls and the church. He is also of the royal line. It is undeniable.' Ealdred held up a hand, summoning someone from the crowd.

A youth stepped forward, not yet matured to manhood, but far from a child. He looked nervous, almost meek, but Styrkar could see some nobility in his bearing.

'Edgar the Aetheling,' Ealdred pronounced. 'Grandson of the great King Edmund Ironside. This must be the man to take on the crown by right of birth and by the grace of God. What say you all?'

A huge cheer went up, filling the great hall to its rooftop. Styrkar could see Edwin and Morcar joining in, and realised this was as much their doing as Ealdred and Stigand. The boy was untested, and far too young to take the crown. He would be a puppet for these men, a figurehead on a throne they controlled. And there was nothing Styrkar could do to stop them.

The gathered throng grew rowdier in their support for the new king, and Styrkar found himself being jostled. There was nothing more for him here, and he turned, desperate to get out of the cloying hall and breathe fresh air again.

He staggered outside. News of the witan's decision was

already spreading, and Styrkar could see people were joyous at the decision. It was clear they could not see ahead to what was coming. Styrkar had faced the Franks on the battlefield, had stood against their horses and their knights and tasted his own blood because of it. If these people thought their troubles were over now some boy had been proclaimed king, they were more foolish than they looked.

'Styrkar.'

He turned at the voice, seeing Edith standing nearby. The concern was obvious on her face as she looked him up and down. When last they had seen one another he had been a warrior, tall and proud. Now he was nothing but a worthless vagabond.

'I thought you were dead,' she said, reaching forward to take his arm, but he pulled away.

He should have been dead. He should have perished alongside his king, but by Fenrir's grace he was still alive, if barely.

'I have to go,' he said.

'But why?' she replied. 'And where?'

Styrkar shook his head. 'I do not know. But I cannot stay here.'

'You can barely walk. Let me take care of you.'

'No,' he said as vehemently as he could, but the word was lost in his parched throat. 'I do not deserve your care. I failed him. I failed you…'

She placed a gentle hand to his chest and he stopped, looking down at her face and the sympathy in her eyes.

'And do you think this is how he would have wanted you to go on? He would have wanted you to live, Styrkar. Not to punish yourself. I am going back to Walsingaha – there is nothing more to be done here. And you will come with me.'

'I cannot…'

'Yes you can. I need you. Ulf needs you, now more than ever.'

The thought of Harold's youngest son almost brought tears to Styrkar's eyes. How would he ever explain to the boy how his father had died? How Styrkar had failed to save him?

'My other sons are fled,' Edith continued. 'My daughters sent to abbeys. I have no one left, Styrkar. You must come. Do not refuse me.'

There was a need within him to accept, but Styrkar quashed it. He did not deserve Edith's kindness. He could never accept her charity after such a failure.

Before he could refuse her, a tall figure pushed his way from the boisterous crowd to join them. Earl Edwin ignored Edith, focusing his attention on Styrkar.

'The Red Wolf lives,' he said. There was a light in his eyes, as though he were joyous to see Styrkar. They had only met once before, when Styrkar had delivered their sister Alditha from the Welsh, but now Edwin spoke as though they were old friends.

'Have you come to pledge your allegiance to the new king?' Edwin continued. 'He could do with a warrior like you.' The earl seemed blind to Styrkar's poor condition.

For his part, Styrkar would rather have shat in his hands and clapped than join this useless pig.

'I am Edith's man now,' Styrkar replied, surprising himself more than anyone.

Edwin raised an eyebrow in surprise, but before he could speak further, several horses cantered up beside them and one of the riders called out.

'Brother. We must leave.' Morcar looked down at Edwin, his expression serious. 'Our sister has remained here for too long. It is time for us to take the road north.'

Styrkar looked to the riders behind Morcar. Atop one of the horse's was Alditha, their sister and King Harold's wife of only a few months. She was heavy with child, her beautiful face flushed with the bloom of it, raven hair cascading down her shoulders.

'Then I wish you both good fortune,' Edwin said, bowing before he turned to mount his horse. 'We would stay, but our sister must be conveyed to safety. She carries Harold's heir, after all, and the longer she remains in the south the more danger she is in.'

For the briefest of moments, Styrkar noticed Edith and Alditha share a look. They had both lost a husband in Harold, and though it was doubtful there was any love between them, they at least had a shared grief. If Alditha remembered Styrkar, she did not acknowledge it as she span her horse and rode away.

Styrkar watched as the riders made their way from Berchastede. Before they had cleared the gates, Styrkar felt his legs almost give out beneath him. Edith was there to catch him, and he leaned into her strong grip.

'Come,' she said. 'Let's leave this place behind us. These thegns can continue their schemes. We will have no more to do with them.'

Styrkar let her lead him away with no word of complaint, only too happy to be done with the games of nobles and kings.

16

WALINGEFORD, ENGLAND, NOVEMBER 1066

Duke William's men were weary, but still ready for a fight. The narrow bridge that led to the town forced them into a funnel, and Ronan peered at the water below, hoping his steed would not pitch him into those freezing depths.

On the far side of the bridge, the filthy peasants of this land watched them. A host of mournful, emaciated faces gazed in awe as Ronan and the rest of the army rode by. There was little stomach for defiance here. William had left a trail of devastation behind him all the way from Dover, and every mile they burned and robbed and raped.

Ronan might have felt an ounce of pity for these people, but they were beneath it. Had they showed more fight he might have had some admiration, but they were a defeated people. They deserved everything they got.

As his horse trod through the mud, he could see that some of the houses of this town had already been burned to the ground in advance of their approach. The townsfolk preferred to set their homes on fire rather than leave them for the foreign invaders.

Well, let them. Let them burn this entire country. William would build it anew and drag these peasants into the new world. They would accept their defeat or burn along with their hovels.

Ronan could see William at the head of their column. He lacked his usual proud bearing, still afflicted as he was by whatever malaise he had contracted in Dover, but it did not stop him leading his conquering army. His flesh was waxy, a sheen of sweat covering his brow, but he fought the illness as he had fought the king of these lands. Ronan was in no doubt he would beat it, just as he had beaten Harold.

The duke reined his horse to a stop, raising a hand for his knights to do likewise. They were at the edge of the town, surrounded by burned buildings. A church stood before them, and a more impressive sight Ronan had not seen in these lands. It was a more sturdy monument than the usual pile of stones that passed for English places of worship.

William signalled to his brother, the Bishop Odo, an educated man who could speak the language of the English. Odo nodded and raised himself in the saddle.

'Who will come forward and speak for this town?' Odo cried in his broken English. 'I have come to accept your surrender. There is nothing to fear.'

Silence. Whoever was in charge here was too fearful to step out of whichever dive they were hiding in. Ronan could understand their reluctance; the reputation of William's army had clearly preceded them.

The duke, however, was not so understanding, and he nodded to his brother again.

'We will not wait forever. If this town does not surrender to its new king, we will burn every building to the ground. We will take your livestock, salt your fields and it will be as though this place never existed.'

Ronan could see the irony – by the looks of it, the people of this place had already started the job. But before William could give the order for his men to begin their pillaging, the iron-bound door of the church creaked open.

An old man stepped out into the cold. He was dressed in the regalia of an archbishop, his white vestments stark against the mud through which he trudged. His hair was thin and grey, face careworn, and Ronan could see the fear in his eyes. Understandable considering the circumstances.

He was followed by half a dozen minor priests who lingered by the door, too fearful to approach. So much for their faith.

'My name is Stigand,' said the old man, his voice weakened by age or fear, it was difficult to tell which. To his credit, he spoke the language of the Franks very well. 'I am Archbishop of Canterburgh. And I welcome you.'

William leaned forward in his saddle. 'I wondered how long it would be before I met a man of seniority in this country. I was beginning to think I would only be greeted by turnip farmers.'

His men laughed. Stigand seemed less amused.

'They are fearful of your wroth,' said the priest. 'But I know you are a man of reason.'

'I am,' William replied. 'But it seems the lords of this land are determined to deny me what is mine by right. I hear rumours they have chosen their own king. Little more than a boy, if the tales are true. So where is this king? Will he face me on the field? Does he have the courage to fight me man to man? I would offer him that at least.'

Ronan could see William sway in his saddle, and for a moment wondered whether the duke could even beat a boy in his condition, let alone a man.

'It was foolish,' Stigand said. 'I advised them against it. I told them such a rash move was folly, but they would not listen. But you have demonstrated your might. There can be no doubt now that it is God's will you become King of England. They will accept this.'

'And so you would renounce this pretender to the throne?'

Stigand nodded enthusiastically. 'Of course. He is but a child.'

William swung his leg over the saddle and struggled down to the ground. Though he was stricken by his malady, Stigand was still intimidated, taking a step away from the duke in fear.

'Pledge yourself to me, Stigand of Canterburgh,' William said, as he came to stand before the archbishop. 'Demonstrate your fealty, here and now, before man and God.'

'I do, sire,' the old man replied. 'I pledge—'

'No,' William interrupted. 'On your knees.'

Stigand stared for a moment, as though he hadn't quite understood. Ronan watched as the priest thought on the demand, as though he might expect William to change his mind, to laugh and say he wasn't serious. But Ronan knew William would never allow such clemency.

His legs unsteady, Stigand struggled to the ground, kneeling in the mud, his white robes soaking up the filth. He clenched his hands together as though he were about to pray.

'I renounce the false king, Edgar, and pledge my fealty to King William of England. I acknowledge his God-given right to rule over these lands and all those who live within its borders.'

He opened his eyes, looking up at William expectantly. It was obvious he was hoping he had left nothing out.

'Get up,' William said. 'You look pathetic.'

As the old man struggled to his feet, Ronan almost felt sorry for him. Almost. These people had been given every chance to accept their new king. The longer they resisted, the longer Ronan would have to keep travelling this piss-hole of a country. The longer he would be forced to teach them what it meant to defy their rightful masters.

'Send word to every priest and thegn. They will pledge their loyalty to me, just as you have. Or they will face the consequences.'

The old man nodded, looking relieved that he had satisfied William's demands. He turned and trudged his way back to the church as William addressed his men.

'You see. The word of an archbishop is truly the word of God. This land is ours by right. The first obstacle is toppled. Now the rest will surely fall in its wake.'

As he mounted his horse again, Ronan was not so convinced this was the will of God. But God's will mattered little next to that of a man like William.

Ronan rode into the small compound they had requisitioned. Patrols were posted all around the town's perimeter, but there was little sign of them being attacked. He had felt a little guilty about leaving Aldus out in the cold, but Ronan's feet were like blocks of ice – his crippled ankle screaming in pain – and he had to get the blood pumping back through his veins. Such were the advantages of his rank.

As he dismounted, a young lad rushed from the stables, ready to take his horse. He looked as pitiful as the rest of these pig farmers, but he had seemed eager to offer his services, which was more than could be said for the rest of the town.

'Take good care of him,' Ronan said in the English language his mother had taught him.

The boy took the reins. 'I will, my lord. You can be sure of it.'

Ronan was about to make his way inside, when he thought better of it. He fished in the purse at his belt and took out a silver coin.

'To make sure you do, lad.'

Ronan sent the coin spinning and the boy caught it deftly, then held it up to the torchlight, gawping as though he had never seen its like.

'Thank you, my lord,' he said.

Ronan left him, satisfied with his benevolence. Hopefully, when he had his own lands and serfs they would all be so satisfied with his generosity.

Once inside he could hear the raucous sound of men celebrating. Clearly they had taken the earlier surrender of the English priest as a sign that this conflict was over. If only Ronan shared their confidence. They had won a victory, that was for sure, but the crown was not on William's head yet.

Opening the door to the huge stone feasting hall, he was greeted by the sights and sounds of merriment. By the smell of it, much ale was being drunk, and the barking of raucous laughter cut through the air. Ronan knew this was nothing compared to the feasting that would happen when these lands had finally been subjugated. The riches with which they would be bestowed would pay for a year's worth of revelry.

He made his way towards the fire burning in the hearth so he could thaw out his frozen limbs, but before he could reach it he caught Brian's eye. The nobleman was in one corner, holding court with some of his lackeys, and he called out to Ronan.

'Come. Have some of this fine ale. It tastes like tepid piss, but it does the job.'

How could Ronan refuse?

He took the seat offered beside his old friend and took a long drink from the cup Brian filled. Tepid piss was probably a little too complimentary, but it warmed his insides a little, so he didn't complain.

'Once we have finished taking these lands, we can have the finest Breton wine brought in from the mainland,' Ronan said. 'Then we'll know we have victory.'

'I'll drink to that,' Brian replied, raising his cup. 'It is less than we deserve after what we've suffered these past months.' He took a deep drink, letting some of it roll down his stubbly chin. 'It has been a hard-won victory, but didn't I tell you we had God on our side? That the duke would succeed in the end?'

'That you did,' said Ronan, and drained his own cup. 'I for one am looking forward to the rewards we will reap. I can only hope the lands and riches we're bequeathed will match the loyalty we have shown.'

Brian nodded, but there was a sullen aspect to him. 'That we should.'

'What's wrong? You don't think we will be rewarded for what we've done. Surely William will be a generous king to his most loyal subjects?'

'I'm sure, Ronan. But I wouldn't build your hopes too much. That's all I'm saying.'

'Shouldn't build my hopes up? I have given as much as any man. I rode with the rest at Senlac Hill. I shed as much blood as you.'

'I know, my friend.' Brian laid a hand on Ronan's shoulder and leaned in close. 'But there is only so much land to go around. And William will have to choose carefully who he gives it to. Only a few can receive earldoms.'

'I am as much deserving of land and titles as the next man. We fought together to claim them. We fought with William before we ever came to this shit-pit of a country. I have proven my worth to him, surely he cannot deny me?'

Brian sighed, looking to the bottom of his empty cup. 'Ronan, you are a bastard. You have no lawful claim to any titles at home.'

'And so is the duke. Yet he claims what is his by right. He above all understands that a man should be valued by his actions above his heritage.'

'And he does. But these lands are currently ruled by men of high standing. No matter that they might seem like filthy peasants to you and I, they are still considered nobles. King William cannot be seen to evict men of high birth from their estates and replace them with commoners.'

'So I am a commoner now?' Ronan could feel anger welling in his gut and he fought to subdue it.

'That's not what I meant, my friend. This is a matter of appearances. About keeping the peace. If the peasants know their current lords are being replaced by men of nobility and breeding there is less chance they will rebel and try to place their own magnates back in their seats of power. I am sure William will find other ways to reward men such as you.'

'Men such as me?' Ronan replied, staring into the hearth. The flames burned as brightly as his rage, but he refused to let it take hold of him.

'Loyal men,' Brian said. 'Capable servants of the crown. You will all get to keep what you earn.'

'I understand,' Ronan replied. And he understood full well. No matter what he did, he would always be seen as the bastard son. Cast aside by his father and forced to walk beside peasants and serfs, no matter what he did to prove himself.

'Anyway, forget this talk of lands,' Brian said, reaching for the ale jug. 'We should be celebrating a great victory.'

Ronan shook his head and rose to his feet. 'I am tired, my friend. I must away to bed.'

'If you're sure? There's plenty of tepid piss still to be drunk.'

'I think I've had my fill,' Ronan replied. 'I'll see you tomorrow.'

Brian bid him goodnight. As Ronan left the place he could not quell the rising anger. The stark cold of the English winter hit him when he left the building and he hoped it might serve to douse his ire, but all he felt was betrayed. He had come to these lands with the hope of making something of himself. Of making his half-brothers realise their folly in turning their backs on him, but it seemed that desire was nothing but dust.

When he passed the stables, he noticed the young lad brushing down his horse. He was diligent in his work, despite the lateness of the hour, but when Ronan saw him dunk the brush in a bucket of water he could contain himself no longer.

He limped to the stable as fast as his cursed leg would carry him.

'What are you doing, idiot?' he snarled.

The boy looked up innocently. 'Taking care of the horse, like you asked, my lord.'

'With water? On a winter's night? Are you trying to kill the bloody thing? If you cover the coat in water it'll freeze to death.'

The lad shrank back as Ronan grabbed the nearest thing – a bridle hung over the stable gate.

The boy backed away. 'I was only—'

He gave out a pained shriek as Ronan whipped him with the leather bridle. It felt good in his hand. Felt good to inflict pain, and he whipped the boy again and again.

The lad shrank back, squealing in fear as he fell into the horse shit, squirming to get away, but Ronan did not relent. Every stroke of the bridle filled him with more of a burning hatred for these stinking people. He was above them. Better than any of them, and yet he was treated as their equal.

Eventually Ronan took a step back, breathing heavily from the exertion, and with a shaky hand, the boy held something up. In the flickering torchlight Ronan could see it was the silver coin he had given the boy earlier.

'That's yours,' Ronan breathed, turning away and limping from the stable. 'We all get to keep what we earn.'

17

WALSINGAHA, ENGLAND, JANUARY 1067

There was a light dusting of snow across the ground and water dripped from the tree branches as it thawed in the winter sun. Styrkar stood and watched the young lad's attempts at chopping wood with a mixture of mirth and pride.

Ulf's stroke was clumsy and wild, but the axe was almost as big as he was, so it was only to be expected. He missed the logs more often than he hit them, but when he did manage to get a stroke on target the axe would sometimes split the wood completely. It was encouraging that he bore such strength at such a young age. Styrkar was sure accuracy would come with practice.

He gazed about the estate. When last he'd been here the place was a hive of activity, servants and reeves going about their business with eagerness. Now the settlement was all but abandoned and had been for the weeks since Styrkar had arrived. Edith had been deserted by those who had professed their loyalty to Harold. Not a maid nor housecarl remained to protect her. Their fear of reprisal from the Frankish invaders had sent them fleeing to the hills, but Styrkar couldn't bring himself to resent them for it. Edith had been the most beloved of the king, the mother of his heirs, and no one knew what this invader William might do in reprisal for English resistance to his claim.

Styrkar did not fear it. Let them come. It would give him a last chance at vengeance, and he would happily die here, as he should have done on the hill at Senlac.

'I'm getting good at this,' Ulf said, more question than statement. Styrkar turned to see him swing the axe again and manage to hit the corner of the log, sending it spinning towards the trees.

'You are,' Styrkar lied.

'When will I be able to swing an axe like my father?' he asked, looking forlornly at the trees where the log had landed.

Styrkar sighed, wondering what the right thing to say would be. He erred on the side of invention. 'No one could swing an axe like your father. He was the mightiest warrior this land has ever seen.'

That seemed to please Ulf, and he nodded enthusiastically. 'And one day, I will be too.'

Styrkar watched with a touch of sadness as the boy went back to his labours. It was true, Harold was indeed mighty, but even the mightiest among them could not cheat death. Harold was a testament to that. And yet Styrkar had cheated death. Whether by the will of the gods or just dumb luck, he was still alive when so many others had perished.

Since he had arrived at Walsingaha his body had begun to recover at a rapid pace. He had piled back on the weight he had lost, his shoulders filling out, his legs becoming firm and steady. Keeping himself busy about the place had built as much muscle as he'd ever had. He even had a slight paunch from Edith's generous cooking, but he was sure that would shrink over the lean months before spring.

Now was the time to build a store of wood for the winter, and later he would take Ulf hunting in the woods. The last of the winter game would be hard to find, but it would not hurt to have one last search.

'All right, I think that's enough,' Styrkar said. Ulf was getting tired and he was finding it difficult to even lift the axe now. 'Let's go and eat.'

Ulf nodded eagerly, handing the axe to Styrkar and grabbing an armful of logs. Styrkar could have carried more in one hand than the boy could take in both arms, but he couldn't fault Ulf's enthusiasm.

When they reached the house, Ulf dropped a log in the doorway as he struggled to open the door. Styrkar felt the heat of the fire strike him as he crossed the threshold and was met by a welcome smell from the hearth.

Edith was still chopping at a bench, her knife cutting expertly through the hide of a squirrel as she skinned it for the pot later. Styrkar was once again struck with a twinge of guilt that such a high-born woman was forced to perform the work of a servant. He couldn't help but feel some responsibility. Had Styrkar done his duty and protected the king in battle, all this would be different, but Edith gave no word of complaint. Her children were gone now, but for Ulf. Her sons had fled and her daughters gone to monasteries at the behest of their grandmother, Githa. All she had left was Ulf and Styrkar, but Edith appeared content with her lot.

She did her best to make this a welcome household, and Styrkar had shown his gratitude as best he could.

Ulf dumped the logs beside the hearth, as Edith took the pot from above the fire.

'Sit down,' she said.

Styrkar and Ulf obeyed. As Edith filled their bowls, he once again noticed the sadness in her eyes that she was always at pains to disguise. When Harold had been forced to abandon her and marry Alditha for the sake of an alliance with the northern earls, the light inside Edith had faded. Now, with the loss of her family, it seemed that light had been extinguished, only to be occasionally reignited by Ulf. She was prone to bouts of silence that would last days, and Styrkar had no idea how he might bring any joy to her. He could only hope that time would see Edith's fire lit anew.

They ate in silence, and not for the first time Styrkar found himself wishing he had the easy tongue of other men. He had always found inane prattle an annoyance, but in recent times, during these long quiet moments, he had thought it might be an advantage to have some skill at conversation. Try as he might, the words would not come, and he sat in hope that Ulf might break the silence, but the boy was more interested in stuffing his face with the hot stew.

The discomfort was eventually broken by the sound of horses approaching. Styrkar stood, sliding his chair back and grabbing the axe from where it rested beside the fire. Edith stood, fear in her eyes. They both knew the danger they faced. The Frankish invaders had done her no harm when she picked out Harold's body from the mass of dead those months ago, but perhaps they had changed their minds. Perhaps with rebellious English magnates not accepting William as their king they had come to make an example.

Styrkar pushed open the door, stepping out into the cold. As the five riders approached he gripped the axe tight, ready to defend the doorway with his life. When he recognised the man at their head, he let out a slow breath of relief.

'I hope that's not for me?' said Cypping from atop his saddle.

Styrkar let the axe hang loose by his side. 'We can take no chances.'

Cypping slid down from the saddle, taking the fur hat from his head. He was big and bearded, and in his day had been a ferocious warrior. Harold had granted him lands for his loyal service and Styrkar had met the man before on many happier occasions.

'None of us can, Styrkar,' Cypping said, as they gripped forearms in the warrior's way. 'Not in these dark times.'

'Cypping,' Edith said, moving past Styrkar to hug the old housecarl. 'It has been too long.'

'It has,' he replied. 'And I'm sorry about that, but there has been much to do in recent days.'

'Please, come in,' she said, guiding Cypping inside.

Styrkar left the axe outside as he was followed in by the other four riders. He didn't recognise any of them, but he was sure Cypping could vouch for each one.

Inside they took seats around the table as Edith fetched bowls for her guests. As she began to ladle stew out for them, Cypping shook his head.

'My lady, you should not be doing that,' he said.

'And who will do it for me?' she answered. When the warrior made to stand, Edith shook her head. 'Cypping, you are my guest. Sit. We all have to accept the changes that have been forced upon us.'

Reluctantly, Cypping sat. When Edith had finished dishing up their meal, she asked the reason for his visit. Cypping's expression turned grave.

'I have unwelcome news, my lady. The Frankish duke has... been crowned king. On Christes Maesse of all days. Every noble in the country has been forced to offer their fealty. William is now the King of England.'

Edith shook her head in disbelief. 'No. I don't believe it. Harold's loyal men must have risen in defiance. Someone must have stood against him?'

'They have been cowed, my lady. William is the worst kind of savage. Even the coronation was marred by violence, and much of the capital put to the flame. None will stand against him; they are too fearful of his wrath. They hold on to their lands only tentatively, and fear disinheritance as much as death.'

Styrkar could see Edith's knuckles whitening in rage. It seemed the only thing that would bring her out of her malaise was anger.

'And you, Cypping? Will the lands Harold granted you be taken? How do you intend to hold on to them, if not through standing up to this tyrant?'

Cypping took a deep breath, staring with trepidation at his untouched bowl of stew. 'I have done everything I can to keep my lands. Been forced to accept terms I am not happy with. But to resist the new king would be suicide, and so I have bent the knee to William, as have all those who wish to keep their estates, and their lives.'

Edith was shaking with rage now, and Styrkar could

sense it was about to bubble over. He suddenly regretted leaving the axe outside.

'So you have pledged your loyalty to the man who slew your lord and master?'

Cypping nodded. 'And much worse, my lady.' The old housecarl sighed with regret. 'Much worse, and I am sorry for it. God knows how sorry I am.'

'What are you talking about?'

Cypping looked at her, a mournful expression on his face. 'King William fears rebellion. There are already rumblings from Ireland that your eldest sons will return to these lands and stake their claim on the crown. Undoubtedly many will rally to their call. Ulf is only a boy, but he also carries his father's legacy. As long as he is free, he could be a danger. The king has ordered him taken as a hostage and has sent me to do the deed.'

Styrkar burst to his feet. Cypping's men did likewise, hands gripping their swords.

Cypping rose slowly, regarding Styrkar with a grave look. 'There is nothing that can be done about this, and I take no pleasure in it. If not me, then it will be someone else who comes for the boy. Someone who is less a friend than I am. You have to understand, Styrkar.'

Across the table, Ulf sat in silence, Edith gripping him close. Both mother and son looked defiant.

'I understand,' Styrkar replied.

He butted the old housecarl on the bridge of his nose. As Cypping fell back, Styrkar rushed at the nearest man, smashing a fist to his jaw before he could clear his blade from the sheath. The man staggered, and Styrkar grabbed him by the cloak and flung him towards the hearth.

As he fell screaming into the embers, a second warrior rushed forward, sword raised. Styrkar ducked the sweeping blow, the sword embedding in the oak tabletop. Grabbing the man by throat and balls, he lifted him above his head, bringing him down across his knee.

There was a satisfying crack of ribs before Styrkar was grabbed from behind. This man was strong, but not strong enough. As another of the warriors managed to draw his sword, Styrkar grappled with the one who held him. Furniture went flying as they toppled towards the door. Styrkar roared as they grappled savagely, bursting through the door and stumbling outside. Both men went sprawling to the cold snow, and Styrkar managed to get on top of his opponent.

He smashed a fist into the man's face, and he whimpered at the blow, but Styrkar did not relent, clubbing the warrior with his fists.

A strike to his head sent Styrkar reeling. He foundered, the world spinning around him, and he tasted blood in his mouth. A blade lay nearby, and he reached out for it but before he could close a hand around the hilt someone stamped a heavy foot over his arm.

Styrkar looked up, seeing one of the warrior's raising an axe high.

'No!'

The man stopped at Cypping's order. Styrkar turned his head towards the house. Cypping stood in the doorway, Ulf held tight in his arms, a knife at the boy's throat.

'I didn't want this,' Cypping said. 'And I don't want to have to report to the king that Ulf died in the fight, but I doubt he'll care much one way or the other.'

The housecarl made his way towards the horses, joined by two of his men who staggered from the house. Styrkar still struggled on the floor, a growl of rage issuing from his throat. He would not let them take Ulf; he could not.

The warrior who stood over him raised his axe once more.

'Stop,' Edith shouted.

She rushed to Styrkar's side, covering him with her body.

'You have to let them go,' she said. 'They'll kill us all.'

As Cypping mounted his horse, Ulf cried out for his mother. Edith stifled a sob in her throat, as the rest of Cypping's men mounted their horses. Styrkar tried to rise, but his head spun from the blow. He could feel blood running down the side of his face, and the need to vomit almost overwhelmed him.

The men kicked their horses, stirring up the snow as they rode south from the estate. Edith rose to her feet, following in their wake as they left with her youngest boy.

Styrkar could only watch as she collapsed to her knees, helpless as Ulf was taken from her forever.

The fire burned bright, but still it did not take the chill from the room. The place was empty without Ulf. A tomb.

Edith sat staring into the flames. Styrkar could see that the light inside her had been extinguished completely now. He yearned to find a way to reignite that spark, but he knew it was useless. He was useless. There were no words that could heal her, and by letting them take Ulf he had proven he could not even help through his actions.

The blood down his scalp had dried, but he would not

tend the wound. He did not deserve it. Let it fester along with the grief he felt. That was what he deserved.

He had loved that boy and would have cared for Ulf like a father. His last gift to Harold. But now there was nothing left. Only the anger.

It still burned inside him, but now it was embers. What good would anger do? It would not help Ulf, nor Edith. For all Styrkar's strength and might in battle, he had yet again proven himself worthless.

Edith suddenly stood. He watched her as she made her way to the far end of the room and entered her bedchamber. Styrkar could hear her rummaging, until eventually she returned, carrying something wrapped in hide. It was three feet long and unmistakably a weapon of some kind.

'Take this,' she said, holding it out to him. 'Harold would have wanted you to have it.'

Styrkar obeyed, laying the weapon across his knees. When he unwrapped the hide he saw it was a sheathed blade.

'No,' he whispered. 'I do not have the right.'

'You have every right,' she replied. 'My sons are gone. You are all that is left.'

Reluctantly, Styrkar unsheathed the blade. It was an ancient weapon, a rune-carved seax. Harold had kept it with pride, a sword passed down through his family line.

'I don't deserve this,' he said.

She stood, staring into the fire. 'Then earn it,' she said. 'Promise me you will use it well.'

'I... I don't...'

'Promise me.'

He had no other choice it seemed. 'I promise.'

She nodded back at him. There was such a sense of loss in her eyes, Styrkar almost broke down.

'Goodnight, Styrkar,' she whispered.

She left him by the fire, closing the door to her bedchamber. For the rest of the night, he sat wrapped in an old woollen cloak by the fire as it burned down to ash, with the sword of his dead king across his knees.

A chill gust of wind blew Styrkar from his dreams.

There was nothing left of the fire, and Styrkar felt the cold of the room keenly. Glancing to his left, he saw the main door was open, creaking in the breeze. To his right, the door to Edith's bedchamber also lay open.

In her grief had she wandered out to freeze in the wintry night? Discarding the woollen cloak he moved across the room and entered Edith's chamber. It was empty, the bed undisturbed.

Clutching the seax tight in his hand, Styrkar rushed from the house and out into the cold morning. A fresh blanket of snow lay across the ground and it chilled his bare feet.

The sight that greeted him froze his heart.

Edith hung from the mighty oak that stood twenty yards from the house. She had fastened the rope tight around her neck and now swung gently in the winter breeze.

Styrkar ran but he already knew he was too late. The seax cut the rope with a single swing and all he could do was watch as Edith's corpse fell to the cold ground.

He dropped the weapon, kneeling beside her body, too overcome to even touch her. When eventually he took her in his arms her skin was like ice to the touch. The rope had marred the flesh of her neck, leaving an unsightly welt, but her face was still serenely beautiful. Styrkar found he could not look into those eyes, and he placed a hand across her face.

He had done this. Beyond all doubt, Styrkar knew that he was the one responsible. He had failed to save Harold, failed to save Ulf and now Edith lay dead in his arms. Looking up at the oak, he knew there was only one fate he deserved.

Styrkar stood, hoping there would be enough rope left for him, when his eyes fell on the seax lying in the snow.

Earn it.

Those had been her words.

Styrkar picked up the weapon, the anger seething inside him. What had been embers began to burn up within, and he realised none of this had been his doing.

One man had done this. The invader. The conqueror. King William of the Franks had done this. He had landed on these shores and raped and murdered his way to the throne until he was crowned as king by traitors and cowards.

Styrkar had made Edith a vow to use the seax well. It was one promise he was determined to keep. He would offer his own benediction to this new king.

He would anoint William's reign in blood.

18

CUDESSANE, ENGLAND, FEBRUARY 1067

Bayard let out a long, satisfied sigh as he emptied his bladder under the cold moonlight. It was a clear and peaceful night, and he would have relished it, if not for the terrible chill of this English winter. Nevertheless, he savoured the feeling of relieving his bladder, even if it had been full of weak foreign ale. Unfortunately that was all they had to satisfy themselves with for now. This English hospitality was for the birds, and Bayard would just have to make the most of it. And make the most of it he had.

Once the last drips had pattered to the frozen ground, he put his cock away and turned back towards the farmhouse. Bayard's eye caught sight of the old man, hanging there in the moonlight. His eyes glared up at the starry heavens, arms tied to the fencepost, making him resemble the scarecrows they had passed in the fields on the ride here. Five crossbow bolts protruded from his chest where Farman had used the old man for target practice. He had proven remarkably resilient, and it had taken all five bolts to see him off, tough old boot that he was. All the while they had laughed. Only Bayard was able to understand a word of the man's mongrel language and he had caught much of the old man's begging and pleading. It had fallen on deaf ears. Their distraction had been short-lived, but the old savage's daughter, or granddaughter – it was difficult to tell – had been a much more lasting entertainment.

Bayard had not taken more than a couple of steps towards the farmhouse before Gyffard came staggering out of the nearby barn. His old friend looked weary, staggering slightly and it brought a smile to Bayard's face.

'Had your fill?' Bayard asked.

His drunken friend patted his stout belly. 'More than my fill. She's almost as wearying a fight as the English army.'

They laughed, before Bayard said, 'Is there anything left for the rest of us?'

Gyffard glanced back at the barn. There was silence from within its dark confines. 'I'm afraid it doesn't sound like it. But you're welcome to the scraps.'

'No thanks,' said Bayard, clapping his companion on the back. The prospect of following Gyffard was not a welcome one, but luckily Bayard and the other boys had taken their pleasure with the girl already. 'You're a bloody animal, you know that?'

Gyffard made some grunting noises to that effect as they entered the welcome warmth of the farmhouse.

Embers still burned in the hearth, blackening the remains of the spitted pig that hung there. In any other place that would have been a waste of meat, but here they didn't care. Overindulgence was theirs by right, more than they deserved after what they'd been through in the past weeks.

To the victor the spoils, and Bayard and his friends had made sure to make the most of the spoils in this place.

The rest of the conrois had left a day ago, pushing on westwards into English countryside. The four of them had decided to linger a little longer and make the most of this place. The ale that was left might be foul and weak, but it would have been a sin to leave it for the local peasants when they inevitably fell on this place like carrion birds.

'More ale,' Bayard ordered, looking around through his drunken fug at the mess they had made.

His squire, young Lovell, scrambled from where he'd been dozing by the fire. He shook the last ale barrel they'd scavenged from a town a few miles back, and there was a sorry sloshing to indicate it was almost empty.

Lovell shrugged. 'Maybe we should bed down anyway,' he said. 'Long ride to catch up with the others tomorrow.'

'Long ride be damned,' Gyffard bellowed, planting himself in the warm chair Lovell had been occupying. 'I've worked up a hell of a thirst, so fill me a cup, boy.'

Bayard took the other seat next to the fire that Gyffard's squire Farman had been occupying. The boy shifted aside without complaint, pulling his cloak tighter around his body as he moved closer to the draughty doorway. Lovell struggled with the barrel, managing to fill two cups with the dregs.

'Maybe you should sing us all a lullaby,' Gyffard said to Lovell as the youngster handed the knights their cups.

Lovell nodded grudgingly. He was clearly tired, but he would always obey Gyffard's instruction lest he get a backhand across his ear.

Bayard settled into his chair. Lovell might be the ugliest

little boggart he had ever set eyes on, but he had the voice of an angel.

While Farman threw another couple of logs on the fire, Lovell began his song. He had a range that went from deep and throaty to high and majestic – most likely an advantage of the fact his balls had only recently dropped. The song he sang was of their homeland, and it gave Bayard a strange longing in his heart. It had been months since he'd seen the green fields of Normandy and he quickly found himself with a lump in his throat and tears in his eyes. Lovell's song even made him miss his mother, which Bayard thought would never happen – he'd hated that old goat. She had always judged him, even from his earliest days, looking down with scorn on his every action. He'd certainly given her plenty to be scornful of since he'd arrived on English shores. Bayard had been sure to leave destruction in his wake the likes of which his mother would have found most shameful.

He'd taken a curious pleasure in those dark deeds, but then these people were barely human. They had to be treated no better than animals just to keep them in line, and they deserved everything they got.

As Lovell continued, Bayard found his eyes growing heavier, until he eventually succumbed to fatigue and the thick, chewy ale.

The room was black when he awoke with a start. There was a dull glow from the hearth, but it didn't give off enough light to illuminate the room. Bayard was freezing, despite the blanket, and as his eyes adjusted to the dark, he could see the door at the far side of the room was ajar. It creaked slightly in the breeze, and Bayard gave a shiver of discomfort. The easiest thing would have been to get up and close the blasted thing, but he was already chilled to the bone under his thin blanket and his head was pounding. If he moved it would be unbearable. God damn this incessant English cold.

He kicked out, connecting with Lovell's leg and the young lad snorted awake. He grumbled unintelligibly, until Bayard gave him another kick.

'What?' Lovell asked.

'Shut the bloody door,' Bayard ordered.

Reluctantly, Lovell got up out of his chair, staggering to the door, hugging himself and trying to rub some heat back into his arms. Bayard could barely see what was happening on the far side of the room, but Lovell seemed to be standing there, a grey silhouette in the dark. There was a sudden gust of air that sent a shiver through Bayard. The door to the farmhouse was open wide and Lovell was just standing in front of it.

'What the bloody hell are you doing?' Bayard whispered through the dark.

He was answered by a strange gurgling sound, as Lovell staggered back from the doorway.

Bayard watched as the boy stumbled towards him, knocking into the table and sending a cup tumbling. As he reached the dim light of the fire, Lovell was gripping his throat, blood gushing through his fingers to drip down the front of his jerkin.

The ridiculous thought that Lovell's singing voice was ruined flashed into Bayard's mind before he surged to his feet.

'Attack,' he screamed. It came out high-pitched and panicked.

In the shadows Bayard could see a huge figure had entered the farmhouse – a giant black outline in the shadows, as though Death himself had come to visit them.

Gyffard was jolted awake, throwing off his cloak and grasping for a weapon. Farman likewise fell off his chair, screaming from the bottom of his lungs upon seeing the dark intruder who had come for them in the night.

Bayard glanced about him. There was no sword at his side, and the only thing to hand was an axe lying on the table. He reached for it, hand stretched, fingers splaying. Before he could close them around the weapon something slammed down on his hand. Bayard had just enough time to see four of his fingers spin away and cover the table in blood before he registered the pain.

With a howl he grasped the stump of his right hand, gasping for air, but it felt like he was drowning. The intruder took the axe from the table, making no sound as Farman rushed to attack. He almost fell over the body of Lovell, who now lay staring at the ceiling, dead hands still grasping his throat. Farman had a sword raised and brought it crashing down. The huge intruder parried the blow easily, blades ringing out in the dark. With a quick strike he buried the axe in Farman's head, then wrenched it free and hacked again.

Gyffard was still fumbling for a weapon when Bayard decided he had seen enough. Still gripping the severed stump of his hand, he staggered through the house. Gyffard had found a blade now and there was a brief clash of steel. Bayard made it to the door, pausing just long enough to hear Gyffard yell for help before he stumbled out into the night.

Three steps across the cold hard earth and he fell to his knees. The sounds of violence still echoed within the farmhouse, but all Bayard could do was grasp his hand, grit his teeth and try not to pass out from the pain.

He glanced about desperately, trying to see where they had tethered their horses, but there was no sign of the steeds. The intruder must have cut them free and sent them fleeing into the night.

As Gyffard let out a strangled cry of agony, Bayard decided he should do some fleeing of his own. Struggling to his feet, he stumbled into the night. He almost tripped as he made his way across the nearest field and a sob escaped from his throat. Looking down, he saw that the stubs where his fingers had been continued to pump blood. He would never hold a spear again, never grasp a rein. But that would be the least of his worries if he did not put distance between himself and the giant in the dark.

As he ran across the field his foot caught in a divot. He went tumbling, hands held out instinctively to halt his fall. Pain jolted up his arm and he yelped like a dog. Rising to his knees he gritted his teeth, grasping tight to his wounded hand, fighting back the tears and the pain and feeling the dampness spread through his leggings as he emptied his bladder for the second time that night.

Bayard breathed deep, knowing he should get up and run, but he already had the feeling that was pointless. A long dark shadow had been cast by the moon. Someone was standing behind him in the cold night, and he knew it was no one friendly.

Slowly, Bayard turned. Silhouetted against the bright moon was a huge, grizzled warrior. The hair hung lank at his shoulders, his beard long and thick. Even in the dark, Bayard could see his eyes burning with hate. In one hand he held an axe, in the other a strangely shaped sword.

'You speak my language?' the warrior asked in the gruff English tongue.

'A little,' Bayard answered.

'Then listen,' the warrior said, before Bayard could think to beg for mercy. 'You and your brethren have brought terror to these lands. That time is over now. Tell your master that the Red Wolf is abroad, and he will show no mercy. Tell your master this time of pillage and death is finished.'

'Yes. Yes I will,' Bayard replied, still grasping his throbbing hand. 'I will do anything you ask. And thank you. Thank you for your mercy. I do not deserve it.'

'No,' the giant warrior replied, shaking his head. 'You don't.'

The axe fell from his grip and he reached forward a powerful hand, grasping Bayard by the hair. The last thing Bayard ever saw was that blade flash in the moonlight, and he screamed for his mother as the Red Wolf took his eyes.

19

SCIPENE, ENGLAND, MARCH 1067

The harsh chill of the winter was gone now, and the nights were milder. There was still a nip to the air, but the conditions were perfect for the hunter. The wild animals of the country could rise from their winter sleep and find game in abundance – but for the Red Wolf the hunt had never stopped.

There was blood on his hands aplenty, but not yet enough to wash away the stain of his shame. Much more would yet be shed before he was satisfied. Perhaps there would never be enough… perhaps he would perish long before his thirst could be slaked. Either way, he did not fear the prospect of death. Maybe it would finally give him the release he yearned for. But Styrkar was not done yet. He had never been an easy man to kill, not even with the entire Frankish army after him, and there would be much more blood spilt before he was sent back to the dirt.

Night laid a cloak of shadow about him, and through the dark he stared at the fort on the distant hill. He had been watching it for two days and two nights and had set the routine of its sentries to memory. It was poorly guarded, most likely housing one of the minor Frankish knights and barely worthy of his notice, but notice the Red Wolf had.

He moved forward from the edge of the wood and out into the surrounding field. As he came close to the fort, he could hear the distant sound of whispered voices. They spoke in English, which Styrkar found curious. He had watched the Franks come and go from this place, their armour and huge horses giving them away. But it seemed they had left Englishmen to guard their fort.

No matter. They were still servants of the new king – traitors to Harold – and Styrkar would have his justice.

He rushed silently to the base of the palisade that surrounded the fort's perimeter. There he waited and listened. Only one guard walked a circuit of the entire wall at this hour and once Styrkar heard him pass he knew it would be time to strike. He waited in the shadows until he heard the footsteps above. Then with the strength and swiftness of the animal he had become, climbed the wooden wall and eased himself over the top.

Through the shadows he saw the sentry walking away and struck silently, grasping the man from behind, securing an arm around his throat and squeezing tight. The sentry struggled, panic gripping him, a hand going to the knife at his side, but Styrkar's other hand grasped his wrist, holding him there until he throttled the fight right out of him. Then he gently laid the sentry down and waited.

Two men talked somewhere in the fort, safe in the knowledge they were protected within the high walls. But they were not safe. The Red Wolf was within their lair now, loose and ready for the kill.

Styrkar silently dropped from the raised parapet and made his way to the longhouse at the centre of the compound. He held a breath as he opened the latch and pushed the door inwards, thanking Fenrir that it made no creak to alert those dwelling inside. When the gap was wide enough he slipped in, closing the door behind him, and there he waited for a moment for his eyes to adjust.

Several candles had burned down to almost nothing, giving off a dim, winking glow. Styrkar could hear the regular breath of sleeping children, seeing their slumbering forms through the dark. Stealing across the room he moved through another doorway, careful not to wake any of those innocent figures, and entered the room beyond.

This one was lit more brightly, the fire still burning in the hearth, and Styrkar moved instinctively towards it. It had been days since he had felt the heat of a decent fire and he lingered by it, letting the flames warm his frozen bones.

By the hearth stood a table and as Styrkar cast his gaze over the empty plate and cup that sat on it, he spied a small pile of coins. He picked one up, looking closely. Though he could not read the marking he knew it was no coin he had seen before. It shone in the firelight; a new-made coin for a new-made king. This was traitor's currency, and he knew he had come to the right place in his search for vengeance.

'Don't you move,' whispered a voice behind him.

Styrkar turned to see a small but stocky man glaring at him from the edge of the room. He held a crossbow tightly in his grip. Styrkar had faced such weapons at Senlac Hill, and he knew how dangerous they could be. There was no fear about the man and his hand did not shake. If he'd wanted to put one of these bolts in Styrkar there was little to stop him.

'How did you know I was here?' asked Styrkar. He was sure he made no sound in the dark.

'I could smell your stink a mile off,' replied the man, his accent very much English.

Styrkar suddenly felt conscious of the fact he had been living in the wilds like an animal for so many days he had lost count. He was filthy from head to toe, his hair lank, his clothes threadbare. He had neglected to care for his weapons and even Harold's precious blade was showing signs of rust and rot.

'I was not expecting this place to be full of Englishmen,' Styrkar said.

'No? Well there are no Franks here. I am the lord of this manor.'

'How? The new king has thrown better men than you from their homes.'

'I have been allowed to keep my property. Albeit at a price.'

'I see,' Styrkar replied, feeling his ire begin to stir.

'Do you, Red Wolf?' said the man.

'You know me?' Styrkar asked.

'A red-haired giant with his wolf-head torc comes to my home looking for blood. Who else would you be? Why don't you have a chair? You look chilled to the bone.'

Styrkar was reluctant, but the crossbow was still pointed at him, and he wasn't about to argue with that. He took the chair nearest the hearth, and the man took another opposite, all the while keeping his crossbow trained on Styrkar.

'Those are foreign coins,' Styrkar said. 'If you have been forced to pay for your lands why would they be in your home? You are clearly no pauper.'

The man glanced at the pile of silver on his table. 'These are new times. And a new king brings a new currency. But all coins are spent the same. I have simply exchanged the old for the new. King William wants every sign of the old king gone and replaced with his own image. That is why I have foreign coins.'

'Traitor's coins,' Styrkar replied. 'You should be fighting this tyrant. Not spreading his image. Not making bargains with him.'

'Why? Because defiance is working out so well for you?' He glanced Styrkar up and down, looking with disdain at the dishevelled shadow of the warrior he had been. 'You are a fighter, Red Wolf. That's all you know. Some of us have to fight our battles in other ways. Not everyone uses the sword and axe to resist a usurper.'

'I don't see much resistance,' Styrkar replied. 'You seem to be doing well under your new king in your warm and comfortable house.'

'New king, old king. They're all the same to me. Do you think most of us care who our king is? Do you think the worker in the field cares whose lands he toils over as long as he can feed his family?'

Styrkar rose to his feet, unable to hold his anger in check any longer. The man stood too, that crossbow still trained on Styrkar's heart.

'The words of a traitor,' Styrkar said. 'Where is your loyalty? Was it the new king who gave you this place? You owe Harold everything, and yet you so easily forsake him.'

'I have forsaken nothing. Harold was a fool. He is the one who made this happen. He rushed to face the invader without first gathering an army large enough to secure victory. This country has burned these past months and it is as much Harold's fault as William's.'

'I will kill you,' Styrkar snarled.

The man brandished the crossbow threateningly. 'I'm not afraid to use this, Red Wolf. You don't frighten—'

Styrkar's hand shot forward. The bow snapped, but the quarrel went awry, shooting over Styrkar's shoulder and embedding in the wall. He wrenched the weapon from the man's grip and cast it into the fire, moving closer as his victim stared, wide-eyed.

Before Styrkar could grasp the man by the throat, he made a dash for the door. Lurching after him, Styrkar grabbed the man by the collar, throwing him to the ground. His head hit the stone of the hearth with a thud and Styrkar was on him, fist pounding. He saw an iron poker beside the fire, grasping it and rising to his feet. The man struggled, trying to rise, blood pouring from his head. Styrkar raised the iron.

'No!'

Styrkar turned, expecting to see one of the sentries come to save his master, but there was a boy standing in the doorway. The lad looked terrified, enough to give Styrkar pause. He looked at the poker in his hand, then down at the man lying at his feet. Slowly he realised what a monster he must seem to this family – a wild intruder creeping in at night to murder them in their beds.

Here it seemed he was the invader, sent to murder and kill. He began to consider the Red Wolf might well be as low and base as any of those sent to rape and pillage this land.

Shouts of alarm from outside wrenched Styrkar from his thoughts. He grabbed the man, struggling at his feet, and brought the seax to his throat. Two armed men burst into the room, pushing the boy aside.

'Stay back,' shouted the lord in Styrkar's grip.

His men obeyed, keeping a wide berth as Styrkar manoeuvred his prisoner towards the door. He pulled the man through the longhouse, past the gawping faces of his wife and children and out into the open air. More guards awaited, but they were none too keen to attack with their master in the grip of such a devil.

Styrkar dragged his victim towards the open gate, through the mud.

'No good will come of this,' the man said. 'It's pointless. All you're doing is digging your own grave.'

'A grave waits for each of us,' Styrkar replied as he crossed the threshold of the fort. 'All that matters is the manner in which we reach it. You have made your choice, traitor. I have made mine.'

When they were far enough from the fort, Styrkar pushed the man to the ground. He considered for a moment what to do. Should he strike with Harold's blade? But what good would that do? Kill this nobleman and there would be another to take his place, and most likely a foreigner.

As the guards moved forward, Styrkar made his decision, turning his back and running towards the distant trees. When he reached them, he could still hear the shouting of men in his wake, but they would never catch up with him.

When he had put a fair distance between himself and the fort, he stood for some time in the dark, gripping that sword to his side, wondering if he should have whetted the blade. But the man's words echoed in his head. 'All you're doing is digging your own grave.' Deep down Styrkar knew he was right; this would only end in his death. And what had he achieved? Harold was still not avenged. Neither was Edith or Ulf.

But what else could he do? Surrender? Give in?

No. The Red Wolf was not done yet. There was no surrender for the beast he had become.

He was not done by far.

20

AMBLESBERIE, ENGLAND, APRIL 1067

The wind blew stinging rain into his face. It soaked him to the bone as he walked, but he did not suffer the weather like a normal man. He was the Red Wolf – neither a man nor a beast. Just an object, left to the wilds. A golem of flesh with but a singular purpose… to kill.

His stomach was empty, for the game he hunted could not be eaten. Styrkar had harried Frankish patrols for more days than he could count. Always striking from the dark, swift and sure and bloody. He had left one or two mutilated survivors to tell of his wrath – to spread word of the Red Wolf throughout the land. To carry that name back to their king so that he would learn to fear it.

Styrkar gripped tight to the seax with his right hand. He had long since lost its sheath, but he did not need it. The weapon was a part of him now – the claw of the wolf. A weapon to send Harold's enemies to their hell.

Wrapped around the fingers of his left fist was rope and cord, and dangling from their ends were the heads of the vanquished. The Red Wolf's trophies. Each grinning skull was a rotting reminder of his victories. The stink was stomach-churning, and he could smell them even through the driving wind and rain. That sweet smell of rot was like an elixir, driving him on, forcing one foot in front of the other so that he might find the next foe and add another head to his grim collection.

Through the grey haze of the rainfall, he spied a building in the distance. At first he thought it yet another fort, like the ones springing up all over these lands, but as he drew closer he saw it was ancient – a stone-built edifice from before the invasion. Before the conquest.

He scaled the hill towards it, slipping on the slick ground, but never taking his eyes from his goal. When he was near enough he recognised the place as a monastery. His heart dropped for a moment – there would be no one to kill in this place. What vengeance was there in murdering holy men? Then again he had nowhere else to go, and shelter from the elements would be a welcome, if only short respite.

With mud slick down his legs and the rain soddening his threadbare garb he stood before the door. All was silent within this sanctuary from the storm.

The door creaked noisily as he pushed it open and stepped into the shadowy confines. It was a high chamber. Rows of wooden pews lined the way before him leading to a vast altar. Row upon row of women sat with heads bowed in worship to the White Christ.

At first he was ignored, the nuns observing their prayer despite the door being flung wide, despite an intruder in their midst. It only took one of them to look and see him, to let off a shriek of panic, before terror spread throughout the rest.

He stood watching as the women fled. Some of them rushed through the open door, braving the elements rather than this killer. Others tried to hide or ran to another part of the building. Only one of them was brave enough to remain.

She stood, glaring without fear, then walked along the aisle between the wooden pews to stand before him. Her face was lined by her years, and she regarded him curiously. He could tell she was afraid, just like the rest, but instead of running she chose to face down the killer who had come to her place of worship. She was either very brave, or instilled with the faith of her god, thinking herself impervious to harm. Admirable or foolish, the Red Wolf was unsure which.

'Leave,' she commanded. 'You are not welcome here.'

He glanced around the place, at the idols of her faith, but did not move.

'You can do no harm here,' she said, as much convincing herself as him. 'We are protected by a far higher power.'

'So were these men,' he replied, lifting the heads in his left hand so she could see them better. 'Didn't do them much good, did it? And they had swords to protect them.'

'This is the house of God—'

'There are no gods here,' he said. 'This house is an empty shell.'

The woman's expression changed to one of pity. Any fear she might have had seemed to leave her.

'I am the Abbess Wynflaed,' she said gently. 'What is your purpose here? Why have you come? If it is to indulge in more violence you will find this a disappointing place.'

Why had he come here? To shelter from the rain? For help? To look for some sign he would never find? He could not answer.

'Whatever it is you seek, you cannot bring those in here.' She gestured to the heads. 'This is a place of worship. Even the slaughter of evil men cannot be condoned in this house.'

She looked at him defiantly, and he found he could not match that gaze. Instead he looked down at the rotting skulls in his grip. They were heavy, a burden he had carried for too long.

He turned and flung the heads through the open doorway and out into the rain. Slowly, Wynflaed walked past him and closed the door against the elements. Then she walked back and took him by the arm.

'Come,' she said, guiding him towards the altar. 'Sit with me awhile.'

He found he could no longer resist, and he let her lead him to a seat at the front of the hall. He sat, for the first time realising how weary he was, as she gently prised the blade from his fingers and laid it down beside her.

'Why are you here, child? What do you seek?'

Again he could not answer. He was here because this place was in his path. What he really wanted was well beyond his grasp.

'I seek to kill the king,' he answered.

He expected the abbess to balk at the suggestion, to tell him such a thing was a sin and he should seek penance for it. Instead she just shook her head.

'You will not find him here,' she replied. 'Or anywhere on these islands.'

'He is gone?' he asked.

'For a time,' said Wynflaed. 'He has sailed back to his homeland, and taken the lords of England with him. A journey to inspire peace in these lands, or so they say. The earls Edwin and Morcar, along with the boy Edgar who they call the Aetheling, have all gone with him. The king seeks to persuade them that standing defiant against him is folly. Or that is what he says. In reality it is a demonstration of his power. They will obey or they will die. That is the new king's way.'

'And who holds sway over these lands in the king's absence?'

'His allies. Fellow dukes and earls from Frankia stand in charge of this land now. Foreign lords hold all the power, while English magnates are cast out. Up and down the country landowners must buy back their holdings from the new king. If they resist they face the sword.'

He thought back to the house he had entered days before, to the English landowner and his foreign silver. For a moment there was a feeling of guilt within him for the way he had treated the man who was only protecting his family and his tenants, but he stacked it with his other sins and thought on it no longer.

'I should not be here,' he said, but as he made to rise the abbess placed a hand on his arm.

'Perhaps this is precisely where you should be, Styrkar.'

Hearing his name, his real name, made him pause and he looked back at her.

'How do you know my name?'

Wynflaed smiled. 'We have met once before. You were

much younger, following Earl Harold like a faithful hound. You look different now, but I would recognise the collar of the Red Wolf anywhere.'

She gestured to the torc about his neck, and he absently placed a hand to it.

'I admire what you have done,' she said. 'Though your methods are questionable, you have done your best to protect the people of these lands, just as Harold would have done. God might forgive a sinner if his intentions are for the greater good.'

'I don't need forgiveness,' Styrkar replied. 'And I do not believe in your god.'

'But he believes in you.'

Styrkar was too tired to argue. He would rather have fought a host of Frankish knights than bicker over religion with some old priestess.

'You are welcome to stay,' Wynflaed said. 'If that is what you wish?'

He looked around the place, listening to the rain pounding on the roof. Then slowly he nodded.

'Good. But we'll have to clean you up first. Come.'

Wynflaed rose to her feet, gesturing that he should follow. She gathered some of her sisters, who seemed less frightened now he no longer gripped a naked blade and a fistful of rotting heads. They looked on him with some pity as they stripped him of his rags, and Styrkar did nothing to resist.

In a small room they had already filled a wooden tub with warm water, and he gratefully sat in it. With every passing moment his beaten and fatigued body succumbed to the heat of the water. As he began to clean the filth from his body and his hair, the nuns took away his old clothes.

Styrkar did not even consider his immodesty in front of these pious women. He gave himself over to them fully, trusting them to see to his battered body. They emptied the filthy brown water from the tub and refilled it, leaving him alone for a while to sit and ponder.

For the first time in days he was not moving, neither hunting nor fleeing from killers. It gave him pause to think on what he had done, on the lives he had taken, on what he had achieved and most of all what he had lost.

The weeks he had spent carrying on the fight and resisting the Frankish invaders had taken their toll on him and resulted in nothing. This was no vengeance; he was merely flogging himself needlessly. He could never avenge Harold or Edith. He could never rescue Ulf. He could not save them, and now it seemed there was little chance he could save himself. He was doomed to fight on and die. What else would he do? Where else would he go?

Styrkar would have wept, but no tears came. The wolf did not weep when it knew its time had come. But deep down, Styrkar realised he was no wolf. That was just a name they had given him. He was a man, not an animal, but he would certainly die like one if he carried on this course.

'Come,' said Wynflaed.

Styrkar was stirred from his reverie, realising the water in the tub had long since gone cold.

He stood and dried himself, donning the clothes she had brought him. They were cut to fit a smaller man, but Styrkar had lost enough weight in the wilds to fit easily into them.

When he was clothed, she led him through the abbey and out into the yard at the rear. The rain had stopped and fire burned in a pit.

'I have already burned those rags you arrived in,' Wynflaed said. 'I wondered if you wanted to cast this into the fire?' She held up the seax. 'It will do you no good, child. Not now.'

He took it from her, looking along the rusted blade. He had neglected it, as he had neglected himself. The fire burned bright, not hot enough to melt the steel, but it would still ruin the finish.

Styrkar shook his head. 'No. I am not sure I am done with this yet,' he replied.

'As you wish,' said Wynflaed. 'But remember, a heavy burden is sometimes better left behind. No matter what it means to you. Now, let's get you fed.'

He paused a while at the fire, holding Harold's blade in his hand. Perhaps she was right, perhaps he should leave his burdens behind. But deep within himself, he knew even if Styrkar could forget them, the Red Wolf never would.

21

DUNHEVED, ENGLAND, MAY 1067

Ronan could see the entire site from atop an adjacent hill. He stood under the sun, drinking in the scene. It was the hottest day he'd spent on these cursed shores and he was determined to enjoy it to the fullest.

The castle's construction was a laborious affair, but he drank in every tedious moment. Ronan had always derived some strange gratification from watching other men work. It was a simple pleasure, and one he was not about to forego.

Of course, the whole experience was made that much sweeter by the fact he had a cup of wine in his hand. It had been shipped in from the mainland in small, precious casks – a welcome respite from sour English ale and their oversweet mead. He raised it to his lips, smelling the rich aroma, tasting the deep flavour. It was like honey on his tongue, and he almost moaned in ecstasy at the taste. It might well have been the best he'd ever drank, or perhaps that was just in contrast to the English swill he'd been forced to endure for months. Either way, he would savour every last drop.

The peace was shattered by the sudden bellowing of the master builder. The man shouted at the English labourers in Frankish, which in itself seemed a pointless act, but it did not seem to concern the man. He had been brought in from Frankia, a specialist who had overseen the construction of numerous forts in Bretagne and Normandy, and clearly he was a hard taskmaster. Unfortunately he had not come up against the dull-witted English before, and he vented his frustrations with quite a fury.

Ronan knew it was a futile act. He could have told Brian that Breton builders and English workers would not mix. The former were too regimented, the latter too lazy, and the language barrier would only result in more misunderstanding. Then again, Brian didn't have much choice. He was hardly going to pay for peasants to be shipped over from the mainland when he had an endless supply of slave labour right on his doorstep.

As the master builder continued to rant, Ronan considered chiming in to help breach the language barrier. He could after all speak both tongues like a native, but as he watched he decided it was more amusing to just witness proceedings.

The man from Frankia was desperate for the English to understand that the mortar they had mixed was deficient. Constructing brickwork with too much sand would eventually lead to the structure's collapse. Of course, the English labourers just glared back in slack-jawed indolence, causing the builder to pick up a trowel and stab the mortar repeatedly to make his point. As he raged, there was a sudden noise from the stone wall they had recently built.

Ronan watched with growing mirth, as the huge wall collapsed behind them, punctuating the builder's point better than any language. As the man began to jump from one foot to the other, incensed, Ronan couldn't help but tip his head back and laugh.

'Let them be, Ronan,' a familiar voice shouted behind him. 'It's bad enough I'm losing money without you laughing about it.'

Ronan turned towards Brian, who sat some feet away. He was in a wooden chair purloined from some unfortunate native, his feet up on an empty wine cask.

'Please,' Ronan replied. 'This is the best show I've seen in an age.'

'Come join us,' Brian said, holding up a jug.

Ronan realised his cup was empty and wasn't about to turn down the offer of having it filled.

He limped back down the hill, the sound of the incensed builder fading. Beside Brian sat his brother Alan. Both were reclining in the sun, as appreciative of the weather as Ronan.

'I'm glad you find my architectural struggles so amusing,' Brian said.

'Apologies, my friend,' Ronan replied. 'I haven't had much to laugh about in recent days.'

'You won't be laughing when it's finished. It will be the most fearsome fortress in all of England. What say you, Alan?'

His brother merely shrugged, seeming to care little about the formidable potential of his brother's castle.

Ronan glanced at Alan, who was chewing on a grass stem. He had never liked Brian's younger sibling. He might have been sitting quietly now, minding his own affairs, but

Alan was as debauched and unpredictable as he was deadly with a lance. It was a volatile combination that made Alan difficult to be around.

As Ronan clacked his cup against Brian's, Alan stood, making his way towards the stump of a tree with an axe protruding from it. He plucked the axe free and flung it at a target board some feet away. Ronan made sure to keep him visible in his periphery. It would not have been out of character for Alan to plunge that axe into the nearest bystander, and right now that was Ronan.

'He is anxious,' Brian said. 'He thinks it is too quiet. That soon we will be embroiled in more war.'

Ronan watched as Alan flung the axe a second time, his aim true. 'Then perhaps not the best time for the king to have left for home.'

'This is home now,' Brian replied. 'And it is in safe hands while we are here. William trusts us to guard his kingdom in his absence, and the more forts and castles we build, the more the English will be cowed.'

'So you think your brother worries without reason?'

Brian shook his head. 'There are sparks of rebellion igniting all over the country. We cannot rest on our past successes.'

'We should be curbing every rebellion with sword and flame,' Alan said, flinging the axe and hitting the target again.

'Indeed,' Brian answered. 'But where to start, brother? As soon as one revolt is curbed, another rises in a different place, like vermin in a field. William would be generous with his rewards for the man who could end these troublesome uprisings.'

Ronan's interest was suddenly piqued. The notion that he could further ingratiate himself with the king made him think on the prospect of quelling his enemies. As though he had not already done enough to prove himself. But if further proof were needed, he should at least try to provide it.

It had already been made clear to him he would inherit no lands, but still Ronan could not subdue the need for recognition and the ambition that festered within. Surely if he demonstrated he was capable, more so than the king's noble allies, then the reward would be great.

'Have you heard of the one they call the Red Wolf?' Alan said, throwing the axe again. It hammered into the target board and there was a crack as the wood split.

'The what?' asked Ronan, still staring at the axe in the wood.

'The Red Wolf. Now there's a head I'd like to take. The Bastard would reward a man handsomely if he could lay that at his feet.'

'Folklore,' Brian said. 'This Red Wolf is just a legend cooked up by the local populace to disguise their rebellious ways. No one man could cause the havoc this Red Wolf has supposedly reaped.'

'Don't be so eager to dismiss the rumours, brother,' Alan replied. 'Our own men have made testament to how real he is. A hero of the English, they say. Eight feet tall, half warrior, half beast. He took the eyes of one young knight. The hands of another. Wears their parts like trophies, wandering the wilds like a devil.'

'Then he is no hero,' said Brian. 'He is just a savage, like the rest of these curs.'

'But still a man,' Ronan said.

'Half beast.' Alan was adamant.

Ronan shook his head. 'I'm not so easily spooked by folk tales. If this Red Wolf does exist he is a man like any other. And he will die like any man. Do you really think the reward for his capture would be so rich?'

'Rich indeed,' Alan replied. 'You think you're up to the task, cripple?'

Ronan ignored the barb. 'Cunning always overcomes the beast, my friend.'

'Cunning won't do you any good, Ronan,' said Brian. 'He is protected by the English wherever he goes. There was talk of him moving from the east into the English flat country, but since then, no word. He has gone to ground, for now, and the English will not speak of him to any of our countrymen.'

'Then lucky for me I speak their language like a native,' Ronan said.

'Ah yes,' Alan said. 'Sometimes I forget you are one of them.'

Again, Ronan did his best to ignore Alan's suggestion that he was half a savage. It was true his mother was one of these English, a refugee from the time of King Edward. But to his own mind Ronan was every inch the Breton knight, even if his flaws were pointed out to him often.

'Then we are agreed,' Ronan said. 'I am perfectly suited to tracking down this Red Wolf.'

Brian laughed. 'You would spend your time with these marsh dwellers? Mix with the peasants to find this outlaw?'

'I will bring this wolf before the king,' Ronan replied, the idea beginning to excite him. 'And perhaps he will reward me with a castle to rival your own.'

As he spoke, there was the sound of rumbling, as another part of Brian's construction collapsed in a heap. The sounds of the incensed master builder bellowed out from atop the hill and Alan began to laugh uncontrollably.

'I hope you have better luck with its construction than my brother,' he said, plucking the axe from the broken board.

Later the three of them ate within the old fort, and that night Ronan could barely sleep for thinking of what he might achieve.

The next morning, Brian informed him where this Red Wolf had last been seen and even granted him a conrois of his own knights to help find him. If Ronan could track this fugitive, it would reflect just as well on Brian.

As he rode out of the settlement with Aldus at his side and twenty men at his back, he could only think of the land and power that would eventually be his.

His thoughts were momentarily diverted when, from the corner of his eye, he saw a body at the side of the road. The man was unmistakably English, and from his garb most likely a labourer who had helped with the building of the castle. A familiar axe was buried in his head.

Such was Alan's way of finding amusement. Or perhaps he was offering a way to motivate his brother's workforce. Ronan could only hope it was not some portent for the mission ahead.

As he left the body behind, he determined that it was not. If anything, it was a portent of his success. For there would be much death if he was to persuade the English to tell him the whereabouts of this Red Wolf.

22

COLESELLE, ENGLAND, MAY 1067

Styrkar had done his best not to outstay his welcome. The Abbess Wynflaed had expressed regret at him leaving the abbey, but he knew it was time to go. Despite trying not to unnerve the nuns he knew his presence was a burden on them. They may no longer have feared the Red Wolf, but if he was discovered by a Frankish patrol there was no telling what they might do.

He had stayed just long enough to regain his strength. The nuns had washed and fed him, even trimming his unkempt beard and oiling his hair. He now wore it in a topknot as he wandered further west, feeling like a new man. The women had seemed proud of their work when they had bid him farewell. Not even Edith had taken such good care of him, but he left before growing too used to their ministrations. It would not do for him to rely on the comforts granted by others. He was still a fugitive, and there was no telling what hardships might lie ahead.

The seax of Harold was given a fresh scabbard from the

stores of the abbey, and it sat comfortably at his hip. It was a reminder that he still had much to achieve, though Styrkar still had no idea how he might accomplish his aims. Edith's words were still fresh in his mind, despite the months since she had died.

Earn it, she had told him. And by Fenrir's teeth he had tried. But he was not done yet. He would not be done until the Frankish conqueror was in his grave and his followers driven from these lands. An impossible task, but Styrkar could not let the weight of such a burden sway him.

He had wandered north for a whole day and night since leaving the abbey, without knowing where he was going. In that time he had encountered no patrols and only seen farm workers on the distant hills and a sheepherder with his flock. It all seemed so normal, as though the battle at Senlac and the death of the king had never happened. When he eventually crested a hill and saw a settlement by a river in the distance, the illusion of normality bedded in even more.

It looked such an idyllic setting, untouched by the ravages that had already afflicted much of the eastern part of these lands. For the briefest of moments, Styrkar yearned to cast aside his weapon and enter this community, forgetting his promise to Edith, his duty to his king. But he could never forget. He refused to.

As he walked down the hill and into the village he was reminded of the times of peace so long ago. Of the days he had accompanied Harold into village after village and been greeted with joy by so many of his subjects. Styrkar had never been a genial man, but he could still appreciate the virtue in others.

Entering the village, the bustle of the place felt alien to

him. He had been wandering, killing, spending his nights in the cold of the wild, and after the violence he had wrought the laughter and mundanity of this place was like being in a welcome dream.

He heard the ring of a hammer, the blacksmith busy at his forge as a few men and women crowded the entrance, eager for his wares. Further on, children frolicked in the road, the high-pitched giggles loud in his ears as they played without a care in the world. A man traded fish at a stall, surrounded by a gaggle of women bartering noisily for his catch. At the end of the road a woman was loudly berating her husband as a sot, while he sat in ignominy taking every word with stoic resignation.

Styrkar almost laughed at the scene but caught himself. He had no right to laugh. He had no right to be here among these people, with their ordinary lives. The animal that lurked within was a danger to these people, and he knew it. Better that he leave them to their normality lest they face the same curse that afflicted him.

Towards the river, Styrkar's eye was suddenly drawn by the noise of raised voices. He could see beyond the hamlet a large stone building on the riverbank. Ropes had been erected atop a pulley, and as he drew closer he recognised the place as a watermill. The wheel sat at an awkward angle, more ropes tied through the spokes, as a crowd of men struggled to lever it into place.

A dog suddenly barked at Styrkar's heels and he started, hand straying to the seax at his side. He gripped the handle, staring down at the dog, fighting the urge to strike it. When the hound eventually ran off into the distance, he knew he had to get away from here.

'Cured fish?' said a voice behind him, and he almost drew the blade as he saw a toothless man holding out a stinking fillet of herring.

Styrkar held up a hand in refusal, feeling more and more unnerved by the place. He walked away, reaching a well and sniffing the bucket to make sure it was fresh before filling his waterskin. He had seen enough of this place; he had to go before he hurt someone.

After walking from the settlement he paused at the water's edge, glancing downriver to see the men still struggling with their waterwheel.

'I told you this wouldn't work,' barked one of them, a short thin man who appeared to be avoiding as much of the manual labour as he could.

'Because you've come up with the best ideas so far,' bellowed another, a balding man with a prominent gut from indulging in too much ale.

'We need to readjust the ropes. The pulley needs to be higher.'

'We just need more bloody muscle. All you've done is stand there and watch.'

The thin man made to answer, but stopped when he saw Styrkar observing them. He raised an eyebrow, and the fat man turned his head, looking on curiously.

'So? You just going to stand there, or are you going to help us out?' said the man with the thick waist.

All Styrkar could do was stare back. It seemed an odd request. Days before he had been slaughtering men in the night, now he was being asked to help out some struggling villagers.

'Is he all right?' said the thin man.

'Maybe he's foreign?' said his friend.

'Do you understand what we're saying?' the thin man said, as though Styrkar might be deaf.

The temptation to walk away and leave these men behind was overwhelming, but Styrkar also felt the need to help. There was something about their struggle, and the fact he knew he could help them, that made him drop the sack the nuns had given him and walk towards the waterwheel.

'I understand you fine,' he said as he joined three other men on one side of the rope.

'All right then,' said the fat man. 'Let's give this another go. On my count, heave...'

He counted down from three. Styrkar pulled on the rope with all his might, the wheel moving easily this time as they muscled it onto the stone supports. More men pushed from the side and the wheel slotted into place.

'There we go!' said the bigger man. 'I told you we just needed more muscle!'

He slapped Styrkar on the shoulder as though they were old friends. Styrkar should have been annoyed at the man's familiarity, but something inside him appreciated the gesture.

'I still think we should have adjusted the pulley,' said his thin friend.

Ignoring him, the big man turned to Styrkar.

'Let me get you a drink,' he said. 'We're headed to the longhouse. We've been at this all day and I think we deserve a reward.'

Before Styrkar could answer, the shorter man chimed in. 'We haven't bloody finished yet. We still need to secure—'

'That's enough for one day,' he said. 'What say you?'

The question was directed at Styrkar. He had never been a drinker. He was a fighter, and the fuddled head mead and ale gave was never good for a man of the sword. But there were no enemies here. No one to fight. Besides, it had been so many weeks since he had spent any time in the company of ordinary folk, he had to admit he missed it.

'I will come,' he said.

With that the big man clapped him on the back, guiding him back towards the hamlet, accompanied by a dozen labourers.

They reached what they called the longhouse, but Styrkar was sure he'd seen more welcome-looking cowsheds. When they decided to perch themselves outside in the sun he felt some relief. The big man, whose name was Osgar, placed a cup of mead in his hand and Styrkar began to relax a little. The labourers introduced themselves, a list of names he would never remember, and began to make small talk in the midday sun until eventually Styrkar was alone with Osgar.

'So where do you come from?' Osgar asked.

Styrkar was unsure how to answer. He couldn't very well explain his relationship to their dead king and the fact he'd left a trail of bodies all the way from Walsingaha.

'I have been wandering since the invaders came. They burned my town close to Lundenburg. I have been looking for honest work since then.'

'Farm work? Well, there's still plenty round here, if you fancy staying. I can put a word in with the local landowner. That is if he still has any farmland by the end of the month. The Franks have been taking over estates all around here.'

'Does that not concern you?'

Osgar shrugged. 'Why would it? They still need men to work the fields. What difference who owns it? The Franks still pay with the same coins. Some of them might have a different head hammered on the front, but you can spend them just the same.'

'But the new king is not of these lands.'

'One king, another king. What's the difference? We still have to rise in the morning, still have to plough the field, still have to mill the flour, still have to make the bread, still have to catch the fish. What does it matter where the king comes from? Is he going to make me work any harder than I already do?'

Styrkar had no answer to that. It was a simple question that could not be argued with.

As the day wore on, they were joined by another man who had helped them with the wheel. Osgar introduced him as Kenric, a small handsome fellow with eyes that lit up when he smiled.

'That's a fair accent you have there,' Kenric said. 'There some Norse in you?'

'A little,' Styrkar answered cagily. 'But I have lived in many places.'

'And where do you think you'll be living next?'

'I have not given it much thought,' he replied.

'A wanderer?' said Kenric. 'Man after my own heart. Done plenty of that myself; moved from place to place. This one's as good as any. Kind of place a man might settle if he had a mind to.'

'I have no mind to settle,' Styrkar said.

'Sure, and why would you? Strapping man like yourself and these times as difficult as they are. But you can't wander forever, and I'm sure there's plenty of work you can turn your hand to. Despite appearances, I'm a hunter.' Styrkar looked him up and down, thinking it unlikely, but he also knew that appearance was not always the measure of a man. 'These are rich lands, and I could use the help. Now, I might not look much of a hunter, but you do. And I could use a capable man to help me. There's too much game for me alone and when there's a wolf abroad they come to old Kenric's door to see it off. I reckon that would be work you're suited to, if you had a mind.'

'I am not so sure it would be the right thing for me,' Styrkar said.

But would it? He had spent time enough hunting men. Time enough slaying his enemies. Would now not be a time to hunt less dangerous quarry? He doubted a wolf would be as dangerous a foe as an armoured knight.

'Well, you can suit yourself, friend. But the offer's there if you want to take it up.'

Styrkar took a drink from his cup. The mead tasted good, and with the sun on his face he felt like he might never want to leave. These people were friendly, and they had welcomed him like a lost brother.

'I'll think about it,' Styrkar said.

As Kenric smiled and called for more mead, Styrkar was sure he would not have to think on it for long.

23

HEREFORD, ENGLAND, MAY 1067

It wasn't just the silence that was uncomfortable as they made their way along the road. The cart bumped and jolted them mercilessly, but Gisela knew her suffering was nothing compared to that of her mistress. As she saw the castle at Hereford appear upon the horizon, she let out a long sigh of relief.

Agnes leaned into her, the old woman clutching her cloak about her as though they travelled through winter snows, and the girl held her close.

'We are almost there, mistress,' she whispered. 'The castle is just ahead.'

The old woman looked up with rheumy eyes, barely acknowledging the sight in front of her, before leaning back against Gisela's shoulder.

As they drew closer to their destination, Gisela could see the huge construction rising before her. An old wooden fort was being gradually torn down and replaced by formidable-looking stonework. Even at a distance Gisela could see men working feverishly on the huge scaffold.

The cart rumbled across a hastily built bridge into the bailey beyond. Once it had come to a standstill, Gisela was quick to climb down, eager to help her mistress from the object of her torture. Agnes struggled, even with the driver's help, the breath coming quick from her as she gingerly lowered herself to the ground.

No sooner had they arrived than a voice called out to them from across the bailey.

'My lady, so glad you have arrived.'

Gisela turned to see Baron Richard approaching. He was much younger than his wife, but still old enough to be greying at the temples. His finery was testament to the wealth and status of the FitzScrobs.

He walked forward to embrace his wife. For her part, Agnes seemed to endure the gesture rather than welcome it.

'Why did we have to come to this damned place, so close to the border?' she asked.

There it was. The baroness wasted little time in making her feelings about their situation clear.

'You know why, my love,' Richard replied. 'I have explained it to you at great length. Once we are settled here you will see the advantage of it. This is truly beautiful country.'

The sour look on Agnes' face said she didn't agree.

'I will take Lady Agnes to her chambers,' Gisela said, before her mistress could complain any further.

'An excellent idea,' Richard replied. 'Stonhild will show you the way.' He gestured to a pock-marked young girl who waited for them beside the main castle structure.

As Gisela guided Lady Agnes towards the building, she found it odd that Baron Richard knew the girl's name. Gisela had been in service to the FitzScrobs for almost ten years and it was unlikely he would have been able to pick her out in a crowd as one of his servants. As the girl guided them silently inside, Gisela guessed the old letch was most likely taking his pleasure with her, despite her ugly face.

They were taken to a room at the corner of the structure. Gisela had to admit the stonework was expertly built but the place was bleak and cold, unlike their home back in the east.

'This place is like a dungeon,' Agnes said as she shuffled to the nearby window and struggled with the shutters.

'We'll make it a home, my lady,' Gisela replied as she helped her close the wooden panels and secure the latch. 'I'll make us a fire and it'll be nice and cosy.'

Agnes pulled a sour expression as Gisela made her way to the hearth. There was wood and kindling and even a flint for the lighting, which was a relief – she didn't relish the idea of wandering this place aimlessly looking for a flame.

In no time she had lit the fire and the chamber began to warm through. The bed had already been made, and Gisela managed to dress her mistress in her night clothes and get her under a thick woollen blanket. Agnes was so exhausted from the journey she was snoring in no time.

Gisela sat in a chair in the corner of the room, gazing at the old woman as the sky outside turned dark. Agnes was old now, and not long for this world. Gisela couldn't help but wonder what might be in store for her in this new part of the country, so close to the frontier, if her mistress were to pass. She would have to find some other way to make herself useful to the FitzScrobs.

As she wondered what she might do, Gisela found herself feeling guilty for it. She could not remember the last time she had considered her own needs before those of her mistress, and the sudden selfishness made her feel a deep pang of guilt.

It was to some relief that Stonhild came to their chamber again later to summon the baroness for dinner. Gisela gently woke her mistress and took pains to wash and dress her, before following Stonhild down to the dining hall.

The table was already laid out and would have sat twenty people. As it was, there were only places set for two.

Baron Richard received his wife enthusiastically and, as was her way, she greeted him with much less aplomb. Gisela helped serve them both a course of rich, thick soup and the two of them ate in silence for a while.

Gisela watched, thinking on how they had always struck her as the oddest couple. It was not often that a powerful man would take a much older wife, but then she had to ask herself if Richard had been all that powerful before the marriage. Most likely he had married out of expedience, but Gisela had never been foolish enough to enquire as to the real reason.

A cold breeze blew through the chamber, and Agnes pulled her cloak tighter about herself.

'This cursed place will be the death of me, Richard,' the old woman said. 'You have brought me to my tomb.'

Richard let out a low sigh. 'How many times, my love? There is no other way.'

Gisela knew the story well. The sitting Saxon lord of Hereford, Earl Eadric, had been evicted after failing to pledge his fealty to the new king, and Willem of Breteuil, a close friend and ally of King William, had been granted the lands in return for his support during the recent conquest. It was no secret that Baron Richard had been ordered to take charge of Hereford while a new castle was constructed.

'No other way?' said Agnes. 'You have always coveted this place. You wanted this more than anyone.'

'While the king is in Frankia, Bishop Odo and Earl Willem are in charge of these lands. In William's absence their orders are to shore up the defences of every frontier. It is a prodigious honour that Willem has granted me. We are here to oversee the protection of the kingdom, my love. It is a great responsibility. You should be proud.'

'Proud?' she said, a little soup dribbling down her chin. 'You have stolen this place from its sitting lord. And not even by force of arms. Someone else had to grant it to you. My father—'

'Yes, my love. I'm sure we all know exactly what your father would have done. Marched on this place years ago and taken it by force. Well, you know it was never as simple as that. We were given our lands by King Edward, and so was Eadric. But now there is a new king. One who demands fealty. Luckily for us, Earl Eadric decided a Norman king was not one he could bow to. I have been granted the place through loyalty, my love. Not theft. And I could not have refused even had I wanted to.'

'As if you would have wanted to,' Agnes sneered. 'We had enough. More than enough, but that has never satisfied you. Don't talk to me of loyalty, when all you really have is relentless ambition.'

Gisela could sense Richard's exasperation, but to his credit he took his wife's barbs as though armoured in mail.

'Times have changed, my love. The old kings are dead. It is the Bastard's time now, and he will brook no refusal. He is stronger and more ruthless than any other king we have served. Edward and Harold were mere pretenders compared to King William. Yes, I am ambitious, but what other way is there? Stand aside and let others trample our lands and our name? William has shown us the way – rise up and take what is ours, or see ourselves cast in the mud.'

Agnes made to answer, but she was cut off when the door opened. A tall figure entered along with the chill breeze and Gisela's skirts wafted about her legs. Her breath was caught in her throat as she recognised the newcomer.

Osbern had always been handsome, but the year or so since she'd last seen him had only made him even more desirable. His shoulders had filled out and the neatly trimmed beard gave him a squarer look to his jaw, if that were possible.

'Mother. Father,' Osbern said, bending to kiss his mother on the cheek.

As he made to sit between them he noticed Gisela standing at the periphery of the room.

'Is that Gisela?' he said with a wide smile.

'It is, my lord,' she replied, feeling a flutter in her stomach.

'How comely you've become since I last saw you.'

She was about to thank him for the compliment, when he turned his attention back to Lady Agnes.

'I trust your journey was a pleasant one, Mother?'

'Hideous,' she answered. 'But I endure.' She gave a withering glance towards her husband, which Richard ignored.

Osbern picked a slice of cooked pork from the platter in front of him, along with a wedge of cheese. His father leaned into him.

'News from the west?' he asked.

'Ah yes,' said Agnes. 'Now you are the sheriff your duties must weigh heavily upon you. I am proud of you, son.'

'Thank you, Mother,' Osbern replied. 'And yes. Our border patrols bring reports daily. Earl Eadric gathers more support by the day. They have begun to call him "The Wild". A name that suits his savage nature. If he is not curbed quickly, we could have a full-scale rebellion on our hands.'

Agnes made the sound of a hissing cat, glaring at her husband. 'And this is the place you summon me to?' she scolded.

Osbern continued before his father could protest. 'There is nowhere safe in the kingdom, Mother. Uprisings are being sparked across the length and breadth of these lands. It is not helped by the king's absence; we need him here to assist us.'

'The king has his own battles to fight,' said Richard. 'And he has entrusted us with this duty. Construction of the castle continues apace. Soon we will be surrounded by strong walls and a fully manned garrison. Let this Eadric the Wild come. He will find we are not some helpless outpost.'

Osbern shook his head. 'Do not underestimate him, Father. I have seen what he is capable of first-hand. He burns and pillages like the Saxons of old. His men are fierce and loyal. He will not be so easily cowed.'

The baron laid a hand on his son's shoulder. 'Fear not. I'm sure the king will return soon, and I have already sent word to Willem of Breteuil that we require more men. I expect Hereford to be flooded with knights loyal to King William soon enough.'

'Enough talk of war and rebellion,' Agnes cut in, before Osbern could outline any further concerns. 'I have not seen my son for an age. It is time you told me what you have been up to these past months. I want to hear it all.'

And so Gisela stood as the conversation turned to Osbern. She heard little of it, too busy was she staring at the young man she had always admired. Eventually, when Lady Agnes grew tired once more, Gisela guided her mistress back to her room and put her to bed.

The place was silent, eerie even, though she put that down to her unfamiliarity with the place. Eventually, she wrapped herself in a cloak and made her way from the bedchamber to take in some air.

Even in its early stage of construction Gisela could tell the castle was going to be a formidable fortification. It was atop a hill, with a view of the surrounding lands. She did not envy the army that might seek to attack such a well-defended bastion.

Despite knowing it might be forbidden, she made her way up to the top of a newly constructed wall, ignored by the few guards who stood in vigil over the place. From the battlement she could see a long way west. Osbern had spoken of rebellion, and she could only imagine the fell deeds that might be occurring even now at the hand of Eadric the Wild.

'It is beautiful country,' said a familiar voice.

Gisela turned to see Osbern standing beside her, and her voice was instantly caught in her throat.

'Beautiful but treacherous,' he continued. 'My father doesn't understand just how treacherous.'

Gisela swallowed, despite her dry throat. 'I am sure he will listen to you, when you explain.'

'I doubt that,' said Osbern. 'He has always coveted this place. Now he has it there will be no dissuading him.' He shook his head. 'Anyway, it has been too long since we last saw one another. Tell me, are you still the same girl I knew?'

'I don't think so, my lord,' she replied.

'No,' he said, with a grin. 'Now you are a woman grown. No longer the freckle-faced girl from the old country.'

'I have not been a girl for quite some time.'

He nodded, but the handsome smile slowly dropped from his face.

'You should not have come here, Gisela. My father should never have brought you and my mother to this place. There is a war brewing, and there might be nothing I can do to stop it.'

'Surely the war is over. The new king has been crowned and the English are put in their place.'

'The struggle is not finished by far. The English will never accept a foreign king. There is trouble coming, for all of us.'

'Then we shall fight,' she replied. 'Together.'

He smiled down at her, placing an arm around her. It was small comfort in this remote place far from everything she knew, but she would cling to it. At least for as long as she could.

24

COLESELLE, ENGLAND, JUNE 1067

He plunged head first into the bush, heedless of the shrubbery that threatened to cut his arms. His big hands closed around the rabbit, and it squirmed and struggled in his grip. Styrkar wrenched the creature free, snapping its neck before it could make a bigger nuisance of itself.

This was not the kind of hunting he had envisioned when Kenric made his offer those weeks before. Styrkar had been expecting to hunt deer and trap wolves, not face conies and the odd angry badger. But then again, Styrkar had never been much of a bowman, and it was hard to bring down game with an axe.

Not that he was in any position to complain about his lot. He was making a generous living from selling skins and meat. The town had welcomed him with open arms, and he had a roof over his head, food in his belly and people he could call friends. The wild thoughts of vengeance he had harboured for so many months were still there, but locked away at the back of his mind. Sometimes he would think on them, and think on acting upon them, but since he had arrived in Coleselle, the Red Wolf had slept. Life went on.

He stuffed the rabbit in a sack along with the others and hefted it over one shoulder. It was full enough for one day, and as the evening drew in he made his way back through the wood towards town.

He was alerted by a rustle from the trees, stopping dead as he waited to see who was coming. When Kenric appeared from amid the trees onto the path in front of him, he let out a slow breath. For a moment Styrkar felt an odd sense of relief; his hand had not even strayed towards the seax at his belt. A few weeks ago, he would have been ready to fight before Kenric even showed himself. Now, he had become so used to the lack of danger he had not turned to the fight-or-flight instinct that had kept him alive for so long. Whether that was a good thing, Styrkar could not say.

Kenric noticed him, a wide smile crossing his face as he held up the sack he was carrying.

'Come see what I've got, my friend.' Kenric beamed.

Styrkar peered into the sack as Kenric held it open. Inside was pigweed, shaggy mane mushrooms, rosemary, nettle leaves and other things he couldn't identify. It was hardly a king's bounty, but Kenric's face told how proud he was of his foraging.

'We will eat like lords tonight,' Styrkar said.

'Lords indeed,' Kenric replied, closing the sack and swinging it over his shoulder. 'When we get home I will cook us up a feast worthy of a coronation. A rabbit stew like you've never tasted. Then we can sell the rest for coin and mead. We are like merchants, you and I. True men of wealth and breeding.'

Kenric smiled up at Styrkar, who didn't feel the need to speak. But then he never did.

'That's what I like about our partnership,' Kenric said eventually. 'These long lingering conversations. They're a constant comfort.'

Styrkar managed to stifle a smile. He had long since grown used to Kenric's endless chatter, and even learned to take his occasional sarcasm on the chin. It had been something of an adjustment. His friend often cut too close to the bone with that sharp tongue of his, and had it been a fellow housecarl who shot Styrkar such a barb he might have reacted differently. But it was obvious Kenric's banter was harmless, and he meant nothing by it.

Kenric continued to talk and Styrkar continued to listen as they took the path back towards their home. When they were within half a mile, Styrkar saw the first cloud of smoke billowing above the trees.

He raised a hand for Kenric to be silent and his friend stopped in his tracks, staring up at the black pall rising before them.

'The town,' he breathed.

Styrkar dropped his rabbits and grasped Kenric's shoulder. 'Stay here. If you see any Frankish warriors hide yourself in the trees.'

'No,' Kenric said. 'I can fight.' There was little conviction in his voice.

Styrkar shook his head. 'I have seen this before. Many times. There is nothing you can do.'

'What about you?'

Styrkar glanced back to the town, feeling his stomach come alive, tasting the cold spittle in his mouth. This was his chance. The opportunity he had been waiting for. The inevitability of his end.

'It has been good knowing you, my friend,' was all he could say.

He raced towards the town, leaving Kenric behind him. As he ran he pulled the seax clear of the sheath, feeling the reassuring weight in his hand. Excitement began to well up, anticipation of the fight, the baresark within taking control. The Red Wolf.

In the distance there was a scream from the village. He couldn't tell if it was man or woman, but it was obvious he was too late to do anything but avenge them. Swords clashed from beyond the trees and he willed himself to run faster, plunging heedlessly through the brush. The closer he got the stronger the stench of smoke, of burning wood. Of death.

Styrkar raced from the tree line, sprinting down the path into town. The flames were high, and it looked like almost every building had been put to the flame. The longhouse burned, the mill along with it, the great wheel he had helped erect now blackened and smoking in the river.

The screaming had stopped, and there were no signs of any marauding warriors as he slowed to a stop at the centre of the town. All that awaited him were corpses.

Styrkar stood amidst the smoke and the heat. Breathing heavily from his run. His eyes scanned the surrounding buildings, but there was nothing left alive. Not even a stray dog to give him hope.

Then the first of them appeared.

He recognised the armour, their mail and helms, spears and shields braced. First one, then half a dozen, then a score. Too many to fight and hope to live. Styrkar gripped the seax tighter, feeling his lips curl back from his gritted teeth.

Let the first of them come. He would show these bastards how the Red Wolf died.

But they did not close in. They surrounded him, keeping a safe distance as they stood and waited.

'Come on,' Styrkar snarled. 'Fight me.'

In answer, a gap appeared in their shields.

A Frankish knight limped forward. He wore no helm and the mail hood was drawn back from his head to reveal a dark mop of hair, shaved at the sides in the Frankish manner. There was an expression of smug superiority to his face. It was a look Styrkar had seen often, just before he turned that smug look to fear, then terror.

'Greetings,' said the knight. 'My name is Ronan of Dol-Combourg.' His English was as good as any native Styrkar had ever heard and he spoke as though to an old friend. It seemed odd as they stood amid such carnage. 'I have come in search of the one they call the Red Wolf. And it looks like I've found him.'

Styrkar did not answer. He stared at the strange foreigner, waiting for him to make his move, but the man only grinned, before gesturing over one shoulder.

A break appeared in the Frankish shields, and a huge warrior stepped through, dragging a body along with him. Despite the prone man's battered and bloody face, Styrkar recognised him as Osgar. The giant knight drove his friend to his knees, grabbing his jaw in one massive hand and making him look up.

'You were surprisingly easy to find,' said Ronan. 'I simply followed the corpses left by a red-haired giant until I came upon this place. Though I must admit I am a little disappointed; you are no giant at all. Just a man, if a little on the large side. But from the collar around your neck, I see I have found the right one.'

'You can talk, Frankish,' Styrkar said. 'Now, can you fight?'

Ronan glanced around at his men. 'We can all fight, my friend. We have nothing to prove on that score. But fighting would be a needless waste. I would rather take you alive.'

'I will never be taken alive. If you think otherwise, you're a fool.'

'Unfortunate,' Ronan replied.

There was more movement, as some of the knights moved aside, allowing Styrkar to see beyond the circle that surrounded him. More Frankish warriors stood beside the collapsed huts, dishevelled villagers on their knees, women and children among their number. The knights had naked blades in their hands and the intent was obvious.

'Drop your sword, Red Wolf, and I promise no one else will be hurt. Refuse, and I promise you the massacre of this place has only just begun.'

Styrkar looked from sallow face to sallow face. All he wanted was the chance to fight to the death, but he knew it was not just his own life he would be paying with. There was more at stake than just a last chance at vengeance. He had lived among these people, and they had grown to know him, to accept him as one of their own. How could he risk their lives? There was no question what these foreign bastards would do; Styrkar had seen it all across these lands and knew he had no choice.

The seax slipped from his grip and stuck in the ground by his feet. Ronan smiled at him as his men closed in. The giant who had dragged Osgar across the ground came to stand before him. Styrkar looked up, waiting for his hands to be bound behind him, but before any of the Franks made a move, the giant struck him a crunching blow to the jaw.

He fell, tasting blood in his mouth, smelling the damp earth beneath him. The village spun, and he struggled to push himself up onto his knees.

'Are you watching?' Ronan shouted as Styrkar floundered on the ground. 'This is the one you call the Red Wolf.'

Styrkar could see more villagers being brought forward to witness his capture. Before he could move, the giant kicked him in the ribs, knocking the wind from his lungs.

'This man is an outlaw,' Ronan continued. 'A scourge upon these lands. Defiant in the face of your new king.' Another kick, and Styrkar felt more pain driven through his body. He became nauseous, the vision blurring at the edge of his periphery.

'This is your hero,' Ronan cried. 'And this is the fate of all those who oppose the new order of things.'

Styrkar had time enough to cover his head with his arms as more of the Frankish knights joined the giant. He had no idea how long they kicked him, but when eventually he could draw breath it felt as though his entire body had been beaten to a blackened pulp.

He could not have fought back, even had he wanted

to. But Styrkar knew the time for defiance was over. If the people of Coleselle were to live, he had to sacrifice himself.

As he lay, beaten and bloody in the mud, Ronan came and knelt beside him.

'Get used to this position,' he said. Styrkar tried to speak, but his face was numb and all that came from his mouth was blood. 'Much worse awaits when I finally present you to the king.'

Blackness began to consume Styrkar's vision, until eventually the mercy of darkness took him.

25

COLESELLE, ENGLAND, JUNE 1067

He was alone in the silence with only his regrets for company. Styrkar's body ached, his ribs felt as though they had been smashed and with his hands bound behind him he struggled to breathe. Every lungful of air was laboured, and all he could concentrate on was sucking in one agonising breath after the other.

The hut was blackened and burned. One timber prop remained, and he was lashed to it. The burned-out roof let in the night air and Styrkar could see a sky full of stars above. He did not know how long he had been here; consciousness came to him fleetingly before he succumbed to the pain and darkness once more. On occasion it had been light, then dark, and he had been awoken by the screams outside or the laughter of a foreign soldier. Now, with the coming of night, all was silent.

His arms strained against their bonds, but the Franks had bound him tight. It only made him regret his easy surrender all the more. Styrkar should have known not to rely on them to keep their word. He should have fought to the death, and to Hel with the consequences. From the noises he had heard, they had made their sport with the surviving townsfolk despite his surrender. Now he waited for his own fate, trussed up like a sacrificial goat. But regret would not help him now. All he could do was hope an opportunity would arise where he could avenge himself. Deep down, he knew that chance was further away than ever.

Styrkar squinted through the shadows as he heard footsteps approaching. With a creak of the timbered floor, someone entered the hut, carrying a torch that made it impossible for Styrkar to see in the sudden brightness. As he glared through swollen eyes, his sight adjusted enough to see the crippled knight standing in the dark. Ronan, he had called himself. His expression was almost sorrowful.

'You look in pain, my friend. I wish there was something I could do to make you more comfortable.' He planted the torch between the floorboards and knelt. 'Would you like a drink?' Ronan waved a cup below Styrkar's nose and he could smell mead. It would have been good to wet his lips with it, but instead Styrkar turned his face away.

'No? To be honest I don't blame you. This is far from the worst thing I've tasted on this island, but it still does not compare to what I'm used to. In my homeland we prefer wine. When I first arrived here I admit, this stuff turned my stomach, but I think I might be getting a taste for it.'

Ronan stood and took a sip, grimacing at the taste. Then he looked back down at Styrkar.

'Tell me, where did you come from?' When Styrkar

didn't reply, Ronan carried on regardless. 'I will make an assumption that you fought in the great battle. You are a warrior, of that there is little doubt, so how did you survive? Perhaps you ran away before the end? That would explain why I don't remember seeing you.'

Styrkar gritted his teeth at the accusation of cowardice, but still he did not speak. Instead he fixed Ronan with a defiant glare, though he knew it was a worthless gesture. It only brought a smile to Ronan's lips.

'Don't feel bad, Red Wolf. Running was the best thing to do. The English were destined for defeat. They stood no chance against our horsemen. Your King Harold was a fool to think he could stand against us.'

'Harold was a warrior king,' Styrkar snapped, unable to hold his peace any longer. 'He had already fought and won a great battle. We had marched for hundreds of miles before we even faced you on the field. Put a sword in my hand and I'll show you what one of his warriors can do. I'll kill all you Frankish bastards.'

Styrkar strained against his bonds but he knew it was hopeless. He was spouting empty threats.

'You were one of his personal guard, I would wager,' Ronan said. 'I already know your name is Styrkar. That one did not take me long to prise from the tongue of this town's elder. That is no English name. Norse perhaps?'

'I am no Norseman,' Styrkar replied. 'I am a Dane.'

'Well, Styrkar the Dane, you may have fought well at the battle – that much I do not question. But you should also have accepted your defeat with grace. You and the rest of your English rebels will find no peace until you bow to the new king. Resistance will not end well for any of you.

William is your master now, and there is nothing you can do about it.'

Styrkar gritted his teeth, tasting the blood on his gums, knowing he should have remained silent, but he could not.

'Harold was not just my king or my master. He was as a father to me. His wife was like a mother. His sons my brothers.'

Ronan raised an eyebrow, looking down with amusement. The expression only served to anger Styrkar even more.

'I hate to be the bearer of bad tidings, but Harold's sons have fled across the sea to the west. They have abandoned this place, and perhaps you should have done the same, Styrkar the Dane. This was not your country and these are not your people. Why would you remain?'

Styrkar knew he should have stayed silent, but it was too late now. He had already begun, and it was most likely that he would die in this place. What did it matter now what this foreign knight knew?

'I had to stay… for Edith. She had lost everything. She was a mother to me and… the boy Ulf. Harold's son. And you bastards took him.' Those last words were spat from bloody lips. Once again Styrkar strained against the rope that bound him, feeling the timber he was lashed to crack under the strain, but still it held him fast.

'And what of Edith?' Ronan asked. 'What changed that you would abandon her for this life of violence?'

The image came back to him in a sickening rush. Edith hanging from the great oak, her flesh pale and frozen in the chill morning air. Her gown fluttering in the breeze as her bare feet swung above the frosted earth.

'She is dead,' Styrkar said.

He waited for the next gibe, for Ronan to find his pain amusing, but when he looked up he saw only sympathy on the knight's face. Ronan took a slow sip of mead before he fixed Styrkar with a mournful look.

'I too lost my mother. Many years ago, when I was but a boy. And I, like you, was taken in by a second father. The Count of Penthièvre is a hard man, but I suffered his displeasure and served as his squire, desperate for approval. I almost had it too, until the day I fell from a horse, foot caught in the stirrup. It dragged me for miles, and when it finally stopped I was left broken. But I could not allow myself to stay that way. Would not let myself be defined by my one weakness. So I understand what it is to feel pain. To feel loss.' With a blink of his eyes the sorrowful look was gone. 'But I have since learned to forget the past. To dwell on your demons only leads to...' he gestured to Styrkar beaten and bloodied and bound to a post '...only leads to destruction. I am not so determined to bring myself low. I have ambition, Styrkar. I am unsatisfied with my lot. It is my goal to live the life of a wealthy man. To have land, power, admiration. Had I fallen into a pit of bitterness I might have become like you, but I learned long ago that you cannot battle against the established rule of law. You have to work within it. What did you possibly hope to achieve, Styrkar? Did you think this Red Wolf would fight his way to the English throne and cut down the king himself?'

'Perhaps not,' said Styrkar, fixing Ronan with as defiant a look as he could muster from his battered face. 'But I would not have given in. I would not have stopped until as many dead foreigners lay at my feet as I could cut down. I would have strangled every last invader with my bare hands given the chance.'

'Then it was fortunate I stopped you,' Ronan replied before draining the rest of his cup and flinging it into the dark.

He reached to his side, and for a moment Styrkar thought he might draw a blade and cut his throat. Instead, Ronan pulled the sheathed seax from his belt, kneeling beside Styrkar and drawing the blade a few inches. The steel shone in the torchlight, the runes carved upon it glittering as though enchanted by ancient druidcraft.

'A beautiful weapon,' Ronan said. 'Was this the sword you were going to murder the king with?'

Styrkar had no idea how to answer. He had not even considered how he might kill a king. All he had wanted was to take as many lives as he could until these foreign knights stopped him.

'At least tell me where it came from. The man who crafted this was an artist. I might well have him make me a weapon of my own.'

If Styrkar told Ronan its heritage he might well have kept Harold's weapon as a trophy. Paraded it around for all to see – the captured sword of a king. Better Styrkar keep his mouth shut – he had already said more than enough.

Ronan shrugged and rose to his feet, sheathing Harold's blade once more.

'No matter,' he said. 'This sword will have to suffice. The sword of the Red Wolf. The first of many rewards for your capture. When I give you to the king, he will gift me a gilded sword of my own, I am sure. Rest easy, Styrkar the Dane.

You will not have to think on your failure for long. With any luck the king will be merciful and your death will be swift.'

With that, Ronan turned and limped back out of the hut.

Styrkar was left alone with nothing but the starlight, and the prospect of a quick death.

26

COLESELLE, ENGLAND, JUNE 1067

Styrkar woke groggily, with a foul taste in his mouth. Blood had dried on his lips and they cracked as he opened them and tried to suck in a shallow breath. When his chest expanded to help relieve his lungs, the cord that bound his wrists cut deeper into the flesh and he winced at the pain.

The stars had gone now, and through the gap in the roof he could see the dark sky reddening with the dawn. It was then he could smell it; burning, but this was no warming hearth, this was thatch and timber.

As his eyes focused he could see smoke drift across the sky, followed by the shouts of panicked voices in a language he recognised but did not understand. Smoke began to fill the hut and Styrkar could hear the crackling sound of flames as they licked at a nearby building.

Panic suddenly gripped him, and he struggled against the cord at his wrist. He was bound tight, and there was nothing he could do but dig the cord further into his flesh, feeling the blood pour down his hands.

He coughed, feeling the pain in his aching lungs. This could not be the way he died. He could not perish, gagging for air in a smoke-filled room. The Red Wolf had to die with a weapon in his hand and a bellow of rage on his lips.

Styrkar shouted out, hoping someone might come for him. He was King William's prize – surely the Franks would not just leave him to suffocate in this hut? Or perhaps Ronan had changed his mind. Perhaps the knight had decided to present Styrkar's corpse to his king, and choking in a cloud of acrid smoke was the most fitting execution.

His eyes were streaming, the tears running down his bruised cheeks, but through the pall he saw someone rush into the hut. The figure fought its way through the smoke, stopping at Styrkar's side. The man knelt, and Styrkar could feel him use a blade to cut at the cords binding his wrists.

He felt relief as soon as his bonds were cut, the ache in his shoulders relenting as he flexed his arms. Before he could examine the damaged flesh of his wrists, his rescuer grabbed him and pulled him to his feet. Together they stumbled through the smoke and out of the hut. Styrkar took in a deep breath of air and coughed from the bottom of his lungs. He spat a black gob of phlegm, looking up to see the face of the man who had rescued him. Kenric stared back, his eyes wide with fear, but there was a determined set to his jaw.

The town was on fire and the flames lit up the dawn. Every building had been set alight, and in the midst of the carnage Styrkar could see men fighting in desperation. It looked as though the Frankish knights had been taken by surprise, and they were at pains to defend themselves against the savagery of the townsfolk. Styrkar could only admire their resolve. The invaders had brought death to their town, and now they were taking their vengeance.

He moved to join them, but Kenric grasped his arm.

'We have to flee,' he said. 'There's no time.'

Styrkar struggled against his friend's grip, but Kenric held on fast. He was stronger than he looked, and Styrkar had no choice but to let himself be led towards the edge of the town.

His senses were assailed from all sides as they stumbled through the smoke and the fighting. For an instant he was back on the hill at Senlac, surrounded by the screaming and the violence, but he managed to keep his wits long enough for them to reach the edge of the burning buildings.

'Come on,' Kenric urged, as they made their way across open ground towards the tree line.

Styrkar risked a glance back, but he could see nothing through the smoke. The sounds of battle had receded now; the crackling of fires was all he could hear.

When they reached the edge of the wood, Kenric paused, planting his hands on his knees and gasping for air. Styrkar hawked another black gob of spit, hands balled into fists. The urge to run back and take the fight to the Franks almost overwhelmed him, but he could see some of the townsfolk fleeing now. They had achieved what they wanted; to spit their defiance in the face of the invaders. To rescue whoever the Franks might have left alive. Now all that remained was to flee.

'We have to keep moving,' Kenric said.

Styrkar didn't try to argue, no matter how much he wanted to exact his vengeance, and he followed Kenric deeper into the wood. They fled west across land he was unused to, their main hunting ground lying to the north and east. Kenric led a fast pace, and Styrkar realised how weak he was from being beaten and lashed to a post. Any other day he would have far outpaced his friend, but today he struggled to keep up.

Eventually they reached a clearing, overlooked by an ancient elm tree, and Kenric slumped down on a fallen trunk.

'What is going on?' Styrkar asked, refusing to sit despite the ache in his legs.

'I met up with some of the others who fled when those knights arrived. At first all they wanted to do was run to the hills, but some of them were angry, their families still in the town. Didn't take long for them to decide to fight back under cover of dark.'

'That was brave of them,' Styrkar said.

'More like stupid,' said Kenric. 'Luckily someone came up with the plan of burning those Franks while they slept, rather than taking them on in a fight. Better to set the whole town afire than leave it to those bastards.'

'That someone was you?'

Kenric shrugged, but his grin took the credit.

'You have my thanks for not leaving me there,' Styrkar said.

'Wouldn't abandon my old mate, would I? I hope you'd do the same for me.'

Styrkar nodded, though to his shame he didn't know if he would. He had been obsessed with killing and revenge for so long, it was more likely he would have perished on a Frankish spear while Kenric choked to death in the smoke of the fires.

Before he could admit the truth, someone came into the clearing. There were two of them, a man and a woman, although they were barely out of their youth. The girl had a desperate look to her, face blackened by soot. The young man's handsome face was marred by a deep frown.

'Is this it?' said the man. 'Are we in the right place?'

'That you are,' said Kenric. 'Where are the others?'

As though in answer, more townsfolk made their way from the trees. Styrkar recognised most of them, ordinary men, women and children he had lived among for the past weeks. Each one bore some scar from their experience, whether a wound or a face marred by loss. Every last one of them had changed from the carefree folk of old. It was a look Styrkar recognised only too well.

Around twenty townsfolk eventually gathered in the glade, and the last of them to arrive was Osgar. His face was still a swollen mass of bruises but there was a grim look to him. From the axe he carried in his hand, Styrkar could only guess that he had taken his vengeance on the Franks.

'What do we do now?' someone in the crowd said.

'The next town is not too far,' replied someone else. 'If we follow the river—'

'We can't go to a town,' a third one interrupted. 'The Franks will follow us there for sure. We have to go deeper into the woods.'

More voices joined in, and before long the whole crowd were arguing and panicking over what they would do and how they would survive this. Styrkar had heard enough.

'You are all outlaws now,' he said, raising his voice above their squabbling. 'For now and forever you will be fugitives from the wrath of the new king. He will not stop until he has tracked you down and made an example.'

If Styrkar had been hoping to inspire them into further defiance against the foreigners, it did not work. A couple of the women began to weep. Men put their heads in their hands in despair.

'There is a better way,' Kenric said, rising to his feet. 'To the west they say a Saxon lord has risen in rebellion. His estates were taken from him and he has retreated to the Marcher Lands. From there he strikes back against the invaders, gathering more support to him by the day.'

'Earl Eadric,' said Osgar. 'I've heard of him. He fights against the new king and it is said the Franks fear him. Kenric is right. We should travel west and find this rebel lord. Pledge ourselves to his cause. Surely he can protect us?'

The crowd seemed encouraged. With little other choice, this seemed their only chance for survival, but Styrkar was not so convinced.

'Will you come with us?' Kenric asked.

Styrkar shook his head. 'I have had my fill of lords and fealty. There was only one king I was loyal to and he is dead.'

'What will you do?'

Styrkar watched as the townsfolk began to gather their meagre belongings, some of them already making their way west through the trees.

'I will recover. Regain my strength, and then I will kill the next Frankish patrol I find.'

'So you'll die?' said Kenric. 'You're a fool, Styrkar. You would throw your life away rather than join with us? Rather than pledge yourself to a man who fights our enemy?'

Styrkar began to see the sense in Kenric's plan. Whoever this Earl Eadric was it was obvious they fought for the same cause. But the prospect of kneeling before another lord angered Styrkar almost as much as the thought of facing the Franks again.

'Are you coming?' Osgar called. The rest of the townsfolk had gathered now and begun the journey west.

'Well?' asked Kenric.

Reluctantly, Styrkar nodded. 'Very well. Let us see what this Saxon lord has to offer.'

'It makes sense,' said Kenric, slapping Styrkar on the arm. He winced at the blow, feeling the rawness of his bruises.

Together they made their way west, leaving the burning town of Coleselle behind them. Styrkar could only hope this Eadric was a man worth making an alliance with.

27

THE MARCHER LANDS, ENGLAND, JUNE 1067

They had walked for four days with little rest. It had been important they put as much distance between themselves and the Franks as possible, and Styrkar had led them at a challenging pace. Mothers and fathers carried their sleeping children when they had to, but on the whole he had been impressed with their fortitude.

When Styrkar found himself in unfamiliar lands, Osgar had taken over, leading them along the hidden paths to the border. They could not walk the main roads and pathways, and had to avoid settlements of any kind lest news of their passing reach Frankish ears. That would have been the doom of them all.

The land changed the closer they got to the Marcher Lands, turning from flat fields and woodland to barren hills. The closer they got to the lands of the Welsh princes, the more vivid Styrkar's memories of this place became.

It had been almost four years since he had last come here. Gruffydd of Llywelyn had proclaimed himself king of all Wales and become a thorn in the side of the English. Harold had no choice but to bring this Welsh warlord to heel. It had been a hard struggle, and Styrkar had carved out his formidable reputation in those bloody days of war. Eventually, Harold routed the Welsh armies to the four corners of their kingdom and was presented with Gruffydd's head by his own subjects. To add insult, Harold had also claimed the Welsh king's wife, Alditha, some years after.

Styrkar had mixed feelings about those days of battle. He had relished the chance to prove himself a deadly warrior, but that reputation had been hard won. The Welsh were fierce warriors, and Styrkar had to become a savage to match their ferocity. The Red Wolf had truly been born in the Welsh mountains. Now, as they neared the Marcher Lands, he could only hope the Red Wolf would rise once more, and this rebellious earl would give him the chance to rebuild his reputation on the corpses of a different enemy.

It was the morning of the fifth day and they had rested briefly in the night, before Styrkar roused the townsfolk of Coleselle. Osgar led the way once more. He was well travelled, spending his early days as a trader, and he had not led them awry so far, so Styrkar had no reason to doubt his sense of direction.

After some time walking a scant path under a dreary sky, Osgar stopped.

'What is it?' Kenric asked.

Osgar gazed at the mountains on the distant horizon to the west. To the north Styrkar could see a distant tower, most likely a church.

'We are here,' Osgar said. 'The Marcher Lands. Beyond those hills in the distance lie the kingdoms of the Welsh.'

'So now what?' Kenric replied. 'How do we find this Eadric?'

Osgar shrugged.

To the south, Styrkar could see a distant plume of dark smoke rising into the grey sky.

'That might be a good enough place to start,' he said, gesturing towards the steady stream of black smoke.

'That could just be the fires of a settlement,' Kenric said.

'Or a burned-out village.' Osgar sounded worried.

'Do either of you have any better ideas?' Styrkar asked.

The silence that followed was the only answer he needed.

Styrkar led them south towards the smoke. The closer they got, the more they realised that this was not the wood smoke of a longhouse or the fire from a smithy. The cloud was thick and drifting a long way on the breeze.

'Maybe we should think about this?' Kenric whispered as they got closer.

'And do what?' Styrkar said.

'How about not walking into a trap?'

'Then where should we go?' Styrkar snapped, fast losing his temper.

Kenric had no ideas, neither did Osgar. Despite the danger, the rest of their motley group followed them, the prospect of a Frankish patrol seeming to frighten them less than another day in the wilderness.

When they were close enough, they could see the wooden walls of the hamlet had been burned, and the blackened skeleton of the village within was visible. There was no sign of life – no wailing villagers, no pillaging Franks.

'You think it's safe?' Osgar asked.

'Only one way to find out,' Styrkar said, striding forward.

He picked his way through the fallen timbers of the gate, conscious that the rest of their refugee band was already following him. If there was someone lurking in wait they would stand no chance, but there was nowhere to run anyway.

Styrkar gripped his axe tight, looking around for any sign of life, but there was nothing but corpses and dead livestock. The bodies lay naked – if they had been Frankish knights then their armour had been stripped from them, but by the cut of their hair, everyone who had dwelt here was English.

Someone shouted out, and Styrkar turned, ready for battle, only to see a group of the refugees falling on the gutted carcass of a pig. There was no telling how long it had lain rotting in the mud, but these people were half starved, and didn't care. They took out their knives and began to butcher the carcass like wolves falling on a doe.

'I see no Franks,' said Osgar, gaping at the carnage. 'What has happened here?'

'Perhaps they took their dead with them?' said Kenric. 'Or they suffered no casualties?'

'Or maybe this was not the work of the Franks,' said Styrkar.

There was a clatter of timbers, and the men spun to see what had caused the commotion. From beneath the collapsed remnants of a nearby hut crawled a young man. His face was soot-blackened, his arms spindly, and he staggered towards them.

'Mercy,' he wailed in a child's voice. 'Please, mercy.'

As he fell to his knees at Osgar's feet, Styrkar could see he was but a boy. Osgar knelt beside him, offering water from a pigskin. The youth took a deep draught until he coughed spittle down his chin.

'What happened here, lad?' Osgar asked.

'They burned it,' the boy replied, through his sobs.

'Who did?' Osgar gripped the boy's arm, as though trying to squeeze the hysteria out of him. 'Was it the Franks?'

The boy began to focus, staring Osgar in the eye before shaking his head. 'No. It was the earl. Eadric the Wild did this. He knew we had given shelter to the Franks, but what choice did we have? They would have killed us if we refused. He came at night, razing this place to the ground so that the Franks could no longer use it and set everyone to flight.'

Once the words were out of his mouth, the boy collapsed to his hands and knees, sobbing uncontrollably. Osgar patted him on the back before rising to his feet.

Kenric turned to Styrkar, a worried expression on his face. 'Eadric did this? The man we have walked a hundred miles to join up with?'

Osgar glanced about the ruined settlement. 'He is as savage as the invaders,' he said.

Styrkar shook his head. 'This was not the work of a savage,' he replied. 'It is a sound strategy. Leave the enemy nowhere to rest or resupply.'

'Are you mad?' Osgar snapped. 'These folk are English. These are the very people he should be protecting.'

'Eadric is fighting a war,' Styrkar replied. 'These people are the casualties.'

'And what about our people? What will you tell them? That we seek to join up with a murderous savage who burns a village to hinder his enemies?'

'His enemies are our enemies, Osgar. Besides, if we do

not find Eadric soon it won't matter if he is a savage or a nobleman – we'll all be dead.'

'He's right,' said Kenric. 'If the Franks find us before we find Eadric none of this matters. He's our only hope.'

That did not seem to satisfy Osgar, and he tramped off to see if there was anything worth salvaging from the burned-out settlement. Styrkar allowed the refugees to search for what they could, but as the day turned to evening he gathered them together, and they headed west once more. They could not very well stay here. If a Frankish patrol was drawn to the smoke of the village they would be discovered for sure.

As the sun fell, they made camp and gathered around three fires. Osgar organised men to stand watch as he had done every other night, and Styrkar sat beside the fire until his turn came, pulling the filthy cloak he had salvaged from the settlement about him to ward off the cold.

The wind blew across the camp, sweeping the fires into dancing patterns as someone began to sing a low and mournful song. The lone voice was joined by a second, until half the camp was singing a soft lullaby to their slumbering children. It wasn't until a stranger stepped from the darkness into the firelight that the singing stopped.

Styrkar's hand went to the axe at his belt, and he silently cursed the men on guard for not doing their job. As the stranger came into the light, striking a hulking figure, Styrkar could see more newcomers lurking on the periphery of the camp.

Though there were more than twenty of them sitting about the fires, the man showed no fear. He was bedecked in furs, a vast mop of hair and beard covering his head. From within a scarred face stared two piercing eyes that shone on the firelight. As he peered through the darkness, Styrkar could see they were surrounded by a savage-looking mob, but they kept to the shadows, hanging back as their leader crouched by the flames.

'Don't mind if I warm myself awhile, do you?' said the warrior as he held up two meaty palms to the fire.

No one was brave enough to object, but Styrkar kept a hand next to his axe. If these were bandits they would find meagre pickings here, but Styrkar was determined he would not give anything up without a fight.

'So what brings you to the borderlands?' the warrior asked. 'This is dangerous country. There are robbers abroad. Welsh raiders and worse. You must be foolish or desperate to trespass in such a woe-begotten place.'

Styrkar glanced across the fire to Osgar. His gaze was lowered, and it was obvious he did not have the courage to speak. Likewise, Kenric kept his peace, which was unlike him. Not that Styrkar could blame the man for not wanting to single himself out.

'We have come searching for Earl Eadric,' Styrkar said. 'They say he fights the Franks, and we would join him in his rebellion.'

The man looked at Styrkar, fixing him with that piercing gaze. 'Eadric?' he said. 'The one they call the Wild? A savage man of violence, they say. A tyrant. A killer. Why would you seek out such a man?'

Styrkar sighed. 'Because the Franks burned our town. Because we have nowhere else to go.' He fixed the shaggy-looking bandit with a fierce gaze of his own. 'And because we would have justice.'

The bandit grinned, revealing a mouthful of smashed teeth. 'Are you a warrior, son? You look the part, at least.'

Kenric rose to his feet, and Styrkar could tell he was fighting his fear. 'This is Styrkar, the Red Wolf. The Franks fear him more than any other. More so than Earl Eadric.'

The bandit seemed impressed as he regarded Styrkar. 'I have heard the name. That's quite a reputation to live up to.'

Styrkar rose to his feet, and the man stood with him. 'I have no worries on that score,' he said. 'So, do you think this Eadric would let us join him?'

The man grinned his gap-toothed grin. Slowly he nodded.

'I reckon I would,' Eadric said.

He stepped forward and grasped Styrkar's forearm. They regarded one another for a moment, as the light of the fire danced in both their eyes.

'Welcome, Red Wolf. And don't worry. There'll be plenty of chances for you to prove that reputation of yours.'

As they grasped arms in the firelight, Styrkar could only hope the chance would come soon.

PART THREE

LOYALTY DIVIDED

28

RECORDINE, ENGLAND, JULY 1067

They waited in the pitch black, each man silent but for their heavy breathing. Behind them the river ran past gently, a dozen boats lashed together and bobbing on the current. Twenty men hid in the reeds, watching as the torches atop the walls of the fort winked in the night.

Styrkar heard the distant sound of laughter. How they loved to laugh, these Franks. They seemed to find mirth in everything; with every meal, with every horse they rode, with every town they burned or woman they raped. They wouldn't be laughing for long.

Kenric moved forward and made to speak, but Styrkar held up a hand for him to hold his tongue. They had been told to keep their mouths shut; any sign that they were here might ruin the whole raid. Styrkar knew better than anyone the importance of keeping your mouth closed and your eyes open, to cage the killing rage that might be building up inside until the right time. It was clear Kenric did not share that experience, but he did as he was bid, and kept his words to himself. Styrkar could sense the fear in his friend, but the man was not alone.

Osgar was not far away, his face half hidden in shadow. Styrkar could see he was gritting his teeth, but his eyes were fearful. In recent days he had shed his oversized gut, and looked more a warrior than ever. Whether he would do more than just look the part remained to be seen.

Not a single man wore any mail and only a few had shields. Their weapons were poorly crafted swords and axes, or weapons for farming or butchery. One man even carried a crooked billet. Styrkar gripped an axe that would have been more suited to skinning bark than taking Frankish heads, but it was all he had and he would make the most of its use.

He could not tell how long they had been waiting in the dark. Styrkar's own impatience was growing, but he fought it back. Eadric had ordered them to wait until the main force gained entry, then upon his signal they should charge. What that signal might be, he had not made entirely clear, but Styrkar was sure he would recognise it when it happened.

From the darkness surrounding the fort, Styrkar saw a sudden movement. Eadric's men were rushing to their positions, and tension gripped the score of men that surrounded Styrkar. This was it; their time would soon arrive.

Two Frankish sentries stood guard outside the gate, idly chatting in their bastard language, and Styrkar could see Eadric's men moving towards them. Four archers drew their bows and the swift volley of arrows saw the Franks fall silently to the earth.

Towards the northern side of the wooden palisade,

Styrkar could just make out men throwing ropes across the top of the fortifications. He felt a twinge of jealousy as they began to scale the wall, wishing he were among their number, the first to whet their blades upon the Franks within the walls.

Silently they crept over the palisade and into the fort. There was more nervous quiet, but for the heavy breathing all around, as Eadric's men did their work. Then the silence was broken.

A single panicked shout split the night air – Styrkar could not make out the words or even the language it was in before he heard a clash of steel. The front gate quivered as though something heavy had struck it from inside, before it was violently flung open.

There was a deep bellow – a wordless cry of rage as Eadric leapt from the darkness onto the path to the fort. His cry was joined by a host of others as his men burst from cover and they charged the gate.

Styrkar watched them rush inside, the light from the fort illuminating the path. Eadric led his warriors from the front, and their shouts of fury echoed across the flat ground to the river. It was as much as Styrkar could take, and he stood, preparing himself to race into the fray.

Before he could take another step, someone grabbed his arm. Looking back he saw Leofstan, one of the refugees from Coleselle, looking at him fearfully.

'We haven't had the signal yet,' he said. It was clear he was in no mood to thrust himself into the violence.

'What more signal do you need?' Styrkar snarled.

He wrenched his arm away from Leofstan's grip and burst from the cover of the reeds. The ground was boggy beneath his feet, but he still rushed towards the open gate. He was encouraged to hear footsteps behind him, as more men followed.

The corpses of the two Frankish sentries lay on the path and he jumped over their arrow-strewn bodies, dashing through the gate, gripping his axe tight in his fist. Inside, all was carnage. The sounds and smells assaulted Styrkar's senses, blinded as he was by the bright light within. Men grunted in pain and anger, swords clashed, the hot sweat stink of men fighting for their lives.

Eadric had taken the Franks by surprise, but they had ordered themselves quickly. To the north end of the courtyard they stood in a shield wall, repelling Eadric's men with their spears. For their part, the attackers threw themselves at the Franks with a ferocity Styrkar had not seen since Senlac. They had paid for that ferocity with their lives, and already half a dozen of them lay dead or wounded on the ground.

Separate battles were taking place all across the courtyard, and as soon as Styrkar's eyes adjusted he saw two men wrestling nearby. As he darted towards them, he recognised Stithulf, one of Eadric's most trusted men, grappling with a knight. They held a blade between them and it was hard to see which of them had the advantage.

Styrkar raised his axe, bellowing with all his might. The Frank had enough time to look at him, a mournful expression crossing his face, before Styrkar planted the axe in his face. He fell back, Styrkar pouncing on top of him, the red rage boiling up inside. With a snarl he wrenched the axe free and brought it down again once, twice, just to make sure the deed was done right.

As he stood, Styrkar could see the courtyard had been reduced to a wild slaughter. The Frankish shield wall had collapsed, and they fought in a desperate melee, one or two of them already fleeing through the gate in terror.

A long axe lay on the ground, the fallen weapon of one of Eadric's men, and Styrkar moved towards it. He dropped the hand axe and picked up the bigger weapon, feeling its reassuring weight in his grip.

Raising it high, he finally succumbed to the hot rage within, unleashing the baresark with a cry of feral hunger. Two Franks stood side by side, desperately defending themselves with spear and sword. Styrkar smashed into them with his shoulder, knocking one to the ground where he fell with a clatter. A devastating backswing caught the second knight, and he let out a choked cry as the axe broke his neck.

Styrkar looked down. The second knight was trying to rise to his feet, shield and spear lost to him. The Frank looked up as Styrkar raised his axe high, giving him enough time to see what fate awaited him, before the weapon came down and crushed his chest.

The cries of the combatants grew more desperate as Styrkar searched for his next foe. He looked for where the fighting was thickest, rushing towards the foreign knights in time to see Osgar take a spear to the chest. His friend fell, but Styrkar was too lost in the haze of battle to care, throwing himself into the fray, his bloodlust taking over.

His axe rose and fell, hacking down any man brave or stupid enough to face him. Blood spattered his arms and chest. He could taste it on his lips, feeding his lust for death.

Someone barged into him, and Styrkar turned to see the face of Eadric, staring with his own wild-eyed bloodlust.

'Good that you could join us, Red Wolf,' he bellowed, before they both tore into their enemies again.

The earl fought with sword and shield, battering at the remaining Franks, forcing them into submission. Styrkar added his axe to the slaughter until finally the surviving knights threw down their arms.

They shouted in their foreign tongue, but the meaning was obvious.

'They have surrendered,' someone shouted.

Still it took some time for Eadric's men to stop their slaughter. Styrkar's blood was up, his hunger not sated, and he heaved in a deep breath, trying to calm the rage within. He was not done yet.

'Get them on their knees,' Eadric ordered.

His men made quick work of subduing the Franks, dragging the helmets from their heads and prodding them with sword and spear.

Styrkar looked down at the dozen men left alive. Most of them averted their eyes to the ground, but one of them looked up, fear marring his youthful features. Styrkar stared back, recognising the terror, knowing the man was beaten, but it was not enough. The wolf within him had to be satisfied.

With a grunt of fury, he raised his axe one last time and brought it down on the hapless prisoner. The rest of the Franks began to beg more fervently as they saw Styrkar murder their fellow knight, but all Eadric could do was laugh at the dark deed.

'The Red Wolf has shown you the way,' Eadric shouted at his men. 'We take no prisoners this night.'

That was all the encouragement his warriors needed,

and Styrkar stood back, watching as the rest of the men fell upon their captives, slaughtering them to the last.

He had little sympathy for the Franks. They had come to do murder all their own, but as he began to calm, as the baresark left him trembling in the night, Styrkar could only regret his rash act.

Other prisoners had been dragged from the huts within the compound now, but these were not foreigners. As they protested at the brutish treatment of Eadric's men it was obvious they were English. Neither Eadric nor his men seemed to care, and they too were driven to their knees in the courtyard.

Styrkar looked away, unable to watch, and as he did his eyes fell on the body of Osgar on the ground. He stared up at the night sky, the spear still protruding from his chest. Osgar had been a good man, but was now just another casualty of the invasion.

'Wait,' Styrkar said, before he realised what he was saying.

'What?' said Eadric. His men stood over the English prisoners, their weapons poised.

'These people are not our enemies,' Styrkar replied. 'They should be spared.'

'They have made their loyalties clear. They are traitors.'

Styrkar scanned the row of pitiful faces. It was obvious there was not a warrior among them. He remembered Osgar's outrage when they had discovered the razed village some days before, and he knew what the man would have thought of this wanton murder.

'Did we come here to kill our countrymen, or kill the Franks? Our cause would be better served by sparing these people. Let them spread word of this victory. Let your deeds be spoken of throughout the land.'

Eadric looked at the sorry group on their knees. It was clear his own lust for slaughter was abating, and slowly he nodded.

'Very well, Red Wolf. Let them go,' he ordered.

The prisoners needed no further encouragement, scrambling to their feet and rushing towards the gate.

'Run, bastards,' Wulfsige shouted after them. He was Eadric's right hand, and a man Styrkar hadn't liked from the moment they met. 'Tell the new king that Eadric the Wild rules these lands now.'

With that he raised his voice, shouting Eadric's name again and again until he was joined by other warriors from the earl's band of outlaws.

Styrkar heard another shout, at first quieter than the rest, then louder, until that too was joined in a chorus.

'Red Wolf, Red Wolf, Red Wolf.'

He turned to see Kenric, and some of the others shouting his name and they didn't stop until the cries of "Eadric" had been drowned out.

When the cheering was done, and they began to strip the Frankish bodies of their mail and weapons, Styrkar felt a strong hand clap him on the shoulder.

'You fought well,' Eadric said, a wide grin now replacing the scowl he had worn during the fight. 'Soon the men will look to you to lead them in battle, and I will become the follower.'

'You have nothing to fear from me,' Styrkar replied. 'I am no leader, and neither would I want to be.'

Eadric clapped him on the arm. 'Sometimes we don't get

to choose what we become,' he said, before joining his men in the pillage.

Styrkar knew he was right. It was obvious Eadric had not chosen to become a chieftain among outlaws. For his part, Styrkar would accept any fate, as long as it meant he could continue to kill the Franks.

29

MERLEBERGE, ENGLAND, JULY 1067

Ronan had lost the trail days ago. Though his men had been angered by that, the uprising at Coleselle had only served to increase their zeal. Many of them were wounded, their brothers dead. More than one of them had burns and scars that would act as constant reminders of their failure. That was good. It would instil the need for revenge against these stinking peasants, and that would make them follow him into Hell if he needed them to.

A burn on Ronan's forearm would serve as reminder enough for him. It was bandaged, and for almost a week he had struggled with a fever, fearing it was infected. But he had pulled through, and now he had an ugly wound to look upon every time he needed some encouragement that the Red Wolf had to be found.

'Where is he?' Ronan said again.

It had been the same question he'd asked in a dozen such places throughout this part of the country. He and his men had left a trail of carnage in their wake, but always the answer had been the same.

'I don't know, my lord,' said the old man.

He was lashed to a waterwheel. It seemed the most inventive way to question these people under the circumstances, and anything that assuaged the boredom was a welcome distraction.

Ronan sighed as he crouched by the mill. The place was relatively peaceful, the rest of the townsfolk would be cowering in their hovels. Just another shit-pit on a long winding road of shit-pits. This one stood out somewhat – it was bigger than the ones before, and there were ancient burial mounds not far from its centre. Testament to this country's ancient and noble history. There was nothing noble about it now.

'Do you need reminding what will happen if you don't tell me what I want to know?' Ronan said.

Some of his men sniggered at the prospect, but Ronan was taking no pleasure in this. He was as frustrated with asking the same questions as the old man was being tied to that waterwheel. Which of them would break first was still a tough question to answer.

'Please, my lord. I don't know who this Red Wolf is.'

Always the same answer in every shitty town. Ronan was beginning to grow angry, and not just with their silence. He'd had enough of this country and its people. They stank and all they ate was bread, hard mouldy cheese and swine. In fact he'd never been to a place that had so many different words for pig.

Of course there was every chance this man was telling

the truth and he really had no idea who the Red Wolf was, but Ronan could not take the chance. Styrkar the Dane had escaped him, and in the process Ronan had been humiliated. He had lost men, but that had paled next to the damage to his reputation. How was he to rise and become a man of wealth and status when the rest of King William's army was laughing at him? He had no choice but to see this through to the end.

'Where is the Red Wolf?' he repeated with a sigh. The words were starting to bore him. 'Where are the other rebels? An entire town went missing, man. Someone must have heard something.'

'My lord, I don't know. We haven't seen or heard a thing. I swear by almighty God.'

'We know they came this way,' said Ronan, the tedium of it all making him angrier. 'Over a score of people must have passed right by here. Do you seriously expect me to believe not one person saw anything? No one heard a baby crying? Not one of these rebels asked for food or shelter?'

'Nothing, my lord. I swear it.'

Ronan had heard enough, and signalled to two of his men. They had jammed the waterwheel with heavy spears and by levering them they turned the wheel, submerging the old man beneath the surface of the water.

He gasped before his head went under, and there was more laughter from the knights surrounding Ronan. Three of them were even wagering whether or not the old fool would still be alive when he came back up.

As Ronan waited, giving the old man long enough to think below the water, he glanced over, seeing Aldus standing there. His old companion gave nothing away as he watched proceedings. Not even a smile or a wink to let Ronan know he was doing the right thing. There was no one to temper Ronan's methods. No one to let him know if this was the right course of action or if he was going too far. Maybe one day, somewhere, there would be a guiding hand – but whoever it might be they were not here now.

'Let him up,' Ronan ordered.

His men levered the waterwheel and the old man appeared from beneath the surface with a splash of water and a gasp of air. He heaved breath into his lungs, making a pitiful choking sound, which might have evoked sympathy from a different crowd of onlookers.

'I swear, my lord,' he gasped desperately. 'I don't know what you're looking for.'

Ronan's hands balled into fists. He had suffered enough of this. 'I've given you every chance,' he spat. 'All you have to do is tell me what you know. Don't you realise how reasonable I'm being? Were I the king you'd have lost a hand by now. Or at the very least an ear. So I'll give you one last chance before I let my men cut your feet off. Where is the Red Wolf?'

The old man sobbed. Whether he was weeping was difficult to tell due to the water dripping from his sodden face. 'My lord... please...'

Ronan let out a long sigh, nodding to the spearmen again. They levered the wheel once more and the old man was lowered into the water. This time he did not have the chance to take a gasp of air.

More bets were placed as they waited. Ronan watched the murky waters as he gave the old man plenty of time to have a change of heart.

'Up,' he said, and his men obeyed.

This time when the man rose from beneath the surface he did not gasp for air. He simply hung from the waterwheel, drenched and limp.

One of the men behind him shouted in triumph and coins were reluctantly exchanged. With a sigh of disappointment, Ronan left them to untie the corpse and made his way back to the town. Another dead end. Another day with no clue as to where the Red Wolf had gone.

He gritted his teeth in anger as he limped into the empty marketplace. He knew the English would be watching him from within their huts, fearfully wondering which one of them would be dragged out next and put to the question, but Ronan had suffered his fill for one day.

As he made his way to the longhouse he had requisitioned for his own shelter, one of his men came racing down the street.

'A contingent of riders is on the way,' the man said breathlessly.

'Englishmen?' Ronan asked, fearing rebels.

'No, they're Normans. I think it's Willem of Breteuil by the look of his standard.'

'FitzOsbern?' Ronan said, immediately thinking that an attack of rebels might be easier to face. 'Gather the men. And be quick about it.'

The man rushed off, shouting for the other knights to muster. Aldus was at Ronan's shoulder immediately, and he felt some relief to have his towering friend at his side.

When his men gathered he was dissatisfied to see hardly any wore their mail. Most had stripped to their jerkins since they had arrived in this place and he would never get them looking like soldiers before the Lord of Breteuil arrived. Nevertheless, Ronan did his best to make sure he and his contingent were at least presentable by the time Willem and his riders entered the settlement.

Willem FitzOsbern looked imperious as he trotted into the town ahead of his entourage. Each one of his men was a disciplined knight – a warrior of distinction – and Ronan couldn't help but feel a pang of jealousy. The Lord of Breteuil reined in his horse, glancing around the deserted hamlet with a disdainful frown.

'My lord.' Ronan bowed as Willem dismounted. 'We weren't expecting such an esteemed guest.'

The Lord of Breteuil was every inch the Norman warlord, striking a powerful figure. Though his hair was thin and greying on top, his thick moustache hung well below his chin, more than compensating for his bald pate.

He scanned the waiting honour guard until his eyes fell on Ronan. He didn't even try to hide his displeasure.

'You are?' Willem asked.

Of course Ronan would not expect this man to recognise him from the battle against King Harold. Why would he? Ronan had only risked his life so his betters could benefit from land and riches.

'I am Ronan of Dol-Combourg, my lord. Son of Rivallon. I fought during King William's victory as part of Brian of Penthièvre's conrois.'

Willem looked unconvinced. 'I have met Rivallon. Don't remember him mentioning a son called Ronan. No matter. What are you doing here?'

Another reminder of Ronan's lack of legitimacy, and why he rarely used his father's name. He bit down the anger it suddenly kindled. 'I am on a mission for Lord Brian. In pursuit of a notorious rebel.'

The Lord of Breteuil gazed about the deserted town. 'And how is the pursuit going?'

'Making more progress each passing day, my lord,' Ronan lied.

'My men have been on the road for two days,' Willem said, clearly unconcerned with Ronan's mission. 'We will stay here the night.'

'Of course, my lord. I will have food and lodging laid on for your men. You will be given the longhouse.'

Willem seemed unimpressed when Ronan gestured to the long wooden hut that stood in pride of place at the centre of the town.

'Most generous,' replied the Lord of Breteuil.

Ronan took pains to make Willem as comfortable as possible. For the rest of the day, he rallied the English townsfolk to raid their food stocks and found someone able to prepare what might pass for a feast.

When darkness fell, Ronan found himself at the table in the longhouse. Willem sat at the head of it, his most loyal knights at his side. Ronan should have left them to it, but the opportunity to dine with one of the most powerful men in England was too good to spurn.

'What brings you from the west, my lord?' Ronan asked, when the conversation lagged enough for him to speak.

A couple of Willem's men glanced towards Ronan, as though wondering what gave him the right to speak, but Willem seemed unconcerned by any lack of etiquette.

'I have been inspecting my garrisons in the Marcher

Lands,' he replied. 'I had to bolster the number of troops garrisoned there due to the recent troubles.'

'Troubles, my lord?'

Willem ran a hand through his impressive moustache. 'A defiant English earl by the name of Eadric. He has raised a rebel army, determined to reclaim the lands he lost to the king. He stands no chance, of course. It won't be long before he gets what is coming.'

Ronan was about to answer that he was having much the same trouble, when servants arrived bearing wooden platters. Each one was a man or woman Willem had brought in his entourage. Ronan could only assume they were English slaves Willem had freed from bondage... and now used as his personal retainers. They served the meagre fare, and Ronan looked down at the soup of barley, oats and rabbit. It almost turned his stomach.

'My apologies, lord,' he said. 'This is the best I could muster at such short notice. I am sure you are used to much better.'

Willem shook his head as he swallowed a mouthful as though it were the finest cut of venison.

'Nonsense. You will learn that any food is the food of lords. When the king and I were but children we spent months in the wilds. Food like this would have been a feast. I have never forgotten where I come from, Ronan of Dol-Combourg, and neither should you. No matter how far you rise.'

'Of course, my lord,' Ronan said quickly conscious of the smirking knights surrounding him at the table. 'I am well aware of your humble beginnings. A remarkable rise to power. Both you and the king are extraordinary men.'

The flattery didn't seem to do him any good, and Willem merely shovelled more food into his mouth. As he watched, Ronan could only feel further contempt. It was true that Willem and the king were friends as boys, that they had been under threat of murder for much of their childhoods, but for Willem to plead poverty was laughable. He was the high-born son of a Norman lord. It was inevitable he would rise to become a powerful man. But then Ronan had witnessed many men from rich backgrounds feign humility. It made their hypocrisy all the more difficult to swallow.

'You mentioned you were in pursuit of a fugitive,' Willem said, wiping his moustache on his sleeve. 'Tell me, how do you intend to track him down?'

All eyes turned to Ronan. How was he to admit that the trail had gone cold? That the fugitive he sought had disappeared, and half a town along with him?

'The Red Wolf is a devious quarry,' Ronan said. 'Ruthless. Savage. But I will find him soon. The English cannot conceal him forever, and a man of such wanton ferocity will not stay hidden for long.'

'So you will continue to burn and torture until you get what you want?'

It seemed a curious question. Willem of Breteuil was no stranger to torture and dismemberment to get what he wanted, so why ask?

'If the English refuse to abandon their old ways and accept the new, they must be forced,' Ronan said, hoping that was the right answer.

'Perhaps,' Willem said thoughtfully. 'Or perhaps it is time we stopped ravaging this land. We intend to be here for some time. The king will have to unite his people sooner or later, or we'll be fighting rebellions for a hundred years.'

'These people are swill-drinking, lice-ridden, pock-marked scum. They are beneath us in every way. With the greatest of respect, Lord Willem, we are their betters and the only way they will come to our side is if we first bring them to heel.'

Ronan stopped to take a breath. He realised he had begun to rant. It was obvious he had spent too long in pursuit of the Red Wolf and it was starting to show.

'I take it Lord Brian is happy for his men to be romping across the countryside, slaughtering the king's subjects?'

It began to feel like Ronan was in a trap. Was Willem interested in his progress, or was he trying to criticise his methods?

'He is happy for us to do the king's work, my lord.'

'Or perhaps he has sent you on a fool's errand.'

Not the first time Ronan had heard that. 'My lord, the Red Wolf is a danger to the king and his men. His rebellion might be small now, but as you have seen in the west – one man can light a spark that sets the whole land aflame. I would stamp out this fire before it takes. No matter how many bog-trotting peasants I have to drown in the river.'

Willem raised his cup and drank deep. All was silent, not even his men spoke among themselves anymore. Ronan began to wonder if he'd overstepped the mark, but then Willem gave a long sigh and rose to his feet. The rest of his men also stood, and Ronan thought it best to do the same.

'We have a long road tomorrow,' Willem said. 'I would retire to my lodgings. Your hospitality is appreciated, Ronan of Dol-Combourg.'

With that he left, and his men followed to bed down for the night. Ronan stepped out of the longhouse, watching as they made their way to the huts set aside for them, marvelling at the discipline and obedience of Willem's followers. If only his own men were so dedicated.

As he watched, he saw someone lingering in the shadows nearby. They looked nervous, which could have meant danger, and Ronan's hand strayed to the knife at his side.

'Please, my lord,' said a low voice. 'I would speak with you.'

'Come into the bloody light then,' Ronan hissed.

The figure moved forward, and Ronan could see it was a young lad he vaguely recognised as one of Willem's servants who had brought their platters at dinner.

'Speak,' he said, as the boy moved his weight nervously from one foot to the other.

'My lord, I thought it best to speak with you in private. I am in service to Lord Willem and while in the Marcher Lands I heard news you might find... useful.'

The boy stopped. It was obvious what he was after, and with a sigh Ronan took a coin from the purse at his belt. He could just have beaten the information out of the lad, but this was one of Lord Willem's personal retainers. Besides, it had been a long day and he was growing weary.

'Out with it,' Ronan said, handing over the coin.

'In the Marcher Lands we heard much of the rebellion. Much of Earl Eadric and his raids on the Frankish garrisons. But I heard another name mentioned. A fierce warrior fighting at the earl's side, known as the Red Wolf.'

The hairs suddenly stood on the back of Ronan's neck. 'Where were you when you heard this name?'

'It was in Hereford, my lord. People were talking about it out of earshot of… your people, my lord. But that was the name. The Red Wolf. They say he is fierce—'

'Yes, yes,' Ronan replied, having heard more than enough. 'You can piss off now.'

He watched as the boy scurried off into the darkness.

Hereford was not too far to the northwest. And it made sense that one rebel would be attracted to the stink of another.

Ronan smiled in the dark. What was it Willem had said? A fool's errand? Well, he would soon see how much a fool's errand it was when he was in the Marcher Lands.

This Earl Eadric and the Red Wolf were in the same place. Perhaps he would soon have the chance to place two heads at King William's feet.

30

THE LONG FOREST, ENGLAND, JULY 1067

Styrkar trod carefully across the dry forest floor. It had not rained for days, leaving the brush dry and brittle beneath his feet, and any noise might scare off his quarry. The bow felt awkward in his hand. He was unused to the feel of it – a coward's weapon and one he had made little use of in the past. Give him sword, axe and shield any day. But this was work unsuited to such weapons.

Kenric stalked through the trees a few feet away, making no sound. He was much better suited to the bow, and his brow was furrowed as he squinted through the woodland. It was as though the raid on Coleselle had never happened, and the two of them were back to hunting in the forests that surrounded the town. The only difference was this time they had much bigger game than rabbits in mind.

The deer was not far away. Though they could not see it, Styrkar knew it was somewhere beyond the mass of trees ahead. They had tracked it for miles and now they were almost upon the beast. It was elusive quarry, but he and

Kenric could track pretty much anything. Spotting and killing it was a different matter, and even with the bow in his hands, Styrkar was not wholly confident they would eat tonight.

Kenric stopped, spotting something up ahead, and Styrkar slowly lowered himself to one knee, peering through the wood. Light shone down through the canopy, casting long shadows and not for the first time Styrkar hoped they were downwind of the beast, lest their scent give them away and put their quarry to flight.

As his eyes scanned the trees in the distance they fell upon a russet hide. Styrkar froze at the sight of the buck and his heart beat all the faster. The animal had not spotted them yet.

He raised his hand in a silent gesture for Kenric to go north and outflank the beast, but he was already moving. Styrkar held his breath as he stepped closer to the animal, using the trees for cover, hiding behind the sturdy trunks but keeping the beast's hindquarters in sight.

When he was within thirty yards he stopped, hunkering down behind low-hanging branches, waiting for the buck to step out from beyond the tree. If he shot it in the hindquarters it might flee, and they would have to track it for miles until it died. Better to wait until its head and neck were exposed and bring the animal down instantly.

Taking a breath, Styrkar nocked and drew, feeling the tension in the bowstring. His aim had never been the best, but he was sure at this range even he could strike the beast.

There was a crack of snapping twigs.

'Shit,' shouted Kenric, as the deer bolted.

Styrkar loosed, a poor shot that narrowly missed its

target. He fumbled another arrow from the quiver, desperate to keep one eye on his quarry before it dashed into cover. He heard the sound of another arrow being loosed as he nocked, but Kenric missed as well. The buck was almost out of sight as he drew again.

An arrow struck the deer before he could even aim. A perfect shot, hitting its target full in the chest. The buck went down in a flurry of leaves, the arrow pierced through its heart.

Styrkar stood, chiding himself for his lack of skill as Stithulf stepped out of the shadows. His wide smile said it all.

'A great shot, my friend,' Kenric said, stepping forward to pat Stithulf on the shoulder. 'We work well together, yes?'

'All you did was put the animal to flight,' said Styrkar shaking his head. 'Stithulf needed no help from you.'

'And what was your contribution?' Kenric said. 'You couldn't hit the side of a pig barn from five paces.'

Styrkar shrugged. 'The bow is not my weapon. Give me a sturdy axe any day.'

Kenric laughed at that. 'I'd like to see you hunt down a deer with an axe, my Danish friend. That would be a feat to behold.'

'I'll give you a feat to behold,' Styrkar replied, already binding the buck's feet. As the two men watched him, he heaved the animal across his shoulders, taking the weight of it on his own. Neither of his friends seemed impressed, but Stithulf was still smiling, pleased with his work and happy to let Styrkar contribute to the hunt in his own way.

'It's a good job you came with us,' Styrkar said to the young warrior. 'Otherwise we would have gone hungry tonight.'

'Glad I could help,' Stithulf replied with a wink.

Though he would never have said it, Styrkar liked the man. He was one of Eadric's most loyal warriors, but Styrkar had grown to know him well over the days he had spent in the outlaw camp. Where the rest of Eadric's warriors had treated the newcomers with suspicion, Stithulf had welcomed them into the fold.

It did not take them long to reach Eadric's camp, and Styrkar had to suffer Kenric's usual blether for a mercifully short time. The settlement sat in the middle of the Long Forest, miles from any kind of civilisation, but it was a bustling community all its own. Eadric's rebels had grown to number in the hundreds and the place had been organised like any other town.

Women tanned and beat hides for armour, scaled and filleted fish and took care of their children while the men sharpened their axes and practised for war. The place was abuzz with life, even ringing with the sound of a smith's hammer as he tempered blades in the makeshift forge.

'I'll look forward to some of that meat later,' Stithulf said, waving them off. 'I must see the fletcher about more arrows.'

Kenric bid him goodbye and Styrkar gave him a knowing nod as they made their way to the stump of a mighty fallen oak. Styrkar hefted the deer carcass onto the flat surface. It had been flattened into a makeshift table, a perfect surface for the butchery to come.

Styrkar pulled his knife as Kenric went to stow their bows and quivers. As he slit the beast's belly to draw out the guts he saw a couple of hounds moving forward with interest, but they kept their distance. They had learned the hard way not to bother Styrkar when he worked.

There were many mouths to feed within the camp, but so far no one had gone hungry. They could only hope that in a few months, when winter drew in and food became sparse, they would have enough stored to survive.

'Butchery suits you.'

Styrkar recognised the voice, and did not turn to acknowledge it. Wulfsige was Eadric's most loyal – the earl's trusted housecarl, but Styrkar could not find it in him to respect the man. He was blunt and disrespectful, and one day Styrkar might well have to teach him some manners.

'The earl wants to see you,' Wulfsige said.

Styrkar opened up the buck from neck to balls and grabbed a handful of guts. One pull and they spilled out onto the ground, causing one of the nearby hounds to keen hungrily.

'He wants to see you now.' Wulfsige was fast losing patience. 'So do as you're bid.'

Styrkar turned, one hand bloody, the other still holding the knife.

'I don't take orders from you,' he replied.

Wulfsige stared, hand on the blade at his belt. Styrkar could see a twitch in his eye, and knew what he was thinking – could he draw his own knife and attack before Styrkar buried his weapon in the man's neck? It was unlikely.

Before either of them could make their move, Kenric appeared between them.

'I can take that off your hands,' Kenric said, trying to be helpful but just getting in the way.

He held his hand out for the knife as Styrkar and Wulfsige continued to stare at one another. The tension was palpable, but Styrkar was not willing to relent. He would be damned if he'd back down to this bastard. Luckily he didn't have to, and Wulfsige moved his hand away from the weapon at his belt.

'Styrkar,' Kenric said, still holding his hand out for the knife.

Slowly, Styrkar handed the weapon over.

Wulfsige backed away, and Styrkar turned and headed off to find the earl.

Eadric's longhouse was on the edge of the encampment. It was a rudimentary building fashioned from crudely carved logs. It looked every bit a part of the forest as the trees themselves. A ramshackle building for a ramshackle war chief.

Styrkar offered a cursory nod to the two housecarls standing guard at the door. They nodded back at him, recognising the Red Wolf and standing aside to allow him entry. When Styrkar walked inside he could feel the stifling heat of the fire burning in the crude hearth. It gave off a warm glow that illuminated the gloomy interior of the room. The place smelled stale – rotting leaves and vegetation. There was no doubt that he was in the heart of the forest.

'The Red Wolf,' Eadric said as Styrkar entered.

The earl was seated on his makeshift throne, staring at a piece of parchment in his hand. He looked up, seeing the big Dane and the blood covering his left hand.

'Been on the hunt, I see,' he said, standing up and placing the parchment down on the long feasting table in front of him. 'You must be thirsty, and I have wine.'

'Don't waste it on me, my lord,' Styrkar replied. 'It has never been to my liking.'

'An acquired taste, I'll admit,' Eadric replied, filling two wooden cups from a battered pewter jug. 'But trust me, it grows on you. And I took this in our last raid on the Franks. It would be a shame to see it go sour.'

He offered the cup and Styrkar took it without further complaint. The earl drank deep, and Styrkar took a sip. The dark liquid was rich and spicy as it went down his throat. The smell of it almost made him gag but he swallowed it down anyway.

'I have received word from the west,' Eadric said, placing his empty cup down. 'From the Welsh princes of Gwynedd and Powys. The brothers Bleddyn and Rhiwallon have answered my call.' He picked up the parchment and held it out for Styrkar to read.

'I never learned, my lord,' Styrkar said.

Eadric shrugged. 'And why would you? What use has a man such as you for reading?' He put the parchment back on the table. 'It is an offer of alliance. The Welsh are to join our fight against the invader.'

'The Welsh?' Styrkar asked. 'They are savages. Treacherous murderers. How can you think they will honour such an alliance?'

Eadric nodded. 'All of that is true, Styrkar, but I do not have the luxury of being able to pick and choose my allies. Look around you. We are exiled to the forest. No one else is coming to stand by our side. And I need strong sword arms and savage bastards by my side if I am to defeat the Franks and reclaim what is mine.'

'You think you can trust them?'

Eadric laughed. 'No, son. I don't think I can trust them as far as I can spit. Which is why I want you by my side when I go meet them. If you're willing?'

'Do I have a choice?' Styrkar asked.

'We all have a choice, Styrkar.'

But did he? Eadric was a man who valued loyalty, and Styrkar admired him for that. It was obvious this was a test of that loyalty. Joining with the Welsh could well have been a foolish move that would see them all murdered in their sleep. Styrkar had fought the Welsh by King Harold's side and he knew full well what savages they were. In this though, he had no real choice.

'I will stand by your side, my lord. If that is what you ask.'

'It's settled then,' said Eadric, a wide broken-toothed grin appearing amidst his shaggy beard.

He picked up the jug and refilled the wooden cups, clacking his against the one in Styrkar's hand before they both downed the wine. This time, Styrkar found himself grimacing less as he swallowed. Perhaps he was already acquiring the taste for it.

When they had eventually drained the jug of its wine, Styrkar left Eadric in the longhouse to plan his meeting with the Welsh princes. Outside in the fresh air, he began to think further on the alliance, but no matter how he tried to convince himself that Eadric was doing the right thing, he could not get over the thought they were putting themselves in more danger.

But it was not Styrkar's decision to make. To his dread, he began to realise that once again he had no choice in this. No choice in where he was forced to go and who he might fight. The Red Wolf was once again beholden to another lord. His fate no longer his own.

31

HEREFORD, ENGLAND, AUGUST 1067

The town of Hereford was only a stone's throw from the castle that loomed over the settlement like a vast defensive bastion, but as Gisela walked along the street there was still an air of tension about the place. The sun beamed, the sky was clear, and in every other way it was a beautiful day, but for the smell. Sewage ran in the streets and the river was used as a privy, but Gisela had long since grown used to the stink of it.

She could already hear the market: the hustle and bustle of the traders and the tinkers, the merchants who had come from far and wide, bellowing their lungs out like their lives depended on it. Hereford was a hub for local trade, linking north to south, and the mix of accents and dialects made strange music.

As she reached the edge of the town she nodded curtly to the men who stood guarding the gate. They recognised her face and that she was a servant of the local lord, and thus knew not to challenge her. It was a luxury she had grown used to, but it did not make her feel any more important. Gisela knew her place, and no amount of deference from the town guards would change that.

Lady Agnes had fallen foul of yet another malady, and Gisela was determined to find some remedy for her mistress. There was bound to be something that she could buy in the bustling market of Hereford to ease Agnes' woes.

Gisela made her way past the stallholders and the market traders shouting over one another for passing trade. Soon she was lost in the crowd, appreciating the anonymity. Though her face might be occasionally recognised she was sure no one knew her name. How she would like to get used to that; to be one of the ordinary folk again, but she knew she was a stranger here and no matter how much she longed for it, would never fit in. As soon as she opened her mouth she marked herself as an outsider, her accent revealing her as a foreigner, an invader.

Nevertheless, she pushed her way through the crowds, determined to reach a meat seller. It would most likely be pig, but perhaps she could purchase a chicken for a broth if she was lucky. Before she managed to follow her nose to the right place, her attention was drawn to a lone stall at the edge of the market.

An old woman stood behind her display of wares. She was silent, not bothering to compete with the other vendors as they shouted their lungs out across the marketplace. Gisela slowly approached, marvelling at the array of fine cloths the woman had for sale. As she looked closer she saw silks and lace, material she had never seen on this island before. Gisela reached out a hand, touching the fabric, feeling it soft against her fingertips. It reminded her of her childhood, of the fine dresses her mother used to make. Gisela swallowed hard at the memory; it brought back only thoughts of sorrow and loss.

'Where have these come from?' Gisela asked.

The old woman regarded her with a smile. 'From the continent, my dear. Brought from as far as Bohemia.'

Gisela regarded the array of material and a plan began to formulate in her mind. She could sew the most beautiful dress from some of this fabric, something her mistress would no doubt appreciate. Perhaps there might even be enough cloth left over for her to make some kind of garment for herself.

She fished in her purse. Lady Agnes as ever had been miserly with the coin she had given and there would not be enough for both food and clothing. Gisela thought about the choice she had to make and it did not take long to decide. Before she could talk herself out of it, she had purchased a short roll of linen and some fine lace. She stuffed them in her bag and made her way from the marketplace, trying not to think about the consequences.

No sooner had she left the safety of the town, and made her way along the road to the castle, than she heard the sound of approaching horses. Turning, she saw a column of riders making their way towards her along the road. Gisela was quick to step aside, allowing the column of knights to ride by, none of them giving her so much as a nod of acknowledgement. At their head rode the only one of their number without a helmet. His hair was dark, his jaw set tight as he rode. There was a determined look to him that Gisela did not like, and she began to get a strange feeling of foreboding in her stomach.

As soon as they were past her, riding hard for the castle, Gisela quickened her pace in their wake. The gate to the castle was already open to welcome the riders, and they crossed the bridge over the moat to the sound of clattering hooves.

Gisela stood and watched. There was nothing unusual about a contingent of knights. Rebellion was all around, and the comings and goings of King William's army had become normality, but she couldn't help shake the discomforting sensation inside her.

Unable to quell the feeling, she made her way into the castle grounds. She could see the knights already being greeted by Richard, the dark warrior who had ridden at their head bowing low before the baron. Gisela did her best to make herself invisible, moving around the perimeter of the courtyard and entering the main tower of the castle. She rushed upstairs, taking them two at a time until she reached the bedchamber of her mistress. Inside, Lady Agnes was still in her bed, although she was well enough to be reading her Bible through narrowed eyes.

'My lady, a contingent of the king's knights has arrived.'

Slowly Lady Agnes laid down the book beside her. 'On what business?' her mistress asked.

'I do not know, my lady. Baron Richard is already speaking with them.'

Gisela knew what she was doing. Lady Agnes' curiosity would get the better of her, and they would both get to find out what was going on. Already her mistress was struggling from beneath the sheets.

'Come then,' she said. 'Let us go and greet these knights. We cannot let my husband be the only one to represent this house.'

'Are you sure this is the right thing to do, my lady?' Gisela said, feigning innocence. 'You are still unwell.'

'Nonsense,' Lady Agnes snapped. 'I am well enough to greet guests in my own home.'

Gisela did her best to dress her mistress and help her from the room. When she had finally guided Lady Agnes to the bottom of the stairs, she could hear voices and some laughter coming from the dining hall.

In her eagerness not to be left out, Agnes almost dragged Gisela along the corridor, seeming to make a miraculous recovery from her ailment. When they entered the dining hall they saw Baron Richard seated at the head of his table, and the dark-haired knight lounging casually in a chair by the hearth.

'Ah, my dear,' Richard said as he saw his wife. 'You must be feeling better?'

'Well enough to greet my guests,' said Lady Agnes as Gisela helped her into a seat opposite her husband.

'May I introduce Ronan of Dol-Combourg,' Richard said gesturing to the knight.

The man stood and bowed towards Lady Agnes. He was unsteady on his feet, and as Gisela looked closer she could see his foot was twisted awkwardly.

'It is an honour to meet you, Lady Agnes,' Ronan said.

'Yes, yes,' Agnes replied. 'And what, might I ask, brings you to Hereford Castle?'

'I am here at the behest of Earl Willem,' Ronan replied. 'We are on the hunt for a notorious outlaw.'

Agnes seemed far from impressed. 'Another one?' she said. 'Doubtless you have heard we have our own trouble with outlaws.'

'Yes, my lady,' said Ronan. 'It seems the country is riven with rebellion.'

'Indeed it is,' said Richard, unwilling to be left out of the conversation. 'Eadric has been most troublesome these past months, but it will not be long before he's brought to heel. His followers will be put down, and every rebel in the Marcher Lands will have his head mounted on the walls of this castle. I have vowed not to stop until every last one of them has faced the king's justice.'

'Then perhaps we can help one another?' Ronan said. 'I am sure the outlaw I pursue has formed an alliance with this Eadric. Thus our troubles are intertwined.'

'And what's the name of this rebel?' Agnes said.

'He is known as the Red Wolf, my lady,' Ronan replied. 'A cunning and brutal savage.'

Richard rose to his feet, looking at Ronan gravely. 'Have no fear. I will offer you any help you need in capturing this Red Wolf.'

Ronan likewise stood and both men clasped hands. 'And I will do likewise in helping you bring this Eadric to task. And as a mark of my respect and gratitude for your help, I would like to offer you something.'

He gestured to one of his men, who held out a weapon bound in hide. Ronan took it and unwrapped the covering to reveal a Saxon blade within. Drawing the sword from its sheath, Ronan held it up to the light, and Gisela could see runes glittering all along the blade.

'The sword of the Red Wolf,' Ronan said. 'I took it from him before he escaped me. Soon I hope to reunite him with it.'

Baron Richard accepted the sword, looking down at it in

wonder. 'A beautiful weapon. Strange that it should belong to such a base savage. This belongs in pride of place above my hearth.'

Gisela expected her mistress to also rise to her feet, not wanting to be left out, but instead the old woman let out a pained cough. Agnes raised a kerchief to her mouth as the coughing continued until she was hacking convulsively from the bottom of her lungs.

Gisela moved to her mistress's side. 'Are you all right, my lady?' she asked.

'Perhaps I am not as well as I thought,' Agnes said under her breath, as she tried in vain to clear her throat. When she took the kerchief away from her mouth, Gisela could see there was blood on the cloth.

'Perhaps you need more rest, my dear,' Richard said.

Gisela was already helping Lady Agnes to her feet. The old woman did not acknowledge her husband as they both made their way from the dining chamber. All Agnes could do was offer Ronan a limp wave of acknowledgement as they made their way from the room and back to her chamber.

By the time Gisela got her mistress into bed the old woman had managed to stop coughing and taken a little water.

'I will make you a tincture, my lady,' Gisela said. 'Honey and mint should help clear your throat.'

The old woman stared out of her window as though she had not heard.

'This rebellion will never end,' Agnes said. 'Even if they track down those outlaws and behead them, there will always be more to take their place. My useless husband could mount a hundred heads on the walls of this castle and it will not bring the king's enemies to heel. The English will never give up. These people might be savage but they are also proud. They will never bow to the rule of a foreign king.'

'I am sure Baron Richard knows what he's doing,' Gisela said.

Agnes did not answer, instead rolling onto her side as though her maid were not even there.

By the time Gisela had been to the kitchen to prepare the tincture and returned to the chamber, her mistress was fast asleep. It was best to leave her that way; at least then she was at peace.

Gisela put the tincture down on a table to let it cool and moved to the window. Down in the courtyard she could see Ronan of Dol-Combourg limping across the courtyard. He was accompanied by a giant knight and surrounded by a score of men in mail. As she watched this fearsome group mount their horses, Gisela could not help but think her mistress was wrong. As proud and brutal as the English were, the Franks surpassed them in every way. For a moment Gisela felt a twinge of pity for any outlaw who might rise against the army of King William, for surely they stood no chance.

32

MATHRAFAL, KINGDOM OF POWYS, AUGUST 1067

They had walked for miles through the night. The relentless sound of rain spattering against leaves plagued them every step of the way.

The last time Styrkar had come to this accursed country he had been accompanied by the constant rain. What was it about this place that the gods would choose to piss all over it every single day?

Styrkar remembered well when he had joined King Harold to crush the rebellious Welsh. He had first bloodied himself in those savage battles, taken his first head and sent that first soul screaming into the afterlife. It seemed so long ago. This time they were not here to destroy the Welsh, but to form an alliance with them. Even the thought of it made Styrkar's hackles rise, but now he followed a different master. One who saw fit to bargain rather than fight.

Somewhere ahead through the dark of the forest, Eadric led his men on. Beside him would be Wulfsige and the other housecarls, all eager to please their master. Styrkar was happy to take up the rear, to hang back in the dark. Though he served Eadric faithfully, he felt no need to impress the man. Besides, it had already been made plain they were not here to fight, but to parlay.

The twenty of them tramped through the thick woodland. Hardly much of a raiding party. If they had wanted to take on the Welsh in battle, they would have come with a much bigger force than this. Nevertheless, despite the fact that they had come with hopes of making allies, it didn't make them any less nervous. This was dangerous country, and the Welsh were as unpredictable as any bandits or cutthroats.

As Styrkar walked, Stithulf hung close to his shoulder. He had his bow drawn despite the rain, not caring that the string might snap if drawn in the wet. Styrkar was reassured by his presence. He had seen just how deadly Stithulf could be with that weapon, and if some Welsh bandit came screaming at them from the dark he relished the thought of Stithulf greeting him with an arrow in the eye.

They carried no torches. Although Eadric had insisted that they were here to form an accord, he still did not want to make their presence known to the whole forest. The Welsh were expecting them anyhow, surely there would be no trouble…

Someone suddenly whispered from up ahead for them to hold.

Styrkar stopped, Stithulf at his shoulder, and they both stared out into the darkness. There they stood in the rain for what seemed an age, listening to the sound of it drumming against the leaves.

Eventually Styrkar could wait no longer. And he moved

up through the ranks of men. He saw Eadric at the front looking out into the blackness of the forest.

'What is it?' Styrkar asked.

Eadric's eyes were hawk-like, glaring through the trees. 'I think we're lost,' he replied.

'So we just stand here in the piss wet?' said Styrkar.

'Do you have a better idea?' Eadric said.

Wulfsige took a step towards Styrkar in a threatening manner, and for a moment he thought he might have to bury his axe in the housecarl's head. Before he had the chance there was murmuring from the men, and Eadric planted a hand on Styrkar's shoulder.

They peered north, and through the trees Styrkar could see a man was approaching. He was small, a spear in his hand, and in what moonlight they could see by, it looked like his face was blackened with mud. All Styrkar could make out were two bright eyes in a dark face. It reminded him of the savages he had fought a few short years earlier, their bodies painted, howling at the sky as they fought like demons.

The man came to stand before them, staring like an animal with prey in its sights. None of them seemed to know what to do until Eadric took a step forward.

'I am Earl Eadric,' he said. 'I take it you've been sent by—'

'I come to bring you before the princes Bleddyn and Rhiwallon,' said the man in his strange accent. Despite the way he spoke, Styrkar was impressed. Every Welshman he had ever met or killed before today only spoke the guttural Welsh language.

Eadric eyed the man suspiciously. 'They only sent one man to greet us?'

The warrior smiled, his yellow teeth bright in the moonlight. 'Just follow us,' he replied.

As he turned, Styrkar heard the crack of flint on tinder, and sparks flashed through the trees. A dozen torches suddenly ignited despite the heavy rain, and in their light he could see that their meagre group of twenty were surrounded. Black figures stood among the trees, every man holding a spear; some had shields. Had the Welsh wanted to fall upon them and murder them in the middle of the wet forest they could have done so easily.

They followed the warrior through the trees for another mile or so. The rain did not relent as they came out of the forest and Styrkar could see a hillfort in the distance.

No one spoke as they made their way towards it, and when they were clear of the forest Styrkar could see he had underestimated the Welsh numbers. There must have been fifty of them.

The path towards the hill fort was lined with spears struck into the ground. Atop each one was a rotting head, dripping in the rain.

'You think that's some kind of warning?' Stithulf whispered to Styrkar. 'They telling us to be scared?'

'Could well be,' he replied.

Stithulf nodded. 'It's bloody working.'

The Welsh did not seem in the least threatened by the English. They had not even demanded to take their weapons, such was their confidence.

As they entered the fort there were yet more Welsh

awaiting. Many of them glared with barely hidden disdain, and Styrkar expected nothing less. They had been at war with the English for centuries, a feud that had outlasted two dozen kings. These warriors would be waiting for any excuse to bury their spears and axes in English flesh. Styrkar could feel that need hanging like a cloud in the air, and the more they glared with undisguised hate, the more he would have happily returned the gesture.

Their Welsh guide stopped before a circular thatched building. He turned to Eadric and said, 'Just you.'

Wulfsige stepped forward. 'I'll be damned if he's going in there alone.'

Styrkar also moved forward to stand at the shoulder of the earl. 'He goes nowhere without us.'

The guide shrugged. 'All right,' he said. 'Then it's the three of you.'

He led them into the circular hut and immediately Styrkar was relieved to be out of the rain. By the light of a torch, he could see a man sitting in a chair at the opposite side of the wide room. He was big, with a beard curling down to his chest, braided hair hanging well past his broad shoulders. As Eadric stepped forward the man inclined his head as though he were weighing the earl up.

Beside the warrior on the throne stood a second hulking figure. This one had an equally impressive beard, but his hair was shaved to the scalp. Tattoos swirled along the sides of his head, his face fixed in a scowl and his hand resting on a wicked axe at his belt.

The guide gestured to the man in the chair with a bow. 'Prince Bleddyn ap Cynfyn of Powys,' he said. The man in the chair nodded curtly. 'And his brother, Prince Rhiwallon ap Cynfyn of Gwynedd.' The big bald warrior didn't move but just continued to glare.

As the scout retreated to the shadows, Eadric took a step forward and bowed. 'My thanks for granting this audience,' said the earl.

'You are welcome,' said Bleddyn. 'We are united by a common enemy. In some kingdoms that would make us brothers.'

'This is no brother of mine,' said Rhiwallon. 'Anyone too weak to fight his own enemies is no man.'

Bleddyn held up a hand to his brother to be silent and Styrkar could see who held the real power between them.

'We all know why you're here, Earl Eadric,' Bleddyn said. 'You wish us to join in an alliance. Yet despite my brother's crude tongue, he speaks truth. Why should we join with you now, when you have been exiled? When your lands and power have been stripped away?'

'Once King William has finished subjugating the English, he will turn his eye west,' Eadric replied. 'The Welsh will be next. You need all the allies you can get.'

Rhiwallon barked a laugh. 'We can defend our own lands,' he said. 'We will not be so easily cowed by the Franks, and we need no help from an exiled Saxon.'

Again Bleddyn held up a hand for his brother to be silent, this time his face creasing in annoyance.

'Calm yourself, Rhiwallon,' said Bleddyn. 'These are our guests. They should be treated with respect. I apologise for my brother's curtness. But he is right in his reluctance. Why would we help a man like you reclaim his lands? What would we gain?'

Eadric ran a hand through his sodden hair and wiped it

on his leather jack before speaking. 'The road to Hereford is long, and William's forces are stretched. With your army at my side there would be much plunder to be had. You could both make yourselves rich with what you pillaged on the way.'

Bleddyn raised an eyebrow. 'You would be happy to see the Welsh ravage your lands after you have spent so many years defending your borders?'

'As your brother is so keen to point out, they are no longer my lands,' Eadric said. 'Now they belong to the Franks.'

'We cannot trust this man,' Rhiwallon said. 'He has nothing. He holds nothing. He is nothing.'

Had anyone said the same about King Harold, Styrkar would have pulled his blade and cut out the man's tongue. Not so now. He could only think that Rhiwallon had a point; Eadric was willing to let his own lands burn to reclaim what was rightfully his.

'Once we have joined together,' Eadric said. 'Once we have decimated King William's army, retaken the Marcher Lands and claimed what is rightfully mine, it will be time for a new treaty. The Welsh will no longer be harried. There will be no threat of invasion from the east. Such an agreement would halt any further costly wars. You will not get such an offer from King William. He will burn your forts to the ground and slaughter your people. With me ruling the borderlands you will only prosper.'

Bleddyn nodded at the words, tugging on his beard as he thought. 'I can see the sense in this,' he said.

'Bollocks,' Rhiwallon said. 'We help this English prick and we get to keep our own lands? We should be fighting, not bargaining. These Saxons are cowards. They don't know how to make war.'

Styrkar had heard enough, and he stepped forward to stand beside Eadric. 'We knew how to make war when your High King crawled from his pig-shit lands and invaded Wessex,' he growled. 'We knew how to make war when we followed Harold into battle and sent Gruffydd's men screaming back to their caves.'

'You think so?' Rhiwallon stepped forward, pulling his axe free of his belt. 'Then why don't you show me how you make war, Red Hair?'

'Enough,' said Bleddyn. 'Calm yourself, brother. We are all friends here.' He shot Styrkar a warning glance before turning his attention back to the earl. 'Eadric is right. We have already seen what this Frankish duke has done to the English. Better a Saxon lord sat on our borders than this ambitious foreign king.' He sat forward in his seat, glaring at Eadric intently. 'What is our plan, Exile?'

'We unite our forces,' Eadric said. 'We ravage the western extent of the Marcher Lands and move east. Once we have taken Hereford and its castle, we will have a foothold in William's lands. He will be forced to bargain, and we give him no other choice but to grant me back what is rightfully mine. With your armies camped deep in his territory he will be forced to pay you both handsomely to return to your homeland.'

Bleddyn smiled. 'See, brother, we will not just get to keep our lands. We will return richer than any Welsh kings have ever been.'

Rhiwallon nodded. 'Very well, we shall see what riches await. But first there will be much killing to do.'

Bleddyn rose to his feet, stepping forward and grasping Eadric's arm. 'You have yourself an agreement, Saxon.'

As they left the hut, stepping back into the rain, Styrkar could not help but feel that a devil's bargain had been struck. Eadric was willing to slaughter his own countrymen to regain his seat of power. He should have spoken up. He should have told the earl that this was destined to end in grief, but what good would it do? He was beholden to Eadric. Had pledged his loyalty to this man and for good or ill he would have to follow him into the slaughter.

As the rain beat down harder in the cold Welsh countryside, Styrkar could only take solace in the fact he was heading for war against his most hated enemies once more.

33

HEREFORD, ENGLAND, AUGUST 1067

They lowered the coffin reverently into the grave. Gisela fought against the tears, but she could not stop them washing down her cheeks as she watched her mistress conveyed back to the earth. The priest spoke his rites as men with ropes slowly put the old woman to her final rest.

There was barely anyone at the graveside. That in itself was testament to the old woman's legacy. As much as Gisela had respected Lady Agnes, she could fully understand why so few had come to see her laid to rest. But despite Agnes' shortcomings, Gisela could not seem to stop the tears. Was she weeping for the old woman? Or were these tears for herself? Now that Lady Agnes was dead, Gisela's own future was in question, though she was starkly aware that this was not the time or the place to think on such things. Better that she turn her attention to remembering. Better that she think on the memory of Lady Agnes rather than lamenting on what might lie in store.

On the other side of the grave stood Baron Richard. He

was weeping too, but Gisela found it hard to believe those tears were genuine. More likely they were tears of relief that he was finally free of the old harpy. When first she came into the service of the FitzScrobs, Richard and his wife had a fraught relationship. In recent years that relationship had grown more venomous by the day. Now the baron was finally free of his shrewish wife, his grief was little more than an affectation.

To the baron's left stood Osbern. He shed no tears, but Gisela knew that he grieved more deeply than his father. His hands were clasped in front of him, the whites of his knuckles vivid in the morning sunlight. Osbern had become cold towards her in recent weeks, and Gisela had put it down to the growing troubles in the west and the responsibility he bore as sheriff. Nevertheless, she couldn't help but be saddened by the distance that had grown between them.

Beside Osbern was his elder brother William. He could barely hide his boredom with this whole affair. Gisela could remember little of him; he had left the household many years before to take up estates of his own in another part of the country. He was a stranger in this place and it showed.

As the priest finished his last rites, Richard, William and Osbern each picked up a handful of earth and dumped it atop the wooden coffin. The finality of it hit Gisela hard, but she fought back more tears, biting her lip, trying to retain some kind of solemn dignity.

When she turned to glance across the graveyard she saw the knight, Ronan, standing some feet away. It was curious that he should be present since he was not part of the family and had not known Lady Agnes at all. As she watched him with growing interest, he looked up and caught her eye. It was difficult to read the expression on his face. Was it one of boredom? Sympathy? It was certainly not grief or sorrow.

Gisela dragged her eyes away from Ronan's, realising the priest had gone silent, the last rites done with. Now the funeral was finished the few mourners who had come were making their way from the churchyard, and Gisela followed towards the waiting horses and wagons that would take them back to Hereford. Ahead of her, Osbern and William walked, deep in conversation, and she found herself close to Baron Richard. He walked alone, but had clearly overcome his grief already. Perhaps she should offer him some solace. Perhaps she should try to make it known how much she was worth to his household?

He glanced at her briefly before mounting one of the wagons. Gisela stood by the side of it and, when the wagon pulled away without Richard offering the merest acknowledgement, it began to dawn on her just how little she mattered.

Gisela waited as the horses were mounted and the wagons began to rumble northward. Just when it seemed she would be left behind, one of the wagons pulled up beside her. Osbern looked down.

'Are you coming?' he asked.

'Yes, my lord,' she replied, taking his hand as he helped her into the back of the wagon.

She sat with the other servants, who kept a silent vigil. Gisela didn't know any of them that well. Her duties to her mistress had kept her separate from the rest of the FitzScrob housemaids and servants, and she began to lament the distance she had put between them. Had she somehow thought herself superior? No, that was not her way. But now in her grief she regretted not having made more of an effort to know them.

As the wagon trundled north, she could not stop herself glancing at Osbern. He sat silently in his sorrow and she yearned to speak with him. The further north they went the more she realised the chance was slipping through her fingers, and she could hold back no longer.

'I am sorry for your loss, my lord,' she said.

At first he did not answer, and she wondered if her words had been lost beneath the sound of the wagon's wheels, until he turned and nodded at her solemnly.

'Thank you,' he said.

More silence. She knew she should have left it at that, but as she saw him suffering there was nothing she could do to hold her tongue.

'Your mother was a kind woman,' she lied. 'It was an honour to be in her service.'

Osbern sighed deeply. 'We both know my mother was many things, but she was not kind. She was spiteful and quick to anger. I often wonder how you managed to last so long in her service.'

'My lord, your mother was always kind to me. I like to think we were friends, in our own way. It was only recently that—'

'Please,' Osbern said. 'Spare me your delightful stories of my mother. There are other things I must think on.'

'Of course, my lord. You must be deeply burdened. I understand the threat from the west only grows worse.'

'It does,' he replied.

'Do you think we are in much danger?'

'For you? There is little danger. Behind the walls of the castle you will be safe enough. Do not burden yourself with it. Better that you think on finding some other way to make yourself useful, now that my mother is gone and you have no mistress.'

It was a needless barb. One that cut Gisela deep. Of all the people she had expected to strike at her like that, Osbern was the last. Perhaps that was why it hurt the most. Or perhaps it was because she knew his words were true.

'How could you think me so selfish?' she said, growing angry at his gibe. 'Why would I think such a thing when Lady Agnes has just been laid to rest?'

Osbern did not answer, and turned his attention back to the road ahead. It was probably best for them both if they spoke no further on it. Gisela looked away, seeing the other servants glance at her furtively. Were they thinking the same? Did everyone wonder what she would do now that she was a lady's maid with no mistress?

The rest of the journey passed in silence, and when they finally trundled into the courtyard of the castle, Gisela could see Baron Richard was already organising the funeral party.

He laughed, his voice echoing around the courtyard, all signs of his grief now gone. Ronan and some of his knights were beginning to make merry and it seemed this time of mourning was to turn into some kind of celebration.

Osbern jumped down from the wagon, not giving Gisela a second glance as he approached his brother William and they began to talk once more. Richard and the others made their way inside to the feast hall and the servants climbed down from the wagon, not one of them offering to help Gisela as she struggled from the back. As she stood alone in the courtyard she suddenly realised she had no friends here. As wicked and spiteful as Lady Agnes had been, it seemed that she truly had been Gisela's only companion in this place.

As the servants began to prepare food and bring meat and wine for the lord of the castle and his entourage, Gisela left them to it. She found herself walking through a corridor of the castle to a room Lady Agnes had spent much time in. She closed the door behind her, taking in a deep breath. On one wall shelves had been erected, leather-bound tomes stacked from floor to ceiling.

Gisela stood in front of the shelves, looking at the spines. She knew her letters but she had never been a voracious reader like her mistress. It had seemed the only pleasure Lady Agnes had ever taken had been from the pages of some book or other. Religious screeds and histories could never hold Gisela's interest though, but with nothing else to do perhaps now was a good time to begin her education. Perhaps there might be something she could learn from these books that would make herself useful to the household.

She heard the door behind her open. Gisela turned, and in the candlelight she recognised the man who entered. Ronan limped in, closing the door behind him, and Gisela regarded him pensively. He was handsome in his own way, but there was an arrogance to him that was all ugliness.

'I never had a chance to tell you how sorry I am that your mistress has passed,' he said.

'Thank you, my lord,' she replied. 'But it seems my grief is not shared by many others.'

Ronan shrugged. 'That's understandable. I'm led to

believe the sharpness of her tongue could rival any blade. She was certainly a thorn in Baron Richard's side.'

'They were companions for many years, my lord. Every marriage has its share of strife.'

Ronan nodded at that. 'That it does,' he said. 'But now it seems Richard's troubles are over. And yours just begun. So what will you do now your mistress is no more?'

Gisela felt a sense of unease growing inside her. What business was this of Ronan's? Why would he even have an interest? Nobody else within the castle seemed to even care. Making such mention of it now would only make her seem selfish, and so she ignored the question.

'Why were you at the funeral?' she asked instead. 'You did not know Lady Agnes, yet you came to pay your respects.'

'I was invited,' Ronan replied. 'The baron and I have much to discuss. No doubt you have heard about the threat from the west?'

'Yes. Lord Osbern has told me about it at length,' she said, though she knew it wasn't true. Osbern had grown distant, no longer the man she had known in her youth. 'He says there is little to trouble us here.'

'Did he indeed? I fear Sheriff Osbern may have been misleading you. There is much for you to fear. Lord Eadric is a fierce and vengeful warrior, and it is rumoured he has sought an alliance with the Welsh princes. They will bring nothing but death and misery with them.'

Gisela tried to swallow, but her mouth had gone dry. Was it the prospect of an attack by the fearsome Welsh? Or was it Ronan's presence?

'I am not scared,' she said.

He took a step towards her, and she could smell a musky

odour coming from him. Not an altogether unpleasant smell, but there was a certain sense of the unwashed about him.

'You should be,' he said. 'There is no telling what they will do when they get here… but I can protect you.'

He reached out a hand and brushed her upper arm. It was all she could do not to shiver at his touch.

'My lord, I—'

'There is nothing for you to fear from the Welsh if you are with me.'

He grabbed her, pulling her close. Gisela tried to push him away, but he was strong. What could she do to resist such a man?

'No,' she said.

He did not speak, instead pressing himself against her. The smell of him was stronger than ever now, and she began to struggle in his grip. Despite her defiance, he was not to be put off and he nuzzled his face into her hair.

She could tell now he was not about to stop. They were alone in this room and the panic rising within her was enough to make her cry out. But no one would come to save her even if she screamed this whole place down around their ears. There was no one in this castle willing to defend her. She would have to defend herself.

She kicked out, remembering his crippled leg, her foot connecting with Ronan's ankle.

He snarled in pain, staggering back and knocking a candle from the table. Once he had released her, Gisela rushed to the door, wrenching it open and dashing out into the corridor.

She ran, not looking back, as he shouted curses in her wake.

Gisela did not stop running, but instead raced out of the castle doors, across the courtyard, through the main gate, over the bridge and down the road towards the town.

There was nothing behind her but pain. It was time to make her own way.

34

LEOFMINSTRE, ENGLAND, AUGUST 1067

The water was freezing, a stark shock to his system. As he washed away the blood, Styrkar could see the swirling mist it left in the river. The dark rivulets were swept away like the memory of his recent deeds. How much of the blood was his, Styrkar had no idea, but the cold of the water served to calm his battle fury and now he had only empty memories of death and slaughter.

When his flesh was clean he climbed out of the river, pausing on the bank. Looking down at his body he felt some relief at the fact that there was hardly a mark on him. There would be bruises in the morning for sure, but now all he was left with was a cut to his forearm. He watched as the blood dripped rhythmically onto the wet grass; a small price to pay. A tiny penance considering how much death he had dealt. King Harold would have been proud. Or so Styrkar tried to tell himself.

He sat on the bank, fishing in the pouch he kept with needle and thread. As he began to sew the wound, feeling the sharp pain of the needle, he knew that the last thing Harold would be was proud. Styrkar could still hear distant screams from the town. The smell of burning timbers was pungent in the air, and a veil of smoke was being gently blown by the wind and swept along the river.

Styrkar should have been revelling in his victory. All he felt was shame.

When the wound was closed, he tied off the thread and bit it free, storing the needle back in its pouch. It was not the first time he'd had to sew his own wounds. It would not be the last.

His weapon lay nearby, a long Dane axe he had taken from a corpse some days earlier. The haft and head were still covered in the blood of his enemies. Or perhaps not. Styrkar wasn't even sure who his enemies were anymore.

Eadric's union of English and Welsh had ravaged their way along the River Lugg. For days now they had fought hard, burned and pillaged. Styrkar had been forced to watch as the armies of the Welsh princes had murdered and plundered, raped and slaughtered. These were Harold's people, and because of that they were Styrkar's people as well.

Had he known this would happen when he joined with Earl Eadric? Had he even cared?

Deep down Styrkar knew what he was doing. He had known what would happen the day he travelled with Eadric to form an alliance with the Welsh, but his obsession with revenge had made him turn a blind eye to it. But he was blind no longer. Now he knew exactly what his thirst for vengeance had wrought.

He dipped the axe head in the water, letting the river wash

away the evidence of his actions. It would do the iron no good – the river water would cause it to rust – but Styrkar didn't care. He just wanted to clean away the memory of what he had done. Of what he had become.

'This was a dark day,' said a voice behind him.

Styrkar turned to see Kenric standing on the riverbank. His was a face usually filled with mirth, but not today. Now his friend looked deeply troubled. It was a look Styrkar had seen often in recent days, and it did not suit Kenric's brow to be marred by so much care.

'I'm beginning to wonder why we're even here,' Styrkar said.

'Then maybe we should leave,' Kenric replied. 'We have enough riches to last us a year, maybe two. There's nothing keeping us here now.'

Styrkar saw a sack at Kenric's feet. Obviously he was not so troubled as to forego indulging in a little plunder of his own.

'I am not finished yet,' Styrkar said. 'There is still much I have to do.'

'What? You haven't killed enough men yet? How many more have to die before you are done with this obsession?'

'It is not the number of men,' Styrkar replied. 'It is the nature of the men I have to kill. When I have found them and put them to the axe, I will be done.'

'Then I hope you find them soon, my friend. Because if you carry on like this, the only thing being washed away by the river will be your corpse.'

Styrkar stepped out of the water and made his way past Kenric and up the riverbank. His friend picked up his sack and followed close behind. They didn't have to go far before they passed the first of the corpses. It lay half off the path, and Styrkar did not have the heart to look as they walked by.

Further on towards the town there were yet more bodies, and this time he could not help but witness the extent of the slaughter. These bodies had already been stripped and lay naked in the road. The Welsh had descended like carrion crows, looting the dead of everything they had, as though robbing them of their lives were not enough.

As Styrkar walked into the burning town the screams were subsiding. Here and there he heard wailing as people begged for their lives and the Welsh took their pleasure on the prisoners. One group had decided to ravage their victim out in the street and it was a sight that threatened to turn Styrkar's stomach, but what could he do? Were he to try and stop them he would end up one more dead and naked corpse in the road.

When he reached the centre of the town, he saw Eadric up ahead in close conversation with Prince Bleddyn. They pored over a map, smiling at one another, nodding their agreement as the Welsh prince patted the Saxon earl on his shoulder in congratulation at their recent victory. Styrkar could feel himself growing angry once more, his lust for violence clearly not sated. As he approached, Bleddyn looked up, and upon seeing Styrkar a wide grin crossed his bearded face.

'The Red Wolf comes,' said the Welshman. 'You were fearsome today, boy. They will tell tales of you, greater than any hero of legend.'

Styrkar stopped beside him, staring at the prince in disdain. Here was a beast of a man, and not just in appearance. He had taken his own share of lives today in the most merciless fashion.

'There are no heroes here,' Styrkar replied, trying his best to quell his rage. 'I see only cutthroats and plunderers.'

The grin fell from Bleddyn's face, and his deep brow furrowed. 'Mind your tongue, pup. Else I cut it from your mouth.'

Styrkar took a threatening step forward. 'I'd like to see you pull that knife before I bury this axe in your fucking head.'

Before either of the men could move, Eadric put himself between them, grabbing Styrkar and holding him back. Kenric joined Eadric, and together they wrestled Styrkar away.

'That's it,' Bleddyn shouted after them. 'Curb your dog, Saxon.'

Styrkar wanted to fight, wanted to make Bleddyn regret his words, but Eadric's grip was like iron.

When the earl had dragged him out of earshot of the Welsh, he turned on Styrkar.

'What the bloody hell do you think you're doing?'

'I could ask you the same thing,' Styrkar replied. 'We are supposed to be fighting the Franks, not slaughtering our own people.'

Eadric turned to Kenric. 'Leave us,' he said.

Without a word of complaint, Kenric tugged at his forelock and retreated out of sight.

Eadric turned back to Styrkar, his expression softening. 'Once we get to Hereford—'

'When we get to Hereford you intend to strike a bargain with the Welsh. You intend to have William pay them off.'

'You think you know me so well, Red Wolf? Do you think me so base? There will be no bargaining with the Welsh. They are a means to an end. I am using them, or are you too stupid to see it?'

'What are you talking about?'

'Once I have taken Hereford and have a foothold back in my estates, I will strike a bargain with King William. If he grants me back my earldom, I will see the Welsh driven from these lands. When I am once more earl, I will visit slaughter upon the Welsh. They will get no reward.'

'So you would swap one foul pact for another? To think I trusted you. I did not come here to kill King Harold's countrymen and I did not come here to bargain with the Welsh or the Franks. I came here to kill the servants of King William and now you tell me you wish to strike an agreement with him.'

'Think, Styrkar,' Eadric said. 'Look at what King William has done. And in such a short time. England is his. It is madness to think we can fight him.'

'You think me a fool?'

'I think you are blind to your need for revenge,' Eadric said. 'I think you are a capable warrior, but you are close to becoming a liability. I think if you cannot follow where I lead, I will have to leave you in the wilds where I found you.'

Styrkar gripped his axe, fighting the temptation to kill Eadric where he stood. Before he could act, Wulfsige was by their side, drawn to the sound of their argument. The housecarl had his hand on his sword, sensing trouble. Stithulf was also with him, looking nervous at the prospect of fighting the Red Wolf.

Styrkar calmed himself. Now was not the time or the place. He had fought hard for days on end and now was time to rest. The hard fighting was still to come.

'I will follow,' he told Eadric. 'But once we have taken Hereford and you have your lands once more, I will not stand by while you bargain with the king of the Franks. After we have taken Hereford, our alliance will be over.'

He turned and walked away before Eadric could answer. There was nothing the earl could say that would calm him or change his mind. And it was unlikely Eadric would even try.

35

HEREFORD, ENGLAND, AUGUST 1067

Milburga was still sleeping in her bed when Gisela rose. Since she had taken lodgings with the old cloth seller it was rare that she would wake first, and she took the chance to dress and open the shutters to their small house. It sat on the outskirts of the town, a modest place for a modest woman, but it was warm enough and it kept the rain out, so what more could they ask?

Gisela pulled the shawl tight about her shoulders. It was a cold morning, but through the shutters she could see the sky was clear and the day was certain to be a bright one. Even had the rain been hammering down she would still have found a reason to smile, but then in recent days she had much to be thankful for.

When Gisela had fled the castle and made her way down to the town of Hereford so many days earlier, it had seemed as though she were throwing herself to the wolves. There had been nowhere to go, she had no friends here, and so she had wandered. It wasn't long before she'd found herself at the old woman's stall she had visited days before, staring absently at the cloths and silks she had on display. Milburga had turned out to be the kindest woman Gisela had ever met.

The old woman had realised without asking that she was in trouble. They had talked at length into the long hours before Milburga told Gisela that she could stay with her. It had not been a request – the old woman was insistent – and Gisela came to learn that Milburga was not the kind of woman who took no for an answer.

'You're up early,' Milburga said.

Gisela turned to see the old woman had risen. 'It is such a beautiful day,' Gisela replied. 'Shame to waste it.'

Before Milburga could agree, there was a knock at the door. The two women shared a confused glance; neither were expecting visitors. When Gisela opened the door to the hut, the face she saw was the last she had expected.

Osbern forced a smile as soon as he saw her, but she easily recognised his discomfort.

'Gisela,' he said. 'It's so good to see you.'

'Is it?' she replied without thinking, but all her pent-up frustration had suddenly risen to the surface.

'Of course,' he continued. 'We have all missed you at the castle.'

She found that hard to believe. 'Missed me so much that it took you days to come and find me?'

Osbern shook his head, his face a picture of innocence. 'I didn't know where you had gone,' he said. 'I thought you had fled the country until I heard you'd taken up with some old merchant in town.'

'Well, now you know,' she replied.

There was more discomforting quiet until Osbern said, 'I am sorry. But with my mother's death and the trouble in the west, I did not think what you might be suffering.'

That was enough to make her feel guilty. Clearly he had no idea about Ronan's behaviour. But why would he? No one had been there to witness it.

'No, I should apologise,' she replied. 'I have only thought of myself.'

'Then we are both sorry,' Osbern said, the handsome smile back on his face. 'So you will come home?'

Gisela suddenly felt a giddiness in her stomach, but it was gone as soon as she thought on Ronan and his men still lurking about the castle grounds.

'I cannot,' she said. 'As long as—'

Somewhere in the town a bell began to ring.

'What's that?' Milburga asked, as she came to the doorway. 'Someone's making an awful racket.'

A look of dread crossed Osbern's face, and he turned to look back down the street.

'What is it?' Gisela asked.

Osbern shook his head. 'No. This cannot be happening. Our scouts should have given us warning.'

Gisela felt a cold dread fill her stomach as to the north of the town she heard shouts of alarm. A scream rose up, long and shrill across the rooftops. It could only mean one thing.

'We have to go,' Gisela said to the old woman.

Milburga stood, looking confused.

Gisela rushed forward and grabbed her hand. 'We have to go *now*,' she said, more urgently.

The old woman let herself be dragged out of the hut. In the road, people were already rushing towards the castle for safety. The bell had stopped ringing, to be replaced by the sound of steel on steel in the distance.

'Help me, Osbern,' Gisela said, but he was already making his way up the hill to the castle.

'They told us we would be safe,' Milburga said in a daze, as Gisela helped her along the main thoroughfare.

'Osbern!' Gisela yelled again.

He stopped, turning to look at her with a desperate expression on his face. Then, without another word, he raced away towards the safety of the castle.

'Damn you,' Gisela whispered, as she practically carried Milburga up the hill.

The old woman did her best to keep up as people began to rush past them. Gisela glanced back. A house was already on fire at the outskirts of the town and she could see a bearded warrior charging up the street with axe raised. His face was painted in pitch and he laughed as he cut down a screaming woman desperate to escape. It was clear they would never make it to the castle before the marauding raiders overwhelmed them.

'This way,' Gisela said, dragging Milburga from the main path and ducking between two houses, their bare feet slopping through the mud.

There they waited, gasping for breath. Gisela could hear Milburga wheezing, and she willed the old woman to be quiet. More shouts and screams pealed out, this time closer, and through the gap in the houses Gisela could see a group of savage warriors sprint past in pursuit of the fleeing townsfolk.

'Wait here,' Gisela said, moving to the edge of the alley to see if their way was clear.

Northward their escape was barred by the wooden palisade that surrounded the town, but the way south was clear. Gisela turned to tell Milburga to follow but she gasped as she was faced by the most terrifying sight.

The fearsome warrior was huge and she barely came up to his chest. His teeth and face were blackened by mud and pitch, eyes staring hungrily from beneath a mop of matted hair, and in one hand he held a cruel-looking axe.

Before she could think to run, he grasped her hair, pulling her towards him. His breath stank of dog as he said something in a guttural language she didn't understand. This was one of the feared Welsh and Gisela fought the impulse to scream as she struggled in his grip.

The warrior threw her to the ground rather than bury that axe in her head, and Gisela felt the cold dread of fear overcome her. He would not kill her yet – but perhaps after he had taken his pleasure.

The raider fell on her, making eager noises in his throat as he tore at her skirts. Gisela tried to kick him away, but he was too strong. Instinctively her hand balled into a fist and she lashed out, striking his bearded jaw. It stunned him for the briefest of moments, but then he grinned wickedly.

A rumbling laugh echoed up from his throat, at the same time as Milburga thrust a handful of darning needles into his neck.

The Welshman roared, rising to his feet and wrenching the needles out. As Milburga reeled back he raised his axe and brought it down on her neck. She was powerless against the blow and Gisela watched in horror as the old woman fell.

As the warrior stemmed the blood running from the

wound at his neck, Gisela knew she had to act. She could not just lie there while he recovered. She had to flee or...

There was a knife at his belt. Gisela scrambled to her feet, wrenching the blade from its sheath. The Welshman did not realise what she'd done until she had buried it up to the hilt in his throat.

He glared, those cruel eyes going cow-like as he staggered, fingers clutching at the knife. The axe fell from his fingertips and Gisela knew she was not done yet. She grasped the fallen weapon as the warrior collapsed to his knees. It was only then she decided to scream, yelling to the heavens as she raised the axe and brought it down on the warrior's head.

The blow took a chunk of flesh but was not powerful enough to crack his skull. As the Welshman reached out to her for mercy, Gisela angrily swatted his hand aside and struck again. This time she buried the axe in his face, hearing the satisfying sound of shattering bone, and the warrior collapsed forward into the mud.

Gisela stared for a moment at the corpse, suddenly catching the breath she had been holding. Then she saw Milburga lying on the ground. The old woman had saved her, and sacrificed her life in the act. Gisela would have thanked her, would have sank to her knees and prayed for her soul to reach Heaven, but there was no time. If she did not flee, then Milburga's selfless act would be for nothing.

As the screams and sounds of battle began to consume the town, Gisela ran to find safety.

Ronan glared down the hill to the houses below. The town was already burning, the alarum having long since gone quiet, to be replaced by the sound of slaughter. Between the distant rooftops the Welsh were coming.

None of the reports had anticipated them attacking in such numbers. The horde was like a ravenous plague, charging towards the castle with all the fury Ronan had been warned to expect from these savage westerners.

To his left stood Baron Richard. The man stared at the same sight, but instead of resolve, all Ronan could see was fear in his eyes.

'Rally your men,' Ronan snarled. 'And close the bloody gates.'

Already a mass of peasants from the town were streaming into the castle courtyard, desperate to reach safety. The knights within Richard's garrison milled around in equal panic.

Ronan reached forward and grabbed Richard's arm, shaking him furiously.

'We need to secure the gates,' he shouted in the baron's face. 'Get your men in order.'

Richard just stared back. If there had ever been an ounce of steel in him, it was melted away now.

Ronan dashed from the parapet, his leg screaming in pain as he limped down the stone staircase to the courtyard.

'Close the gate,' he barked at a group of men-at-arms.

They looked back at him helplessly, seeming reluctant to lock out the fleeing peasants.

'The gate,' he screamed again. 'The fucking gate.'

He heard a pathetic voice wailing something about the townsfolk being slaughtered, how they couldn't leave them outside, when Aldus appeared.

'Get the men,' Ronan ordered. 'And close that damned gate.'

Aldus nodded, pushing his way through the crowd. Ronan could see his own men trying desperately to reach him, but the throng of peasants was too thick.

He stumbled, jostled by the crowd, looking desperately at the wide-open entrance. Then he heard them; a low roar of hate issuing from beyond the castle walls. The Welsh were here.

All he could do was watch as they reached the open gateway, cutting down the host of fleeing peasants in their path. Ronan tried desperately to wrench the sword from his belt, but a panicked man barged into him in his eagerness to escape the slaughter, and the sword spilled from his grip.

He backed away, eyes widening as the attackers cut their way inside, hacking a path through the hapless peasants, desperate to get to more worthy foes. The press of bodies was too thick for him to flee, his leg screamed out in protest, and it was all Ronan could do to keep his footing. The Welsh would be on him in moments.

Aldus grasped him about the shoulders, pulling him through the crowd. An arrow whistled overhead, narrowly missing the giant knight, who continued to wade heedless through the mass.

'On me,' Ronan bellowed, when Aldus had managed to clear a space around them.

His men responded, joined by some of Baron Richard's garrisoned troops. There was fear in their eyes, but that would serve them well – desperation always made men fight the harder.

'Lock shields,' he ordered. 'Aldus. Take some men and close that bastard gate.'

The giant nodded before he and half a dozen others began to make their way around the edge of the courtyard.

'Advance,' Ronan said from behind the ranks of men.

Obediently they moved forward. The peasants had all but been slaughtered now, and beyond the shield wall in front of him, Ronan could see the Welsh. They had gathered in a mass just inside the gate and were bellowing in a foul language, readying themselves for battle.

'Stay in formation,' Ronan said. 'This rabble will attack en masse. They will break on our shields.'

Then there was no more time for orders. The first of the Welsh charged, throwing themselves at the shield wall. The first two were impaled on spears, before the rest managed to slam into the solid nest of shields. Ronan felt the impact, yearning desperately for a weapon. The men in front of him grunted as their shields were battered by axe and sword. Arrows and rocks flew overhead, clanking off the conical helmets of the knights and Ronan had to duck to avoid an arrow to the eye.

Though the Welsh attacked furiously, the shield wall held. Little by little they wore down the Welsh numbers, a scream here as one was speared in the face, a shrill cry there as another took a sword to the skull. Ronan's men were winning, pushing the enemy back, and he allowed himself to take a breath in relief. It didn't last long.

A deep voice roared, and the shield wall buckled as a single axe slammed into its midst and hacked down a knight. Ronan recognised the axe wielder, and cold dread gripped his heart.

The Red Wolf hacked to left and right, lopping off an arm, crushing a skull and shattering the defensive line. With the integrity of the shield wall breached, it all but collapsed. Two more knights went down, overcome by the rallying Welsh, and Ronan staggered back as he saw what was about to happen.

The Red Wolf burst through the centre of the wall, and glared, locking eyes with Ronan. Styrkar made a terrifying sight, his body spattered with gore, his face a mask of furious intent.

Ronan ran.

For all his leg was crippled he fled like the devil himself were in pursuit. Pushing his way past cowering peasants he sped up the stairs towards the parapet above. There was nowhere to escape to – he knew that – but in his panic all he could do was delay the inevitable.

When finally he scrambled to the top of the staircase he risked a glance behind him. The Red Wolf was coming, axe in hand, his stride measured as though savouring the moment.

Ronan cursed the day he had ever heard the name Red Wolf, as he raced along the battlement. Reaching the top of the north bastion he saw there was nowhere else to go but down.

The sound of the battle in the courtyard was muted now, as though taking place far away. Ronan gripped the merlons, looking down to the ground far below. Could he survive such a fall?

'You think to rob me of the right to kill you?' Styrkar's voice bore a barely controlled menace. 'Take the fall and you might not die right away. Get on your knees and I'll make it quick.'

Ronan turned to face his end. Even with fear tearing at

his every fibre, he was determined to offer this scum no more glory than he was owed.

'Get on with it,' he replied, spitting on the ground before the axeman.

Styrkar took a step forward, but a sound from behind alerted him. Aldus raced towards them along the parapet, gripping shield and sword.

The Red Wolf turned to face the giant knight, Ronan seemingly forgotten. He raised his axe and smashed it down on Aldus' shield, and Ronan was shocked to see his huge friend stagger back under the force of the blow.

As the two fought, Ronan glanced about the bastion, his eyes falling on a crossbow left abandoned by one of Baron Richard's men. He rushed forward, hands shaking as he picked up the weapon, fumbling at the quiver by its side. Behind him he could hear the brutal sound of axe on shield, Aldus grunting as he tried to fight back. There wasn't much time.

Planting a foot in the stirrup, Ronan pulled the string back over the lock. His crippled leg screamed at the effort, but he managed to cock the weapon, hefting it to his shoulder as he slammed a quarrel in place.

The two fighters had dropped their weapons now, giant and Dane grappling at the edge of the battlements. Ronan aimed, but he could not shoot without risk of hitting Aldus.

With a roar, Styrkar slammed the huge knight against the stone, one thickly muscled arm smashing that helmeted head against the battlement again and again.

Aldus was defeated. Ronan had no choice.

The crossbow sang a sweet note as it unleashed the bolt. It tore through the chainmail at Styrkar's shoulder and he roared in pain, losing his footing. As he fell he held on to Aldus with an iron grip, both of them toppling from the parapet.

Ronan could only watch in horror as his closest friend and most hated enemy disappeared over the wall.

36

HEREFORD, ENGLAND, AUGUST 1067

He was shrouded in darkness. Something rang in his ears; piercing shafts of sound that threatened to split his skull.

Styrkar opened his eyes, sucking in a breath that sent pain galloping through him. He groaned, trying to move, but it was as though he were buried beneath a pile of earth.

Was he dead? Had they found his body and already thrown him into a pit with the rest of the day's corpses?

As his eyes focused he saw he was lying at the bottom of the wall. Beneath him was the giant Frankish knight, eyes staring up at the sky, mouth gaping as though he had screamed his last until the breath was snatched from him. Styrkar almost laughed at the ridiculous look on his enemy's face. But now was no time for mirth.

Styrkar tried to push himself to his feet, but pain screamed in his shoulder. Reaching up a hand he could feel the shaft of a quarrel protruding just to the left of his shoulder blade.

Hopefully it had not cracked the bone, or it was unlikely he'd ever be able to use his arm again.

Crawling off the Frankish giant's body, he tried to stand. Thankfully his legs still worked, and he struggled to his feet, but his left arm was numb from the shoulder. He winced in pain as he tried to move it, struggling to massage some life back into the useless limb, but it was no good. Before he could think more on it there was a hiss and something thudded into the ground not far from him. Glancing up, he saw Ronan glaring down, crossbow still in his hand.

Styrkar stumbled away from the wall, almost tumbling down the hill towards the town. He grunted as he went, every step sending pain coursing through his arm. Gritting his teeth against the agony was all he could do as he stumbled from the castle and the din rising from within it. The fight was still on, but he knew he could add nothing more to it. And if he did not find cover soon, it would not be long before Ronan found his mark.

As he stumbled back into the town, he slowed to lean against a hut and catch his breath. A quick glance back told him he was out of range of the bow. Only now did he realise how hurt he was. The wound in his shoulder was not his only ailment, but it was hardly surprising, looking at the height of the wall he had fallen from.

Gingerly, he limped his way along the road through the centre of town. He could still hear the sounds of houses being ransacked, some of the Welsh so eager for plunder they had forgotten they were here to take the castle. From somewhere there was a scream of alarm. Styrkar couldn't tell if it was man or woman, but it was suddenly cut short by the sickening thud of a weapon.

As he walked, his mind growing foggy with delirium, he was suddenly reminded of a town many years before. He had staggered in a daze then as he stumbled between burned houses, listening to the slaughter and the misery. Styrkar had only been a boy when Hedeby was razed by the king of Norway, and the memories of it had always been distant. Now, as he staggered along the ravaged streets, those memories came back all too vividly.

Styrkar stumbled from the well-worn path, falling against the door of a house. All he wanted was shelter, somewhere to rest awhile and clear his head, and this place seemed as good as any.

He opened the door, taking a painful step inside before quickly closing it behind him, shutting out the noise. His shoulder still tormented him, every breath sending pain coursing through his body. The bolt protruded three inches, meaning there was still three inches of shaft buried in his flesh, but he would have to see to it later – now all he wanted was respite.

There was a chair placed beside a winnowing fire and he shuffled towards it gingerly, unable to quell a sigh of relief as he lowered himself into it. Within the darkness of the room he tried to control his breathing, wondering if he would ever be able to muster the strength to eventually stand.

Styrkar closed his eyes, trying to shut out the memories. He had come here to reap vengeance. To kill without mercy. Eadric had led him and he had followed like a faithful dog. After so many towns burned, after so many innocents killed, he realised he was following an unworthy master.

What had he done? This was not what Harold would

have wanted; for him to leave a trail of his dead kinsmen in his wake. Neither was it what Edith wanted when she told him to earn the blade he had lost. Styrkar had failed them both.

A sound alerted him, a soft shuffle in the darkness that made him open his eyes. Styrkar rose to his feet, the chair toppling behind him as a figure came rushing at him from the shadows.

All he saw was the knife, and he acted on instinct, hand flashing forward to catch his attacker's wrist. Still the blade scraped against his mail and bounced up to nick his jaw. Only then did he see it was a woman who had come at him from the dark, eyes wide and desperate.

They stared at one another as Styrkar fought the pain in his wounded shoulder. She was held fast, but still she struggled, trying to wrest her arm from his grip. She was young, terrified, and Styrkar knew it was he who had caused this. He and the warriors who had come to this place with no thoughts but to destroy.

'Let me go,' she said. Her words were forceful but Styrkar could still hear a tremor in her voice.

'Are you going to stab me if I do?' he asked.

She didn't answer. Still, he loosed his grip on her wrist and she took a step back, holding the knife out threateningly.

Styrkar was done with fighting. If this woman wanted to cut his throat then let her. Perhaps it was what he deserved.

Slowly he turned, picking up the fallen chair and righting it, before slumping down once more. It creaked beneath him, built for someone with much less bulk and not wearing heavy mail.

She was still staring at him, still holding the knife out defiantly, but she did not attack.

'Am I your prisoner?' Styrkar asked.

Slowly she lowered the knife. 'You are no Welshman,' she said.

'I am a Dane,' he replied.

She looked at him curiously. 'Then you are far from home.'

'I am. Further than you know.'

'What are you going to do?'

It seemed a curious question. 'I am going to sit here awhile and rest,' he replied.

'I mean with me? What are you going to do with me?'

Styrkar shook his head. He could tell what the woman meant. The Welsh had fallen on the town with all the savage fury of their kind. Men had their throats cut; women were raped. The thought of taking a woman against her will sickened Styrkar to his stomach, and he was not about to murder the helpless. Not anymore.

'I'm not going to do anything with you,' he said.

The tension seemed to leave her, and Styrkar felt some relief as she lowered the knife.

'What is your name?' she asked.

'My name is Styrkar,' he replied. For a moment he was tempted to tell her he was the feared Red Wolf, but that ruthless warrior seemed far away now.

'I am Gisela,' she replied. 'You are wounded, Styrkar. You need help.'

It seemed an obvious statement. 'And will you help me, Gisela? Or will you send me the rest of the way to Hel?'

'Perhaps we could help each other?' she said. 'Get me out of this place and I will see to your wound.'

'You are a healer?'

Gisela inclined her head. 'Of a sort. I can bloody well try, at least. And I don't see anyone else here to help you. Will those Welsh bastards see to your care? Somehow I doubt it.'

Styrkar doubted it too. He struggled to his feet, feeling the pain more keenly now the red rage of battle had passed. The woman raised the knife once more, as though he might attack her.

'Do you want to get out of here or not?' he asked.

Without another word she moved to his side, bracing her shoulder beneath his good arm and guiding him out of the hovel.

Outside, the sound of battle from the castle had subsided. Two Welshmen ran past, fleeing with the booty they had ransacked from the town.

'This way,' Styrkar said, guiding her deeper into the mess of houses so they would not be seen.

Gisela helped him on, moving towards the gates of the town that now lay burned and broken to the north. Through the gaps in the houses, they could see more warriors fleeing the battle, heading back to the boats that were moored by the river.

'Wait,' Styrkar said, and they stopped at the edge of the town, hunkering beside a building whose thatch was still smouldering.

More Welsh ran past, this group panicked, and from the direction of the castle Styrkar heard a horn blow. The sound for retreat.

'We have to go now,' he said, leading the way as Gisela

helped him across the road. They struggled through the gate. To the west was the river; to the right he could see a copse of trees. If they could make it there, they could hide as Eadric's army fled to their boats.

'Styrkar!'

The voice called out before they could take a single step towards safety.

Styrkar turned to see Stithulf approaching along the path and he cursed beneath his breath as he saw Wulfsige not far behind him.

'See you've claimed your own reward,' Stithulf said. 'Come, we have to get to the boats. The earl has ordered us to withdraw – the bastard Franks managed to close the gates. The men still inside the castle have been slaughtered. A scout has reported Frankish reinforcements approaching from the east, so we don't have much time.'

He began to lead the way east. Styrkar glanced down at Gisela, seeing the fear in her eyes.

'What are you waiting for, Red Wolf?' Wulfsige asked. 'Were you going to run away with this one? Keep her all for yourself?'

The housecarl laughed at that, and Styrkar had never wanted more to squeeze the man's throat shut.

With no other option he made his way towards the boats. Gisela began to tremble as she helped him along, and he wanted to tell her to flee, but more raiders had come now, surrounding them. If she fled they would chase her down with ease. When finally they reached the river it was too late for her to escape.

Styrkar struggled to sit at the stern of the first boat, Gisela taking the seat in front of him as Welsh raiders and English rebels began to flock to the riverside. They quickly took up oars, making their way from the bank with all speed. Before their boat was pushed off, Styrkar heard a familiar shout.

'Wait for me!'

He looked up to see Kenric racing as fast as he could, laden down with loot from the town. Styrkar's friend managed to board, just before the boat made its way along the river.

'You look like shit,' Kenric said unhelpfully, as he slumped in the seat beside Gisela.

'He is wounded,' she said, her eyes fixed on the bottom of the boat.

Kenric moved to Styrkar's side, examining the quarrel still protruding from his shoulder.

'That needs to come out,' he said.

Styrkar would have congratulated his friend on his talent for stating the obvious, but all he could do was look at Gisela, her forlorn expression filling him with guilt. When she looked up at him, Styrkar mouthed that he was sorry. The girl just glanced away, watching the river as it rolled past.

'Well, brace yourself, my friend,' Kenric said.

Before Styrkar could protest, Kenric gripped the shaft of the crossbow bolt and wrenched it clear of his shoulder. Styrkar had only a moment to feel the agony that coursed through him before he blacked out.

PART FOUR

BLOOD PRICE

37

THE LONG FOREST, ENGLAND, AUGUST 1067

He awoke on the floor, drenched and shivering. Styrkar's room was dark and cold, and what little light there was seeping in through the gaps in the poorly constructed hut told him it was daytime. The reassuring voices he heard outside told him he was safe. But he didn't feel safe.

With the fever that had assailed his body he felt weak and vulnerable. Though he was over the worst of it, he still felt sick, the wound in his shoulder still aching. His whole body felt bruised, as though he'd been kicked from one side of the Marcher Lands to the other, and his throat was dry as a nun's crotch.

His constant companions were the flies that buzzed all around. The bloated things would occasionally land on him irritatingly as they probed for rotting flesh. Well, they would have to wait. He was not a corpse yet.

Peering through the scant light he saw a jug and a wooden cup had been left by the side of him. He reached out, hand shaking as he grasped the cup. When he stretched for the jug his limbs ached, fingertips managing to grasp the handle before it slipped from his grasp, spilling the contents on the floor. With a sigh, he rolled onto his back.

Styrkar had never felt so weak. He had been wounded before – his scarred body was testament to that – but never had he been reduced to such a pathetic state. But where before he had been treated by King Harold's best surgeons, now he was among a rabble of cutthroats and rapers, with not a skilled healer among them. Styrkar realised he had few true brothers here, and only regretted it had taken him so long to realise it.

The door swung open, letting in a cooling breeze that made Styrkar shiver. He looked up from where he lay, lamenting he had no weapon nearby and hoping he wouldn't need one. When he saw Kenric's smiling face in the doorway he allowed himself to sink back to the straw mattress.

His friend entered, wrists and forearms adorned with bronze bands, and he had found a mismatched ring for every finger. At least one of them had benefited from Eadric's campaign of raiding.

'Feeling better?' Kenric asked as he approached.

Styrkar wasn't entirely sure. He couldn't remember how long he had lain there slipping in and out of consciousness or whether he could even stand.

'I've brought you a gift,' Kenric continued. 'Something to make you feel better.'

He turned, gesturing to the door, and Styrkar could see another figure behind him. When she walked into the dull light, Styrkar recognised her immediately.

Gisela looked sullen, but he could see a flash of concern about her as she looked over his clammy body.

'I mean, I know she's not really a gift,' Kenric continued. 'She was yours to start with, but I've kept her safe while you've been… lying here. No one else has touched her.'

As Gisela knelt by his side, Styrkar tried to rise, but she gently pushed him back to the ground.

'How long has he been like this?' she asked.

Kenric shrugged. 'A few days.'

'No one has been taking care of him?'

'I stitched his wound,' Kenric said, as though he were proud of the fact. 'But other than that, wasn't much we could do.'

Gisela rolled Styrkar over, sniffing at his bandaged shoulder before reeling back. 'It's not infected, but it needs cleaning properly. And he needs to be washed – it stinks in here. Go and get me water. Hot water and clean rags.'

Without a word of argument, Kenric scurried off to do her bidding. Styrkar was surprised at how forcefully she had commanded him, and how quick he was to obey.

Gisela tore a strip of cloth from her skirts, picking up the fallen jug and wetting it in the dregs. As she began to dab at Styrkar's forehead he could not help but stare at her. Over the past days her face had become grimy, her hair tangled, but she was still as beautiful as the first time he'd laid eyes on her.

'I'm sorry,' Styrkar said, as she tended to him.

A smile crept up the side of Gisela's face and for a brief moment, Styrkar felt some lightness to his mood.

'For the smell?' she asked.

'For bringing you here,' he replied. 'I would not have—'

She placed a finger to his lips, her skin soft against his. 'Stop talking. This isn't your fault.'

He lay back, allowing her to minister to him, all the while feeling more guilty. He could tell she was not speaking the truth. Of course it was his fault, and yet still she treated him with kindness. No one had shown him such care since the nuns at the abbey. Since Edith…

The thought of his dead mistress filled Styrkar with a sudden grief. Later he would not know whether it was at the thought of Edith, or the fever from which he was recovering, but a tear ran from his eye and down his face.

'Don't worry,' said Gisela, her hand wiping the tear away. 'You will recover.'

In that moment, Styrkar wasn't sure if he even wanted to. He had failed. His path to vengeance had only led to yet more suffering, and what had he accomplished? Nothing but to spread misery in his wake.

The thought of it angered him. He was wallowing in his self-pity and knew that was not his way. He was Styrkar the Dane, the Red Wolf, not some miserable pig farmer from the arse end of nowhere.

He tried to sit, and Gisela said, 'No, you have to rest.'

'I have rested enough,' he replied, pushing her hand aside and moving to sit with his back against the wall of the hut. His head spun for a moment, bile rising, but he swallowed it down and fought to retain his faculties.

'You're a stubborn one,' she said.

He could not argue with that. 'You have a Frankish edge to your voice,' Styrkar said, doing his best to divert attention from the nausea. 'Is that where you're from.'

'A long time ago,' Gisela replied. 'I was born in a place called Flanders. When my parents died I was sent to serve in the house of the FitzScrobs. When they came to these islands I came with them.'

'So, you are a slave?' he asked.

Gisela shook her head. 'No, I am a servant. There are no slaves in Frankia. We do not allow such a barbaric practice where I am from.'

'Slave, servant. What's the difference?'

'The difference is, I am free.' Gisela lowered her eyes. 'Or at least, I was.'

Styrkar wanted to tell her once more how sorry he was, but words were no use now. They were both prisoners in their own way, only Styrkar's chains were not about his wrists.

The door opened once more, and Kenric came in, struggling with a pot of hot water. It still steamed as he laid it down by Styrkar's side.

'See, you're looking better already,' he said. 'And just in time. Earl Eadric is gathering his men for a witan.'

'To discuss what?' Styrkar asked.

'My guess is what we should do next.'

Styrkar pulled the woollen blanket aside, feeling the cold against his flesh. Ignoring it, he tried to struggle to his feet and despite Gisela's protestation he managed to stand.

'You need to rest,' she said.

'I need to be at the witan,' Styrkar replied.

'She's right,' Kenric said. 'You look fit to drop.'

Styrkar fixed him with a baleful look. 'Help me or get out of my way.'

That was enough for Kenric, and he nodded his agreement. Despite Gisela's objection, they both quickly washed him.

The warm water was invigorating, and Styrkar began to feel whole once more. Once he had struggled into clean clothes, he felt ready to take on almost anything. Walking would have to do for a start.

Outside the hut, the fresh air made his head spin, but he gritted his teeth and forced one foot in front of the other. It didn't take him long to discover the location of the witan – voices were already raised and he walked through the sparse woodland towards them.

Eadric sat on a log surrounded by his men. Wulfsige was at his shoulder, and opposite sat Bleddyn and Rhiwallon.

'We need to take the fight back to them,' Rhiwallon growled, rising to his feet. His men murmured their assent.

No one seemed to notice Styrkar as he came to stand in the midst of the warriors.

'It's too late for that,' Eadric said. He looked weary, and if Styrkar hadn't known better he'd have thought the fearsome earl defeated. 'Our scouts have already told us that Hereford has been heavily fortified. An entire garrison patrols its outskirts. We could not get within a mile of the place before meeting an army of Franks.'

'Then what do we do?' Rhiwallon demanded. 'Sit here in the woods and wait for winter? We did not come here for the meagre spoils you have provided, Saxon. We came for riches.'

'And riches you shall have,' Eadric replied.

'From where?' The Welsh prince spread his muscular arms wide. 'Is there silver in the trees?'

'Your prisoners,' Eadric said.

'Our slaves? Most are worthless.'

'Many are Franks,' the earl replied. 'Their countrymen

will pay much more for their return than you can get selling them to the Irish. And when we bargain with the Franks for their lives we will negotiate a deal for you and your brother to return to your lands in the west. That was always part of the arrangement.'

'When we had taken the city of Hereford,' Rhiwallon said. 'But we have no city. All we have is this stinking forest.'

Eadric shrugged. 'It's not the position from which I wanted to make the bargain, but it is all we have.'

'We might as well have surrendered,' bellowed Rhiwallon. 'I say we take the fight back to them. Attack them at night. Blacken our bodies and—'

'No, brother,' Bleddyn said. He looked almost as battle-weary as Eadric. 'The Saxon is right. Attacking the Franks in their castle is impossible. But we might be able to salvage something by bargaining with them now.'

Rhiwallon shook his head. 'But, brother—'

'I said no,' Bleddyn growled. It was enough to silence Rhiwallon. 'The only problem we have now is sending a messenger brave enough to meet with the Franks. Someone who does not fear death. Who would take a message…?'

Styrkar had already stepped into the centre of the clearing. This was his chance to make up for his mistake. His opportunity to see Gisela to safety, and he would trust no other with it.

'I will take the message,' he said.

Eadric smiled. 'You look like the dead,' he said.

'There's enough life in me to strike a bargain with the Franks,' he replied.

Rhiwallon laughed at that, as Bleddyn eyed him suspiciously. 'Why would you volunteer for this?' asked the

Welsh prince. 'They're just as likely to take your head and mount it on their gates as listen to you.'

'Does anyone want to go in my place?' Styrkar asked. There were no willing volunteers. 'Then I'll leave in the morning.'

He turned and made his way back to the hut. The nausea had struck him again and he needed to lie down before he fell. Kenric was quickly at his side and helped him back to the hut.

'Are you mad? Bleddyn speaks sense. They'd more likely murder you where you stand than hear you out.'

'You'd better hope they don't,' Styrkar replied.

'Why's that?' He could already see a worried look on his friend's face.

'Because you're coming with me.'

38

HEREFORD, ENGLAND, AUGUST 1067

Ronan hung at the back of the short column of riders. He would have preferred his own knights, but the FitzScrobs had insisted that it was their men who would lead the contingent. Having Aldus by his side would have made him feel safer, but his friend was dead, slain by the Red Wolf. Hopefully soon there would be a reckoning for that.

Aldus had been his constant companion, the only man he had ever relied on. Now all that was gone. Ronan tried to ignore the gaping chasm the loss of his friend left, but no matter how he tried to focus on the task at hand he could not shirk the image of Aldus falling from the summit of the castle wall. The grave they had dug for the giant had been suitably deep and Ronan had struggled against his tears as the last rites were spoken. But he could not allow grief to cloud his mind. Ronan had always been a man of singular purpose, and right now he had a job to do.

Of course, Baron Richard was not with them. This was a

dangerous mission. Why would he risk himself needlessly? Instead, his son Osbern led the column as it rode along the river.

Ronan had taken an instant disliking to the man, but he kept up the façade that they were friends. Osbern was an idealist. He respected this land and its people. Obviously he had spent too long here and been drawn in by the primitive charm of the place. He would do everything he could to secure a peaceful outcome, apart from what was most expedient. They should have been hunting down these rebels, not bargaining with them. They should have been mounting heads on walls, burning settlements, interrogating prisoners. But here they were, riding to make peace.

Eadric had sent a written message. A meeting was set up. Now they were making their way through the peaceful countryside to parlay with one of his rebels. As they rode the few short miles from Hereford, no one would have known that a few days before this land was riven with rebellion, houses burned, villagers slaughtered. Their contingent was a mere half dozen men – exposed, vulnerable, and most likely doomed. But still Ronan had come. If this was the only chance he had to put an end to this whole affair then he would do so.

Their meeting place came into view up ahead. Only half the church was still standing, the rest having been consumed by the woodland. Even in its heyday, Ronan would have thought it was a dilapidated affair: stones piled haphazardly, wood nailed in with little care for the longevity of the place. It sickened him yet further. How little regard the people of these lands gave to the construction of their places of worship. They would soon learn what real churches should look like. Buildings of awe and wonder. Places to be revered.

That would come later. For now they had to stamp out further resistance, and Ronan was keenly aware that this was not the way to do it.

Osbern held up a hand for the column to halt before calling on them to dismount. Ronan climbed down from his steed and limped his way to the front as Osbern glared at the church.

'Could be a trap,' he said to the sheriff.

Osbern nodded. 'Could be. But what choice do we have in this?'

'We could set the place on fire. We could take captives. We could make them tell us where Earl Eadric is hiding.'

'And in the meantime he slaughters his prisoners,' Osbern said.

Ronan couldn't see the problem with that. 'Well, you're in charge,' he said, taking a step back and letting Osbern lead them on.

The half dozen men drew weapons and brandished their spears. Ronan didn't bother drawing his own sword but kept a hand on the hilt. If they were about to be ambushed in any significant numbers it was doubtful their weapons would do them much good.

Osbern led the way through the churchyard. Here and there was a stone marker, worn down by age. Ronan limped on through the grass, his eyes fixed on the gaping entrance to the church. It smelled musty inside, rotten. The woodland had encroached on the old building, making it one with the surroundings. As they entered, a bird tweeted in the crumbling rafters and a rat scurried across the floor. Ahead of them a hulking figure stood waiting.

'You are Eadric's man?' Osbern said, brandishing his sword.

It seemed pretty bloody obvious.

When the figure stepped forward into the light lancing through the broken roof, Ronan felt a squall of anger well up inside.

Styrkar looked gaunt about the face, but his shoulders still bulged within the mail coat he wore. A hand-axe hung at one hip, a sword at the other, and he carried a wicked-looking Dane axe across his shoulder.

'Who else's man would I be?' Styrkar said.

Ronan bristled. Here was the bastard who had slain his childhood friend. He had buried Aldus only a few days previously, a mighty grave for a mighty warrior. And the killer now stood bold as brass, showing not an inch of repentance.

'What's your name?' Osbern asked.

Before he could answer, Ronan stepped forward. 'This is Styrkar the Dane,' he pronounced. 'Though you might know him better as the feared Red Wolf.'

Osbern tightened his grip on the sword he held. Ronan thought how pathetic Osbern looked. It was obvious the Red Wolf could have murdered them all where they stood had he a mind to.

'Eadric only sent one man?' Osbern said. 'That's an arrogant move, even if that man is a renowned killer.'

'Who says I'm alone?' Styrkar said.

A second figure stepped out of the shadows. He had

a bow drawn and trained on the knights, each finger of his hands bearing a shining ring. Despite his confident expression Ronan could see those hands were shaking.

'Lower your weapons,' Osbern said to his men. Reluctantly they obeyed. 'We are not here to fight. We are here to bargain for the release of our people.'

'Wise,' Styrkar said. He did not lower the axe.

'So what does your master want in return for the prisoners?' Osbern asked.

'He would have a hundredweight in silver for each one. Any less and you get them back in pieces.'

Ronan laughed. 'Are you mad? These are not nobles you hold. They are peasants.'

Styrkar regarded him coldly. It was obvious he recognised Ronan but made no reference to their previous meeting. Ronan had never wished more that he was a better shot.

'That's the price. Take it or leave it.'

'We will pay,' Osbern said, before there could be any further argument. 'The only question is where?'

'There is a tributary six miles along the River Lugg. By an abandoned mill. Bring the silver on boats, just you and the rivermen. If we see any armed warriors all you'll get back are corpses.'

'We will need time to gather such wealth,' Osbern said.

'You have two days,' Styrkar replied.

'We need more time than that.'

Styrkar shrugged his broad shoulders. 'You have two days, or Earl Eadric gives his prisoners to the Welsh.'

Osbern shook his head, but Ronan knew there would be no further bargaining. He stepped forward.

'We will bring your silver. But know this, Red Wolf. You will never be safe from me. I will find you. There will be no place far enough you can run to escape me.'

Styrkar regarded him gravely. 'Who says I will run? Once this is done, I may well come to find you.'

'A day I will look forward to.'

Osbern and his men backed away. Ronan glanced at the archer, committing his face to memory – another rebel he would put to the sword should he have the chance.

When they were outside the church Osbern hurriedly led the way to the waiting horses. As they mounted up, Ronan couldn't help but gaze back at the church. How he would have loved to rush inside with his men at his back and cut down that Danish bastard where he stood. The pride of the man, the sureness. He would have wiped that smug look of arrogance off his face all right, and nailed his head to the nearest gatepost.

They rode south towards Hereford in silence after Osbern had sent one of his men ahead to inform his father of the bargain they had struck. All the while, Ronan could not help but think his plans to raise his station were being blown from his grasp like ashes. As much as Styrkar had proclaimed his intention to track Ronan down, he knew he could not trust the words of the rebel. If he didn't do something, the Red Wolf could easily slip the noose and disappear into the wilds forever. Then where would he be? Just another knight in Brian's conrois. Committed to serve in this pitiful country until old age. There had to be something he could do.

The town of Hereford was quiet as they rode past. The burned thatch had been stripped from most of the houses and the sound of saws and hammers echoed out over the wooden palisade. Ronan had not appreciated how alive this place had been when he first came to the castle. Now a pall of misery hung about the town. These people would remember what Eadric and his Welsh allies had done here. Only good would come of that. King William's name would be spoken of with respect now. It was not he who had ravaged the place, but a Saxon lord. These people would give praise to the king now and beg his protection. It sickened Ronan to his stomach how fickle they were, but the survivors would learn the benefit of loyalty in time.

In the castle courtyard he dismounted and followed Osbern inside. There had been much slaughter here, much bloodshed on the cobbles, and Ronan had no wish to tarry and remind himself of what he and his men had suffered. The heads of those Welsh they had managed to kill still adorned the gates, rotting in the breeze. If Ronan had his way there would be many more before this business was finished.

Baron Richard sat in the feasting hall, his chair by the fire, and fur blanket over his knees. There was nothing inclement to the weather, but the old man was showing his age now more than ever. It seemed the past few days had tarnished his sheen.

'Father,' Osbern said. 'We have met with Eadric's emissary. He demands a hefty ransom, but I think if we act fast we can gather the silver he demands and secure the captives.'

Richard continued to stare into the fire. Ronan stood behind Osbern and noticed the glint of the weapon that had been mounted in pride of place above the hearth. The sword of the Red Wolf taunted him. It sat as a reminder of the man he had taken it from. The man who had murdered Aldus. Now more than ever, Ronan yearned for his justice.

'Where and when is the exchange to take place?' Richard asked, still staring into the flames.

'Two days from now, along the River Lugg,' Osbern told him.

Richard nodded. 'Then I will send men along the river and this dark business will be concluded. We can leave this behind us. The rebellion will be over.'

Ronan could have laughed. If Baron Richard thought a few weights of silver would see this rebellion quashed he was a fool. But there was no way Ronan would tell him that. The exchange would give him an opportunity. Perhaps his last chance to finally accomplish what he had come here for.

'If I may, my lord,' Ronan said. 'I would be happy to make the exchange.'

Richard looked up from the fire, gazing through the shadows at Ronan. 'You? But this is not your concern. Why would you put yourself in such danger?'

'I am a servant of the king,' Ronan said. 'It is my duty.'

Osbern and Richard exchanged a relieved glance before Richard said, 'You have my thanks, Ronan of Dol-Combourg. Your bravery becomes you. I will make sure Earl Willem hears of your selflessness.'

Ronan bowed low. 'Your servant,' he said, before turning and making his way from the feasting hall.

As he limped towards the garrison to prepare his men, there was a flurry of excitement within him. Ronan was no one's servant. And when he had the Red Wolf's head, he would no longer be just another anonymous soldier.

Yes, he would take Richard's silver along the river, but it would act as nothing more than bait. If Eadric wanted his ransom he would surely come collect it himself, and Styrkar would be alongside him. There would be no reward for these rebels. If they thought they were safe hiding behind their prisoners, Ronan would be sure to show them their mistake.

39

RIVER LUGG, ENGLAND, AUGUST 1067

The boats followed the course of the river southward. Styrkar sat at the prow, watching the trees on the riverbank for any sign they might be ambushed. The Franks would be foolish to try anything; Eadric had already promised to execute every last prisoner should they be attacked. Still, it did not make Styrkar any less vigilant.

There were over a hundred prisoners in all, crammed into the five boats, surrounded by Eadric's men. On the bank, following them as they rowed, were more than a thousand Welshmen. Bleddyn and Rhiwallon had not trusted Earl Eadric to return with their silver and Styrkar could hardly blame them, he had already learned how treacherous the earl could be. Plunder was the only reason the princes had come to the Marcher Lands, and to return empty-handed was not an option for either of them.

Styrkar turned to look at the prisoners and saw Gisela at the front of the boat where he had put her. She was chained at the wrist to another prisoner, and Styrkar would have spared her that indignity but he had no choice in the matter. Eadric had ordered every one of them shackled. If something went wrong, he had instructed his men to pitch them all into the river.

'Not long now,' Styrkar said to her under his breath. 'Soon this will all be over and you will be free.'

She nodded her thanks to him, but he could still see the fear in her eyes. It pained him to think that he had caused this. That after making her a promise back in Hereford town that he would help her, now she was chained and her life hanging at the edge of a precipice.

Someone called out from the bank, and Styrkar turned to see the wreck of the mill up ahead. This was it. They would soon find out if Eadric's plan would work.

There was no sign of the Franks, and Styrkar's unease began to deepen. As they reached the mill and secured the boats to the shore, he jumped to the riverbank. Eadric was already standing some feet away, eyes scanning downriver. Wulfsige and his other housecarls lingered close by, and Styrkar moved past them to stand beside the Saxon lord.

'What now?' Styrkar asked, fearing that Eadric's nerve would give out and he would execute the prisoners anyway, or hand them over to the Welsh.

'Now we wait,' Eadric replied.

Wulfsige stepped forward, a deep frown on his scarred face. 'We should never have come here. We cannot trust the bastard Franks.'

Styrkar could see he was twitchy and nervous, hand on the axe at his belt. He was ready to run or fight, and waiting here at the riverbank was only making him more anxious.

'We wait,' Eadric said.

'For how long?' Wulfsige asked petulantly. Styrkar couldn't blame him – it was a question they all wanted answered.

Before Eadric could speak, a Welsh scout came barging through the trees, pointing back along the river.

'Boats,' he said. 'They're coming.'

Eadric turned to his men as word of the approaching Franks spread throughout the Welsh ranks. 'Keep your heads,' he ordered. 'We collect the silver as planned. First sign of an ambush, we pitch these poor devils into the river.'

There was a ripple of assent as his warriors drew their weapons. From the boats there were wails of fear as the prisoners lamented what might happen should something go wrong.

Styrkar watched as half a dozen boats were rowed upstream. The boatmen pulled hard on their oars, struggling against the current. Eventually, they moored on the opposite bank and the boatmen quickly debarked. Through the trees, a group of armed men appeared, Ronan limping at their head.

The Frankish knight spread his arms as though presenting the boats and the riches within. Styrkar could see that sheets of cloth had been bound across their contents.

'Here it is,' Ronan called out across the river. 'We have brought what you asked for.'

'And so have we,' answered Eadric, gesturing to the prisoners.

'So how should we proceed? I suggest you send us the prisoners first.'

'Of course you do,' Eadric shouted, before whispering,

'Frankish bastard,' under his breath. 'How about we send our boats one by one? And at the same time?'

Ronan shrugged like a man without a care. 'However you wish, Earl Eadric.'

He turned and gave orders to his men. Two of them waded into the water, pulling a weighted rope tied to the prow. One of them swung it about his head before flinging it across the river. At his order, one of Eadric's housecarls waded in to retrieve it and began to pull the rope across.

'You,' Eadric said to the men sat aboard one of his own boats. 'Row!' He gestured across the river.

'How do we get back?' one of them asked.

'You can bloody swim, can't you?' Eadric growled.

There was no further argument, and the men began to row across the river. The two boats crossed paths, prisoners and silver moving slowly across the river until their prows bumped against the bank almost at the same time. As Eadric's men leapt from the boat full of prisoners and began to wade back across, Styrkar could see the men and women being unloaded on the other side.

Wulfsige had already waded in knee-deep to check the boat of silver, and he cut the ropes that secured the hide covering. The bottom of the vessel was lined with shining ingots, and Wulfsige looked up with an ugly grin.

'We're bloody rich,' he said.

Before anyone could stop them, some of the Welsh fell on the boat, swamping it and unloading the silver as though they were ravenous for it.

'Shall we send the rest?' Ronan shouted.

Eadric dragged his eyes away from the boat full of silver. 'Yes,' he replied. 'Let's get this over with.'

The Franks hastily lashed the boats full of silver together, again flinging a rope across the river. Three of Eadric's men waded in this time to pull the hoard across, so eager were they to take their share. Meanwhile, Eadric ordered the four remaining boats full of prisoners to be lashed together at prow and stern. Rather than risk his rowers this time, he also had a rope flung across the river.

Styrkar could only watch as Gisela was borne away. She turned her head to look at him and he nodded to reassure her. In return she raised her hand, the most subtle of gestures, bidding him farewell.

As Eadric's men pulled on the rope, they were joined by a couple of the Welsh warriors, grown impatient by the wait. Styrkar could hear them straining and shouting encouragement to one another. As the two rows of boats began to pass one another, they suddenly stopped.

'Pull harder,' one of Eadric's men barked.

'It's snagged on something,' said another.

Try as they might, the warriors could not get the boats to budge. Meanwhile the prisoners were slowly being dragged away to the other bank.

Rhiwallon stepped forward, his brow creasing in concern. 'Get the frigging silver,' he bellowed, pointing at the boats.

His men needed no further encouragement, dropping their weapons and plunging into the river, some not even bothering to remove their mail as they waded in at chest height to reach the boats full of loot.

Styrkar could only watch as more and more men began to swarm the boats, pulling themselves from the water. They savagely cut the ropes, dragging back the strips of hide that covered the silver. The disappointment on their faces told a grim tale.

'There's nothing here,' one of them yelled back furiously.

'What's that shitty smell?' he heard another one say.

Before anyone could answer, Styrkar saw a line of Frankish knights step forward from the opposite tree line. Every man carried a loaded crossbow, the head of each bolt aflame.

'Get off the boats,' Eadric screamed, but he was already too late.

The Frankish loosed a flaming volley across the river. Some of the quarrels splashed harmlessly into the water, their fires sizzling on the surface, but others hit the mark. As soon as they thudded into the pitch-covered boats they ignited. A wall of flame erupted on each boat, the men on board consumed by fire. Their screams pealed out as some of them leapt into the dark waters to extinguish the flames.

Styrkar spun around at the sound of beating hooves. He had barely enough time to raise his axe as a row of mounted knights burst from the surrounding woodland. Welshmen were speared on lances, others hacked down by axe and sword, and in the confusion many of them were put to flight.

Styrkar felt consumed by rage at the betrayal, leaping forward, axe swinging to hack the first knight from his horse. The man was pitched back off the saddle, and Styrkar finished him with a devastating blow to his skull.

'Get the prisoners,' he heard Eadric shout.

Turning, he saw that in his cunning, Eadric had also tied a rope to the rear of the boats containing the prisoners. Half a dozen of his men were now splashing through the water to grasp the rope and pull the prisoners back. Across the river, Styrkar could see Ronan's men still struggling to pull them across, but they were no match for the strength of the Welsh.

Battle erupted all around as the mounted knights ran rampant, but Styrkar ignored the melee. He peered through the flames, desperate to see if Gisela was safe.

The prisoners had drawn level with the flaming boats, and many of them were screaming with alarm, shielding themselves from the fire. As he watched, Styrkar saw one of the prison boats catch alight. The chained townsfolk within it desperately tried to put out the fire but it was no use. Gisela was at the front, doing all she could to stamp out the flames.

Styrkar dropped his axe, rushing to the water's edge. The rope connecting Gisela's boat to the rest had burned through and it began to drift, still on fire. There was no time to strip off his mail coat, and Styrkar plunged into the water, wading desperately towards the boat before it was consumed by flames and sank to the bottom of the river. He saw one of the prisoners pitch over the side in desperation, dragging another with him as he fell, the heavy chains pulling them both to their deaths.

Styrkar grabbed the rope to the burning boats, pulling himself along it, reaching the first flaming vessel. Despite the heat he pulled himself up, feeling the fire lick at his clothing. He ran across the chain of vessels, leaping from one to the next, desperate to reach the final boat as it was dragged away by the current. The fire set his leggings alight, but he ignored the searing heat that burned his flesh as he ducked a tirade of fiery crossbow bolts. One leap and he managed to grab Gisela's boat, and with a final burst of effort pulled himself on board.

'Help us,' someone screamed, as he felt the heat from the fire, smelled the stink of burning wood.

The prisoners were chained together at the wrist, there was no way he could release them all. Before he could think what to do a flaming bolt whistled past his ear and Styrkar ducked. The man chained to Gisela stood up, eyes wide in panic.

'We have to get—' was all he had a chance to say before a quarrel buried itself in his chest.

The man slumped to the bottom of the boat as more flaming missiles impacted against the hull. Styrkar pulled the axe from his belt, grasping the dead man's arm and hacking it off at the wrist. Gisela gasped in horror, but Styrkar had no time to reassure her as he grabbed her and they both plunged into the dark waters.

He lost his grasp on her as he fought to stay afloat, the heavy mail dragging him down. Styrkar thrashed in the water, legs pumping frantically but he could not touch the bottom. Submerged as he was, he could see nothing but distant light above him.

Water gushed into his nose and mouth and he began to panic, arms flailing as he desperately made his way towards the shore. His foot caught the bottom and he propelled himself towards shallower waters, but he was tiring fast. He could not give up. The shore was not far away, but try as he might he could not reach it. Darkness began to consume him, his lungs bursting, and he started to drift out of consciousness.

A hand grasped his collar, hauling him out of the depths. Stithulf and Gisela pulled his head above the surface and he coughed up a gout of river water.

Styrkar crawled up the bank, retching all the while as the sounds of battle coalesced in his ears. Someone was shouting for retreat, and as he looked up he could see the Frankish horsemen running amok, the Welsh routing through the trees. The cloth of his leggings was blackened and the flesh of his lower leg raw from the flames, but he managed to stand.

'We have to get out of here,' Stithulf said, hauling Styrkar after him.

There was no arguing with that, and Styrkar stumbled behind his friend. Gisela ran with them as they made their way through the trees, flaming bolts still peppering the ground all around them.

One glance back, and he could see Ronan standing on the opposite bank. The treacherous swine glared intently at the carnage, and for a moment Styrkar considered racing back to face him. But now was not the time. All he could do was flee, and hope he would get another chance to bury his blade in that crippled bastard's heart.

40

HEREFORD, ENGLAND, AUGUST 1067

Ronan lost only a score of men before the rebels finally fled into the woods. Mainard had reported the numbers but he'd hardly listened. The only man he was interested in was Styrkar, and as he trod the riverbank, searching the bodies, he became more dismayed when he could find no sign of him.

Another failure. It nestled within him as he ordered his men to mount up, eating at his insides as they made their way back towards the castle. Ronan had barely acknowledged the fact that they were being followed by the score of prisoners liberated from Eadric and his Welsh allies.

He glanced back along the sorry column, ignoring the bodies of his men slung across the backs of horses and the wounded slumped in their saddles. All he could focus on was the wagon full of FitzScrob silver. Here were riches beyond his imagining... and he could imagine a lot. Ronan could become a wealthy man back in Bretagne with such a hoard, but try as he might he could not think of a way he could keep it for himself. His men would not help him without taking their own cut of the booty, and word would find its way back to the FitzScrobs if their silver disappeared and Ronan were suddenly to turn up back home a rich man.

Still, the temptation to take the silver and run was overwhelming. And who deserved such a reward if not him? Before the temptation became too much, Mainard kicked his horse forward to ride beside Ronan.

'What do we do with the prisoners?' he said in a low voice.

'What do I care?' Ronan replied.

'You might if word gets back to Baron Richard of what happened. We were supposed to make the exchange for the prisoners, not ambush the rebels. We've lost men, a lot of the townsfolk have died, and the rebels have fled. If we—'

'All right,' Ronan snapped. 'I get the picture. We passed an abandoned longhouse on the way here. The roof had enough thatch left on it to catch ablaze.'

He glanced at Mainard, hoping he didn't have to explain any further, and was pleased when the young knight nodded and reined his horse around to let the others know their plan.

Ronan plodded on. He knew any more thoughts of theft and flight were pointless. Now all he could do was hide the evidence of his treachery.

When eventually the house came into view, Ronan was surprised at how little he felt about what they were about to do. He had watched before as towns and villages had been put to the torch. As William's faithful had raped and murdered, and all in the name of making him the rightful king. God's chosen. And every time he had felt the sickness in his stomach lessen. Now there was nothing but a slight grumbling of hunger.

Ronan pulled his horse to a stop. With a gesture, he ordered Mainard to herd the prisoners inside. His men went about the task with eagerness, shoving the frightened civilians with their spears, persuading those reluctant to obey with a mailed fist.

At first they were docile enough, but within moments panic began to spread. Women shouted in alarm, clutching children to their breasts as their men began to get more aggressive. They were subdued at the tip of a dozen spears, but by the time Ronan's knights had corralled the last of the townsfolk inside there was a clangour of desperation.

Ronan sat in silence and watched as his men secured the door, barring it shut. Hands clawed at the gaps between the lintel, and a well-placed axe hacked off a few fingers to demonstrate there was no escape.

Torches were lit, and his men stood back. They had followed William's army from the coast of Normandy. Fought hard for months. Rampaged and slaughtered throughout the English countryside, but still they paused, unsure of whether to act.

'Burn it,' Ronan ordered.

His men obeyed, flinging their torches atop the thatched roof, and Ronan watched as the flames licked at the dry straw, spreading quickly.

Subdued panic turned to hysteria, as the men, women and children inside the house began to scream in terror. Ronan signalled to his crossbowmen to make ready, and a score of them lined up in front of the burning building, locking their strings and loading their quarrels in anticipation.

Pitiful pleas for mercy were lost amid the cacophony of voices. Someone banged against the door as smoke began to billow through the gaps in the wood. Ronan could hear coughing and vomiting from within.

It did not take long until the whole building was in flames, and the tumult of noise from within began to die out. The door shook as someone inside threw themselves against it. Again and again it trembled until eventually the wooden plank barring it shut cracked and broke.

The first man out stumbled blindly, only to be cut down by half a dozen crossbow bolts. A woman followed closely behind him, but Ronan's men did not discriminate and she too was stuck like a flailing pin cushion. Then came the burning figures.

A man screamed, body consumed by flames, his cry of agony cut short by a single quarrel to the chest. Ronan could see his men hurrying to reload before any more dying men followed. With a bellow of anguish, another man rushed out to stand before them. His arms were held out as though exalting the sun and his dying squawk slowly faded before he dropped to his knees. One of the crossbowmen aimed but Ronan held up a hand.

'Save your quarrel,' he said, as the burning man squirmed on the ground in a vain attempt to quell the flames. 'No need to waste it now.'

No one else tried to escape. The building had gone quiet but for the crackle of the fire. Ronan couldn't tell how long he sat watching as it burned, the roof turned to ash, the timbers blackening before they collapsed inwards. When he was satisfied the deed was done, he signalled for his men to continue their way to Hereford.

The castle was all but deserted when Ronan returned. Once the wagon full of silver was rolled into the courtyard, he dismissed his men and dismounted his horse. A brief glance about the castle grounds, the high stone walls and the fortified ramparts, and Ronan knew he was done with this place. It had served its purpose. The Red Wolf was gone now – Eadric and the Welsh with him. What came next, Ronan could not say, but he'd at least rest awhile before he decided his next move.

Inside, the feast hall was empty – no servants or maids to fetch him the food that would sate his growing hunger. Ronan picked up a poker, stoking the waning fire before he threw on another log and then sat himself in the chair closest the hearth. Baron Richard's chair.

Ronan could only think how much better suited he would be to sit in this seat. The chances of Earl Willem granting him these lands and this castle were all blown to the wind now. He was nobody once more – just another nameless soldier in King William's army. At least his days of grovelling at the feet of the FitzScrobs was over. They were useless to him now.

On the table was a gilded brass jug and cups to match it. He picked up the jug, sloshing the dregs of the wine at the bottom before pouring them into a cup and raising it to his lips. The wine tasted bitter, but he swallowed it down with a grimace.

'What is this?'

Ronan looked up to see Baron Richard standing at the threshold, glaring with disdain as Ronan reclined in his chair.

'This?' Ronan said, holding up the empty cup. 'Quite possibly the shittiest wine I've ever tasted.'

'What are you doing here?' Richard asked, struggling forward to lean against the feasting table. He looked worse by the day, and Ronan realised he wasn't long for this world. It was a notion that brought a smile to his face until Osbern appeared. Richard's heir stepped forward, clearly as confused as his father why Ronan was here resting in their feast hall.

'Where are the prisoners?' Osbern said. 'Were you successful?'

Ronan inclined his head, glaring back into the fire. 'That depends on your definition. Were we successfully ambushed? Then yes. Did I successfully secure the kidnapped citizens of Hereford? That would be a no.'

'Then where are they?' Richard said with growing horror.

'Oh, I'd say half of them are at the bottom of the River Lugg. As for the rest? By now they'll be on their way to the slave markets of the Welsh coast.'

'You bloody fool,' Richard growled, slamming his fist into the table with all the menace of a flower girl at a wedding.

'Don't fret, old man,' Ronan said with a dismissive wave of his hand. 'Your silver is safe. Or most of it, at least.'

'What do you mean "most"?' Osbern asked, but his father ignored him, stumbling closer to Ronan.

'To hell with the silver,' Richard said. 'Those people are lost. They were under my protection. I trusted you, and you have failed me.'

Ronan gritted his teeth, standing up and feeling how heavy his mail was. He needed a rest. Needed to strip down and bathe and drink and forget. But here he was, arguing with some sick old fool and his idiot son.

'Failed you?' he said, fixing Richard with a deathly gaze. 'I do not serve the FitzScrobs. I am Ronan of Dol-Combourg. I rode in the conrois of Earl Brian of Penthièvre. Friend and confidant to the King of England. I fought to secure these lands for the Duke of Normandy while you were shivering in your shit-pit waiting for the outcome. I serve William, not you. And you keep your castle and your lands at his pleasure. Don't presume to lecture me, old man, or I'll have you beaten till you're pissing blood.'

Richard was shaking. To his credit, he held Ronan's gaze as the anger bubbled up within him.

'You can't talk to my father that way,' Osbern said. 'You go too far.'

Ronan glanced back at the fire. Above it still sat the sword of the Red Wolf in pride of place. He took a step towards the hearth, the sword within arm's reach.

'I'll talk to you and this decrepit old fool any way I please.'

'Get out of this house,' Osbern said, marching forward as though to throw his insolent guest out himself.

Ronan grasped the sword. For the briefest of moments he appreciated how perfectly balanced it was, before he swung it. Had the blade been drawn it would have hacked deep into Osbern's skull, but still in its sheath it only managed to smash his nose.

Osbern staggered back, hands covering his face as blood dripped through his fingers. Richard cried out on seeing his son struck so violently, but it only served to spur Ronan on.

He advanced on Osbern, ignoring the pain in his crippled leg, feeling all his frustration begin to manifest into violence.

'The English would consider this a sacred weapon,' he snarled, bringing it down on Osbern's head. There was a hollow sound as the reinforced scabbard cracked against his skull. Osbern whimpered as he fell to his knees.

'It was wielded by one of their heroes,' Ronan continued, bringing it down again.

Osbern whimpered as the blow fell, cowering on the ground like a whipped dog.

'And now it sits in a house of cowards and weaklings.' Another blow, another crack and Osbern went still.

Ronan looked up to see Baron Richard staring in terror, a hand clamped over his mouth to stifle a cry for mercy.

'I think I'll look after this, Baron Richard,' Ronan said, brandishing the sword like a club. 'What say you?'

Richard nodded, before dropping to his knees to tend his wounded son. Ronan considered unsheathing the blade and leaving this house with no masters, but the consequences of that would be much worse than beating its heir to a pulp. Instead, he limped from the room and into the abandoned courtyard.

As he walked to his horse, he knew chances of any repercussions were small. William was already subjugating this land with fear. It was the most effective way to silence an enemy…

And if the FitzScrobs knew anything, they now knew fear.

41

THE LONG FOREST, ENGLAND, AUGUST 1067

He winced at the pain, gritting his teeth against it. His leg stung, the pain intensifying as Gisela removed the dressing. The agony of it made Styrkar want to scream.

'Don't be such a child,' she said, as she dipped her hand into the bowl and liberally wiped some stinking unguent all over the burn on his shin.

Styrkar growled deep within his throat as she applied the foul-smelling paste. He had watched as she made it, adding honey, wine and bran, thinking it might be something pleasant to eat until she had added pig fat, foraged herbs and some mouldy bread. Still, he didn't argue as she ministered to him.

The tincture began to sting worse than the burn and he grunted in pain, instantly regretting it. He hated showing weakness in front of anyone, least of all her.

'I know it hurts,' Gisela said. 'But I would have thought a man such as yourself would be used to being in pain.'

'Lucky I have you here to tend me,' he said.

She stopped and glanced up at him, raising an admonishing eyebrow. 'Indeed. But let's not make a habit of this, shall we.'

He found himself nodding, and she carried on. Once the ointment was spread, she took a fresh binding and wound it around the leg before neatly tying it off. Then she rose to her feet.

'Can you stand?' she said.

Styrkar struggled as she helped him rise. It was painful to put weight on the leg, but at least he could still walk. The ointment was already soothing the pain of the burn and leaving behind an intense itch.

'Thank you,' he said to her.

Gisela shrugged. 'It's nothing. I learned to make ointments from my mother, a long time ago. I have been tending a sickly old woman for many years, so you make a welcome change.'

'No,' Styrkar replied. 'I mean for saving me. I would have drowned in the river if not for you.'

She looked up at him, holding his gaze in the dank light of the hut. 'Then I suppose we're even. I would have burned in that boat, or drowned, if you hadn't come for me.'

Styrkar felt his stomach tighten as he stared at her. He wanted to take this woman in his arms and hold her close. He fought the temptation to reach forward and kiss her. Gisela didn't make the feeling any easier as she looked at him, her expression turning expectant. Slowly she reached a hand up to brush his bearded cheek and Styrkar felt his skin tingle at her touch.

The door to the hut burst open, bathing them both in daylight, shattering the moment.

Kenric stood there, short of breath. 'You have to come,' he said. 'Now.'

For a moment Styrkar thought about donning his mail and racing from the hut but it was obvious they were not under attack.

'What is it?' he said, moving towards the door.

'Trouble,' Kenric replied.

As Styrkar left the hut he glanced back at Gisela. She stood watching him, and for that briefest moment she seemed the most beautiful thing he had ever seen.

'I'll be back soon,' he said, before closing the door and following Kenric through the camp.

Already he could hear angry voices through the trees, and both men quickened their pace. Kenric led him to the centre of the camp, where Welsh warriors stood in a circle alongside Saxon housecarls. Beyond them, Prince Rhiwallon was shouting in his language to the baying howls of his men. Styrkar pushed his way through the warriors to see Eadric, Bleddyn and Rhiwallon standing among them.

'This is not over,' Eadric barked, the heavy furs that adorned his shoulders making him look more bear than man. 'We had a bargain. It is not done yet.'

As Rhiwallon continued to curse in Welsh, Bleddyn shook his head.

'We are finished here, Saxon. We have lost enough men. The silver we took at the river won't even begin to cover the losses we have suffered. The slaves don't come close.'

'Slaves?' Eadric said. His hand was on the axe at his belt, and Styrkar could sense the potential for violence heavy in the air. 'They are my prisoners. Not yours.'

'Consider them recompense for my dead warriors,' Bleddyn said.

Eadric fixed him with a malevolent gaze. 'And what about *my* dead warriors? Do you think I should just suffer their loss? Disappear into the wilds? Let the Frankish bastards forget I was even alive?'

'You are beaten, Saxon,' Bleddyn replied. 'Your best bet is to return to the castle, fall on your knees and beg forgiveness from the Frankish king. See what scraps he might throw you to end your rebellion.'

'So you think me a dog now?' Eadric said, voice lowered and thick with menace.

Rhiwallon had gone silent and Bleddyn regarded the earl with a baleful stare. Styrkar knew neither of these men would back down. A fight was inevitable, and he began to regret not donning his armour and bringing his biggest axe.

'They are not your slaves,' Eadric said, breaking the silence. 'And neither are they my prisoners. Now they are a message. I will show the Franks we are not beaten. I will take the head from every captive and deliver them back to Hereford. I will show the Franks we are not beaten. Flee if you want to, back to your mountain holdfasts. But know this: England will remember how you were defeated. How you gave up and fled the fight.'

Rhiwallon bristled, half pulling the sword from the scabbard at his belt, but his brother Bleddyn clamped a hand down on it.

Slowly he nodded. 'You shame us, Saxon.' He and Eadric stared at one another for what seemed an age. Then a smile cracked across Bleddyn's bearded face. 'But I admire your steel. You're right, a message is what's needed. Our fight is not over yet.'

He held out a hand and Eadric grasped it. The two men then hugged like old friends before Eadric turned to his men.

'Gather every prisoner in the clearing,' he bellowed. 'And bring me my fucking axe.'

Styrkar was already retreating through the crowd as the surrounding warriors howled their approval. He rushed across the camp, back towards the hut. Kenric was nowhere in sight and he cursed beneath his breath. He had to get Gisela out of this place, but now it seemed his only ally had fled.

Gisela was lighting a fire as he rushed in. She looked up in alarm as she saw the grim look upon Styrkar's face.

'We have to leave,' he said.

'What's happened?' she replied.

'There's no time.' He grasped the short axe leaning against the wall. Before he could reach for his sword, the door to the hut opened.

He and Gisela froze as Stithulf entered. With him were two more of Eadric's men, Hairud and Osbarn – solid warriors who Styrkar had fought beside half a dozen times. Men he knew and had trusted with his life.

'Styrkar,' Stithulf said with a nod. His voice was friendly, but Styrkar could see he was nervous, his hand hovering near the knife at his belt. 'Earl Eadric has ordered—'

'I know,' Styrkar said.

'So she has to come with us.'

More silence as Osbarn and Hairud drew their weapons, slowly moving around the edge of the hut to flank him.

Stithulf glanced at Gisela, then back at Styrkar, hand slowly moving to that knife. He looked anxiously at the axe in Styrkar's hand.

'None of us have any choice in this,' Stithulf said. 'You know that, don't you?'

'I know,' Styrkar replied.

Stithulf was right – none of them had any choice at all, least of all Styrkar.

Before Stithulf could clear the knife from its sheath, Styrkar darted forward, slamming the axe into his neck. There was a crack of bone as Stithulf's clavicle split and the head of the axe sunk deep. Styrkar didn't try to wrestle it clear, but instead stripped the knife from Stithulf's belt as the man fell.

Osbarn was closest, and Styrkar barged a shoulder into him before he could strike. They both crashed into the wall, shaking the rickety hut violently and dislodging straw from the roof. Styrkar drew the knife blade across Osbarn's throat and he let out a strangled cry as blood gushed down the front of his mail shirt.

As Hairud rushed in, axe raised, Styrkar grabbed Osbarn and used him as a shield against the attack. Hairud's axe hacked open the back of Osbarn's head and his gurgling ended.

Styrkar dropped Osbarn to the ground, grappling with Hairud. The man was strong, but not strong enough as they fell to the ground, losing a grip on their weapons. Hairud growled as he tried to grasp Styrkar's arms, but the rage was on him now. He wrenched an arm free and punched Hairud in the face. The sting in his knuckles only spurred him on further and he punched again, this time in the man's throat.

Hairud's grip loosened as Styrkar unleashed all the Red Wolf's fury, pummelling the throat, crushing the windpipe, beating and beating until his foe struggled no more.

He breathed hard as he stood, scanning the ground to make sure the three men were not about to rise. Stithulf's dead eyes stared at the roof of the hut. He had been a good man, a friend even. But that body served as a reminder to Styrkar that the Red Wolf had no friends. Looking up at Gisela he saw the expression of horror on her face. For a moment that expression stung more than any wound. She had seen the fury of the Red Wolf and it terrified her.

Styrkar held a hand out to her. He would not have blamed her had she screamed in fright at that and fled from the hut to face Eadric's axe, rather than go anywhere with him.

Instead, she stepped forward and took his hand. Styrkar picked up a fallen sword before opening the door to the hut, leading her out into the open air.

The camp was in turmoil, the distant screams of the prisoners echoing through the trees as they realised their fate. Eadric had wasted no time, and Styrkar could already hear the cheers of the Welsh as the earl put those helpless townsfolk to the axe one by one.

With the camp distracted it did not take Styrkar long to guide Gisela to the edge of the woodland. There stood three horses tethered to a post and he quickly untied one of them. After helping Gisela onto the steed's back he made to untie a second, but a furious voice stopped him in his tracks.

'Treacherous bastard,' came the cry, and Styrkar turned to see Wulfsige rushing towards them.

The housecarl carried axe and shield, wearing his mail

shirt but no helm. Still, he was better equipped than Styrkar, but the Red Wolf's rage did not care for armour.

With a low growl emanating from his throat, Styrkar charged to face Wulfsige, battering his sword against the housecarl's shield. Wulfsige planted his feet, taking the rain of blows, the wood of his shield splintering under the onslaught. Then with a grunt, he swung the axe, and Styrkar had to stagger back or risk being hacked apart.

'I've waited a long time for this, you Danish wanker,' Wulfsige snarled. 'I'm going to add your head to Earl Eadric's pile.'

Styrkar tensed, readying himself to attack again when there was a sudden hammering of hooves. Kenric steered his rampant horse in between the two warriors, shouting for Styrkar to, 'Come on!'

He did not hesitate, leaping up onto the horse's back as Kenric kicked its flanks.

Gisela rode close behind as they sped away, and Styrkar could hear Wulfsige cursing him for a coward as they fled. Once, that might have shamed him enough to leap from the horse and fight the bastard, but not now.

He and his friends had escaped. And for the first time since he could remember, Styrkar felt free.

42

BRIEN, ENGLAND, SEPTEMBER 1067

The horses plodded their way steadily along the undulating coastline. Gisela gripped Styrkar's waist, her head resting against his back as he led them further south. Their only hope was to put as much distance between them and Eadric as possible, and never look back.

At various points they had seen signs of the Frankish occupation – a stone construction in the distance, or a patrol which they had given a wide berth. Other than that, this country was sparsely populated. The odd town sat on the edge of the coast, fishermen plying their trade, but Styrkar had no interest in stopping. They had to remain anonymous, hidden. If there was any chance of them avoiding Eadric and the Franks they had to be as ghosts.

'Looks like we're being followed,' Kenric said on the second day.

Styrkar was alarmed until he saw the animal watching them from a distance. A single wolf was dogging their tracks as they made their journey along the seafront. There was no sign of the rest of its pack, and Styrkar wondered if it too was an outcast. If so, then the beast was in fine company.

On the third day they reached a promontory on the headland. Overlooking the sea stood an ancient ruin, white walls long since dulled by the coastal wind, columns weathered by the salt spray. Nevertheless, it had a roof of sorts, and the three of them were in dire need of shelter.

Styrkar nudged Gisela awake and the three of them climbed down from their horses. As Kenric hobbled the steeds, Styrkar and Gisela entered the crumbling house. Though much of the old building had been consumed by the landscape, there were signs that this place had once been opulent, perhaps even the dwelling of a wealthy magnate.

'This is an old Roman villa,' Gisela said. 'Perhaps a thousand years old.'

'Roman?' Styrkar said.

Gisela smiled at his ignorance. 'Warriors of an ancient empire,' she replied. 'Their armies once conquered these lands.'

It sounded a familiar story. 'And what happened to them?' he asked.

'The same thing that happens to all empires... it collapsed and eventually fell to ruin.'

Styrkar reached out a hand to touch what remained of a picture on the wall. It was made up of dozens of tiny shards of marble, many having fallen and shattered on the ground, but he could still see the image of a woman staring back at him. For a moment he wondered who she might have been, and what part she might have played in this Roman Empire. Had she been important? Had people spoken her name in reverence? As he stared at the face looking back,

Styrkar realised that now, a thousand years on, it no longer mattered. She was dead and gone, as one day they all would be.

A sharp wind suddenly blew through the ruin, and Styrkar went to find wood to build a fire, as Kenric joined him.

'We've had a good run, you and I,' Kenric said.

Styrkar looked at his friend, who squinted out at the sea. 'We have,' he replied.

'I think it's time we said our goodbyes.'

'You're leaving?' Styrkar hadn't realised how much he had grown fond of this man. How much he had depended on him.

'I like you, Styrkar.' Kenric smiled. 'But you're a dangerous man to know. I think I'd prefer a quieter life from now on. Besides, you won't want me hanging around now…' He nodded back towards the Roman ruin where Gisela was tending to the horses.

Styrkar shook his head. 'No. We are just—'

'Tell yourself that.' Kenric slapped him on the arm. 'Keep up that grim façade, and you'll be a lonely man forever.'

Styrkar wanted to tell him there was nothing between him and Gisela. That he was only protecting her out of duty. He knew it was a lie.

'Goodbye, my friend,' Kenric said.

Styrkar watched him say his goodbyes to Gisela, who hugged him close, before he mounted one of the horses and cantered off southward along the coast. When he looked back at her Gisela smiled, and before he knew it Styrkar was smiling back.

As night drew in, they made a fire, the wind buffeting

against the stone frame of the villa. Gisela sat close and he began to regret not hunting for something they could eat.

'I am sorry for this,' she said to him, breaking the silence between them.

He looked down at her, those delicate features beautiful in the firelight.

'You have nothing to be sorry for,' he replied. 'I made my own decision.'

'But you abandoned your people. You killed them to protect me.'

'They were not my people. Not my friends. I was only...'

What? Using them for his own ends? Or was he the one who had been used? As he thought on it, he knew he had been in thrall to Eadric. Blinded to his ruthlessness by an all-consuming need for revenge. Eadric was a leader who would have seen his own countrymen slain to satisfy his thirst for power. Styrkar could never have been loyal to a man like that for long. It had always been destined to end this way.

'Then you have no one?' she asked.

'Not anymore. I was King Harold's servant. He was my family, as were his wife, his sons. Now they are gone and I am...'

'Lost,' she answered. 'As am I.'

She shivered, and he moved closer. He had wrapped the horse blanket around her, and she placed it around his shoulders to shield them both against the autumn cold.

'Perhaps we are not lost. Perhaps we are just free,' he said as he looked into the fire. 'We have both been slaves. Shackled in chains of our own making.'

Gisela smiled at that. 'And now those chains are broken?'

She raised her hand to touch the iron torc at his neck. Styrkar raised his own hand, feeling the collar and the hardened skin beneath. Without pause or regret, he grasped the band and pulled it from his neck, setting it down beside him.

The wind howled through the villa as they hunkered closer beneath the blanket. As they did so, she placed her hand in his, sharing their warmth. When her head began to nod, he gently laid her down beside the fire, wrapping her in the blanket and placing his arms around her. Within moments he could hear her gentle breathing as sleep took her.

Watching the fire wane, it was as though a weight began to slough from him. No longer did he feel the hunger for vengeance that had plagued him for so long. Now all he wanted was to protect this woman, who had shown him nothing but kindness, despite what he had put her through.

But it was not just Gisela he wanted to keep safe. For so long he had roamed the land searching for something he could never attain, and all the while he had not cared whether it killed him. Now, in this ancient house, as the wind blew in from a rough sea, he wanted to live. Wanted to do something other than kill. He wanted to grow old in peace.

Sleep took him quickly, despite the howling winds, and the dreams he had were no longer of death and slaughter. It was not a nightmare that he later woke from as he felt a gentle hand brush his face.

Styrkar could see the dawn rising over the distant coastline and in its light Gisela was looking up at him, her gentle smile making his heart beat faster. She leaned closer to kiss him and it felt sweet, the hairs on his neck standing on end as the thrill ran through him. He held her tight, her kiss becoming firmer, more insistent as they lost themselves in one another.

Styrkar forgot the rest of the world, his past, even what his future might hold. All that existed was here and now, and the woman he held in his arms.

When finally they had ended their lovemaking, and the sun was high in the autumn sky, Styrkar could hardly catch his breath. Gisela lay still in his arms and their bodies were covered in a thin sheen of sweat, made chill by the sea air. He wanted to weep for the years he had denied himself such pleasure, and all for what? Loyalty to his masters? Pursuing a goal he could never reach?

'What now?' Gisela asked. She was wrapped within his arms, the single blanket curled tight around them both.

Styrkar shook his head. 'I had not thought beyond the day,' he replied. 'It has never been a decision I've had to make. I have always acted on the will of other men or fought to avenge the dead. But that is the past now. As for the future… I do not know.'

'We could sail away from here,' Gisela whispered, looking out beyond the villa at the calm coastal waters. 'Across the sea to Flanders where I was born. No one would know you there. And it is unlikely they would remember me. I was a girl when I left.'

Styrkar thought on it. England had been his home for years, and before that the lands of the Norse.

'Maybe this place is as good as any,' he said. 'We have the sun. We have the sea. We have a roof.' He gestured up to the rotten beams above them and she laughed.

'A few days ago I might have thought that lacking in ambition,' she said.

'And now?' he replied.

She turned to face him, taking his bearded chin in her hands and planting a lingering kiss on his lips. 'Now I would be anywhere, as long as it is with you.'

At her touch his heart beat faster once more. Styrkar had never realised that this was what made a man whole.

He unwrapped himself from her arms and told her to wait for him while he found them some water. Later he would hunt, or fish, but for now they had given themselves a thirst that needed slaking.

Taking an old jug that had been abandoned within the ruin, Styrkar walked towards a stream they had passed not far up the coastal path. When he eventually found it he knelt, filling the jug before pouring it over his head. The cold water revived him and he closed his eyes, letting the sun bathe his face in light. He opened them to a subtle noise.

Further upstream, he saw the lone wolf that had followed them for some miles. It lapped up the stream water before stopping and fixing him with a suspicious gaze.

The two stared at one another for some time, before Styrkar held out his hand to the animal. It shied away at first, but when Styrkar made no attempt to approach, it overcame its doubt and padded forward, sniffing at the outstretched hand.

'You have lost your tribe too, my friend,' Styrkar said.

He lowered his hand, and the wolf came closer, sniffing at him before reaching forward with its head. It sniffed at his beard before licking Styrkar's face. He bent his head, feeling the creature's soft fur against his forehead. Then, in silence, the wolf bounded away and ran off along the coastal path.

Styrkar watched it go, and for a moment he envied the creature its freedom. As he filled the jug once more and rose to his feet, it was only then he realised there was nothing to be jealous of. Styrkar was as free as any wild creature. He was shackled to no master – be he alive or dead. The only one he bore any loyalty to now waited for him along the coast, and Styrkar knew she would never ask anything of him but to love her.

It was an obligation he was more than willing to complete.

43

DUNHEVED, ENGLAND, DECEMBER 1067

Ronan watched as the finishing touches were made to the castle's construction. It seemed the Breton architect had finally managed to find himself the right labourers. Ronan thought back to the dead man he had seen in the ditch so many weeks ago. Perhaps the English workforce had been uniquely motivated and spurred on to new heights of industriousness by that example. Or perhaps Brian had seen fit to pay them a fair wage for their labour. Either way, their efforts were now bearing fruit.

Ronan sliced another piece of apple as he watched the men work, and took a bite. It tasted sour in his mouth, but he ignored the fact. It was only apt, since it matched his mood. He had failed, and watching the construction of this symbol of King William's might was doing nothing to alleviate the fact. The Red Wolf was gone. Earl Eadric disappeared in the depths of the forest. The Welsh still harrying settlements along the English borderlands. Ronan had tried to make a name for himself, to prove he was worthy of a redoubt such as the one being completed before his eyes, yet he had only proved himself lacking. The fate that awaited him now was beyond his control.

Most likely he would end up as some kind of glorified tax collector, roaming the land, demanding tribute from the peasant lords who still held on to their estates in the region. Perhaps he would always be a messenger boy for better men.

He tossed the apple away, wiping his knife on his sleeve and sheathing it. Damn this place. And damn the day he had ever come here.

Before he sank too far into melancholy his attention was diverted by the sound of approaching hooves. Brian led a column of horsemen from the east, back early from his meeting with the king, so recently returned from Normandy.

Ronan limped towards the castle entrance to greet his lord, bowing his head as the earl dismounted.

'Magnificent,' Brian said, looking up at the construction of his castle. 'I trust you've had no trouble?'

'None, my lord,' Ronan said. Brian had left him behind to oversee the final part of the building works, rather than accompany him to the capital to greet the king. Yet another lash of the whip of ignominy.

'Well, consider yourself fortunate,' Brian said as he handed the reins of his horse to a squire. 'The rest of the country does not remain so unmolested.'

'Trouble brewing?' Ronan asked as he accompanied Brian in through the main gate.

'That's one way of putting it,' Brian replied. 'Wholesale rebellion might be another.'

'This was to be expected,' Ronan said, limping along as best he could to match Brian's long stride. 'The English were never going to go down without a fight.'

And hadn't he witnessed that first-hand.

'Not just the bloody English,' said Brian. 'Eustace of Boulogne landed a fleet at Dover not so many days ago.'

'Was there battle?'

Brian shook his head. 'The fortifications at Dover were enough to make him rethink an attack. But the threat was there.'

'But why?'

'The English lords who still hold power and wealth have offered much recompense for foreign aid. And they don't care where it comes from.'

'But Harold is dead. His followers fled. These troublemakers are a disorganised rabble.'

'Not so, my friend,' Brian said, leading them inside.

The main hall was sparsely furnished, with no hangings yet displayed on the walls. Ronan was sure Earl Brian would see to that soon enough, and before long there would be captured banners and weapons nailed to every stone.

Brian pulled a chair up before the cold hearth as more servants scurried from an adjacent room to light a fire and bring him wine. Ronan stood uncomfortably until Brian gestured for him to sit.

'Not far from here lies the town of Exonia,' Brian continued. 'A fortress, or what passes for one in these lands. King Harold's mother, Githa, has chosen to bar herself inside and she has birthed a nest of rebellious snakes within.'

'So? Why not just burn it to the ground?' Ronan said, suddenly seeing an opportunity.

'If we make a martyr of that woman it will unite every rebellious lord in this country. Those who are now willing to put aside the sword and kneel before King William will rise up in righteous fury.'

'So what's the answer?'

Brian shrugged, taking a sip of wine and letting out a long sigh. 'For now, her vengeful spite is contained within the walls of Exonia. But she will have to be dealt with eventually. In the meantime, the king has done his best to persuade, bribe and threaten the other English lords into pledging their fealty.'

'The sooner they are ousted the better.'

'If only it were so simple. The English peasants are not so easily bought. And if they see the country being sold to Norman and Breton nobles while receiving nothing themselves then rebellion will split this land apart. We have to keep those English lords on side. At least for now.'

'And how does William seek to do this?'

That brought a smile to Brian's troubled features. 'What we have always done, my friend. A promise of marriage. William's daughter Adela has already been betrothed to the English Earl Edwin.'

'He's handing his daughter over to some Saxon pig?'

'I doubt it. It's just a ruse while he gains a foothold in the northern region. He will string this betrothal out until he has gained enough power. I doubt he would ever allow it to happen. Even William is not so ruthless as to condemn his own daughter, and why would he tie himself to these people by marriage?'

Stranger things had happened, but Ronan guessed they would have to wait and see. William had a strong affection for his children, but his affection for the crown of England ran much deeper.

They both drank, and when their wine jug was empty, Brian called for more. The fire had warmed the room, though the bare stone walls still seemed stark and empty. Ronan would have waited longer for the right time to ask about his own fate, but if he had learned one thing over the years it was that there was never a right time.

'So there will be rebellions aplenty,' Ronan said. 'And much work to do?'

Brian nodded as he stared into the fire. The wine had almost got the better of him, but the Lord of Penthièvre had never had the strongest tolerance.

Ronan could wait no longer. 'And what part will I play in all this?'

Brian fixed him with a curious expression, then a smile broke on his face.

'You will be at my side, Ronan. As you always have been.'

'So I am still in favour?'

Brian laughed. 'When were you ever out of it?'

'I only thought, my failure at Hereford—'

'Failure? The rebel lord Eadric was sent skulking into the forest with his tail between his legs. The Welsh still harry those lands, but they will be put in their place soon enough. You did not fail, my friend.'

But he had not captured the Red Wolf. It might not have seemed so important to a man like Brian, but to Ronan it cut deep.

'I would appreciate another chance,' he said. 'I would have an opportunity to distinguish myself for our king.'

Brian did not answer, but instead looked back to the fire, pursing his lips in thought.

'All right,' he said eventually. 'I will tell you something, but it is to go no further than these walls.'

Ronan moved in closer. Brian's secrecy was pointless anyway – the servants within this place were always listening out for something to fuel their gossip.

'Word has reached the king of a conspiracy against him.'

'From within our ranks?' The notion was shocking, but not altogether impossible.

'No. Only a fool would try and betray William. The consequences would be dire for anyone who tried, and our king has been most generous to his followers.'

'Then from who?'

'Harold's sons fled these lands after their father was defeated in battle. It is widely known they sought sanctuary in the court of the Irish King. Rumour has it they are mustering for war; a counter invasion. Harold's son Godwin would have the crown for his own head, and the Irish King Diarmait would help put it there.'

'But where will this invasion take place? And when?'

'That's just the thing,' Brian said. 'No one can say. And were we to try and send a spy to find out, they would not last a day in the mistrustful court of Dublin.'

'No. I imagine they would never trust a stranger in their midst.'

'Indeed. And so the king must wait for Godwin's fleet to land on his shores before he can respond. For the man who could give William fair warning, the reward would be great indeed. For the man who could rid him of these troublesome heirs before they set off from Irish shores, he would grant half a kingdom.'

'And you think I could help you accomplish this?'

Brian shrugged. 'You are cunning, Ronan. You always have been. A man who finds ways to get what he wants, despite the poor hand dealt to him.'

The reference to his crippled foot was obvious. Ronan might have bristled at it, had he not accepted long ago that it was true.

His thoughts went to Styrkar and to the sword Ronan had taken from him. The Red Wolf had admitted that Harold was like a father to him, his sons like brothers. That rune-carved weapon was far too precious to be the sword of a mere housecarl. Perhaps it had not always belonged to that red-haired brute.

Regret began to creep back into him as he thought how close he had come to capturing the Red Wolf. If Ronan had his hands on him now perhaps there would be a way he could use the man to solve the king's conundrum. But Styrkar was gone.

'If there is a way, I will find it,' Ronan said.

Brian reached over and nudged his shoulder. 'Ah, forget it. This is an impossible task. Even for you.'

'Perhaps,' Ronan replied. But he would never accept anything was impossible.

They went back to their drinking. As much as Ronan tried to put the thought of infiltrating King Diarmait's court from his mind, he could not. But the solution was beyond him.

The night drew in, and Brian's head began to nod, his long journey from the capital catching up with him. Ronan left his lord to rest beside the fire and made his way out into the cold winter air. His leg began to throb, always worse in the cold, and Ronan gritted his teeth against the pain, refusing to succumb to it.

Before he could reach his garrison, he saw Mainard approaching. The young knight seemed agitated about something, and for a brief moment Ronan hoped he had come to tell them of a nearby uprising. Something that might relieve the mundanity of this place and give him a chance to vent his frustrations.

'A man has asked to see you,' Mainard said.

Ronan's head was fuzzy from the wine and he was unsure if he heard the words right. 'To see me? Here, in this place?'

'Yes. Asked for you by name. Says he has information.'

'What man?'

'Some Englishman. Says he knows something of value to you. If you can afford it.'

'Does he indeed?'

'I know. I would have had the insolent bastard flogged, but I thought you'd want to speak to him first. Shall I have the men soften him up before you see him?'

Ronan considered it for a moment, but the past months of violence had not done anything to elevate him above his peers. Murder and pillage had not seen him rise in standing. Perhaps from now on he should step more lightly.

'No,' Ronan replied. 'I'll speak to this Englishman. If what he's got to say is not worth the price, then we can move on to the flogging.'

Mainard nodded enthusiastically, leading the way through the dark. Ronan followed, half hoping that the man's information was worthless and he'd have the excuse he'd need to relieve his boredom.

44

BRIEN, ENGLAND, JANUARY 1068

The rabbit-skin cloak was wrapped tight around his shoulders as Styrkar worked away at the wood. The winter air was chill, but so far the season had been mild. Nevertheless, he was thankful for the crackling fire that warmed the room.

In one hand he held the small knife, in the other was the wood he was gradually whittling away at. As always, he'd had no idea what kind of figurine he was carving when he began, but gradually a gull was revealing itself. A head, a wing, tapering tail feathers all appearing as though he had no control over what he was creating.

Before they came to this place it had been years since he'd last carved, and he had forgotten what a simple joy it was to create something from a simple block of wood. The process allowed his thoughts to drift and a smile crossed his face as he fashioned the final touches.

Gisela had helped turn this old ruin into their home. Together they had restored it as best they could – thatch for the roof, stone to rebuild the walls, timber to make the door. At first they had still spoken of leaving, of taking a boat across the sea to Flanders where they might start anew, but those conversations had waned. Now this was their home. Remote and peaceful. Styrkar had never thought that this might be a life he would crave, but most men had no idea what they truly wanted until it was forced upon them.

When he had finished carving out the gull and smoothed over the rough edges with a stone, he stood and placed it on a shelf alongside the other animals he had carved. Wolf, bull, squirrel, raven. All stood side by side on the mantel. Styrkar held his hands out to warm them on the fire as he looked proudly at his creations. He had spent so many years destroying, he had never learned to appreciate the simple pleasure that could be gained from creating something.

A fleeting thought crossed his mind that perhaps, in the coming months, he might be able to carve something for a child, but he dismissed it as soon as it came. He and Gisela had not talked about such things, and Styrkar did not want to encourage those thoughts. Did not want to raise his hopes of something that might end up dashed. He was happy to simply exist without thinking too much on the future.

The door to the villa opened, and Gisela entered. Her face was flushed from the cold, her body encased in layers of bulky animal skins. She had been skinning a fox outside and her hands were still moist from the labour. It was something Styrkar would have preferred to do himself, but she had insisted.

'Someone is coming,' she said.

Immediately Styrkar reached for the crude axe he had made and walked out into the cold air. Along the coastal path he could see a lone figure making his way south, approaching with haste.

'Who could it be?' Gisela asked. She had followed him out into the cold. Styrkar would have preferred her to stay inside where it was safe, but he had learned the hard way that she was not a woman to be told what to do. It was a quality he couldn't help but admire in her.

As the man came closer, Styrkar recognised him beneath the heavy hood of his cloak.

'Kenric,' he said, feeling some relief that it was a friendly face.

When Kenric was within a few yards a smile crossed his lips, but Styrkar noted it did not reach his eyes.

'It's good to see you,' Styrkar said, as he approached.

'The feeling's mutual,' Kenric replied, stepping forward to grasp Styrkar in a hug.

'Come inside,' Gisela said. 'You must be freezing.'

They stepped into the villa, and as Gisela threw another log on the fire, Kenric hunkered down in front of it, rubbing some heat into his limbs.

'I didn't know if you'd still be here,' Kenric said. 'Part of me was hoping you'd be long gone.'

'Then why have you come?' Styrkar replied. 'I take it your journey has been a long one. Why make it if you were unsure you'd even find us?'

'I wanted to warn you,' Kenric said, rising to his feet and fixing Styrkar with a grave expression. 'It's the least I owe you, friend.'

'Warn us of what?' Gisela asked.

'Earl Eadric is hunting you. He has travelled south with

some of his housecarls and the fiercest Welsh hunters the Prince of Powys could spare. He wants revenge on you for murdering his men and deserting him. Wants revenge on both of you.'

'And how does he know where we are?'

Kenric looked to the ground. His shame was obvious. 'I was hunting to the north. Minding my own business, you might say, when they found me. Wanted to know where you were and I did my best not to tell of it. They beat me, tortured me, but I'm no warrior, Styrkar. I'm not like you. When I said I last saw you to the south, Eadric made me show him the way, but I managed to escape. Took the road here as quick as I could manage to warn you.'

Styrkar stepped forward, and Kenric recoiled as though he might be struck. Instead, Styrkar gripped him by the shoulders. 'You have my thanks, old friend. I do not blame you for this.'

Kenric nodded, but he still looked deeply ashamed of what he had done.

'Where is Eadric now?' Gisela asked, the fear palpable in her voice.

'Not far north of here. Only a few miles. The Franks are building a fortification, and Eadric chose to camp there. They might still be waiting, so if we leave now we can be miles from here by the time they arrive.'

'All right,' Gisela said. 'Then we will run.'

'No,' Styrkar replied. He hadn't even given his answer any thought, but then he didn't need to. He was done running. From his past, from the Franks. He would not run away from this.

'What do you mean, no?' Gisela said. 'Are you not listening? Eadric is only miles from here. He could be on his way now, with killers by his side. You cannot fight them all.'

Styrkar looked at Gisela, seeing the fear in her eyes. The desperation. He knew if they fled now, it would not be the last time. They would live their lives in fear forever. There had to be an end to this.

'Kenric, you must stay here and protect Gisela.'

'No,' she said, moving forward and grabbing him by the fur cloak she had made. 'You're not to do this.'

Styrkar ignored her, keeping his focus on Kenric, unable to look his lover in the eyes. 'Tomorrow, if anyone comes down that path but me, you are to take her far away from here. Across the sea to Flanders if you can.'

'You won't do this,' Gisela cried, and as she began to weep he held her close, so the sound of it was muffled against his chest.

Styrkar felt something inside him break, but in this he knew there was no choice. If they were ever to be free he had to face up to his past one last time.

He took Gisela by the shoulders, then placed a hand beneath her chin so she was looking him in the eye.

'I will be back,' he said.

She did not reply, but instead reached up to kiss him urgently. When she was done, she turned and fled to another room in the villa.

'Sure you don't want me to come with you?' Kenric said.

'We both know there's not much point in that,' Styrkar replied.

'Want to borrow my bow?' he asked, patting the weapon slung across his back.

'There's even less point in that,' Styrkar said. 'I couldn't hit a pig barn from five paces, remember?'

Kenric shrugged at the truth of it.

Styrkar placed his axe in his belt beside the tiny knife he wore. Before he left he paused, picking up the torc he had placed away on a shelf. As he fixed it around his neck, old memories returned. Memories of enslavement, of duty, of his thirst for revenge. When this was all over, one way or another, he would fling the thing into the sea. Right now he needed it, for what was the Red Wolf without his iron collar?

'I'll see you tomorrow, friend,' Kenric said, as Styrkar opened the door to the tiny house he had made.

He paused for a moment on the threshold, dismissing the nagging urge to stay. To gather his things with Gisela and run. Then he closed the door behind him.

As he made his way north he hardly felt the winter chill. No sooner had he begun to walk the long coastal path than he saw a companion dart from the brush, padding alongside him.

The wolf looked up eagerly, as though they were on the hunt together. It looked thin, like it had not eaten for days.

'Not long now, my friend,' Styrkar said, his words leaving a trail of mist as he thought about the death he was about to deal. 'Soon you will get to eat your fill.'

45

WORLE, ENGLAND, JANUARY 1068

Kenric had been right, the hunters were not far north. By the time Styrkar had covered the ten or so miles along the coast, night had fallen, then all he had to do was follow the fires in the distance. They had not moved yet, as though they were waiting for something, or someone. Surely they could not have known he was coming? Kenric had told him Eadric was keen to pursue his quarry. If he knew where Styrkar was, why did he wait here?

Styrkar put those thoughts from his mind as he crept through the dark, the outline of the half-built fortifications coalescing before his eyes. There was no need to think on such things now – he had to focus on the job at hand. The job of killing.

The sound of voices pealed out through the dark. These men were not expecting to be attacked, not anticipating that the hunter might become prey.

Earthworks had been built around the base of the hill, some of the wooden timbers already erected. The skeleton of the castle sat atop a steep mound, offering a perfect view of the surrounding countryside. When its construction was complete, this would be a formidable bastion to attack. But it was not completed yet.

The closer he got, the louder the noise grew. English and Welsh voices competed on the night air, as though their uneasy alliance meant the only way they could fight was by drowning one another out with their din. It would be to Styrkar's advantage.

He crept closer, pausing in the dark as he saw a bulky warrior patrolling the fort's perimeter. An axe was slung over one of his shoulders but from his vantage point, Styrkar could not see if he was armoured. Instead of a helm he wore a thick hat of fur to ward against the cold. It was all the opening Styrkar would need.

As the man walked past him, just visible in the ambient light from the camp, Styrkar darted forward. He had a chance to see the warrior's eyes widen as Styrkar fell on him from the shadows, knife stabbing out to pierce the man's throat. They both fell to the ground and Styrkar clamped his hand over the man's mouth to stifle his gurgling cries. He struggled, but with all Styrkar's weight upon him there was nothing he could do but exhale his last blood-filled breath.

When the warrior was still, Styrkar stood, waiting in the dark. A howl of laughter from the camp told him they had not heard the murder, and he picked up the man's axe and stripped the sword from his belt. The man wore mail beneath a thick fur cloak, but there was no time to don it. Styrkar had to keep moving, had to be swift with the killing.

Climbing up past the earthworks, he looked across the

flat top of the mound. Three fires burned, half a dozen men hunkering around them, sharing their skins of ale and the skewers of meat they had cooked. Horses were tethered at the other side of the camp, whickering nervously as the warriors cajoled one another.

Styrkar could have rushed in, could have cut down at least two of them before they knew they were even under attack, but the rest would have overcome him in no time. There had to be another way.

Silently, he crept around the edge of the camp. Scaffolding had been erected to support the building of ramparts, and as he ducked beneath the timbers he came upon a bale of straw. Barrels of pitch sat next to it, used to seal the gaps between the timbers of the palisade.

Lifting one of the barrels he hefted it, testing the weight. He could easily throw it across the camp, but whether his aim would be true was another matter. Quietly he cracked open the lid, raising the barrel to shoulder height before he let fly.

Pitch spilled onto his furs as he launched it across the camp. It came down beside one of the fires, spilling its load and scattering flaming tar across the camp. One man was caught in the flames, burning pitch sticking to his legs and igniting his cloak.

As the man screamed, Styrkar sent another barrel flying. This one shattered in the midst of another fire, the pitch spreading to ignite the scaffold erected nearby.

The camp erupted in confusion, a couple of the men trying in vain to douse the flames that were consuming one of their number. Styrkar took his chance, darting forward, a growl issuing from his throat as he raised his makeshift axe and buried it in the head of a bellowing Welshman. Before his victim fell, Styrkar darted off into the darkness.

Eadric was on his feet now, shouting at the warriors, but his voice was lost amidst their panicked cries.

As Styrkar stalked the perimeter in the blackness, one of the Welsh fled from the camp in a panic. Styrkar lurched from the shadows, sword flashing across the warrior's throat. The Welshman staggered back, gurgling his last.

One of Eadric's men screamed that they were surrounded, as the remaining Welsh bellowed in their own language.

'Stand your ground,' Eadric ordered, but it was too late.

The nerve of the Welsh warriors gave out and they scattered from the camp, fleeing into the surrounding dark. Only Eadric, Wulfsige and one of his men stood firm.

Styrkar saw no need to wait. He could not tarry, or the Welsh might regain their courage and return. He charged, raising the Dane axe high. The last of Eadric's men turned, only managing to vainly raise his arm as Styrkar brought the axe down, caving in the front of his head. As he fell dead, Wulfsige bellowed, rushing at Styrkar and battering him back with the boss of his shield.

The axe went flying into the night, and Styrkar pulled the sword from his belt as he staggered backwards. The flames of the fire had taken now, the scaffold along with the half-built palisade was burning furiously.

Wulfsige came again, his axe flashing in the firelit night, and Styrkar was forced onto the back foot. He staggered, the flames licking at his clothes and igniting the pitch that had spilled on his fur cloak.

As the fire singed his face and beard, Styrkar dropped the sword in his hand, slapping at his cloak in vain.

'Come on bastard,' Wulfsige bellowed with relish, charging in one last time, raising his axe for the killing blow.

Styrkar tore off his cloak, flinging it at Wulfsige. The flaming furs wrapped around his shield, fire licking at his face and as he staggered back, Styrkar leapt forward, shoulder crashing into his chest and knocking him back to the ground.

Wulfsige grunted, Styrkar's full weight on top of him. The temptation to smash the man's face with his fists was almost uncontrollable, but Styrkar's instincts were screaming at him.

He rolled aside, just as Eadric charged in, axe raised.

The earl brought the weapon scything down as Styrkar dodged, the blow that was intended for him hacking into Wulfsige's chest. The housecarl let out a piteous squeal as his ribs were crushed, his last breath squeezed from his lungs by the axe head.

Eadric struggled to pull the weapon free, planting a foot on his still-writhing housecarl. Styrkar jumped to his feet, scrambling across the camp towards a burning corpse that lay by the fire. The flames licked at his arm as he grasped the man's sword from its sheath and wrenched it free.

No sooner had he grasped the weapon than he was forced to duck another swing of Eadric's axe, the earl growling savagely. Styrkar leapt back out of range and the two men stood assessing one another.

'It didn't have to come to this,' Eadric said.

'It would always have to come to this,' Styrkar replied. 'You should have let me go. Should have forgotten you ever laid eyes on me.'

'Some things can't be forgotten, Red Wolf,' Eadric said, hefting the axe once more and advancing.

Styrkar waited, picking his moment as the axe came crashing down. He dodged, feeling the air part as the axe missed by a hair. Then he darted forward, sword flashing to slice into Eadric's thigh.

The earl bellowed, incensed at the wound, limping after Styrkar and swinging the axe about his head like a berserker. Styrkar dodged through the flames, ducking and swaying aside as the axe split the air around him. Eadric was breathing heavily now, and with one last burst of effort he leapt through the flames at Styrkar, bellowing his terrifying war cry.

Styrkar swung, his eyes never leaving the axe, as he cleaved the haft in two. Eadric barely had a chance to realise he was holding nothing more than a useless stick as Styrkar smashed the pommel of his sword into the earl's face.

Eadric fell back, crashing to the ground. There he floundered, spitting blood and teeth as Styrkar stood over him victorious. When the earl looked up at him, there was a crimson smile on his gap-toothed mouth.

'Get on with it,' he said. 'Don't gloat, boy. It's beneath you.'

Styrkar's hand twitched, as though the sword yearned to strike the killing blow. Instead, he lowered the weapon.

This was what Eadric wanted; to perish in battle at the hands of a fierce warrior. But Styrkar was no longer slave to another man's desires. No longer blinded by loyalty and the lust for revenge. He would decide his own fate now, and he stared down at the beaten warrior. The only sound was the crackle of flames and the panicked cries of the horses still bound to the burning palisade.

'You are beaten,' Styrkar said. 'Coming after me was foolish.'

Eadric laughed again and it turned into a hacking cough as he spat out more blood. 'It looks that way, boy. Enough talk. Strike the blow.'

'No,' Styrkar replied. 'I will not. And because I have spared your life you will vow never to come after me again. You will forget the name of Styrkar the Dane. Go back to the Marcher Lands and lament the day you ever thought you could kill me.'

'Kill you?' Eadric laughed again. 'I was not sent here to kill you, Red Wolf. I was sent to catch you.'

Styrkar shook his head. 'What do you mean? I was told you were hunting me. That you wanted vengeance.'

'I wanted silver, boy. Days ago I was sent a message by the Franks. Told where your lair was. Offered a reward to bring you to them.'

'But Kenric—'

Eadric began to laugh again. It sounded hollow as it rose over the sound of the flames.

'Looks like I'm not the only one who's been betrayed by someone he thought a loyal friend,' Eadric said. Styrkar could see the pleasure in the earl's eyes, and he fought back his rage. His thoughts turned immediately to one person...

Gisela.

Styrkar raced across the burning fort towards the horses. The rope binding one of them to the scaffold was on fire and the beast was consumed by panic. He grasped the rope, hacking it free and wrestled the horse away from the flames.

Its eyes were wide as it nickered in fright. Heedless of its fear, Styrkar leapt up on its back, loosening the rein and letting it run into the night. Guiding the horse south along the coastal path, he let the beast's terror carry him back home.

46

BRIEN, ENGLAND, JANUARY 1068

Styrkar reached the villa just before dawn. He jumped down from the horse, expecting it to carry on its flight, but the animal had run all the fear out of itself, and instead stood panting in the darkness.

As he rushed to the door of his home he considered approaching with stealth, but there was little point now. Anyone inside would have heard the horse approaching. Besides, they already knew he was coming – they would be ready and waiting.

Styrkar kicked the door aside, the sword gripped in his hand, girding himself at what he might see. The villa was empty. In the hearth, the fire had almost burned out and there was no sign of Gisela or Kenric.

When Styrkar made his way back outside the sun was glowing red as it started to rise over the distant horizon. He would have shouted for Gisela, but he knew it was pointless. She was not here.

He mounted the horse once more, putting heels to

flanks, riding on further south. As he urged the steed to a gallop, his eyes peered through the dark, the rising sun illuminating the land around. It was desolate, not a soul in sight, and Styrkar struggled to quell the panic welling up within.

Then he saw it, a mile or so in the distance. A church standing on a hillock not far from the sea. In the dim light of morning he could see torchlight emanating from inside. There was no other choice but to urge the horse closer, riding the beast almost till it dropped, in his eagerness to reach the place.

It was a small chapel he knew, long abandoned. In all the time he and Gisela had shared the nearby villa he had never known anyone occupy the place. No one worshipped here, but now there was a light beaming from inside, as though drawing him like a beacon. When he got close enough he could see almost a dozen horses hobbled by the side of the building. Frankish warhorses, by their size and barding.

He breathed deep as he dismounted, approaching the entrance with care this time. The door stood ajar, and Styrkar pushed it aside, hearing the hinge creak ominously.

At the far side of the tiny chapel, he saw her. Gisela was flanked by two Frankish knights, their blades unsheathed. All Styrkar could do was focus on her, wanting to speak, to tell her she would be all right. Instead, he stood in silence, sensing more men in the shadows around him.

'I was beginning to think you weren't going to make it,' Ronan said, limping from the darkness. He toyed with something in his hand, and as he moved further into the light, Styrkar saw it was one of the figurines he kept atop his mantel. A small wooden wolf.

'I am here now,' Styrkar said, still gripping his sword at his side. 'You can let her go.'

Ronan grinned and shook his head. 'I think not.'

As Styrkar's eyes adjusted to the gloom, he could see perhaps ten knights surrounding him. Then Kenric stepped from the shadows.

'Betrayer,' Styrkar snarled, wanting to dash forward and strike the man down, but knowing it would only lead to his death.

'I'm sorry, old friend,' Kenric said.

'Why?' asked Styrkar.

Ronan stepped in front of him. 'Why do you think? For the coin. Your friend Kenric came to me some days ago, offering your head in exchange for... what was it? Three bags of silver?'

'Four,' Kenric said. 'And it was gold.'

'Ah, yes. Four bags of gold for the head of the Red Wolf.'

'So why not just kill me?' Styrkar asked.

'Because you're little use to me dead,' Ronan said. 'But how was I to take you alive? If I fell upon your little home with my men, there would have been slaughter. You would have fought us to the death. So I had Kenric here send an offer to Eadric. If he could capture you I would reward him. His lands would be returned and all would be forgiven. Should he have succeeded in your capture, all the better. If not, I could simply walk into your home while you were away and take what you value the most.'

'What if we had just fled when Kenric told us we were being pursued?' Styrkar said.

Ronan smirked. 'The Red Wolf? Flee in the face of danger? Don't make me laugh. I knew you would rush to face such a threat, and from what Kenric told me, you would do what you could to protect the handmaid here.' He gestured to Gisela. 'We've met before, by the way. Did she never tell you? She once resisted my charms, but obviously she prefers... a more savage lover.'

'Eadric or one of his men might have killed me,' Styrkar said.

'It was a calculated risk,' Ronan replied. 'And one that has clearly paid off. I have you here, impotent. And it has not cost me a single man, or a single penny.'

Kenric cleared his throat. 'Almost. Look, as impressed as I am with your cunning, my lord, I think it's time I was paid and on my way.'

Ronan shrugged. 'Of course. Your reward.'

He gestured to one of his men, who stepped towards Kenric, swiftly pulling a knife and plunging it into his ribs. Kenric gasped and Gisela raised a hand to her mouth to stifle a cry.

Styrkar watched as Kenric sank to his knees. He felt nothing. If his treacherous friend had ever bothered to ask, he would have explained how remorseless, how underhanded, these Franks were. Kenric had learned that lesson on his own.

One of Ronan's men dragged Kenric into the shadows of the church where he moaned piteously, slowly breathing his last in a dank corner of the forgotten chapel.

'Is Earl Eadric dead?' Ronan asked, giving no thought to Kenric's dying gasps.

'No,' Styrkar replied.

'Pity. I could have claimed that victory as my own.'

'What now?' Styrkar asked, growing tired of Ronan's

imperious tone. He wanted this over with, for good or for ill.

'Now you're going to perform a service for me. Or I'll cut your woman's head off.'

Styrkar still had the sword in his hand. He made the briefest calculation of whether he could reach Gisela before one of the Franks could kill her. Perhaps. Perhaps not. But he would never have been able to fight his way out and protect her at the same time.

'What would you have me do?' Styrkar asked.

Gisela shook her head, the tiniest gesture, but Styrkar had to ignore it.

'The sons of Harold Godwinson reside at the court of King Diarmait,' Ronan said. 'Word has it they plan to stage an invasion of their own. You will go to Dublin, seek them out, discover where and when they plan to attack and bring that information to me.'

'So the armies of King William can lie in wait?' Styrkar replied.

'Precisely,' Ronan said with a grin. 'You're obviously not as stupid as you look.'

Styrkar glanced over at Gisela, who stood in silence, still flanked by the armed knights. Her eyes glistened in the torchlight as she fought back her tears, and he could only admire her bravery. He wanted to tell her how sorry he was that he had brought her to this. Styrkar had only ever wanted to protect her and now her life hung in the balance, all because of him.

'I will do as you ask,' he told Ronan.

'A wise choice,' the knight replied. 'Now, let's waste no time. A boat is already waiting.'

One of Ronan's knights stepped forward, reaching for the sword Styrkar held in his hand, and he allowed it to be taken. Before they could usher him from the chapel he fixed Gisela with a determined look.

'I'll be back soon,' he said.

'And I'll be waiting,' she replied.

Ronan's men led him out into the crisp morning air. They mounted their horses and Ronan led the way south. Styrkar did not allow himself to glance back at the chapel as they plodded along the path, lest his desire to fight for Gisela's rescue overwhelm him.

They rode south until the sun had risen fully from beyond the horizon. A brusque wind was blowing in from the north as they finally reached a shallow inlet. Styrkar saw a small boat waiting for them, two oars aside and a furled mast in its centre. Three boatmen were already preparing to set sail.

Styrkar dismounted, eager to be on his way, and Ronan climbed down from his own horse.

'Don't think about betraying me, Styrkar,' he said. 'She's only safe as long as you do as I ask.'

Styrkar did not answer as he began to cross the beach. Ronan fished in the bag at his horse's saddle and took something from within. He followed Styrkar across the shingle and waited as he climbed aboard the tiny vessel.

'If you get the chance to kill any of them, feel free,' Ronan said. 'And if you want, you could use this.' He unwrapped the sword he had taken from his saddlebag. It was Harold's seax, the one Ronan had taken from him so many months before.

'It took me a while, but I eventually worked out who this

really belongs to. Perhaps the blade of King Harold will help you persuade his sons you are on their side.'

Ronan flung it into the boat, and Styrkar caught it, holding the weapon in his hand and suddenly regretting the day he had ever laid eyes on it.

'Safe voyage,' Ronan continued, as one of the boatmen pushed the vessel clear of the beach and jumped inside. 'I hope you can sail.'

Styrkar ignored Ronan as he laughed at his own quip. Instead, he took up one of the oars, and with the other boatmen he pulled hard, propelling the small vessel away from the shore.

No, Styrkar could not sail, but he could pull an oar. It had been the one thing he was good at before he ever came to these shores.

Setting his jaw he rowed hard, eager to reach Dublin…

To betray the men he had once called brothers.

THE STORY OF THE RED WOLF CONTINUES IN BOOK TWO:

SHIELD BREAKER

Glossary

Baresark – Legendary Norse warriors who fought without armour.
Berserkergang – A violent fury said to overwhelm some Norse warriors in battle.
Conrois – A group of between five and ten Frankish knights, who fought together as a unit.
Fyrd – A civilian army consisting of freemen drawn from the shires.
Hel – Or "Helheim", the Norse realm of the dead.
Housecarl – A nobleman's personal bodyguard.
Jarl – A Norse or Danish chief.
Seax – A single-bladed Saxon weapon, used as a knife or short sword.
Thegn – A noble given lands by the king in return for service during times of war.
Torc – A ring of metal worn about the neck.
Witan – Or "Witanagemot", a meeting or council of senior Saxon nobles.

About the Author

RICHARD CULLEN originally hails from Leeds in the heartland of Yorkshire. If you'd like to learn more about his books, and read FREE exclusive content, you can visit his website at **Wordhog.co.uk.**

Credits

Editing by: Holly Domney, Helena Newton and Annabel Walker
Production by: Rebecca Clark
Cover Design by: Nick Venables
Marketing by: Jade Gwilliam